SAVE OVER £6!
When you subscribe to SHE from only £6.45 by quarterly Direct Debit

Treat yourself or a friend to a subscription to SHE and save a massive £6.50 a year on the full subscription rate. What's more you can spread the cost over the year and pay just £6.45 every quarter by Direct Debit.

Subscribers enjoy:

* Saving £6.50 a year
* That's just £2.16 an issue (usual price £2.70)
* FREE home delivery
* Spread the cost – just £6.45 by quarterly Direct Debit
* Just £25.90 a year by all other payment methods

Call our order hotline now on **01858 438844**
quote 6426/6427
Lines open weekdays: 8am–9.30pm;
Saturdays: 8am–4pm

You can also subscribe securely on line, simply visit www.subscription.co.uk/she and quote the ref 6426

Hurry! This offer must close 31st December 2002

This offer is available for UK subscriptions only and closes 31st December 2002. Acknowledgment of all orders will be sent within 14 days. The full UK subscription rate is £32.40. For subscription enquiries please telephone 01858 438838.

D1176136

Praise for *My Canapé Hell*

'A spirited satire on celebrity culture . . . A dark, insider's view of fashionable stars and happening bars, the book crackles with acute observation and hilarious one-liners'
Wendy Holden, *Mail on Sunday*

'A bitingly funny satire . . . sharp, witty and vastly entertaining' *Heat*

'One of the funniest books of the year' Shebah Ronay, *Mirror*

'A wickedly incisive wit dissects the highs and lows of the cocaine and champers set' *Cosmopolitan*

'Comic look at the perils of the celebrity circuit . . . Horribly fascinating' *Elle*

'Relentlessly of-the-minute . . . a modern morality tale with a happy ending' *Daily Mail*

'Wicked' *Image*

'Absolutely hysterical, I could not put it down' Candace Bushnell, author of *Sex and the City* and *Four Blondes*

'Funny, with a wry insider's view of the newspaper world' *She*

'If I were going to read a book it would be this one' Caroline Aherne

Also by Imogen Edwards-Jones

SHAGPILE

About the author

Imogen Edwards-Jones is an award-winning journalist, columnist and broadcaster who writes for many national newspapers and magazines. She is the author of two highly-acclaimed novels, MY CANAPÉ HELL and SHAGPILE, available from Flame. She was born in Birmingham and lives in London.

To Me

(Without whom none of this would have been possible)

Acknowledgements

I would like to thank Kenton for his advice, love, support and tolerance beyond the call of duty. I'd like to thank Sean, Claudia, Steve F, Kris, Ciara, Daisy, Ant, Jamie T, Xander, Mark W, Tom, Ben M, Beatie, James P, Alek and Sarah V for their stories, anecdotes and jokes that I have stolen with impunity. I'd like to thank Mike and Michelle for the bank holiday weekends they have lost because of this book, also Laurie, Cathie, Katyn, Ruth and Alex for taking my calls. I would also like to thank Caroline and Craig for their time and advice and Jo and Tim for the loan of Lucky Cottage, their swimming pool, and their bottomless drinks cabinet. And finally I'd like to thank my wonderful family for all their support and their ability to listen to the most turgid of stories, plus Simon Trewin for his marvellousness and Phil and all at Hodder for their help and guidance.

Prologue

Rehab was inevitable. A year of drinking, smoking and eating fried quails' eggs with lump fish roe on polenta biscuits is enough to make anyone have to hide from the world and paint images of their inner child using only their left hand. Sitting alone in my dormitory, devoid of stimulation and stimulants, with only *The Road Less Travelled* for company, it's the first time in nearly twelve months that I've been able to take stock of what really happened to me and the people I met on this journey into the inner recesses of celebrity. What a protracted and disgraceful journey it was. Full of lies, vacuity, broken promises, betrayed secrets and blind ambition, all punctuated by the photo opportunity and the pursuit of fame. I lost real friends on the way, made a myriad of false ones, developed confidantes who became too famous to acknowledge me and had a potential boyfriend die in the most sordid of circumstances. And it was all supposed to be such fun. Or at least that's how it started out . . .

It's one of those busy, important press days, where everyone on the desk is worrying about sequins and pink chiffon. A typical dank, grey and drizzling September afternoon outside, yet we're already packing up the red maribou mules and thinking of spring. Maya Franks, the well connected twenty-three-year-old work experience, is efficiently weaving her way between the desks, handing out free Kiehl's samples. In black polo neck, dark hair smoothed back into a ponytail, her denim clam-diggers are so tight you can see her thong. Meanwhile Andrea Adams, the heavily streaked, overly scented, fortysomething head of the Style Desk, is ingeniously using her bra cups as ashtrays. Puffing away like a beagle, she's tactfully giving her equivalent of good phone – a long litany of sighs, huffs and morgue-like silences punctuated by an – 'Oh, sure, I can see it on my desk – naat.' Andrea, somewhat unfortunately for a Style Editor, is famous for cottoning on to things just a bit too late.

I should know. I've been sat opposite her so long I've got pins and needles in my arse. Well, actually it's been nearly a year. Nearly a year since I made the grave error of going to an all-night party, and offering to share my experiences with the readers of *The News*. Nearly a year since my keenness prised me away from the dusty confines of deputy junior crime reporting. Nearly a year since those honest, earnest days spent scribbling away in magistrates' and coroners' courts, until I became one of those cheap Vauxhall-league transfers to Style. Since then, I've championed the 'what normal people look like in designer clothes' corner. I've been dressed up in hipsters, bumsters, I've donned blonde and dark wigs to see if blondes really do have more fun. I've spent a whole day in Naomi Campbell shoes, gone to Tesco's in a transparent dress, test driven the micro skirt, the tube skirt, the split up the side skirt and all in the name of fashion. Then at the beginning of every week I've sat and stared at my cursor as it's willed me to write something of import and interest. Winking at me like a Bangkok whore, it's promised so much more than it's ever delivered.

'Oh, God,' I mutter. 'Let's see if she really notices. "Gone are the days . . ." I start to type with ostentatious zeal. "Gone are the days . . . when . . . when women only ever had one style of skirt in their wardrobe, um, now," I pause. "Now . . . they've got two."'

'Oi, Abigail,' barks Andrea from over the other side of her terminal.

'Mmm?' I reply, recoiling slightly as a cloud of acrid breath floats over the computer. Andrea's had another of her liquid lunches.

'How are yer doing over there? How much longer are you going to be?' She coughs and starts patting the top of her desk. 'I haven't got all day, these pages need to go soon.' She exhales loudly, finds what she's looking for and sparks up another cigarette.

Andrea is always slightly hysterical of a Monday afternoon. She has a whole week to decide how to fill her page and can never make up her mind until she's seen what's been in the Sundays, particularly *The Sunday Times* Style Section. Nearly ten years in the job, seven of which have been spent on *The News*, and she'll change her whole layout if she's gone long, flowy and floral and those 'wankers' on the Style Section have gone short and utilitarian.

'Right,' she announces. 'I'm just off to the News Desk to see if there's anything important we've missed.' She stands up, throws her butt into her coffee with an extinguishing sizzle, and makes her way over to the fag free zone that is News. Out of the corner of my eye I can see her flirting heavily with Justin Connolly, the Deputy News Editor, who looks like an acne-plagued twelve-year-old in his father's shirt. Nephew of someone in management, it's obvious he doesn't know how to handle this large woman as she leans over him, serving up her breasts on a nylon and lace platter, pointing her backside, the shape of a mature Conference pear, to the rest of the newsroom. Justin's ears turn plum, as he flicks his thin fringe right and then left and then right again. Even from my distance you can see he's stammering. Andrea stands up, snakes her skirt back into place on her well-clad hips and makes her way back through the office. She's brandishing a large shiny photograph and looks really quite excited.

'Right, Abigail,' she announces before she sags back down in her seat. 'Stop what you're doing immediately, this has just come in off the wires. Liz Hurley . . . at a première, cleavage, you know, the full Versace plunge. I want 800 words about how women in their thirties should cover up. You know, um, something along the lines of Audrey Hepburn versus Paula Yates, how to dress when you're not in your twenties.'

'Oh, OK, fine,' I hear myself saying. 'A sort of . . . "Gone are the days when women knew how to dress . . . now they look like underwired trouts escaped from the farm?"'

'Yeah, yeah, terrific,' nods Andrea. 'By four.'

With almost an hour to go, I sit back and take the opportunity to contemplate the essentially male-dominated office. Rows and rows of grey plastic desks, manned by flustered-looking blokes in ill-fitting suits, each sporting a computer, a telephone, piles and piles of paper and the occasional spider plant in the final stages of atrophy. It's not the most beguiling of environments. Not exactly conducive to creativity. For all its flashy liberal views, *The News* still exudes the classic playground mentality of girls against boys. With women consigned to the naturally frivolous departments, or those with caring, sharing, health or educational overtones. Apart from the odd exception, it is usually the men who get let in on the hard stuff. A year of journalism school in Cardiff does nothing to prepare you for a future in skirt lengths. It fills you with romantic ideas of John Pilger civil rights stories, government conspiracies, worthy investigations into corrupt international conglomerates. Fortunately it doesn't take long before such stupid notions are knocked out of one's fluffy female head. As I sigh, bemoaning my fate, the telephone goes.

'Abigail Long?' says a clipped voice the other end.

'Yup.'

'Tricia here, from the Deputy Editor's office.'

'Oh,' I say, suddenly sitting up straight as if I'd been caught thieving. 'Oh, yes, yes, that's me,' I embellish, stammering like a pubescent on her first date.

'The Deputy Editor says he'd like to see you tomorrow morning, after conference, if that's convenient for you?' she says in such a way that suggests it should be.

'Course,' I say, feeling like I want to throw up all over my console. 'After conference, that's fine . . . Um, did he say what he wanted me for?' I venture.

'Er, no, not exactly,' replies Tricia, implying she knows exactly why I've been summoned. 'See you tomorrow then?' I could swear she's smirking. 'At 11.30,' she adds, before putting the phone down.

Not exactly? Not exactly? What on earth can that mean? My mind lurches to overdrive. Not exactly. Well, I'm obviously going to be fired. That's it. My piss-poor career, like a spring lamb unaware of mint sauce, cut short in its prime. And all I have to show for it is a pile of cuttings about the pros and cons of wearing American tan tights. Good for nothing except a junior post in the twizzeting world of Style. No one gets called into a meeting with Gavin West, the grim reaper of Fleet Street, unless it's to be fired. I hadn't seen the guy since I was hired and he found the time in his lunching schedule to meet me. Oh, God. Gavin West. Gagging Pest. As he's known by the News Desk secretaries for his legendary ability to frot you in the lift on his way up to the fourth floor. Gavin West, the man who's reduced even the toughest political columnist to tears over an expenses claim. 11.30 a.m. 11.30 a.m. . . . I should go and get catatonically drunk while I'm still employed.

It's a long and lonely walk to the tube, especially if it's raining, but most especially if you're about to be fired. On leaving the concrete cube that is *The News* building, I was expecting to feel some sort of elation. After all, it's the last time I'll make this tiresome trip along this pavement. The last time I'll be coiffed and douched by a passing juggernaut. But no. All I feel is that I've been mugged from behind by a passing hangover. Sick, weak and concussed with headache, I contemplate a homeward-bound short in the mock-Elizabethan Parrot and Crab on the corner, but it's chucking-out time in the City and the pin stripes are beginning to choke up the pubs. All I can hear is the leather-soled clicking of their expensive shoes, as they stream past me down the steps towards the ticket machines.

The Central Line is predictably crammed with steaming coats and commuters jabbing each other in the kidneys with collapsible brollies. I squeeze my way aboard and hang all the way home. Voiding my head of all cognitive thought, I attempt the horoscope in someone else's *Evening Standard*, but in the end I allow my head to loll so much to one side that by Queensway I suddenly catch myself dribbling on my own shoulder. That's it, I think, negotiating my way through two armpits before I find my way out on to the platform. Time to call a life management crisis meeting down the pub.

The Cock and Bottle is a rarity in London's 'fashionable' Notting Hill. Just off the new bohemian shopping strip of Ledbury Road – where you can buy such sartorial essentials as flower pot handbags and faux fur sling-backs – it serves real lime-less beer, has a swirl spirit-soaked carpet, pork scratchings, locals, and a small telly in the corner for football. I think it even mounts its own team, sometimes on Sundays, for some sort of inter-brewery derby thing in the park, although I couldn't swear to it. Sunday and I are not the best of friends. It also boasts a highly competitive quick fire quiz, with an elusive cash prize, that people actually travel across London to take part in. But otherwise it's cosy, pleasantly quiet, and perfect for a life crisis meeting.

Prised into a corner, in an ethnic Peruvian fun-coloured cardigan that strangely regurgitates rogue long black hairs, I'm already on my second vodka and third packet of crisps. I've always found machine-eating salt and fat helps in a trauma. I'm not really one of those catering tins of Celebrations, Gloria Gaynor type of girls. For me, a family-size bag of cheese and onion goes a long way to helping take disappointment square on the chin. That and half a bottle of vodka.

Not one to cry wolf, it's rare for me to call a crisis meeting of any description. Three last year. And only one this. But actually in comparison to the other three – being chucked, being asked to leave the flat I shared with my lifelong friend from university who wanted her lover to move in and, oh, joining the Style Desk in the first place, this one really is quite important.

What will I do if and when I'm fired? I can hardly go back to teaching English as a foreign language down the Brompton Road again. For a start they won't have me. Being caught in a clammy teenage clinch with Carlos from Ecuador was not, and I am the first to admit this, the most professional behaviour. Anyway I just couldn't bear the long, disappointed, punctured Lilo of a sigh I'd get down the telephone when I informed my mother. 'Twenty-eight years old, dear,' she'd say. 'No flat, no boyfriend to speak of and oh, now no job . . . we are doing well, aren't we? Are you sure you don't want to come home and start life all over again?'

My father, of course, wouldn't mind particularly. He'd mutter something placatory and then add something along the lines that I should talk to my mother as she'd know what to do. I'm amazed he's ever achieved anything at all, my dad, judging by his inert and ineffectual behaviour, and suffering, as he does, from a terrible selective deafness. Quite how he managed to juggle the milk quotas enough to afford to send me and my older sister to that nice day school in Taunton is a miracle of creative European subsidy accounting. Plus the £25 a week he gave me while I was studying English at Bristol University. It's no wonder he's got a bad heart and uses his aural affliction to avoid tension and argument at all costs. Anyway he's totally useless in a crisis, as I found out when I phoned weeping from the tube after the Carlos clinch. Caught him between milking shifts, heating up some soup for lunch, told me to have a stiff drink down the pub and ring back at four when my mother would be home. Let's hope this lot are more useful, I think, shovelling in another handful of crisps.

First to arrive is James Moore. The lovely James Moore, long limbed, blond, funny, rubbish and one of my oldest and dearest friends.

'So-o-o sorry I'm late,' he announces, mounting a foot stool.

'But Chelsea were on Sky and I had a double on Wise to score first and Chelsea to win 5–1. I knew it was an outsider but it came in. Can you believe? I should be rich. Five hundred quid. But then I realised I'd ticked the wrong box and said that Wimbledon would win 5–1. So I thought, shag it, gave up, couldn't get a cab and now here I am. Got a fag?' he asks, almost without drawing breath. 'Anyway what's the crisis? Are you pregnant?'

'Of course I'm not. I haven't had sex in over six months,' I say. 'Anyway, if I were, you'd be the last person I'd call. You're totally crap when it comes to all things corporeal.'

'Now that's not true,' he says holding up his hands in a double stop sign. 'When Alex was bitten on the neck by a rat while we were sleeping on the beach in Villefranche, I held his hand when they gave him his rabies jab in hospital. That was terrible. I was nearly sick. But I held it in.' He looks very hurt indeed.

'Actually it's work,' I say between crunches of cheese and onion.

'Oh, work,' he tuts. 'Now that reminds me, before we get on to you. Can we do me? Um, what about this for a feature idea?'

'Feature idea? Thought you were going to spend four months living and sleeping with the Tamil Tigers in Sri Lanka?'

'I am, I am, but not for a while anyway ... the BBC are still thinking about it ... In the meantime I'm really broke, obviously, so how about this for a chink-chink-chink money-spinner article that requires no research whatsoever? Single mothers: why does everyone hate them? They're OK ... After all, and here's the catch,' he says raising his right index finger in anticipation, 'I was brought up by one.'

'What, a single mother?'

'No-o, silly, a mother.' He looks keenly for an answer, nodding his head. 'No?' he says, sounding slightly defeated. It is so tragic, I can't even be bothered to reply. 'No? No. You're right. Maybe it needs a bit more work. Drink? Oh, you've got one. Back in a sec.'

James gets up, goes to the bar and immediately enters into some long complicated conversation with the barman, sharing with all and anyone who'll listen his betting problem. James is one of nature's chatters. It's his legendary desire to engage with everyone around him that always lands him in trouble. If he'd kept a quiet and low profile, he'd never have had all those problems in Thailand. If he hadn't been showing off in some low rent bar, about his new-fangled scuba diving skills, then the local Mafia boys wouldn't have got the wrong end of the stick and been convinced he was investigating their off-shore heroin smuggling. They wouldn't have stolen his computer, his passport and his money and then the British Embassy wouldn't have had to smuggle him out of the country for fear of his assassination. When all the time James had been doing some nice, genteel travel piece on seahorses. But then again, if that were the case, then James wouldn't be nearly so entertaining.

He describes himself as a 'cocktail correspondent', or at least his friend Alex does, and he spends his time living what the rest of us would quantify as 'pub plans'. Ideas that shouldn't normally leave the beer mat upon which they were hatched. Yet somehow, bizarrely, and in a manner that is totally beyond James's own comprehension, he does manage to pull off the occasional scam. He's been nominated for a BAFTA. He didn't get it, obviously. But he went to the black tie ceremony and lost with tremendous grace and humour and came back the next day and told us all how he'd peed next to Jeremy Paxman and it was no wonder the man was so confident.

'So work then?' says James, finally returning to his stool, his pint of lager a third drunk already.

'Yes,' I say. 'I think I'm going to be fired.'

'Who's going to be fired?' announces Wendy, throwing one half of her fuchsia pashmina over her shoulder. 'Hi, James. Sorry, what's that? Who's going to be fired? Come on, spill, spill,' she continues, flicking her ash on the floor as she sits down.

'Well, me,' I say.

'You!' she says. 'What are you thinking? Of course you're not. You're the most talented writer I know.'

'I'm the only writer you know.'

'They can't do without you on the ... the ... where d'you work again?'

'The News.'

'Yes, yes, *The News*. They can't do without you on *The News*. Only the other day I heard how fabulous you were from someone, somewhere at something or other. Anyway, whatever. Don't talk bollocks. They won't fire you. They can't. They need you.'

They don't, of course, but Wendy's always like that. Full of frantic hyperbole. Wendy Slater is a bit part, daytime television presenter on *This Morning*, who works maybe once every two to three weeks, and hates her job with a cynicism that belies her generosity in all things, other than vox-popping the general public as to their opinions on the day's hot controversy. As clever as she is thin, she is appallingly bad with secrets, especially when drunk, and particularly with ones concerning herself. Although she pretends to love scandal, eyeliner and the latest in Jimmy Choo, she's actually at her most content lying on her sofa reading Renaissance art books on Florence.

'Now, why d'you think they're going to fire you?' she asks, emptying the contents of her handbag on the table as she reaches for her ringing mobile. 'Only my agent and he can wait,' she says, pressing the 'busy' button. 'This is much more important,' she announces, nodding a thank you as she accepts her vodka and bitter lemon that James has gone and bought her.

'You haven't got pissed and shagged someone, have you?' she asks with predictable directness and vulgarity. 'Thrown up at work? Well then, what are you talking about? Oh, hang on there ... message,' she says, as her phone bleeps rudely on the table. 'One sec.' She places the set to the side of her head. 'I'm going to give myself a cauliflower ear if I'm not careful,' she says, inhaling deeply on her Marlboro full strength as she concentrates. 'Oh God, fuck off, fuck off, fuck off,' she says, dropping the phone back down on the table as if it's just contacted a virulent social disease. She curls her lips and takes a swig.

'Fuck off, what?' says James.

'Fuck off, they want me to do one of those bra and pants shoots for *What Men Want*. You know, that piss-poor wank-mag that parades as new laddism,' says Wendy, sighing loudly and stubbing out her cigarette.

'Oh, I love that magazine,' says James. 'In fact I love them all. They've always got some really foxy bird in her underwear doing the washing up or something. My favourite was Anna Friel, she looked amazing. Isn't she a lesbian?'

'That was only her character in *Brookside*, you idiot,' sighs Wendy. 'Anyway I'm not going to do it.'

'Do what?' says a voice.

'Oh, finally, you deign to show,' I say to Colin as he slips in beside me and kisses my cheek, removing his long black leather coat as he does so.

'I know, I'm sorry,' he says, his pale blue eyes grinning his apology. 'But I had Polly Friend on the phone in some sort of crisis and couldn't get rid of her.'

'You're not still in love with her, are you?' I sigh, looking towards the Lord.

''Fraid so,' says Colin. 'What can I say? She makes me laugh.'

'I make you laugh and you've never fancied me,' says Wendy, making what we all agree to be a very salient point.

'Polly's got bigger tits than you,' says Colin, with a wide smile as he steals one of her cigarettes.

'Polly Friend, Polly Friend, all I hear these days is Polly bloody Friend,' parrots Wendy. 'I mean, what's she ever done? Except star in a sexy credit card ad and show off her assets in *What Men Want*.'

'She's actually really nice,' insists Colin. 'And she's had a really hard life.'

'Oh, my heart bleeds,' I say theatrically.

'Who's Polly Friend?' says James, perking up a bit after his pint.

'Who's Polly Friend?' says Wendy in mock shock horror. 'Who's Polly Friend? Where've you *been*?'

'Ivory Coast.'

'Course you have,' she mumbles and lights another cigarette.

Colin starts to laugh. It's contagious. He has to be the sweetest, kindest, most gentle man in London and that's not because he's my friend. Rather handsome, Colin Chapman is the fortunate owner of that black-hair-blue-eyes combination most girls fall for. As a result, he has an awful lot of gratuitous, meaningless sex on more than a bimonthly basis. However, he's always falling in love with girls who, it would be generous to say, are insane. And the more nuts they are, the more he falls for them. Anyone simple and straightforward, who wants to make him a nice pasta supper with a side salad and a bottle of wine, never gets beyond the initial penetration.

If I knew his mother, I'd blame her. For him to have ended up this way, he must have had an upbringing as natural as Pop Tarts. But just so long as you don't go to bed with him (and I haven't), he's wonderful. The sort of bloke who will sit for hours in Jigsaw while you try on clothes and give you a genuine well-informed opinion on each sortie from the cubicle. And he's got a cult following in Primrose Hill. His comedy act – of a comedian who can't tell jokes – goes down well with those clever enough to understand. Channel 4 keep saying they're very interested.

'Guess what?' I say.

'What?' says Colin.

'Wendy's been asked to do a bra and pants for *What Men Want*.'

'Have you?' says Colin with a smile seductively unfurling across his face. 'Yum, yum. Finally we'll get to see you without all those jumpers on. Can I come down and hold the powder brushes and ice cubes and generally spy or something useful?'

'No, you bloody well can't, and anyway I'm not doing it,' flounces Wendy. 'First of all, no matter how much airbrushing and lighting and clever creative camera work they say they'll do, I'll look crap because I don't have the chest for it. And secondly I've got a degree for chrissake. I mean, what does it say to other women? Schoolgirls even? Women may have hurled themselves in front of horses and gone bra-less for decades but these days "Girls! To get ahead, get your kit off"?'

'Since when have you been a teenage role model?' teases Colin.

'I know, no one has ever heard of me or is likely to, the way things are going, but I have principles.'

'Principles?' James starts to giggle. 'You were very principled this morning taste-testing cook-in sauces in Stockwell.'

'What were you doing watching daytime TV?'

'Well, you know . . .'

'Anyway, at least I had my clothes on.'

'Why not do it? I think you're making a great mistake. I think it's a great opportunity to launch yourself a bit and get a higher profile,' says Colin. 'Polly did it.'

'Precisely.'

'Precisely, what does that mean exactly?'

'Precisely . . . nothing. I don't know, I just don't think it's a very good idea for me,' says Wendy as she starts deleting messages from her phone for want of something to occupy her.

'More drink anyone?' offers James, standing up and making his way over towards the bar. 'Ah, oh dear, I've only got a fiver left,' he says, hopefully rummaging around in his rather thin coat, emptying pockets for something he might have squirrelled away earlier for safe-keeping. 'Unless someone offers to give me a lift home, or something,' he says hopefully. 'Either that or I could cash a cheque, um . . . if I had a book, that is.' He smiles. 'I'll just go to the bar then, shall I? Who's got some money then?'

Wendy brings out two crisp twenties. Everyone looks impressed.

'Wha-a-at?' she says. 'I've just been to the cash point.'

'Hand one over then,' says James, holding the large crisp piece of paper to his nose and inhaling deeply. 'I lo-o-ve the smell of money,' he announces. 'Just a pity I never have any. Vodkas all round, is it?' We all nod. 'And mine's a pint,' he says with total relish.

'So, right,' says Colin. 'Seeing as you dragged me all the way over here . . .'

'Up the road . . .' I correct.

'What's the crisis?'

'I think I'm going to be fired,' I say. Three vodkas in and it doesn't sound so bad.

'And the evidence for this is?' says Colin, reaching for another of Wendy's cigarettes.

'Oh, I don't know,' I reply. 'Gavin West wants to see me in his office tomorrow and that usually means a monstering of some sort.'

'You never know,' says James optimistically. 'He might want to make you Arts Editor or something glamorous like that. And if he does, promise to give me a job? God knows I could do with someone recognising my very hidden talents.'

'You can all have jobs,' I say generously. 'But he won't, it'll be a plain and simple firing, you mark my words.'

Tuesday morning, and I'm as fragrant as a pub carpet. Eight vodkas, plus the pineapple martinis we made back at James's, and death by nasal hair extraction would be less painful. There is something about a bowl of semi-putrid fruit and a cocktail book (from last year's stocking) that brings out the Tom Cruise in every bloke. Nothing like being fired with a hangover, I think, as I walk slowly towards *The News*. My head rattles at each impact with the pavement. My mouth, dry as a cocktail bar in Saudi, has barely managed to manufacture a downable bolus all morning, which means the bacon sandwich in my hand has become more of a hindrance than a help. By the time I finally make it to my desk, Andrea's already there, collecting ash in her cleavage and flicking through the new *Vogue*.

'Bad night?' she enquires. The fag in her mouth conducts an orchestra.

'Two in the morning,' I say, adding an hour for rock and roll effect.

'Seen your Liz Hurley's been flagged on the front?' she says, not bothering to look up.

'No? Has it?' I reply, trying to sound keen.

'"Liz's Frock Shock Horror". Don't you read your own paper?' she says.

'Not if I can avoid it,' I say, realising perhaps a bit too late that it's not the most diplomatic of things to say.

'Well, you should,' says Andrea, irritated. 'Coffee?' she asks, swiftly pushing her seat back with both feet. 'I'm going to the canteen,' she adds, holding out her hand.

'Oh, yes, right,' I say, looking for my purse. 'Double cappuccino with no sugar, and maybe one of those oat things,' I add, handing over a pound coin.

'Right you are then,' she mumbles, walking off, still reading her magazine.

Half an hour to go and I think I'm sweating alcohol. Either that or there's something decidedly dodgy in the bin under my desk. No second thoughts, it's definitely alcohol. I catch a glimpse of myself in the office window. Face puffed with toxic shock. Mouth like a sink plunger. Shoulder-length hair in a centre parting, just the wrong side of wash day. Large black comfort polo neck. Cheap pair of Lycra'd trousers going at the knees. 'You should always dress like you're employable, even if you're not,' counsels Wendy. Well, I've singularly failed to do that today, I think, as I scan the neighbouring desk for *Hello!* magazine.

'Yuck, late night?' says Maya Franks, placing her peach perfect behind on the chair next to me.

'Oh, yeah,' I say. 'Met. Bar, three o'clock,' I lie.

'Really?' she says, sounding impressed. 'I've never been in there myself. What's it like?' she quizzes, wrapping her legs round themselves three times over in her enthusiasm.

'Oh, well, you know, um, bit of a student disco really,' I say, repeating what Wendy had repeated a couple of weeks ago.

'Oh, God, how exciting,' she continues. 'Anyone in there? You know . . . famous?'

'Only the usual,' I say, slightly beginning to wish I hadn't gone down this route.

'Like who?' she persists. Irritatingly.

'Oh, you know, Meg, Noel, Rufus.'

'Rufus Sewell?' she says. 'I thought he was filming in Italy, or at least that's what they said in *OK!* magazine.'

'Yeah, yeah, well he's back now,' I mutter. 'But to be honest with you I didn't stay very long.'

'Just until three,' she says.

'Yeah, yeah, three,' I say. 'Um, seen the new *Hello!*?'

'It was here earlier,' she says distractedly, getting up and mincing over to the other side of the office on a hunt.

Showing off to the work experience, I think. Abigail, that's truly pathetic. Anyway, there's only another twenty or so minutes left in this place. I'll just sit and smoke a lot and wait for my meeting with Lucifer.

'Oi, Long,' comes the aggressive Liverpudlian tones of Andrea as she meanders back through the office ladened down with Styrofoam and Cellophane. 'Fattening thing for you,' she shouts, hurling a Tracker bar across Classified and Arts.

'Cheers.'

'Anyway,' she says, as she sits back down and hands over the coffee, 'shouldn't you be making your way up to the fourth floor by now?'

'Fourth floor? How d'you know about that?'

'Oh, a little birdie,' she smiles, reaching for her golden box of B and H.

'Which little birdie is that exactly?'

'Tricia,' she announces triumphantly.

I should have guessed. They've been best mates since their days on the *Mirror*. In fact, most people think that it's Andrea's friendship with Tricia that helped her get her job and, by implication, keep it.

'Run along now,' she says. 'Luck,' she adds somewhat sarcastically.

I peel myself out of my chair and start walking towards the lift. Horrible grey carpet squares in this office, I shan't be sorry to miss those. Fat bastard in charge of News, I won't miss him. Pretty foppish boy who does the book reviews and gets drunk with me at the Christmas party, I wouldn't mind seeing him again. Nice mumsie woman in charge of Health who caught me crying in the loo once, she might sign my leaving card. Camp columnist who I always thought was gay, but who turns out to have two children and rather an attractive wife, I'd like to see him if only to compare student tattoos again. As for the rest of them, I wouldn't recognise them if I ran them over.

Wendy's always telling me off for being too hearty and red-cheeked and obviously new to London. Maybe they smelt the fear when I first arrived a year and a half ago. Either way,

I had sandwiches at my desk for the first three months on News. No one could quite understand how thrilled I was when I was sent off to do the courts all day. I only had to come back to the office at around four, so there was none of that who-to-have-lunch-with embarrassment. Until I went to that rave, that is, and then the whole horrible office process started over again.

The lift makes a loud microwave sound when I reach the fourth floor.

'Are you coming out or staying in?' asks a sensible-skirted, beige-looking woman holding files.

'Oh, out,' I mumble, staring at the executive red carpet. 'Oh,' I turn, just as the doors begin to close, 'which way is Gavin West's office?'

'Right,' shouts the voice just as the lift slides shut.

The fourth floor is quiet and there are two expensive, well-maintained and obviously regularly sprayed rubber plants in large white pots at either end of the landing. There's a sweet smell of fresh paper and Tipp-Ex. I turn right and knock on the open door.

'Ah, Abigail,' says a woman in a pair of navy shoes with elasticated fronts who I presume to be Tricia. 'He's expecting you,' she says in a sibilant heavy voice that makes her sound like a caring, sharing saleswoman in an intimate feminine hygiene advert. She hands me a warm, milky coffee, in an asylum green cup, that's small enough to imply I won't be staying long. 'Well, in you go,' she hurries efficiently.

Gavin West is dressed in a multi-coloured Allied Carpets jacket of found-threads, a lemon yellow shirt and a taupe tie that announces he had eggs for breakfast. He's writing on his computer, half hidden by an enormous leather padded framed photo of his blue-rinsed wife. He doesn't bother to look up. Instead, he gestures to the sofa, and continues for another three silence-filled minutes. He presses some important keys and sits back, very satisfied.

'Now . . . Abigail,' he announces, stroking the corners of his flavour-saver moustache, moist from the coffee he's drinking. I swear I could almost hear the stirring of one of his legendary hard-ons. He's reported to get a bad case of pyramid pants, particularly with women as he gives them the bollocking of their lives. 'Now Abigail,' he says again, 'have you enjoyed your time at *The News*?'

Past tense, past tense, that was definitely the past tense. I smile so wide and tensely the right side of my face begins to twitch. 'Oh, I love it here very much,' I trill. 'Such a great newspaper, so many opportunities, such good friends and everything.'

'Oh,' he says, holding my stare, 'that'll make what I'm going to say a bit difficult.'

'It will? Shame,' I say.

'What?'

'Oh, um, that's a shame because I've really enjoyed working here and working for you and working generally . . . and I'd . . . I'd like to thank you for the opportunity . . .'

'I'm not firing you,' he interrupts in a sarcastic yawning voice. 'You'd know if I were.' He smiles at the potential pleasure of such a scenario. 'No,' he says, 'I'm offering you a column.'

'A column?'

'At no extra cost to the newspaper obviously, but a column all the same. And we might, if you're lucky, put your photo on it, and all that jazz,' he says, getting up from behind his desk, smoothing down his trousers and fiddling with the brown leather plaited buttons on the sleeves of his jacket.

'Terrific,' I say.

'You see,' he continues, starting to pace the room in his aerated slip-ons, 'it has come to my attention that the readers are interested in celebrities.' He stops and, by way of emphasising the enormous profundity of his point, turns to face me. 'You know, famous people. *Hello!* magazine and . . . and . . . the other one . . . are all the rage. And, as I said to my good friend Michael Winner the other day when we were in the Mirabelle with Jenny Seagrove, Joe and Joanna public are fascinated. They want to know about Phil Collins, they want to know about Cliff Richard, and those . . . Spice Girls. They want to know what they think, where they eat, what they do in their spare time. Fame is no longer a by-product of talent – an irritating thing that happens on the way while you achieve your ambition – it's the ambition itself. Schoolchildren now just want to be famous. They don't want to walk on the moon any more, discover cures for cancer, write symphonies. They want to be photographed on holiday.' He starts pacing again. 'And I want to capture this market, Abigail. I want you to do something up to the minute. With it. Hip. You're the girl to do it.' He winks. 'I want you at all those parties and openings and things. I want you to mix with the stars, find out what they think about the hot topics of the week. And then report back to readers of *The News*.' He pauses and clears his throat. 'You can't have expenses, obviously, because of the cutbacks, but this is your big chance, Abigail.' He turns to face me, marvelling at his own marvellousness. '"Abigail's Party",' he announces, laughing at his own joke, doing the big-name-in-lights thing. 'That'll do.'

I don't know what to say. So I just sit with my knees slowly approaching my ears as I sink into the sofa unit. I smile.

'What are you waiting for?' he asks, totally carried away by his own enthusiasm. 'You'd better get on to Descartes right away.'

'Descartes?'

'The PR company,' he says slowly, like he's trying to communicate with the hard of hearing. '"I Am – Therefore I'm With Descartes", that PR company. Only the most important brokers of celebrity spin in the country.' He sighs with ostentatious irritation.

'Oh, right, thanks very much,' I say as I get to my feet.

'Oh, by the way,' he says as I'm halfway towards the door. 'You're on six weeks' trial, no promises and, oh, clear your desk, dear, you'll be working from home.'

★ ★ 2 ★ ★ ★ ★ ★ ★ ★ ★ ★

Richard and Judy are having an intense conversation with slimming specialist, Rosemary Connolly, about the pros and cons of cottage cheese, while I'm on hold for the fifth loop of some supposedly relaxing whale-soundz track. Lying on my sofa, piling cigarette butts up in a stolen Conran ashtray, I'm holding for Damon Dupont at Descartes, as I have been more or less all morning. No amount of redialling helps, for hardly has the telephonist time to get to the 'car' part of the company name and it's straight to the whales. Occasionally she tempts me, raising my hopes, by calling me back from my electronic hades and asking me who I'm holding for. But then it's straight back to the whistling, another fag, more *This Morning* and pressing questions like how d'you makeover a child's bedroom with only £25? What's the latest shape for eyebrows and why is Richard still sporting that lady hair circa 1986 bouffant?

Must really strim my legs, I think, picking off the remnants of last summer's lime green nail varnish that still stubbornly cakes the end of my toenails.

'Damon Dupont,' comes a brusque but not unattractive voice down the line.

I sit up, knocking the ashtray and all its contents on to the floor.

'Oh, hello, I've been holding for you for . . .'

'Hang on,' he replies, 'my other line's going . . . Dupont.' I can hear him efficiently in the background. 'Yup . . . yup . . . three . . . no, I can't do any more.' He sounds increasingly tetchy. 'No-o-o . . . it's not worth talking to anyone else . . . it's full. Look,' he sighs finally, 'we've had Health and Safety on to us already . . . three, that's my limit. Right. OK. Bye.' He puts the other phone down. 'Yes?' he huffs into my middle ear.

'Hi,' I start again. 'My name's Abigail Long and . . .'

And I lose him again. His mobile starts to vibrate on top of his desk. 'Hi . . . yep, fine . . . love you too . . . call you back,' he says. 'Right, yes, Abigail Long from *The News*?' He's back with me again.

'Oh, yes,' I say. 'Um, I've got this new column thing . . .'

'I know.'

'You do?'

'It's my job,' he monotones, bored with the way this conversation's going.

'Gosh, you're on the ball,' I gush. 'I only got it yesterday.'

'What can I do for you?' he continues, ignoring any attempt at small talk or bonding in any way, shape or form.

'Um, well I was wondering, someone told me that you're in charge of the *Love Letters* première tonight and I'd . . . I'd love to come.'

There's a long pause. I can't resist the temptation to vomit into the void. 'I've read some very nice things about the film,' I say, half-wittedly.

'I'm not in charge of that side,' he corrects like a pedagogue. 'I'm doing the PR for the party.' He pauses. 'And the thing is,' says Damon, slowly. 'We're not sure we really need *The News*. The *Mail*, *The Sun*, *The Times* and the *Mirror* are all covering it with their regulars and, well, to be honest, your circulation's down, a diminishing number of ABC 1s . . . I mean, what have you got to offer that I can't really get just as easily elsewhere?'

I'm now totally thrown and try to laugh through my embarrassment. 'Oh, um, a nice column saying how marvellous the whole thing is?' I punt.

'Well,' he sighs, shuffling paper.

'I could fax it to you before I publish?' I lie, astonished at my own compliancy.

'You're not exactly flavour of the month here at the moment,' he continues, unimpressed.

'I'm not?'

'The Liz Hurley piece you wrote yesterday? Caused us all sorts of trouble.'

'It did?' I say, frantically trying to remember exactly what I'd written.

'Yes,' he replies curtly. '"Liz's Frock Shock Horror". Not popular. Particularly with the boys at Warner's. Anyway,' he mumbles, like his mind's been lured away in some other direction, 'all I can give you is one ticket to the party. Not the film. And,' he pauses, 'obviously in the light of Liz Hurley, Gwyneth Paltrow is strictly off limits, and I will be there to make sure that she is. You may, however' – I start brushing the ash off my trousers. He's beginning to sound like he's orienteering a coachload of packed-lunch swinging schoolchildren at Slimbridge – 'You may, however, speak to – and I suggest that you do – the other hot new Brit Pack actors in the film, particularly Jack Morris and Hamish Rowland, also the writer/director Jason Phillips and the producer Vince Graham.'

'Oh, thanks very much,' I enthuse effusively over a list of names I'd never heard of. Except, of course, Jack Morris, 'Britain's Leo DiCaprio' as all the teen mags have dubbed him, and possibly Hamish Rowland who could be, if I remember correctly, the younger brother of Oscar-nominated sister, Patricia Rowland. 'D'you want my address to bike the ticket round?' I venture, bravely.

'Er, no,' he coughs. 'You can collect it from me on the door. Bye.'

'Oh, Damon . . . Damon,' I shout.

'What?'

'Where is it?'

'Where's what?'

'The party?'

'Oh, right,' he says, possibly sounding apologetic. 'Um, the old gas works, Cleveland Road, Pimlico, starts at 10.30. It's black tie.' Before he puts the phone down, I can hear his mobile revving up again. 'Damon . . .'

So that's it, I think, one solitary ticket to *Love Letters*. The hottest première of the week and I'm going on my own. I lie back on my biodegrading, borrowed from home sofa with cover-all ethnic throw and stare at 'crimper to the stars' Nicky Clarke combing 'products' through some model's hair. Dressed in his signature leather trousers, apparently because they don't attract hair clippings, he snips 'movement' into the back of the head, adds some Charlene Tilton flicks to the front and completes his 'you too can do it at home' compare and contrast with the latest off the catwalk in Paris.

I'm only half watching, really. I'm waiting for Wendy to appear. She'd called earlier, all sweaty and hysterical, saying they were making her dress up as a tomato to coincide with National Tomato Week and spend the morning in Lakeside, Thurrock, asking the man in the street if they could tell the difference between a Spanish – raised on nothing but water and chemical grow-bags – and an English Evesham organic. It's the sort of item my father, if he were ever to watch, would thoroughly approve of.

While I lie back and wait, glancing occasionally at the remnants of the Kelloggs Barbecue Beef Super Noodle supper that float on a film of old cold grease, currently clogging my 'seventies apricot formica surround sink, I realise I'm actually quite nervous about tonight. I start pacing around my extremely small bed-sit apartment, which takes all of five seconds. The result of living in a fashionable area is that you have no room for anything. Boxes of old records are piled high either side of the telly. Covered in material they pose as tables. Since my ex-flatmate pinched the stereo before slinging me out, I no longer have any use for them. Actually the place was rather bijou and smart before I moved my stuff in. But somehow trips abroad have managed to clutter the place with useless hessian and wooden artifacts. A trip to South America was particularly messy. Pink and yellow candlesticks don't look half so cool on a chipped Ikea black ash table as they did in a Guatemalan market. The cramped boarding school for bacteria that pretends to be my kitchenette boasts three matching mugs, a Chilean poncho wall-hanging and a cornucopia of china gleaned from various grandmothers' garages all over the country. It's not what one would describe as a shag pad. Even in my most Mata Hari of moments I always, if at all possible, play away. Bring a bloke back here and there is a distinct possibility he will never return.

I stop my exhausting pacing and lie back down on the sofa to contemplate the fact that I have never been to one of these celebrity party events things before. I've never shared canapés and flutes with the stellar. And to be honest it's all beginning to feel a bit daunting. It's not as if I'm particularly keen on famous people. I have gawped at a few in my time. Jason Donovan in Sainsbury's, Ralph Fiennes in Urban Outfitters, Posh and Beckham by the luggage carousel in Florence airport. I'd accidentally once, when not so much slurring as gobbing drunk, asked Damon Albarn what he did, three times in as many minutes. He, I have to say, or so I was informed afterwards, was pleasant enough to reply that he was in a pop group called Blur each time I asked.

But I've never really hankered after the whole flash bulb frisson. Although I did once, aged eight, do a fifteen-mile sponsored walk for charity, with my leg in plaster, and ended up in the local newspaper. Plump and mousey, it was such a plain photograph that my mother actually refused to put it on the kitchen notice-board. Come to that, I remember once writing in to *Top of the Pops* and asking to be in the studio audience. So embarrassing. Fortunately, no one had videos then, but apparently you could see me, in the background, sporting a perfect pert Purdey haircut, shoulders moving from side to side, catching flies with my mouth, occasionally biting my bottom lip, performing white man's overbite like a groover, while watching Legs and Co. high kick and hand clap along to the number one. But that's it.

Except for the *Blue Peter* badge incident, that is. About which I am a bit ashamed. It was a simple and jealous reaction to when my elder sister, Joanna, wrote a long and complicated letter, with wax crayon illustrations, on the history of dwarf bunny rabbits (she had three) for which she received a plastic ship badge and a letter signed by Biddy Baxter practically by return. Smarting at her success and having no such hobby, I wrote something far more underhand. Something quite awful along the lines that, because I didn't have a *Blue Peter* badge, I was being picked on at school. They sent me one immediately, accompanied by a whole sheet of bullying helpline numbers. It was hideous. Years later, I still have dreams about teams of social workers coming up the drive, holding clipboards, peering over their half-moon specs, looking terribly concerned.

'No . . . no . . . it's a lie,' I scream, tying reef knots in my duvet with my flailing feet. There's a sharp intake of worthy breath. 'So you lied? To *Blue Peter*? Why?' they cross-examine me. 'An untruth! To Biddy Baxter! You deserve to be punished.' I have woken up in ponds of sweat, yelling. 'No! No! No! Biddy, I'm sorry . . .'

So tonight is going to be a bit of an ordeal. For a start I won't know or recognise anyone, especially out of their film, authorial or televisual context. Wendy's the one with a Rolodex of *Hello!* faces, plus total recall program welded into the hard drive of her head. She is the only one who's good at remembering the difference between a soap and a pop star. She says you can always tell when they morphed from one into the other by their hair: curly or unkempt equals soap and smooth as a baby's behind is pop. The major examples she cites of this tried and tested makeover are Kylie, obviously, some blonde from *Coronation Street* called Tracy Shaw and, of course, Martine McCutcheon whose fifteen-minute moment was punctuated by some fairly unsubtle hair extensions, before she went on to become queen of gala performances.

Either way, it's simply not my thing. I don't even have the wardrobe to cope with crisis meetings down the Cock and Bottle, let alone a black tie bash in some disused gas works in Pimlico. And when I do go out I somehow only ever manage to exude all the chic of an M11 road protester. Fortunately, I think, I'll be working, so no one's going to give two farts in a public urinal what I look like. That's what I hope, at least. I sigh and roll over on to my side, propping my head up with my left hand, lounging back on what effectively is my day-bed, only to catch the credits on *This Morning*.

What happened to Wendy? Judy's half-smiling gently at the camera waiting for her goodbye to appear on the autocue. Richard's fiddling dramatically with his ear-piece. He so likes to show the rudiments of a live broadcast.

'Wendy? Wendy Slater, are you there?' he shouts down the satellite link to Lakeside. 'We overran on fat-free Sunday lunch,' he explains. 'We're at the end of the show, but we've just got time to ask you about the results of your taste-test this morning. Is it the English organic or the chemical Spanish that people prefer?'

Wendy's grinning like a serial killer with a knife in the toaster.

'Sorry?' she smiles.

Richard's cliff-hanger of a question bounces around the solar system, desperately trying to find a satellite and then Thurrock. It fails. Wendy's looking as keen as a twenty-seven-year-old woman can look with Princess Leia earphones and scarlet spheres painted on her cheeks. Suddenly there's a high pitched squeak as Richard's question finds the Lakeside shopping centre, mutates and with the reverb all Wendy and the viewer can hear is, 'Fat free . . .'

'Oh,' says Wendy, confused by such an inappropriate question. 'They both are . . . relatively,' she lies, accompanying her falsehood with one of those back to studio nods.

'Thanks very much, Wendy,' picks up Judy, with a pleasant sort of with-wings smile. 'Back tomorrow with Sex Change Secrets, when Dr Raj Persaud will be discussing how to cope when your partner turns out to be not who you thought they were . . .'

My phone starts ringing.

'Aaaaaaaaaah, bloody hell, that's embarrassing,' screams James without bothering to introduce himself or the subject. 'That's got to be the worst thing I've seen in ages,' he announces, almost spontaneously combusting with glee.

'I know, I know, I know,' I laugh, joining in. 'Poor Wendy.'

'Fuck off, poor Wendy,' says James. 'What the hell was she wearing?'

'She had two bloody great diaphragms over her ears,' I giggle. My phone starts bleeping.

'James,' I say. 'Got to go, the other line's going.' I hang up.

'Hi,' comes this sad little voice. 'Was I totally rubbish?'

'Wendy? No . . . you were great. Poor you . . . are you OK?'

'Did I look awful?' she asks. 'They insisted on the hair.'

'The hair was cool,' I say. 'In fact so cool I think I might copy it. Zoë Ball's always got hers like that.'

'She's got short hair.'

'Well, not far off that anyway.'

'Where are you going tonight?' she asks. 'D'you fancy one of those your-career's-not-really-crap drinks?'

'Can't,' I say. 'I've got to go to the *Love Letters* première.'

'Wow,' she exclaims, sounding genuinely impressed. 'Lucky, lucky you. Those tickets are like gold dust, people are killing each other for less in the office today. Everyone who's anyone's going. How on earth did you get one? Have you got an extra? Can I come with you?'

'You can't.' I'm genuinely upset. Wendy would make it fun, amusing and bearable. 'I'd so love you to come with me. I won't know anyone. I'm really nervous, actually. Between you and me I'm really dreading it. I've got to talk to celebrities and everything and I so obviously won't recognise anyone. They're all going to hate me. It's going to be hell.'

'Oh, my canapé hell,' mimics Wendy, totally unsympathetic. 'How did you get a ticket, that's what I want to know.'

'That bloke, you know, at Descartes, Damon Dupont.'

'Oh, him,' Wendy whistles through her teeth. 'I hear he's really handsome.'

She wasn't wrong. Standing in the doorway to a huge aircraft hangar of a building, toyed with by blasts of damp wind, is Damon Dupont, or at least I presume it's him. Tall and blond with the sort of square, stubble-free jaw modelling careers are made of, he's surrounded by a tightly packed group of some seventy people, all glamorously dressed, all waving giant quill invitations made from stiffly laminated paper, all vying for his attention. Intently listening to his Madonna mike earphone headset, he's wearing a navy, calf-length cashmere coat, he's chain-smoking cigarettes and looks totally unmoved. As I make my way up the ramp in a pair of impractical, already painful shoes, I'm overtaken by two blacked out Mercedes saloons which each disgorge a brace of sequin-soaked females, stellar enough to set off flash-bulbs. Flanked by fat-necked blokes in cheap suits, they are immediately ushered through the throng which parts, as though ordered by Moses, and closes as quickly behind.

The quill waving continues unabated and Damon looks at his watch. It's 10.45 p.m. and the queue's already chomping at the bit, gagging to get in. The concept of arriving fashionably late is obviously meaningless at already fashionable parties. For unless you are gifted with photo opportunity, it appears the later you are the less likely it is that you'll make it in – flashy waving of laminated quill ticket notwithstanding. I, of course, don't even have one of those. Piped into a rather unforgiving black dress, borrowed from Wendy in the final desperate furlong, with a Club Class air stewardess plunge at the front and a skirt that stops fashionably but unattractively around the knees, I approach the mêlée. Their demeanour and the sound of their slapping invitations suggest farmed salmon gasping for air. It is situation impossible. No amount of pushing, shoving, hair flicking and pouting is going to get me to the front at the court of the king. Even those sneaky, sideways routes around the edge of the crowd, are littered with desperadoes suffering silently from asphyxia as they voluntarily squeeze themselves up against the barriers.

Suddenly, scuttling in from the right arrives a Dupont acolyte. In the same sort of, but obviously cheaper, navy coat, with derivative hair, he's clutching a clipboard and sporting a similar but seemingly less powerful Madonna headset. Alone and unarmed, he's walking towards the group with a relative lack of purpose. I spot my chance.

'Excuse me.' I rush over with all the elegance of a pre-op Brazilian transvestite. Focusing on the rabble ahead, he looks a little taken by surprise at the tangent of my approach and jumps. 'I'm Abigail Long,' I continue, 'from *The News*. I haven't got an invitation but I spoke to Damon today who said that I should come and get one from him at the entrance.'

'Right,' says the acolyte, looking confused by the speed of the delivery and the amount of information he's just been confronted with. 'What did you say your name was again?'

I repeat it. He starts to flick efficiently through his clipboard, running down the list of names with his finger. He then sifts through a bunch of envelopes fastened to the back of his board. 'Um, nope, nothing,' he says.

'It really should be there,' I insist. 'I spoke to Damon literally just this morning.'

'One minute,' he says and starts to fiddle with his earphones.

'Dupont . . . Dupont,' he radios to his colleague, who is all of fifteen feet away. 'Dupont . . . Dupont . . . this is Weston, Weston . . . are you receiving?'

Damon looks like he has an irritating gnat in his ear and starts tugging at his earlobe.

'Dupont . . . Dupont, this is Weston . . . Weston, are you receiving?' repeats Weston.

'What?' comes a shout so loud down the earphones that I can hear it and Weston winces.

'Um, I've got . . . Abigail Long.' He looks at me to see if he has the name right. I nod. 'From *The News* here, she says you have her ticket.'

'That's an affirmative, Weston. Repeat affirmative,' says Dupont. 'Where are you? Over.'

'Um, over here,' says Weston, with a hearty chummy wave. Damon looks up and is obviously annoyed at our childish proximity. He beckons us over and starts trying to shift the crowd.

'Gangway, gangway,' he shouts, making parting gestures with his arms. 'Let the girl through, gangway, gangway . . . Look,' he yells. 'Let the girl through, all right?'

To whistles, the crowd parts again. I can sense their disappointment at not recognising me as I squeeze my way towards the entrance.

Once inside, the place seems cavernous and empty. The loud classical music echoes. Standing by the door as I ditch my coat, my eyes become accustomed to the dark and start to take in the ostentatious decor.

The black velvet marquee roof is peppered with a myriad of white fairy lights, giving the twinkling impression that it's 'a night of a thousand stars'. The romantic theme, presumably taken from the film, is continued with four huge silver cupid-struck hearts about twenty feet across that are suspended from either corner of the hall. In the centre is the largest mosaic disco ball I've seen since *Saturday Night Fever*. As it spins, it sends small dainty squares of white light flying around the room. It is enchanting. The whole thing feels so deliciously ethereal that it's as much as I can do to stop myself from spinning round and round like the fat girl who's just turned sixteen in *The Sound of Music*. I'm having a classic Cinders moment and it feels wonderful. I look round, my fingers outstretched, looking for a sympathetic face to share my enthusiasm with.

To my right, just by the entrance, is a twenty-five-foot fountain, with three whirling pools full of floating rose petals. Encrusted with silver leaf seashells, its flow is symphonic. To my left, and scattered at various seemingly indiscriminate intervals, are huge stands of flowers – white lilies, pink roses, something unrecognisably exotic – with swathes of rambling ivy wrapped around the tall and dramatic cast-iron stands. A powerful smoke machine, hidden away in a corner, occasionally hisses a spiral of pseudo early moorland mist. It creeps across the room and curls around the ankles of a group of toned men dressed in white loin-cloths, with silver laurel crowns and jaunty silver bows and arrows slung over their shoulders, carrying trays.

'Gosh, what are those?' I say, eyeing the elegant wraps layed out in spirals on the silver platters.

'Chicken fajitas,' proffers a Brummie Cupid, desperate to lighten his load.

Damon directs me past. Obviously serious about me not meeting with Gwyneth, he has swapped places with Weston at the door and is, with his palm flat in my back, escorting me in through the sparse crowd towards the long luminous bar. Close up, he is even more delightful than his square-shouldered cashmere coat suggested. Straight nose, a gentle, some might say naughty, curl to his lips, he exudes the beguiling potent charm of someone easily in control. He is uncommonly tall and uses his six foot three or four inch height like some wary sentinel, keeping a sharp eye out for celebrities.

'Beer?' he says, looking over my shoulder as we arrive at the bar. 'Or vodka?' As he smiles in the neon glow that underlights his face, I notice one of his front teeth shines a capped lime green.

'Vodka would be lovely,' I say, brushing off the thin layer of disco purple dust covering my dress.

'Mate,' calls Damon, waving his hand in the air at a resting Cupid behind the bar. 'Two vodka gimlets, over here, when you're ready.' A pair of pectorals in Sumo-style up-the-crack pants, on recognising the boss, springs immediately into action.

'Vodka gimlets?' I quiz.

'Trust me,' winks Damon, in a manner that implies one should most certainly not. 'They're delicious.'

And they were. Moments later two short fat clear drinks arrive in an iridescent glass. Strong and limey, they take a whole minute and a half to drink.

'D'you want another one of those?' asks Damon.

'Mmm,' is about as much as I can manage as I drain the glass with all the fervour of a tramp on meths.

'Fag?' says Damon, rattling a soft-pack of white-tipped duty-free Marlboro lights, obviously stylish spoils from his last trip abroad.

'Where've you been?' I ask by way of making conversation. Damon is not exactly a chatty font of rib-tickling anecdotes. In fact, although certainly charming, he spends most of the time on the look-out for the famous, scouting over my left and right shoulders and quite cannily using the mirrors behind the bar to check on his reflection.

'Sorry?' he says, leaning to hear my question. He smells subtly of the sweet cinnamon spices of expensive aftershave.

'Where've you been?' I repeat.

'Oh, God,' he exhales expansively in my face. He shouldn't do that very often. Garlic, Airwaves, Doritos and a passing fajita are not the most captivating of combinations. 'We-e-ll, we had this press trip to Amsterdam where I took four hacks for a Dutch Eurotrash special,' he says, suddenly becoming animated. 'Christ, some of the things we saw. Antoine couldn't believe it. And he's seen some things doing that show. Jean Paul came along for the ride. It was just wild.'

'Sounds amazing,' I smile. 'This place is filling up a bit now, isn't it?'

'Yep,' says Damon, doing a 360 degree recce. 'Shall I tell you who's here so far?' he suggests. 'Then we'll go to the VIP area.'

'VIP?' I say. 'Oh, you mean this isn't it?'

'You're joking, aren't you?' replies Damon.

'Course,' I lie, fumbling for my notebook.

'Right, ready?' he asks. I nod. 'OK, in the far corner below the heart you've got Chris Eubank, Patsy Palmer and Sid Owen and oh, yes, with a new wig do, Barbara Windsor.' I scribble away. He ticks off on his fingers. 'By the pink inflatable sofa there's Tony Slattery, Alan Davies, and Graham Norton, and Steven Beckett from *The Bill* is just coming in and he's next to Peter Davidson and Raquel from *Only Fools and Horses*.'

'Who?'

'Raquel from *Only Fools and Horses*,' he repeats as if by saying it slower and louder I might somehow know who she is. 'I've seen two of the All Saints around, the one who had the baby and one of the sisters – Nat/Nicky – can never tell them apart, they both look like Dani Behr. Anyway,' he continues. 'We're expecting Denise Van Outen and Jay Kay, obviously. Zoe Ball now that she doesn't have to get up in the morning. Um, Johnny Depp.'

'Johnny Depp?'

'Well, he's filming here at the moment, so what else is he going to do in the evening except watch telly in his hotel room?' Damon pauses for a second and then frowns. 'Then of course, you know, the regulars in the black and white section of *Hello!* magazine, the fillers at the back of *OK!* who always seem to arrive at the same time and together. But don't for one second think they like each other,' he smiles, waving a cautionary finger. 'It's only because on their own they won't make the paper. Here they come,' he starts to giggle. 'Christopher Biggins, Tamara Beckwith, Yasmin and Yasmin, Tara Palmer, Henry Dent Brocklehurst and oh, where is she? . . . Oh, oh, panic,' he comes over all of a sarcastic tiz. 'And relax . . .' he announces, 'his lovely wife, Lili Maltese. Right,' he says, suddenly clapping his hands, 'follow me.'

The party is, by now, well and truly and tightly packed out. From the perma-spinning disco ball it must look like a marauding mass of sequin-clad woodlice, all mounting each other in a frantic bout of air kissing, networking and bitching.

'I thought Gwyneth looked ghastly,' opines a mountain of blancmange in a baco-foil frock as she stains her trucker's cigarette with another ring of lipstick. 'I've never seen some-one look so much like a man in drag. No tits at all. And did you see her frock this evening? Big mistake.' Her coterie of girl chums squawk with the euphoric delight of Bernard Matthews' farmyard on Boxing Day.

'So what did you think?' asks one tight snake-skin jacket to another.

'Well,' queens the second, 'I couldn't quite get my head around four blokes all being in love with Gwyneth and then I thought the letter writing competition thing at the end to choose which one wins was a little weak. But Jack Morris is handsome, don't you think? He really is the dark Leonardo for the Millennium. We should get him for the magazine.'

Another five more minutes of barging and we finally arrive at the foot of a red roped-off staircase that is guarded by what look like two friends of Mike Tyson in black ties.

'You wait here,' orders Damon, as the torsos give way and he mounts the stairs. 'Don't move . . . I'll be back.'

Standing alone on the wrong side of the cord of fame, with my fixed version of an approachable smile playing on my lips, I move from one hip to another trying to look busy. But after about precisely three minutes, it becomes too apparent to the surrounding throng that I'm a Billy-no-mates. And much like I'd been the perpetrator of a revolting macrobiotic fart, the circle around me widens as the stench of my unpopularity disseminates.

Peter Andre arrives. Sporting a nice shiny chest, he tries to charm his way upstairs. The Friends of Tyson grunt and mutter something about a special pass. He looks totally bewildered.

'A pass,' he pronounces, stumbling over the words. He starts patting the pockets of his combat trousers in such a way one presumes he doesn't have responsibility for his own house keys, let alone a VIP pass. He looks around for help, and is soon ushered away from humiliation by his hair stylist intent on an alcoholic mission. Just as I contemplate taking out my notebook to give myself a sheen of journalistic credibility, a *Brookside* thesp turned just-charting popster arrives with a

Saturday Magazine happy snap camera, recording his stellar-studded week for posterity.

'D'you mind?' he asks, handing it over, as he wraps his arm around the GMTV showbiz presenter who is wandering around with an aimless camera crew in tow.

'Course not,' I smile, thrilled to be engaging with anyone. They pout and preen and pretend they know each other and as I hand it back, I spot an interview opportunity.

'I'm sorry to do this,' I fawn, 'but I'm Abigail from *The News* and I just wondered what you thought of the film.'

'Oh, right,' he says, rearranging himself in his thigh-length leather jacket and running his hands through his stiff gelled hair. 'Hang on a sec,' he frowns. 'What did I think of the film? What *did* I think of the film?' He places his finger theatrically on his chin. 'I know, I know ... "Not only is it fun to see, it's fantasy,"' he announces and then leans over. 'Get it? Fun to see ... fan ... ta ... sy ... Good, isn't it?' he nods. 'Roger Moore said that at the première of *Dr Dolittle* and I've remembered it ever since.'

'Thanks,' I smile, slightly bewildered. 'Um, very good.'

'Cheers,' he says, turning away. 'Oh, when will that be in then?' he asks.

'Oh, some time next week,' I grin.

He seems pleased and runs off, shouting in the direction of Peter Andre, waving his camera. I take out my notebook, start curling my hair around a finger in pseudo deep thought and commence jotting down the canapés. Fajitas, obviously, plus sesame prawn squares, deep fried pineapple chunks with cheese fondue dip, asparagus tips wrapped in Parma ham, fried courgette flowers with tomato salsa, dates stuffed with cream cheese. I've been here for about twenty minutes, like a private investigator on a stake out, and a small pile of cigarettes have piled up at my feet. I'm beginning to think about my flat, a Cuppa soup and sneaking off home, when finally Damon appears at the top of the stairs and waves me up. The FOTs give way and at last I make it into the inner sanctum of the party.

It's less crowded than downstairs. Away from the networking hoi polloi, this is an area where the truly famous can relax, rest their stellar karma and feel blissfully at home. Six groups of handsome fat sofas covered in plump silk cushions are arranged like individual sitting rooms for their comfort and convenience. The two bars run the length of a raised platform in the middle of the party and are manned by frantic looking waiters who shuttle back and forth mixing fresh raspberry cocktails. Robbie Williams is in the middle, surrounded by a group of about eight boys who are all laughing hilariously at some joke he's just cracked. All I can do is stare. Tight black tee-shirt, black silk combat trousers, trainers, eyes the colour of a Camel lights packet. He's so much more handsome in the flesh than any of those magazine covers suggest. He smiles at Damon. I grin right back, overcome with teen scream. God! This job is just fabulous.

Lulu comes over and kisses Damon's earlobes.

'This is Abigail,' he announces.

'Oh, God, hi,' I say biting my bottom lip. 'Just love all your stuff,' I suddenly hear myself saying.

'Thanks,' she says before disappearing.

Johnny Vaughan's on a sofa drinking beer with Denise Van Outen and Samantha Janus. Ewan McGregor's holding court with Jonny Lee Miller, Sean Pertwee, Jude Law and Sadie Frost. Melanie Sykes is at the bar with some bloke. Was that Kate Moss? Suddenly the whole platform is coming into focus and it's terrifying. Someone's superglued my feet to the floor. I'm finding it impossible to move, speak or function in any normal capacity. Instead I just smile inanely like a carer in the community at a patient. As I gawp around again I suddenly spot her. In the furthest corner of the area, sitting bolt upright, in a special VIP VIP cordoned-off area. It is Gwyneth. Glass of what looks like mineral water in hand, she is entirely alone, except for what looks like her swizzle stick of a personal assistant. Long blonde hair as straight as Ernie Wise, she's wearing a silver sequined strappy dress that falls in two triangles over her chest and obviously cost a four-figure sum. Damon follows my eyes.

'Right, Abigail,' he says efficiently. 'You're not here to enjoy yourself. Follow me.'

As he makes his way to the far corner of the bar, he's

accosted by a blonde with upwardly mobile breasts and nostrils bizarrely frosted like a margarita glass.

'Damon,' she slurs, wrapping herself round him like a squid. 'I haven't seen you since Val d'Isère?' she giggles, flossing up her hair. Damon barely flinches and hardly gets eye contact as he peels her off. 'Oh, all right then,' she says, falling back into her mules. 'Give me a call,' she adds, making a finger and thumb sign to her right ear. 'And make sure you do, you big D boy, you.' She waggles her finger and walks off to envelop someone else.

'OK then,' breezes Damon, approaching a group of three attractive young men and a short bloke sitting in a group at the bar, who all leap to attention at the sound of his voice.

'Hamish, Vince, Jack, Jason, this is Abigail Long from *The News*.' They all smile, they all say hello and they all hold out their hands to be shaken. 'Abigail,' continues Damon, 'the stars of *Love Letters*, Hamish and Jack, the producer of *Love Letters*, Vince Graham, and the writer/director, Jason Phillips.'

'Hiya,' I say with all the sophistication of a page three girl.

'Abigail's got this new column,' explains Damon. 'All about celebrities.'

'Well, you don't want to waste your time talking to us then,' laughs Hamish Rowland, nodding towards the rest of the section. Brown slightly curling hair, huge brown eyes with the sort of long, thick curling eyelashes Bambi fixations are made of. As he smiles and blinks in front of me, he looks very like his elder, famous sister.

'Oh, I don't know? We got a *GQ* cover,' chips in Jack. Shorter and darker, with the face and the skin of a girl, Jack Morris is every inch the new DiCaprio. His face is set to be blu-tacked to the wall of every pubescent girl's bedroom in the country and he knows it. 'And I've done *The Big Breakfast*,' he grins. Fortunately for all his girlie prettiness, he also possesses a great deal of what could be described as wide-boy, Cockney charm.

'Abigail . . . it is Abigail, isn't it?' says Vince, heaving himself off his chair. 'Which of us would you like to interview first? You do know that the other two lads, Tom Blend and

Miles Renton, are both filming Stateside at the moment with Tim Roth and Pacino. Pop that down in your pad, won't you? Anyway, I think you should do Jack first obviously, then Hamish, then Jason, and then meself. Is she doing Gwyneth?' Damon shakes his head. 'Oh? Right you are then. Well, you know, I can fill you in with all the details that any of them miss. Sit yourself down here then, and you too, Jack. Drink, Abigail? Cocktail? Or a nice glass of dry white wine?'

I'm stuck for the next hour, sitting on my bar stool, cross-examining four men in turn about a movie I haven't seen. 'You were great as . . . ?' I start with Jack.

'Simon,' he says. 'The mean and moody one who wins in the end when he writes the poem.'

'Course,' I smile. And so it goes on. Jack is amusing and sharp, a chain-drinker and smoker. He is extremely attractive and obviously very naughty indeed. He does back-to-back cigarettes and raspberry martinis throughout our twenty minutes. By the end he is swaying slightly on his seat and obviously well lubricated. 'Fucking love you,' he says, leaning in at the end of our chat. 'Come and have a few jars when you've finished,' he suggests, before planting a rather moist sticky kiss on my jaw. I don't quite know where to put myself.

Hamish is altogether a different story. Irritatingly shy, he says nothing but repeats back my questions with a musing curl to his lips and a gentle blink of his lashes. 'What is love?' he says. 'And come to that what are letters?' But he's so classy and handsome that somehow he gets away with it. I giggle and laugh and flick my hair. Forty minutes in this seat and suddenly I have become fifteen. 'I'm terribly sorry, I'm not usually this difficult,' he whispers as he gets up to leave. 'It takes me a long while before I can trust people. Terrible habit,' he says with a wide beguiling smile. 'Must get over it.'

The writer/director is just paranoid and overly keen that I like his film. 'So which bit's your favourite?' he asks as soon as he sits down. Sparking up a cigarette, he hunches forward awaiting my verdict.

'Well,' I say extremely flustered. 'No,' I pause, 'much more interesting, what's your favourite part?' And he's off, giving me the minutest detail of the plot, the turns, his influences, how he lined up the shots, the lighting. 'Many people said that I couldn't pull it off because I'm only thirty-two and it's my first film, and I've always said who needs a course at UCLA when you've got a Blockbuster video card. If you could put down that I'm Britain's answer to Quentin Tarantino I'd be most grateful.' He looks up, his grey eyes bloodshot with worry, tension and booze.

'Quentin Tarantino? I thought *Love Letters* was an E.M. Forster meets an Anthony Minghella meets a costume drama?' I say, repeating an overheard.

'It is, it is,' says Jason, rocking backwards and forwards in his chair. 'But you know . . . ?' He stares at me, arms outstretched like it's the most obvious connection in the world. 'Quentin and I . . . both worked in video shops,' he finally spells it out.

'Oh, right,' I shrug. 'I'll be sure to note that down.'

Fortunately at the moment Jason chooses to flounce off, Vince arrives. 'Ignore him,' he says, 'he's just a little tense.' And that's it. He settles down, puts his packet of Silk Cut Ultra on the bar and proceeds to begin every sentence with Gwyneth. How attractive she is. How thin she is. How clever she is. How generous she is. This he punctuates by flashing some golden handcuff thing masquerading as a timepiece. What fun she is. How popular she was on set. 'All those stories about needing a car to drive her to the set on other films?' he asserts. 'She walked everywhere!' She wasn't arrogant or aloof. Sometimes she even joked hilariously with the crew.

'She sounds great,' I say. 'Maybe we should call her over for a chat, seeing as she's so friendly.'

'Sure,' announces Vince, letting himself down from his stool. 'Oh,' he turns back. 'She's gone.'

'Gone?' I say. 'But it's not even midnight.'

'She's going to the shows tomorrow in Paris,' explains Vince. 'That's the main reason she accepted the flight over here. Probably gone for an early night,' he smiles. 'We needn't though, need we?' He pats my thigh and goes over to the bar and orders a warm magnum of Moët. 'Abigail,' he beckons on his way over to a selection of sofas, 'come and join us.'

The invitation, despite the slug trail Vince leaves behind him, is irresistible. Champagne, pretty boy film stars, this has to be a girl's idea of heaven. Even if Hamish Rowland does get up and move to the other end of the sofa as I sit down.

'D'you know?' says Jack, leaning over and practically placing his head in my bosom. 'I've never really met a posh bird like you before.'

'I'm not really very posh,' I correct.

'You're a fuck of a lot posher than me,' he says. 'East End market trader's son, me. No money, no GCSEs, no nothing. D'you know how I got this part?' he grins.

'No.'

Sitting up, he flicks his ash on the floor before turning to face me. 'I was trading perfumes down Oxford Street,' he laughs. 'Just before Christmas. What? Nearly two years ago now, and me and this mate, we'd been edged off our patch in Brick Lane by some group of tossers, and we thought, fuck it, let's flog some Diorissimo on Oxford Street. So Derek was look-out, checking for filth, and I was giving it some, you know, gob and then these film geezers turns up. They hang around staring and talking to each other so long I think they're undercover Bill and they're going to nick me. Anyway they walks up and asks me if I want to be in this film. I, of course, tell 'em to piss off, and they says they're serious. I still tell 'em to piss off again. That I'm not interested in any bullshit shit. Eventually they go off and get this script to prove they're fucking serious. Bloody amazing.' He rolls his eyes in disbelief. 'And then sure as Bob's your bloody muvver's bruvver, here I am.' He winks and takes a swig of champagne. 'Bloody peach. Don't you think?'

'That's an amazing story,' I say, becoming more enthusiastic the more I drink.

'Is that not one of the best stories you've ever heard?' says Jack, leaning in slowly and staring provocatively at my lips.

'Yes,' I say, beginning to feel quite hot and heady and short of breath. Jack Morris is really one of the most attractive young men I've met. Everything I've ever read or heard about him is more than true. 'It's most certainly one of the best I've ever heard,' I smile. 'Yes, it certainly is.'

'Did you just say "ears"?' says Jack puzzled.

'No,' I reply. 'Yes, it's most certainly . . .'

'Christ, that's funny,' continues Jack. 'Posh people say "ears" instead of "yes". Ears,' he repeats, putting on a Little Lord Fauntleroy face. 'Oi, Hamish,' he shouts up the sofa. Hamish looks up from his obviously profound and intense conversation with Jason. 'Ears, Lord Fonters here, terrible pleased to meet you, I am sure.' Hamish smiles and laughs hollowly and then gets back to his conversation. 'Ears,' continues Jack, lying back down on the sofa, laughing at his own joke. 'Bloody love posh people.' He throws his pretty square jaw back, looks at the thousands of fairy light stars and sighs. 'D'you know how to take the engine out of a Ford Cortina?' he asks.

'Sorry?' I say. I've got room spin and I'm finding it slightly hard to concentrate sitting so close to him.

'I can only do a Ford Cortina,' continues Jack. 'I rebuilt one from scratch when I was eighteen. Well, when I say scratch, I remade the body and then nicked the engine. I took nearly all night because we was crap. I've got a mate who can do a Beetle in about an hour. They're very easy, Beetles, apparently, although I've never done one. Cortinas take fucking ages.'

For the next two hours we drink another bottle and a half of warm champagne and I hear in the minutest detail how to remove a Cortina engine nut by nut, bolt by bolt, spark plug by spark plug, washer by washer. It's fascinating. Hamish leaves about ten minutes into the marathon, Vince and Jason go about half an hour later. Eventually it's three o'clock in the morning. Robbie Williams and everyone else have long since gone and it's just Jack and me on the sofa laughing hysterically about gear shifts. Damon, still totally sober or at least by comparison, comes over and announces to Jack that his car's ready to take him home. Jack struggles to his feet, putting a euphoric arm around Damon's shoulder.

'Hang on a sec, Damon, mate,' he says, grinding to an unsteady halt. 'Look, Amanda,' he tries to stand straight, 'I've had a bloody great evening. See you around,' he smiles slowly. 'And Amanda,' he nods. 'Remember "ears".' He creases up with laughter and is led away.

I collapse back into the sofa and stare at the stars. I could fall asleep here, I muse. I wonder if anyone would mind. What an amazing evening, I think. I can't wait to tell Wendy. She'll be so jealous. Johnny Depp never showed, but getting drunk with Jack Morris – it's every girl's dream. Will I ever see him again? Does he fancy me as much as I fancy him? God! How the hell am I going to write this one up in the morning?

★ ★ 3 ★ ★ ★ ★ ★ ★ ★ ★ ★ ★

Three weeks later and I'm standing in Trafalgar Square, cold, tired, and crying my, by now rather diminutive, eyes out. I've just spent the evening in the company of a theatre PR so jaded by his job he could hardly be bothered to control his sneer long enough to speak. He emitted an occasional long, bored and nasal whine when I asked him admittedly the most ill-informed of questions. But other than that he looked down his not insubstantial nose at me and then proceeded to introduce me to some of the most powerful, yet tacit, members of theatreland who all feigned a disinterested deafness to my less than probing questions. In short it was a crap night out.

Truth be known, I never thought the launch of a musical could be so dull. First off the Book of Job is not the sort of biblical bodice-ripper that naturally lends itself to a melody – but the fact that Boyzone might be covering the closing number, in their bid for the top slot in the Christmas charts, means that minibus loads of pre-teens are guaranteed to choke up the stalls with their Anaïs Anaïs deodorant and deposits of chewing gum. Secondly, unlike all the other theatrical launches I've been to so far (one), no one seemed to have bothered to book an aftershow venue. So instead of some of us being able to sneak off immediately afterwards, we were imprisoned in the darkened theatre – like veal calves on the way to France – our captivity only made mildly more palatable by green plastic tooth mugs of champagne that Indian-filed along the aisles while people were still applauding curtain down. With all of us safely locked inside the theatre, becoming increasingly compliant through alcohol, they let open the doors into the foyer and the circle bar, so we could circulate, snacking off maharajas' cushions laden with cheese straws as we went.

It was not exactly a Hollywood stellar-spotter's dream. I spied Barbara Windsor, but I'd spoken to her at the Kouros shower gel launch at Heaven night club two days previously. She was, as ever, with Martine McCutcheon, who I'd also interviewed at Heaven. Michael Winner, Will Carling, Cleo Roccos, Dr – DJ – Foxy, and Chris Tarrant were all readily sharing their views on musicals. Then I saw Polly Friend, in some spray-on red sheath, with a to-the-navel plunge, capitalising on her new, totally nude *What Men Want* front cover. I introduced myself as Colin's friend which proved enough to bring her eyes into focus and force a smile to break out on her overly pumped pillow lips.

'So what d'you think of my full bush shots then?' she whispered, raising a finely pencilled eyebrow.

'Great,' I lied, not actually having seen the magazine.

'D'you know,' she continued, 'not only did the stylist wax it into shape but he even ran a comb through it and used some Pantene hair spray!' She giggled. 'Bloody amazing, don't you think? It's the closest I've ever come to a fannicure.'

'So what did you think of the show?' I asked, laughing as I got my notebook out.

'What show?' said Polly, a bit confused.

'The one you've just seen.'

'Oh, I didn't bother to see it,' she yawned. 'I've just come from the Café de Paris where I've been presenting a cable TV award and I'm down here for the photo op. But I can lie, if you want, and say it was brilliant?'

'Would you?' I smiled keenly. 'That'd be great.'

Ever since my initial success at the *Love Letters* première, where even the normally churlish Gavin West had to admit he was pleased, *The News* have been expecting miracles. 'More of what Gwyneth Paltrow was wearing stuff,' briefs the rather jovial Marcus who looks after me on Fridays over the phone. (Andrea Adams and her push-up ashtray and Maya Franks and her fat-free figure are blissfully a thing of the past. Andrea complained she was too busy to look after my column as well as her page, so I was somewhat surprisingly moved to Monday's pop page.) 'We loved all those great quotes, like the one from the *Brookside* boy. Shame you didn't really speak to that Jack Morris bloke, he gets bigger by the day.' Marcus is really very sweet. Not only does he just love celebrity gossip, but he gets me invitations, laughs at my pathetic jokes and he saves me from having to talk to the repellent Gavin West. 'West says,' muttered Marcus earlier in the week, 'West says you should go to more parties, he doesn't think that one a week is enough, and would like you to do three or maybe even four. He also says you're not talking to enough people. He wants more of the stuff like when you spoke to Johnny Vaughan and Robbie Williams at *Love Letters*.' I daren't tell even Marcus that I'd made that bit up. Not having either Williams or Vaughan down as *News* readers, and after a couple of hours of panic, with only a half page on canapés as notes, I didn't think either of them would care they were quoted saying the film was 'fascinating', that 'British Film was definitely here to stay', and that 'Gwyneth's accent was spot on . . . again'.

But apart from a few of those ad libs here and there, most of what goes into the paper is true and it requires hard work. Getting hold of the invitation in the first place, ringing round all the PR people – persuading them to part with a ticket, persuading them that a couple of paragraphs in *The News* is a fine and wonderful idea. Then after arriving at the party it's a question of getting near to stars – circumventing their support system of publicists, friends, girlfriends and significant others and then, after overcoming my stage fright, trying to come up with a question worth answering. Some evenings it doesn't work. Some evenings I go through the whole process and come back with nothing.

So I've been out almost every night since I started. And it's all proving a bit much if I'm honest. I haven't seen or spoken to Wendy for days. James does still call every morning, but my stories aren't quite gelling with his. I've bumped into Colin a few times, once at the book launch of a friend of his where we ate three bowls of Twiglets, drank a lot of box wine and laughed at this tall shark of an agent with ears like the world cup, as he tried to steal the author, right in front of this nice bloke from Peters, Fraser and Dunlop. But apart from that it's a bit of a lonely business. Being neither famous nor fabulously big breasted means that I have limited party appeal. Once I have served my PR plugging purpose, I'm not exactly the person to be seen with, especially when there's a whole MTV station of thrusting VJs with cantilevered cleavages prepared to go down on all fours and bark for a Polaroid moment with anyone from BBC Children's *Broom Cupboard*.

Most nights I have fallen into a bit of a routine. Bowl of something cheap and indigestible on the ethnic wrap sofa, while watching the local early evening news. A sweaty blind panic as I realise I'm about to be late again. A sniffer dog search through my wardrobe working out what is fragrant enough to wear. Two minutes spent star jumping in front of the bathroom mirror to try to see below my waist, as I've long since given up on a full length, on the pretext of what I don't know won't hurt me. A chiropractor's nightmare of a sprint in inappropriate footwear up the road. A long tense wait for a taxi, a quick attempt at slapping on some slap-on using the plastic partition as a mirror, and I have so far always managed to arrive just in time for the speeches.

The next three hours are spent pleasantly smiling, trying to ask my questions, looking occupied and drinking as much free alcohol as possible. In my solitude, I've even begun to make friends with the paparazzi. They're out even more nights a week than me and appear to have no real friends or life at all outside work. A few of them have begun to sniff my name as I arrive. A veritable fag-fuelled fount of information and gossip, the paps know who's doing who, before they do. Although at first glance they appear as inhospitable and charmless as a pack of wolves, rabid for new flesh, they are in fact as malleable and easily led as sheep. All it takes is for someone's flash to go off accidentally and the rest of them follow, frantically snapping away, elbowing each other out of the way like piranha fighting over a corpse, calling out for their particular close-up, and it's not until the poor unsuspecting sound man has filed past that anyone will admit to not knowing who the hell he was. But in their social solitude they have developed a fine line in gallows humour. The banter, the quips and deadpan comments keep them warm in their roped-off pen, as they stamp around in the cold waiting for the shot.

Then as it nears midnight and the bona fide famous leave, it's time for my solitary walk through the West End in search of the ever elusive cab. The quest somehow always ends up in Trafalgar Square, and the steps outside the National Gallery. So here I am again. Cold, tired and with my arm in the air like an uncoordinated cowboy lassoing the on-coming traffic with increasing desperation. I contemplate a wet walk along Pall Mall. Past the line of imposing gentlemen's clubs with their well kept brass and shiny painted sexually discriminating doors. I have often wondered, in a more paranoid moment, if I were raped and bludgeoned on their doorsteps whether they'd let me in and – if they did – whether they'd force me up the backstairs while making sure I didn't have a mobile phone. But tonight I can't even be bothered to walk that far. I've got a Tyneside blister on the back of my right heel and it's been threatening to pop since the entrance to the National Portrait Gallery. I lean against the wall, light another undeserved cigarette and contemplate my fate, while waiting for something shiny and black with a light on to come by.

It wouldn't be so bad if I had someone waiting for me when I got home. Someone funny and understanding like James. Someone to share the anecdotes of the evening with. Someone to squeal with when I say I've met Jude Law. Someone to tell what Posh Spice was wearing. Even someone who's fast asleep would do. Warm bed, cold buttocks, are an extremely desirable combination, especially when they're a dim distant memory. Instead there's a large, badly sprung, soft cheesecake of a bed, where I can sleep like a starfish for the surplus of space. I inhale and stare at one of the bronze lions gleaming like a seal in the rain.

In the distance I can hear the irregular slapping of drunk shoes on a puddled pavement. The sound bounces off the surrounding brickwork and obscures their direction. Looking back down towards Pall Mall I see a slightly familiar silhouette, brolly-less but in a smart ankle-length raincoat, making its way, in not the most economical of routes, towards me. About thirty paces behind is another similarly dressed but shorter, plumper and definitely more pissed character. As the streetlight strikes the pointed cheekbones of the first, I recognise it as Jack Morris. Jesus, Jack Morris weaving his way towards me. The closer he gets the more apparent his alcoholic intake – he's lost control of his neck, and his head, now uncontrollably heavy, is rolling from side to side as he tries, in vain, to suppress tonic water burps. I move into the streetlight and grin hopefully.

'Wow,' he says, coming to an abrupt halt like he's walked into a glass wall. 'It'ss you,' he grins. His eyes are glassy and exude the multi-facet focus of a fly. 'It's her,' he shouts to the other figure behind him. 'Ears!!' he yells again, sticking his own out like Dumbo. 'The poshsh bird from the paper,' he smiles. 'We're on our way to Art House,' he announces like a boasting schoolboy.

'Where?' I say, feeling altogether much more animated.

'Art House, the members' club in Old Compton Street. D'you want to come? Vince is the member. Oi, Vince,' he shouts behind him, cupping his mouth like he should be dressed in lederhosen. 'D'you mind if Amanda joins us?'

'Abigail.'

'What?'

'Abigail.'

'Oh right,' he shouts again. 'If Abigail joins us?'

In the orange glow of the streetlight, I can see the stoutness that is Vince, giving an expansive double-handed thumbs up, as he zig-zags up the slight incline, dancing with a fictitious Ginger Rogers, or perhaps Patrick Swayze. It is difficult to work out which way Vince swings. Or whether, it suddenly occurs to me, there is more to his relationship with Jack, who is notoriously too pretty for his own good, even when spectacularly inebriated.

'Fan-fucking-tastic, then,' says Jack, linking my arm in his. 'You, mate, are coming with us.' He grins. 'It's a bit of a trck. You don't mind, do you? Sober us a bit,' he laughs. 'Give us a chance to drink more when we get there.'

'Trek, you say?' I smile. 'No problem at all.'

'Wait for me,' huffs Vince, like the very unfancied horse coming up the rear.

'We've been in bloody Duke's all evening,' slurs Jack.

'Where?' I ask.

'Duke's Hotel,' enlightens Vince, as he reaches the brow of his very small hill with a huge sigh of achievement. 'London's best kept secret,' he winks. 'The best vodka martinis the capital has to offer.'

'I only had three and one with tonic,' shares Jack. 'But bloody hell, it's like I had a bath in vodka and drank it fucking dry.'

'You get so pissed so quickly it's like being back at school,' giggles Vince, proudly putting his hands in his pockets. 'Wow, Christ, my phone!' he says, suddenly discovering his own mobile in his own pocket. 'Great game, great game,' he says. 'Who shall we call?' He's now looking so naughty, I can tell that it's going to be someone important. 'Jack Nicholson,' he announces with a flourish.

'Bloody hell, mate,' says Jack Morris. 'Not Jack bloody Nicholson. How the hell have you got his number?'

'Oh, I don't know,' mumbles Vince, scrolling through his directory. 'Some pissed bloke sold it to me at a party for a fiver or something.' He presses the dial and puts the phone to his ear.

'But you're a film producer?' I say.

'I know,' he smiles. 'Pathetic, isn't it? Hang on . . . hang on . . . it's ringing . . . Hello,' he says, keeping it together but for only a second.

'Nicholson residence,' comes the transatlantic reply.

'Can I speak to Jack . . . ?'

And that's as far as he gets. The next second he's doubled up in pain on the steps, tears rolling down his face, he can't speak, breathe, inhale or exhale for his own hilarity.

'*Love Letters* will be the first and last bloody film you ever do, mate,' screams Jack, almost beside himself with the joke, slapping me on the back for good measure.

'I think perhaps I should go home,' I say, suddenly feeling bored and slightly out of synch with the joke.

'No-o-o,' says Jack. 'You're coming with us to Arse House. Isn't she, Vince?'

'Yeah, yeah,' agrees Vince, wiping away a few rogue tears.

'I'm sorry, I'm sorry,' he repeats. 'But it never fails, that gag. It gets me every time. Look, I promise, we'll behave. Promise, promise, promise.'

Art House, or Arse House as Jack insists on calling it all evening, is the sort of trendy Soho members' club that appears in Style magazines. Unlike the more established variety which have their steady stream of grown-up celebrities, gently spiced with the odd Hollywood director or passing icon of the silver screen who happens to be filming in the country, Art House is the new kid on the block and it shows. Rather than the battered Home Counties inherited furniture chic of other establishments, this office conversion has all the sit-soft comfort of a first class airport lounge. A central corridor down the middle of the room – separated by half walls – divides the main bar area into a selection of padded booths, each with their own round table and low watt light fitting with mock candle effect. Packed like a Friday night pub just before last orders, the chilled air conditioning sets the cigarette smoke hard in the atmosphere but does nothing to deter the dense collection of midriff-touting young lovelies, louching around on the sofas, horizontal with Sea Breezes.

Each of these private members' clubs has its own unique selling point. Groucho's is the old establishment plus a snooker table, Soho House is the pushy establishment plus a private cinema, Teatro's is the young establishment with a huge dining room and Art House's unique selling point, as far as I could work out, is the new establishment, plus a load of girls dressed in push-up bras.

At first glance, no one appears to be instantly recognisable. Then gaggled together in one tight-knit corner just by the bar I notice two members of the latest combat trouser-sporting girl band. Just Girls, who are reputedly modelled on the All Saints. Dressed unusually in floor-length skirts and bikini tops with woollen cropped cardigans, Becky and Shandy (ex-models turned pop stars) are, judging by the hysterical squeals and broken glasses, having a shots drinking competition with some TV presenter's wife who's always photographed shopping.

Jack is beside himself with delight. Like a four-year-old released, unfettered, into the pick-and-mix, he goes from table to table, flirting, pouting and flaunting his new found celebrity. 'Christ, Abigail,' he puffs, throwing himself down on a pouffe next to me after a particularly strenuous bout of hair flicking. 'I'm knackered. I should really be getting back to Mile End, but I'm far . . . too . . . wankered.' He exhales, loudly, lies back, and puts his hands down his trousers. 'Got any coke?'

'I'm sure they've got some at the bar,' I say.

'Not that sort of coke,' he laughs. 'You know, coke?' I obviously look confused so he enlightens. 'Chang, Bolivian marching powder, Gianlucca Vialli – you know, charl-i-e,' he says, sitting up. 'Cocaine.'

'Um, no,' I say. ''Fraid not,' I say, suddenly sounding like an extremely posh public school teacher with a mouth like a cat's arse.

'Can you get any?' continues Jack, flicking dust off his trousers, like he's discussing loaves of bread. 'Call up a dealer? Girl about town like you must have numbers coming out of her ears.'

'Er, no, not really,' I shrug. 'I really wouldn't know where to start. Never taken it myself.'

'Oh, OK,' says Jack, looking totally nonplussed. 'Bet Vince has got some,' he announces and walks off.

Whether it was Vince or someone else, Jack seemed to find what he was looking for. Fifteen minutes later, he's back chatty as a children's TV presenter. 'So tell me about you?' he starts with a surprisingly unthespian opening gambit.

'There's not much to tell . . .' I start with the usual typical middle-class understatement that is supposed to make the listener goad you into sharing and revealing more. Jack is obviously not versed in such gauche social niceties and takes this at face value.

'Oh,' he says, sounding genuinely disappointed. 'Never mind then,' he shrugs. 'D'you want to see a photo of my kiddie?'

'You've got a child?'

'Yeah, nearly two.' He rummages around in his wallet. 'A

boy,' he says. 'Ray,' he sniffs. 'Named after Ray Winstone,' he laughs. 'So I suppose, in a way, I've always, psychologically speaking, wanted to be an actor. Amazing isn't it how fate somehow rears its mug when you're least bloody expecting it? You know, like with Ray, I wasn't really expecting him, and then Janine fell pregnant, and I have to admit I wasn't, you know, the best pleased of blokes. A father? Fucking me? I'd only been seeing her for three months, you know, Janine. Met her in my local down Mile End. Eyes met across the crowded bar sort of thing, like in the films, and I thought she's the dogs that girl. Chatted her up and before I knew it she was ironing my shirts, doing the tea. Fan-fucking-tastic. Now we've got Ray and I tell you I wouldn't be without him for all the tea and china in the world. You know, because I don't come from a big family myself, just me and my mum. My dad left just after I was born . . .'

Jack's Jerry Springer confessional is relentless. Occasionally he stutters as his gurning teeth are moving too quickly for him to get the words out. His legs are bouncing up and down as he speaks and he's kneading the soft furnishings. Every minute or so, he exhales loudly, emptying his lungs of adrenalin, and snorts back the thin slither of snot that keeps threatening to pour out of both his nostrils.

'Bit of a sob story, don't you think?' he smiles. 'Anyway looks like me, doesn't he?' He flashes the photo of a blond curly-haired boy in a red velvet bow tie. Apart from the colouring, the likeness is more than striking, it's uncanny. The same plump girly Lancôme lips, the short neat nose and the same straight heavy brow that movie star looks are made of.

'He looks gorgeous,' I say, moving in closer for a more focused view.

'Mmm,' says Jack, somewhat distracted. 'Not as gorgeous as those two.'

Following his glance, it is easy to see what he is talking about. Making their way over, ushered along by a pink and keenly sweaty Vince, and a portly bloke with carp lips and freckled slobby forearms like a trout, are two fantastic looking members of the female species with twin pairs of self-supporting tits the size of grapefruits.

'Jack, Jack,' huffs Vince, triumphantly, 'let me introduce you to Marianne, a dancer at Secrets who's tipped to be the new Triumph bra model, and Mandy, the presenter of *Desperate and Dateless* on Nova TV.'

Both their faces crack, with collagen-enhanced difficulty, into weirdly crooked smiles. Jack's off the pouffe in a flash.

'Ladies,' he bows, with exaggerated reverence. 'Pull up a pew.'

'I know you,' teases Marianne, pointing a square tipped French polished nail in Jack's direction. 'You're that Jack Morris, aren't you? I recognise you off *GQ*.'

'Right first time, ladies,' smirks Jack. 'I'm the one and the same.'

Mandy and Marianne giggle.

'Oh, me and my manners,' says Vince all a fluster. 'Trevor Future, I'd like you to meet Jack Morris and um . . . Abigail . . . Abigail . . . what did you say your surname was again?'

'Long,' I smile. 'Abigail Long.'

'Trevor's our manager,' explains Mandy. 'He's just totally wonderful and a real poppet.'

'I wouldn't go that far, sweetheart,' smarms Trevor, looking the other way as he holds out a cold, dank palm for me to shake. 'I just do my job and what's good for me is good for you, which is good for me. It's all just business.' He leans over to bite Mandy's earlobe. 'It so happens that I love my business a bit more than the next man.' The two girls laugh again. Neither of their citrus stacks moves.

A nervous-looking waiter comes over and is suitably obsequious when Trevor flashes his gold American Express card and orders a bottle of the best house champagne. Dressed in a wide striped suit pushed up almost to his elbows New Romantic style, with a French blue shirt that strains slightly around his expense account paunch, Trevor Future cuts an unattractive dash. His mouse hair is oiled flat, drizzled along a side parting, it's then carefully swept across his scalp towards his left ear. He has, even in the dark light of the club, a faint seasoning of dandruff across his shoulders. For a man who must be knocking the right side of forty-five he hasn't worn well. His fingernails are bitten so completely to the quick that the tips of his fingers turn up in protest. Although most certainly showered, preened and producted every morning, he still gives the impression of a man in need of a bath. It does, as Wendy would say, take more than a bar of soap to scrub one's soul. He takes a fistful of peanuts from an earthenware bowl in the middle of the low slung table.

'So,' he crunches. 'How d'you know these two blokes?'

'I met them at the *Love Letters* première,' I explain.

'Oh, right,' he says uninterestedly. 'I was there,' he announces, spraying the table with a slurry of spit and nut crumbs. 'With another one of my girls, Bernadette. Got her photographed with Robbie Williams, made *Bizarre* the next day. Total result,' he smiles, gathering another fistful.

'What exactly is it that you do?' I quiz.

'I'm a star-maker,' he replies nonchalantly. 'More commonly known as a manager, of course. I run Future PR. You've probably heard of us?' I look blank. 'Well,' he continues, slightly put out as he refills his fist, 'I take yer average girl next door and make her into The New Girl Next Door. You know, aspirational, tits, lips, backside, that sort of thing. I turn her into a game show hostess, and from there she might present some kiddie programme, she gets her kit off for some magazine, has a celebrity boyfriend and then it's a one-way ticket to £5000 PAs and a *Hello!* magazine spread.'

'I never knew secretaries were paid that much,' I smile.

'Personal appearances,' he sighs. 'Opening supermarkets, Renault motivational tours, that sort of thing. But between you and me, you can do all the promotional work you want, you can liposuction the life out of them, but it's the celebrity boyfriend that turns a girl next door into The New Girl Next Door.' He winks, nodding over at Jack.

While Trevor and I have been talking Mandy and Marianne have, through a series of skilled, well practised pincer movements, networked Jack into a corner. He is sitting bolt upright, still gurning and sniffing, but with an increasingly stiff smile squatting on his face. While Jack looks fearful, the girls both work their non-biodegradable charms as overtly and seemingly as competitively as possible. Mandy has his left thigh, while Marianne clutches his right – a piece of gold-effect nail jewellery rattles on her little finger each time she squeezes. Like a spectator at the Wimbledon Men's Final, his head whips from one side to the other, reacting to each demand, question and flirtatious giggle.

Mandy is the more provocatively dressed of the two, although the difference is only marginal. A curly dark demi-wave falling to just below her shoulder blades, she's in a maroon strappy dress made of some sort of shiny elastane material that's cut as low down the back as it is down the front. Flaring out into a full skirt, it stops just above her surprisingly hefty knees. She has bare legs and smooth shins that look like they've at least spent three afternoons a week at an electric beach. Marianne, on the other hand, is in a black floor-length evening dress, with reinforced cups to show off her assets. Her ironed straight copper hair swings around her shoulders, occasionally sticking to her heavily glossed lips. They both exude the unobtainable fantasy of a men's magazine. It's obvious that Jack, although not totally relaxed, is beginning to preen in all the attention. In fact it's Vince who's becoming increasingly annoyed. Three more trips to the gents in incontinently quick succession, Vince is emboldened enough to make his move.

'So, Marianne,' he purrs, leaning over and placing a hot, puffed hand on her thigh. I swear she recoils slightly at his touch but her polished professional smile stays in place. 'I think you've got the most perfect set of talents for the movies,' he smiles, a fine half moon of sweat on his top lip catching the dimmed halogen light. I lean in, totally fascinated. And while Trevor drones on, taking me through the list of his clients, most of whom as far as I can work out do bra and pants work for various male publications, I listen with half an ear while concentrating on the casting couch in action.

'Did you know that I'm the producer of *Love Letters*?' continues Vince. 'Took that lad Jack off the streets and totally made him into who he is. From trader to *GQ* cover boy in two years – not bad going, don't you think?'

'I thought it was Eric Fellner who produced *Love Letters*,' responds Marianne, taking a sip from her flute.

'Yes, well,' stutters Vince, 'I was one of the original producers.' He shifts in his seat, realising perhaps too late that

Marianne was sharper than her curves suggested. 'I was the one who found the writer/director Jason Phillips, and, um, all the other actors. Gwyneth and I are very close, she gave me this watch, you know.' He flashes his gold cuff. 'Gwyneth is such an amazing girl . . . have you met her?' he asks Marianne. She can hardly be bothered to respond to such a fatuous question and drinks more champagne and wrinkles her nose up at Trevor. 'No, no, silly me,' continues Vince. 'Course you haven't. Well, when I was in her Winnebago one afternoon . . . eating sushi . . .'

Sitting opposite him, despite his many loathsome attributes, I couldn't help but feel sorry for Vince. Not one of nature's most gifted men, in every sense of the word, I suspect, he is so far down in life's pecking order that he hasn't even managed to hone a line in banter. Some short, wide men with golden watches and thick waists can be extremely amusing and entertaining. But Vince has somehow not learnt the difference between chatting up and showing off. He still suffers from the playground illusion that if he boasts enough about the size of his red tractor the rest of the class will be impressed. He thinks if he talks about his film and Gwyneth enough, Marianne will somehow overlook the fact that he is a pink porker with nothing but coronary potential and drop her thong – if she were wearing one, but judging by the Stone-ing I got when she crossed her legs earlier, I suspect she isn't. Poor bloke, I think as I sit there getting increasingly morosely drunk on bottle upon bottle of house champagne, he hasn't even managed to work out that no matter how many times he mentions the fragrant Miss Paltrow, Marianne is not going to ride his two-backed beast. She is so obviously network-shagging Trevor Future that it would take the truly sensually afflicted not to notice. But as it is, the more Vince flirts, the more Trevor smiles and the more irritated Marianne becomes as her partner (business and sexual) seems disinclined to stand up for her honour.

While the three to my right fence each other with increasingly less accuracy, my evening, to put it politely, is quietly going pear-shaped. Having bumped into Jack Morris so fortuitously in Trafalgar Square, I'd been fantasising that the fickle hand of fate had some reason to connive that our paths crossed. He – a lonely handsome actor under a street lamp – me, a lonely weeping columnist also under a street lamp, it was surely a given that we should disappear into the night, only to re-emerge on the cover of *OK!* magazine as we welcome the readers into our lovely home? Instead, he's got a wife, a child, and now he's flirting with a spandex-clad babe with all the culture and sophistication of the Solihull synchronised swimming team. To say I'm disappointed is more than an understatement. I'm furious. But rather than retiring gracefully, returning home and maintaining some kind of dignity, I decide to do exactly the opposite. And not only do I stay around to witness the glaringly obvious denouement, I erroneously decide to throw my hat into the ring as well.

'Jack,' I say, slurring slightly. He ignores me. 'Jack,' I repeat louder. Again the same reaction. 'Jack, Jack, Jack.' I start tugging at his slightly shiny trouser leg to make entirely sure that he can't ignore me.

'What?' he replies, swinging round in alcohol-fuelled irritation.

'Um, did you like the column about when we met?' I smile, pushing my elbows together between my knees, competing with the saline opposite. I know I didn't really write about our conversation. I remember thinking it better to make a few things up rather than betray confidences. But still I hope he might have read at least something I've done.

'Column?' he quizzes, looking confused.

'You know, Abigail's Party in *The News*?'

'Oh, that,' he shrugs. 'Don't read *The News* myself.' He makes as if to turn back. 'But I'm sure it was very good,' he adds politely, before sating himself once more on Mandy's more obvious charms.

I'm left to scratch my ankles for want of something to do. Sitting back up, I try to light the wrong end of a cigarette, which I fortunately get away with, but end up having to down another unnecessary glass of bubbly to calm my nerves as a result. Lounging back into the biscuit velour, I contemplate my next move. Jack suddenly announces he needs another slash and is immediately followed to the gents by Vince and Trevor, who troop along behind, picking their noses in anticipation.

Left alone with the two Ms, I find my conversational abilities run as smoothly as a sprinter through golden syrup. In fact, if I'm being honest, with the departure of the boys, none of us is gifted in this department any longer. Marianne serves herself some peanuts. Mandy picks fluff off her dress. I light another cigarette. We all smile a lot.

'Oh,' says Mandy, after three minutes of sweat-inducing silence. We all lean in, grateful for an entree. She looks horrified by our sudden and profound interest. 'Oh,' she repeats. 'I was just wondering where Abigail's eye make-up comes from because from here it looks . . . really nice.' We all lean back, our over-enthusiastic interest thwarted.

'D'you think so?' I inadvertently start smudging it with my right index finger, before consuming a mouthful of peanuts. 'It's just a little something I picked up in Boots.'

'Boots!' repeats Marianne, in a manner that sounds like I'd just announced to the rest of the world that I had congenital herpes. 'I haven't been there since, phew, I don't know when . . .'

'Been where?' says Jack, with a large sniff and an overly wide grin.

'Nowhere,' I say, mortified by the profundity of the conversation he's interrupted.

'No, no, ladies, none of this coy stuff, I'm a man of the Millennium,' he insists. 'Where haven't you been, Marianne?'

'It's really not very interesting,' I continue, as Marianne simply smiles rather than come to the rescue in any shape or form. 'Very dull indeed.'

'Abigail was just telling us all about her trip to Boots,' informs Mandy, with unnecessary smugness.

'Boots?' says Jack, looking pole-axed with boredom.

'Yes,' continues Mandy, crossing her legs, 'she had a very interesting experience there today, apparently.'

'Right,' he says. 'Um, what's in your teeth?' he adds, looking at me. 'At the front?' I run my fingers over the front of my teeth. 'Oh, peanut skin,' he laughs.

And with that, all thoughts of *OK!* covers, guest make-up

reviewing slots on *Lorraine Live* and giant golden key gifts from David Frost and Loyd Grossman went out of the window. Plump, drunk, with peanut teeth, the purveyor of rib-tickling anecdotes about Boots the Chemist, I'm not exactly the sort of person you'd be thrilled to see when the screen goes back on *Blind Date*. And Jack, riding high on what I presume to be drugs and attention, wastes no time in making my presence appear mildly irritating. He turns his back entirely, wraps his legs around Mandy's knees and starts talking her through his new Prada outfit.

'I've got the shoes . . . the shirt . . . the tie . . . and the suit . . . it's just a shame they don't make the bloody pants, isn't it?' he laughs.

Bless him, really. I mean I've only met him once and even then it was almost entirely on a work footing, and he's been unnecessarily delightful and accommodating all evening. Picking me up off the streets, taking me here, I don't know what I was thinking, hanging around like an unfortunate smell, ligging along like some provincial groupie, gathering the stellar crumbs from underneath the table. But that's the problem with celebrities. You walk into a party and you think you know them. They, of course, have no idea who the hell you are, but you genuinely think that they are your friend, or at least a mate of your sister, or a school pal of your dad's. You spend your life reading about theirs – their likes, their dislikes, where they like to shop, their top five restaurants, who they love, why they love them, who they loved first, where, how and when they lost their virginity, the secret tips about the area they live in. It is frankly more than you know about your best friend. Unlike all other new relationships, in a celebrity encounter you start from a position of prior knowledge and received opinion. They tell you stories you've heard before. They share secrets you already know. And you always strike up a conversation like you've only just left. Quoting back bons mots you've read in the paper. No matter how unimpressed or detached anyone pretends to be, it normally takes five minutes before 'I really like it when you . . .' or 'It was so funny when you . . .' slips out.

I'm not part of Jack's world, and it's ridiculous to think that

I could be. Surrounded by previously unobtainable women, his is now a lifestyle magazine existence that few can join in on. I sit there, pulling individual eyelashes out, summoning up enough energy to collect my coat. It would have been cheaper and altogether kinder on my liver if I hadn't decided to link arms and burst my blister by walking to Art House in the first place. Wallowing in self-pity, I notice the vodka shot-fuelled girl band and the shopaholic celebrity-by-proxy wife giggling their way over to our table.

'Jack Morris,' purrs Shandy, borrowing Becky's shoulder for support, 'we girls were wondering, as it's nearly 2 a.m., if you wanted to come to the Met. with us. Our management have just booked us a suite and we thought we might have a few nightcaps downstairs before partying on.'

'Yeah . . . partying on . . .' The celebrity shopaholic punches the air with animated glee. She is close to finding the carpet a comfortable resting place.

'Vince? What d'you think?' asks Jack, surrounded by cleavages. 'The Met. and then home?'

Jack has become a Chief Indian who is rapidly acquiring too many squaws. Mandy and Marianne look seriously put out. They've put in an hour and a half of ground work, fought off his slimy hirsute friend and not even a photo op between them. Their whole evening of hard graft is about to come to naught. Trevor springs into action.

'Ladies, ladies,' he says, taking a centre position within the group. 'Why don't you lovely girls head off and we'll finish up here and join you in a minute. My driver's outside, so if you take a cab, we'll meet you there and party on.'

'Party on . . .' repeats retail bird, trotting out her maxim for the evening.

Becky, Shandy and the shop girl look mildly confused at such deft organisational skills this late in the proceedings.

'Oh, OK, then,' says Shandy after a minute's furrow-headed reflection. 'So we'll see you down there then?' Trevor nods efficiently and ushers them away with a wink to his girls whose shoulders visibly lower with relief. 'Yeah, yeah,' he adds. 'See you in five.'

With the girl band dispatched, the spandex twins shimmy

with extra confidence. Their hired Rottweiler has successfully fought off the competition and now they can relax in the knowledge that there's a fresh steak to share between them. As everyone sits back down again, enveloped once more by the fecund velveteen cushions, Jack sniffs loudly and gets a second wind from apparently nowhere and refuses to play ball.

'So are we off then?' he announces, standing up and pulling his shiny sweaty trousers out from around his balls. 'I quite fancy the Met. Bar. I've never been.'

'It's really dull,' says Mandy, exhaling on her cigarette with exaggerated jadedness. 'Full of Radio 1 presenters on their night off.'

'Really?' gums Jack, sounding keen. 'I quite fancy Sara Cox.'

'Yeah,' agrees Vince, throwing his chin back so vigorously as he nods that I spot a large white lump clinging to the rim of his right nostril. 'Me, too.'

'Well, the Met. Bar it is then,' says Trevor, with surprising calm. 'We can't have you never having been there now, can we, my son?' he adds, patting Jack on the shoulder like a small boy. 'Let me just get the bill, and give those girls time to arrive before us and I'll escort you there myself.' He smiles slowly at Mandy and Marianne whose eyes are narrowing in puzzled disbelief. 'There are always a pack of paparazzi outside, snapping away. Famous boy like you, Jack, needs someone to take him in.' The girls relax. The plan understood, they start to jostle for position once more.

The bill arrives and everyone looks the other way. Trevor makes as if to pick it up.

'Abigail,' he says, handling it like a snotty tissue. 'You can get this on *The News*, can't you? Entertainment is the bread and butter of journalism.'

'Course I can,' I lie, searching in my purse for my Switch card. Handing it over to Trevor, I mentally cross my fingers that it will work.

'Switch,' he says. 'How quaint.' Handing the bill back to the waiter, he adds, 'There's an Amex behind the bar. Can I have it back?'

As the waiter disappears, they all get up to leave.

'All right if we leave you here?' suggests Trevor in a manner that implies it will have to be. 'Only I don't think I'll be able to fit us all in my car.'

'Oh, no, fine,' I say bravely. 'No, no, I'm sure I'll be able to order a cab from here.'

'Abigail, are you sure?' quizzes Jack, hanging his head like a disappointed child; his bottom lip protruding, he flutters his eye lashes and then smiles. He walks over, his arms outstretched, and wraps me in a heady mixture of sweat, cigarettes and fading aftershave. Kissing and nuzzling each side of my neck, he whispers in my ear. 'I've had the most wonderful evening and you're totally gorgeous.' He lies with such charm. 'We should meet up when no one else is around and have a few jars. You know, just you and me both. I never did get to find out your secrets.' He winks. 'I'll call you.' He smiles so beguilingly, holding both my elbows, staring into my soul.

'I thought you were going back to Mile End?' I mutter, staring back into his pale grey eyes the colour of wet stone. A flicker of irritation crosses his face.

'Far too late for that now,' he smiles. 'Far too late for that.'

4

'Egg and chips?' says an unreasonably chirpy voice down the telephone.

'Whaat?' I mumble half-coherently into the receiver. My whole body is shaking with toxic shock, as I roll over and pat around on the floor under my bed for a very old, very greasy pair of thick glasses. My dry hair smells of old ashtray, my skin's sweating alcohol and even I'm finding my own breath offensive. My Mickey Mouse alarm clock with the broken second hand shows nearly 11 a.m.

'Who is this?' I say, locating my glasses and orientating myself a bit more successfully.

'What d'you mean, who is this? Who is this? Who ... fucking ... is ... this?' squeals the voice, climbing octaves with increasing indignation. 'Abigail Long, I never had you down as a superficial bitch. How wrong I was. Who else is going to invite you out for an adipose-inducing egg and chips at this time in the morning? Tom ... bloody ... Cruise? It's Wendy, you witch, and I'm mortally offended.'

'Wend, oh, God ... hi, sorry. It's just that you woke me up and I've got a bit of a hangover, I had a late one ... last night,' I mutter, my dry lips finding it hard to form vowels.

'You've always got a hangover,' she sighs, mildly irritated. 'At least for the last two months anyway. So who were you out with last night?'

'Oh, God, you know, the usual sort of vampires,' I say, evasively.

'No, I don't know, that's why I'm asking.'

'Um, I don't know,' I sigh, trying to remember. 'Oh, I know,' I announce, probably sounding a bit too relieved that I had some sort of recall. 'First off it was one of those chick-lit book launches about fat thighs, low self-esteem and vomiting.

Written by one of those media multi-taskers who do a little bit of TV, radio and writing all rather badly. A twiglets and wine box affair. But since she is rumoured to have shagged Will Self, the liggerati were out in force, Poor Salman, Arts Spice Melv B. and, um, Martin Amis.'

Wendy exhales loudly down the phone. 'There's no need to try out your column on me,' she says, her lips audibly tightening.

'I'm not,' I protest, half-lying as I riffle through the damp notepad that's curling and crumpled by the bed, half-forcing my addled head to remember. 'Then,' I pause, the front of my brain actually furrowing under the strain, 'then some musical awards ceremony at the Dorchester. Where a load of fifty-year-old men with demi-waves in glittery showbiz velvet jackets collected door stops for rock songs that had had loads of airplay in Dakota. Then,' I pause again, piecing it all together, 'then, um . . . I bumped into a couple of people at the awards and we went to Art House, followed by Soho House and then eventually on to some all-night actors' club called Jilly's, or something, in Soho with um, er, Jack Morris.'

'Don't um, er Jack Morris me,' squeals Wendy, her lips popping around a cigarette. 'Have you shagged him yet?'

'Course I haven't, we're just mates.'

'Oh, yeah, such good mates that all you ever do is bump into each other at parties and talk about the last party you went to. Honestly, Abigail, there was a time when you used to find those sorts of evenings intimidating.' She puts on an especially posh accent. 'Now it's all "Oh he-e-ell-o-o, da-a-rling, have you met La La?"'

'Oh, piss off, Wendy,' I laugh. 'They are extraordinary, even you have to admit it.'

'Maybe,' she agrees. 'But . . .'

'Are we having egg and chips or what?'

'See you there in ten minutes?'

'A word of warning, I will look like something the cat threw up. Can you cope?'

'It'll be nice to see you.' Her voice smiles. 'Oh, James and Colin are coming as well.'

James and Colin. I've seen Colin around at a few envelope

openings, here and there. He's particularly fond of cheesy award ceremonies for cable companies featuring *Now* magazine regulars and loads of cheap white wine. But it's been almost a month since I've seen James.

In fact, I think that's probably the longest we haven't pressed the flesh, so to speak, since I met him in the Bake and Take in Bristol nearly ten years ago. Our eyes met over the tricky decision between a reckless cheese puff or yer normal, bog standard Cornish pastie. Post-pub and James, I remember, was slightly the worse for six pints of lager top. He had one of those fluid, alcohol-fuelled smiles that seemed to slip and slide all over his face. His eyes were glazed and shiny. He was, of course, chatting. Propped up on the fruit machine, in an atmosphere moist with alcohol fumes, steam and airborne fat from frying chips, he seemed totally oblivious to the inevitable tension of a take-away at chucking-out time. While the rest of the queue were looking at their shoes or vacantly staring at yellow-stained posters advertising virulent green side dishes, he was earnestly asking whoever was closest to him what he should choose. Fortunately for him it was me, and not the heavily pierced rocker smoking a roll-up next in line.

'So what d'you think?' he asked. 'Cheese or Cornish?'

'Cheese or Cornish what?' I replied. I remember, he wasn't traditionally handsome. His shoulder-length blond hair was sneakily beginning to dread-lock itself. His tie-dye shirt was large, red, pink and in need of a wash. But his manner was charm itself.

'Poof,' he said. 'Should I have a cheese poof or a Cornish poof?'

'I've heard Cornish poofs are hard to handle, particularly at this time of night,' I replied.

'Is that so?' he said, cocking his head to one side to digest this new fact. 'Mmm,' he mused. 'What are you having?'

'A big bag of chips,' I replied.

'Oh, God,' he said, holding his head in mock confusion. 'That's a whole new ball game. Chips. Chips. A big bag of chips. What should I do? I can't stand choice. I've often thought that I live in the wrong country, you know. I'd have done so well under Communism. No choice, everything in brown paper packaging. It would suit me down to the ground. Have you ever been to Eastern Europe?' he asked and then continued without waiting for my response. 'I went on this package to Poland once. God knows why. I think my mum won it in some charity raffle. Amazing place. Really beautiful women. Big fat salamis, great churches, lots of Catholics . . .'

'Can I help you?' said the skinny teenage boy behind the counter with more acne than an Australian soap star.

I ordered my chips and James did the same and we walked and talked our way to a bench about four minutes round the corner in Victoria Square. For about the next hour and a half we sat there, laughing and talking total rubbish. I found out that he was from Hampstead, North London, reading History, that he was the eldest of four, with three younger sisters, that his mum made cakes on Sundays for afternoon tea and that he was fond of marijuana and could roll a joint while changing a tape and driving. From that moment I fancied him. I suppose I always have. He's never noticed, of course, being James. The number of times that I have hinted – obvious as a cold sore – and he's never taken me up on the offer. Even that night, I remember holding my head up, puckering my lips, waiting for a slightly salty vinegar snog. But James had looked terribly perturbed.

'Oh, God, are you all right?' he'd asked somewhat alarmed. 'Is there something terribly wrong with your neck?'

And that was it. Forever friends, flatmates, holiday companions, confidants, pal-you-bore-when-pissed-about-your-parents, sofa-you-sleep-on-when-drunk-and-lost-your-keys. And now best mates. Bloke I haven't seen for nearly a month.

Must sort that out, I think, as I make my way towards Coins Café.

The closest thing that Notting Hill has to an American diner, rumour has it that Coins opened up a couple of years ago, ostensibly as a basement hairdresser's, with a coffee shop on the ground floor. The coffee shop took off and, sidetracked by such delicious temptations as thick lattes, fresh fruit and yoghourt and full English breakfasts, people forgot to go and have their hair cut. So now it's a place for people with 'projects' to meet. Surrounded by clipboards and paper and chewed up pens, they sit and chat, earnest and intense, for hours, until they have to go and meet someone else for lunch. Nestling quietly in among the 'project people' are the NA contingent. Their only habit left is coffee and a steady stream of nicotine which they consume with an unnervingly urgent passion. Handsome and louche, they naturally gather in self-supporting groups to trade lighters and juggle mobile phone conversations. Then, of course, there's the occasionally employed – like Wendy, Colin, James and me – who meet for late breakfasts, compare hangovers and trade stories from the night before. These conversations are usually a litany of non sequiturs that are served and volleyed like ping-pong balls, but whose accuracy varies according to the eve's alcoholic intake and how many distracted hungry glances you make towards the painfully slow kitchen.

For a cold, wet Thursday morning in early November, Coins is remarkably full. Through a gap in the steamed-up fug on the plate-glass window, I spot the usual array of gangs and groups, plus a couple of stray black polo-necked characters who somehow manage to make one coffee last as long as their *Independent* crossword. Over the loud hissing and belches of the coffee machine, the clatter of plates, the rabid barkings of the chef and the general low hum of gossip-fuelled banter, I hear Wendy cooing from the brown plastic padded banquette in the far corner. Sitting below the wall-length mirror, framed by the orange walls and an oil painting rattled off by some less than talented local artist, she looks shower fresh, as she waves her slim hands. Her damp hair pulled back into a ponytail, her teeth vigorously brushed, her armpits most certainly deodorised, she looks the antithesis of how I feel.

'Oh, dear,' she announces as I approach. 'That has to be one of the saddest sights I've ever seen.'

'What d'you mean?' I say, failing to carry my hangover with any amount of grace or dignity. As I lean in to kiss her cheek, she recoils.

'I don't think that's strictly necessary,' she says, putting both her hands up, shielding her face, as if my condition were contagious. 'Can't we just shake hands or something?'

'Don't be mean,' I moan, sitting down on a sort of rock-hard pine milking stool designed with high turnover in mind. 'I'm in a frail enough state to cry or have a complete sense of humour failure if you carry on.' I swear my bottom lip starts to quiver as I fight the tidal wave of self-pity that's welling up inside me. I'm really not joking. One more jolly aside from Wendy and it's tears all over the black Formica table and a flouncy ponce home. Fortunately, for all her quips, Wendy's a sensitive enough soul to realise that I was about as capable of dealing with her teasing as a surly six-year-old after a doughnut-free trip around Sainsbury's. Colin, on the other hand, is not.

'Jesus Christ,' he announces loudly to the whole café. Dressed in a black calf-length leather coat with dark ruffled bedroom hair, he looks smugly post-coital. His thick navy jumper deepens the normal pale blue of his eyes. 'I can tell you had a quiet night in with a pepperoni and a Danielle Steel,' he sniggers as he budges Wendy along the banquette. 'Are you still pissed? Because you smell like Oliver Reed's underpants.'

'Right, that's it,' I announce, getting up from the table. 'I was coming out for a quiet heart-attack-on-a-plate and instead I'm getting the fourth from a load of reprobates who wouldn't know abstinence if it mugged them in a Texaco forecourt.'

'Wow, hold on a sec there, Abigail, where's your humour?' says Colin, immediately getting up from his seat, his arms outstretched, pretending to look soft, sweet and somehow desirable. 'Or are you saving all of that for your new celebrity chums?'

'I don't have any celebrity chums,' I whine, exhausted by the non-stop piss-taking.

'Of course you don't,' says Colin, fluffing the top of my hair. 'Little canapé warrior like you. Never met anyone who'd make a Biz-bit in *The Sun*.'

'Anyway, you're the one who's bestest friends with Polly Friend, the Mons Veneris de nos jours,' I say, narrowing my eyes and squinting through my smudged frames.

'Actually, they're not talking,' pronounces Wendy with total delight, flicking her ash into her saucer as if to punctuate her point.

'You're not talking?' I squeal, with total shock-horror-probe excitement, placing my hands on my cheeks, Munch-style. The relief of passing the buck is worth a certain amount of tactlessness.

'Er, yes,' says Colin. 'I'd rather not talk about it.'

'He'd rather not talk about it,' mimics Wendy, enjoying a good stir. 'He'd rather not talk about it because, truth be known, Colin doesn't come out of the story terribly well. Do you, Colin?' He says nothing, but starts playing with caramel and white sugar lumps in the neat porcelain bowl on the table. 'Well, do you, Colin?'

'Not terribly well, no.' He looks up, his blue eyes smile through his lashes. 'But I do feel very, very wretched about the whole thing.' He shivers. 'Not one of my proudest moments in the Rolodex of shame.'

'What exactly did you do?' I quiz, intrigued by Colin's uncharacteristic display of contrition.

'Oh, God,' Colin sighs, gathering his head in his hands.

'Oh, can I tell it? Can I tell it?' Wendy's flicking hair and ash everywhere in her enthusiasm. Colin looks at her. It would be rude to turn her down. Out of all of us, with her gross ability to exaggerate, Wendy does tell great stories.

'Go on then,' he nods. 'But no random lying.'

Wendy looks hurt but decides to let it pass. 'Last week,' she starts.

'Last week?' I say, leaning into the table. 'I can't believe I don't know this already.'

'Shut up,' says Wendy. 'Last week, OK, Colin gets this panic phone call from full-muff-shots, Polly Friend,' she mouths to me by way of explanation. 'Anyway, instead of cutting her arms in ritual self-loathing as she usually does . . .'

'She does what?' I say.

'Oh, yeah, old news,' continues Wendy, swatting away my interruption with total boredom. 'News of the World. Big story. Everyone knows. Anyway . . . what's my name? Oh, yes. Stop interrupting, Abigail, you're ruining my flow . . .

So anyway . . . in lieu of the usual forearm thing, she decides to pierce her own navel. Weird, I know, but that's famous people for you – too much time, not enough friends, family in Nottingham. Anyway, it goes a bit too far, and there's blood all over the floor, she can't deal with it, she can't stem the flow. So she rings up Colin. Why? Who the hell knows? But she does. She asks him to drive her to the hospital. She claims she can't call an ambulance or anything because she's too famous and it might get into the papers . . .' Wendy sniggers, but puts her hands in the air to prevent any possible interruption. 'It's all obviously bollocks but, hey, Colin turns up, like the lovely nice pal that he is, and drives her to the hospital. Anyway, next to him in the casualty waiting room is this girl . . .'

'Oh, God,' I say. 'I can guess what's going to happen next. Colin . . . ?' I smile.

'Whaat?' he protests.

'You really are like some revolting little Jack Russell on heat, cocking your leg on any convenient lamp-post.'

'Actually it was a tree,' continues Wendy.

'A tree?'

'Oh, yes,' she grins, raising her eyebrows, relishing her tale. 'While Wonder Muff was having one stitch in her navel, Colin here was shagging some strumpet up against the tree in the communal gardens opposite.'

'Her name was Belinda and she worked for an advertising agency in accounts,' declares Colin. 'She'd broken her thumb and needed a good strapping.'

'Like anyone's interested,' I say.

'Belinda was it?' exclaims Wendy. 'Thanks for that added detail. So, then, Colin turns up, looking almost as well shagged as he does now, but with the added bonus of mud all up his trousers, down his back and all over his arse. Wonder Muff comes out of her cubicle, signing autographs, pretending she's an extra in *ER*, expecting tea and sympathy. She sees Colin. It's immediately obvious what's happened and she huffs off.' Wendy's eyes widen in delight. 'Non-speaks ever since,' she grins, shaking her fag packet in delight. 'Isn't that great? So who's for egg and chips then?' she adds, waving at a passing waitress.

'Colin,' I smile, 'you're so naughty.'

'It is a bit bad, isn't it?' he giggles. 'But she had such nice breasts I couldn't resist her.'

'What? Nicer than Wonder Muff?' says Wendy, distractedly looking in her bag for more cigarettes.

'Well, they were real,' says Colin. 'So much nicer than the silicone ones that are like trying to chew knee caps.'

'So has Polly Friend got fake tits then?' I ask, probably a bit too keenly.

'Um,' says Colin. Even Wendy moves in for this one. 'Um, oh, yes,' he admits finally.

'Bloody well knew it,' announces Wendy. 'Knew it. They were too high and round like light bulbs to be real. Quite a good job though. Not that obvious. How many people know?'

'Only a few friends,' says Colin. 'And her manager, Trevor Future.'

'Oh, I've met him,' I pipe up.

'You've met everyone,' says Wendy. 'So, is James coming? Shall we order for him, d'you think?' she asks Colin. 'I'm starving and we're getting nowhere at this rate. Ah,' she says to a passing waitress, 'three egg and chips and one full English. Plus lattes all round. Please. Thanks. And could you possibly be as quick as you can, because I am quite literally about to pass out with hunger.' The resting model smiles, mutters something in heavily accented English and disappears into the kitchen.

Wendy lights up another cigarette and exhales across the table in my general direction. I feel very queasy indeed. Colin sits and picks fluff off his rather expensive looking trousers. For lack of something to say, I look down and start cleaning my own fingernails with a stray used toothpick I find on the table.

'Um, so what have you been doing, Wend?' I mutter into my bosom.

'Oh, you know, this and that,' she replies, her head moving from side to side in defiance.

'Been on *Richard and Judy* much?' I ask. 'Only I get up a bit late these days to see it.'

'I've noticed that,' she announces.

'What?' I say defensively.

'That you've been getting up later and later. I presume it's because you're staying out later and later,' she continues, beginning to sound like my mother.

'A bit,' I say. 'But it's all part of the job,' I add feebly.

'Ri-i-ight,' she says, looking over my shoulder towards the kitchen for our order.

Colin's not coming to my aid in the slightest after the last debacle, he's rather enjoying not being centre of attention. Instead, he wanders over to the large window sill, in the front of the café, and riffles through the newspapers. Just as things look like they are about to get really rather gauche indeed, I suddenly spy a friendly face smiling and waving through the fug.

'Look,' I say, with relief, 'there's James.'

'Oh, about time too,' says Wendy, her increasingly crabby mood obviously on scatter-gun effect.

'Guys, guys, guys,' says James. '*Soo* sorry, I'm *soo* late,' he says, sitting down next to Wendy and slapping her on the thigh as he leans over to kiss her on both cheeks, making loud 'mwaws' as he does so. 'Hey, you,' he says, grinning broadly at me, as he punches my upper arm. 'I haven't seen you since . . . since,' he winks, 'since we had sex.' It's an old joke we overheard at some party years ago, but we both laugh. 'No, seriously, when was the last time we saw each other?'

I shrug and frown. 'D'you know, I've got alcoholic amnesia. I can't remember but I have a feeling it was at the Cock and Bottle.'

'Oh, I know, I know,' he says, jabbing the air like the school swot. 'After Colin's gig with all those suits from Channel 4 in the back row with their tongues down their researchers. Then we all went back to mine, discussed what we'd do to get real jobs that paid us proper money and given the choice between Jabba the Hutt and John Prescott, you said you'd rather shag Jabba the Hutt. Wendy had Danny de Vito or Andrea Dworkin and chose to be neutered outright.'

'Did I?' says Wendy, cheering up a bit. 'I must have been pissed because I'd shag Andrea Dworkin any day of the week.'

'Would you?' I say.

'I'm gagging to have lesbian sex,' announces Wendy, rolling her eyes and making sure that at least three other tables overhear her modern, liberal and entirely untrue statement.

'It's just that no one's ever offered me fishy fingers.'

'Fishy fingers,' says James, his nostrils flaring with repulsion. 'You're filthy, Wendy Slater, you really are.'

'I know,' she smiles. 'Aren't I just.'

'You're not sharing your lesbian fantasies with the group again, are you?' sighs Colin, sitting down with a copy of *The Sun*. 'I keep setting you up with loads of lesbians on the stand-up comedy circuit and you're always suddenly unavailable.'

'That's because they're always suede-heads, with bodies like pint glasses and curtain rings through their labia,' dismisses Wendy. 'Give me some nubile Storm model with a penchant for toe sucking and suddenly rearranging my sock drawer won't be nearly so fascinating.'

The resting model arrives at the table and puts all the plates in the middle, cleverly avoiding the complication of who's ordered what. She must be all of eighteen years old with myopically pale eyes, and translucent skin with high cheekbones and lank hair with a centre parting. She looks Slavic and as thin as a cocktail stick. I fear for her spine as she bends down with our chip-laden plates.

'Hiya,' smiles Colin. 'Would you like a lesbian affair with my friend here?' he quizzes in matter of fact tones. Wendy kicks him one under the table. 'Ouch,' he squirms, rubbing his shin. He is undeterred. 'My friend here is rather keen on "coming out" and wonders if you would help her?' he smiles.

The resting model looks extremely confused. This is a line of conversation that is definitely off-menu and she is linguistically incapable of dealing with such deviation or, in fact, such deviancy. 'I will go ask the manager,' she replies, all pouting and perturbed, in a soft, flat voice that sounds like it's rolled over balls of cotton wool.

'Yeess,' hisses an efficient looking plump bird, with round hips and shiny Cox's cheeks. For a manager she obviously does a lot of food tidying in the kitchen. 'Can I help you?'

she says, sucking in her cheeks and looking boredly towards the ceiling.

'Oh, yeah, hi,' says Colin, suddenly sounding splendidly Home Counties. 'Love the food,' he says, licking his lips. She seems to warm to him. Well, most girls do. 'My friend and I were wondering if there were any chance of getting some fish fingers around here?'

James howls with laughter, Colin smirks, Wendy giggles, I smile and the poor manager walks off absolutely none the wiser. It's a good bonding moment. I relax, as much as I can on my stool, and enjoy feeling truly part of the foursome for the first time in nearly a month.

'Guess what?' says James, his egg swilling around in his mouth like yellow and white pants in a tumble-drier.

'Mm?' says Colin, a bit too keen on chips to speak.

'I'm off to Sri Lanka in a couple of weeks,' announces James, in a manner so glib and uninspired that he could have been discussing floor matting. 'For six months, maybe more.'

Everyone puts down their knives and forks and shows the contents of their mouth in shocked unison.

'Six months, maybe more,' repeats Wendy, the first to speak. 'No one took this BBC thing seriously,' she adds, by way of statement of fact, rather than malicious putdown. 'And it's almost Christmas.'

'But Sri Lanka's miles away,' I protest, 'and dangerous, and lonely. It's not that thing that you're planning to do with the Bengal Tigers, is it?'

'Tamil,' says James. 'Tamil Tigers.'

'Whatever, you can't leave.' I know I'm whining but there's very little I can do about it. 'James, you can't,' I say. I feel genuinely hurt and upset and beginning to sweat in my panic. 'You can't leave me here all on my own. Who am I going to talk to every morning? Who's going to discuss *Richard and Judy* with me? Who's going to take my calls at 2 a.m. when I'm miserable and I don't know what I'm doing with my life?'

Colin's the only one who manages to smile. And it's not one of those weak, covering-your-tracks smiles, it's wide and broad and full of generosity. 'M-a-a-te,' he says slowly as he gets off the banquette, 'put it there.' His palm is firmly outstretched. 'About bloody time, too. I knew you'd get it. We'll miss you, of course. But after coming so close to winning an award with the first one, it was only a matter of time before they gave you another one to do. Congratulations, you're a total star. You see,' he says to Wendy and me, 'you see what you can get when you put your mind to it and don't deviate or get distracted in any way. "Dedication," as the late great Roy Castle used to say, "Dedication's what you need" ... if you want to ... um, spin a lot of plates at once ...' he laughs. 'No, seriously, well done.' He raises an eyebrow. 'That's bloody shown the rest of us, hasn't it?' He nods as he sits back down again. 'Time for us to piss on the pot or get off, methinks.'

The mood turns strangely subdued. Somehow our breakfasts aren't so tasty after all. Wendy's the first to give up. Lighting a cigarette, she uses her yolk as an ash-tray. I've come over all emotional. But I tell myself that it's mainly out of self-pity, too much vodka and the sudden cramping and churning in my stomach as my food hits my festering acid guts. James doesn't really know where to put himself, all his opening gambits fall flat on the table like a wet plaice. Colin comes up with a bright idea that we should all try to plan some sort of leaving party for James.

'Tequila,' suggests Wendy, always one to get the ball rolling.

'With vodka chasers,' I add, for something to say.

'A nice quiet dinner with all of us together,' suggests James rather sweetly. There's a collective yawn. 'Oh, OK, nightclubbing at Brown's?' he says, hurling in a rogue idea from nowhere.

'Brown's?' says Colin, slightly shocked. 'Have you ever been?'

'Um, only once when very, very pissed,' admits James. 'And never into the private final circle of Dante's Inferno bit at the top.'

'Forget nightclubbing,' says Wendy. 'Very last week. Why don't we go to a Steak House for prawn cocktails, ribs, Black Forest gateaux, and a bottle of Blue Nun.'

'Did that the other day,' says Colin. 'And it turned out to be a rather expensive and indigestible joke.'

'I know, girls in nipple tassels,' adds James, spinning his own chest as he enjoys the attention.

'A load of pole dancers,' embellishes Colin, going with the flow. 'What d'you think the collective noun for a lot of pole dancers is?' he muses suddenly. 'A crotch?' He shakes his head. 'Or a thong? No?' His lips curl, as a thought suddenly occurs to him. 'I know,' he announces, 'it's a Stringfellow of pole dancers. A Stringy of Pole Dancers.'

As we all laugh, a bit too glad of the weak joke, out of the corner of my eye I see Jack Morris shamble in. Sitting down in the opposite far corner, he's accompanied by a smaller, more languid, decadent-looking bloke in a voluminous cream shirt that, despite the cold weather, hangs open almost to the waist revealing a toned and rather darkly haired chest.

I don't quite know what to do or where to put myself. It's not often that *Home and Away* combine in one café. On closer, subtler, through-the-fingers-of-my-right-hand inspection, Jack looks terrible. He's in the same clothes he wore last night. His tight black tee-shirt and Armani suit trousers look like they've spent the last four hours crashed out on the sofa. His dark hair sticks up at the back. His tongue is hanging out. Thick and furred, like the bottom of a kettle, even his own mouth is trying to disown it. So it hangs loose, limp and horribly dehydrated. Wendy's the first to spot him.

'There's your friend Jack,' she says triumphantly, wiping a post-hysterical tear away from her eye, as she tactfully indicates with the whole of her head. 'Yuck,' she pronounces, scrunching up her face. 'Doesn't look half as good as he does in his photos. Is that another actor he's with? I vaguely recognise him from some posing pouch shots in the hunk of the month section of *Elle* or *Marie Claire* or one of those girlie mags.

'Well?' she smirks. 'Aren't you going to say hello?'

A pair of dysentery-brown tracksuit bottoms large enough for a herd of backsides, a 'Kensington Posh Tart' tee-shirt (size 8 years) covered in toothpaste, tomato sauce and some indefinable other, and a pair of baby blue Birkenstocks, with all the allure and panache of a Dutch geography teacher on a hiking holiday. I'm patently not dressed for networking. Besides, I can smell last night's show-off cognac. My hair is beginning to coagulate and even after my breakfast I can't vouch for the toxicity of my out breaths. I'm hiding, staying put and no amount of Wendy wind-up is going to make me walk over there and make a complete fool of myself.

'Not such good friends then after all,' mutters Wendy, quietly to herself but loud enough for the whole table to hear.

'He looks like quite a nice bloke,' offers James generously. 'If a bit hungover. Wonder what he was doing last night?'

'Why don't we ask Abigail?' smiles Wendy, raising her eyebrows.

'No-o?' says James, leaning in, his eyes widening with incredulity. 'You were out with him last night?' He shakes his head in disbelief. 'Isn't he the star of *Love Letters* with that thin blonde bird . . . what's her name?'

'Gwyneth Paltrow,' says Colin helpfully.

'No, no, not her, you know, thin and blonde . . . ?'

'Gwyneth Paltrow,' says Colin again.

'No, no . . .'

'No,' Colin insists really quite loudly this time, 'Gwyneth Paltrow.'

'Yeah, her,' nods James.

'Don't you read my column?' I ask.

'Er . . . no . . . not really,' continues James, gawping like a goldfish terminally short of air. 'I haven't seen the film, mind you.' James starts to whisper like a wildlife expert observing a rare and wonderful wild creature that might, at any given moment, take flight and disappear. 'But someone at the BBC was talking about it last week. Apparently it's really very good and, um, "hot".'

'It came out three months ago,' says Colin, who's so cool in the glare of celebrity that he's burning neat round holes in his napkin with his lit cigarette.

'Oh, Abby, please go and say hello,' mumbles James, still transfixed.

'Go on,' says Wendy for entirely different reasons.

Colin pretends not to care as I stand up. Squinting through my smeared specs, I make my way over, trying to hold down my egg and chips. I can feel the other three watching my back, not wanting to miss a trick.

'Oh-hi-Jack-fancy-seeing-you-here.' It all comes out as one long sentence delivered at such a pace and such a distance he fails to react. 'Um, hi . . . Jack . . . Abigail,' I say enthusiastically and perhaps more helpfully. He looks up. His eyes are dulled with hangover cataracts. His face slowly cracks into a smile.

'Ears?' he asks almost as much as says.

'Hello,' I say, trying to sound jolly and pretend that such foxy attire with Everest specs is de rigueur in West London. 'Strayed a bit off your patch?' I grin.

'Yes,' he agrees. 'Got very drunk at that actors' club, Jilly's, and met up with a load of mates and we all went back to Linus's. Stayed up till 8 a.m. this morning. Oh, this is Linus, by the way.' He indicates opposite. 'A mate of mine – Abigail.'

'Oh, hi,' says Linus. His drawl is deep and dramatic.

'Take a seat,' says Jack, moving along the bench. I smile across towards the opposite side of the room. James gives a massive thumbs-up. Wendy, for all her winding-up earlier, gives a huge grin and Colin just winks.

'Now what can I have here?' mumbles Linus, moving down the menu with his index finger. 'I'm organic these days,' he continues. 'In fact I'm so bloody organic that the stuff I buy biodegrades before it leaves the bloody shop. I mean, there I was with a perfectly perky bunch of carrots from Planet Organic on Westbourne Grove the other day. A five-minute walk home, and they were as limp as a choir master's wrist when I got them in the door. But you know,' he smiles earnestly and then whispers, 'anything to stop the cancer.'

'Cancer?' I say, sounding frightfully concerned.

'Yup.' Linus's voice wobbles slightly. 'I've just been reading that fabulous Ruth Picardie's book and I think I've got it. You know . . . the big C.' He lets his head fall, positively overcome with his own melancholy.

'But she had breast cancer,' I say.

'I know,' says Linus, shaking his head. 'I've definitely got it . . . you know, too.'

'I think you need breasts to get breast cancer,' I explain.

'Do you?' he says, hunching quizzically. 'Now do you? Do you, really?'

'I think breasts are more or less essential where breast cancer's concerned,' I reply.

'Well, thank God for that.' Linus relaxes back on his milking stool with a huge flourish. 'That's one less tumour eating away at me.'

'You could always get it in your bollocks,' suggests Jack.

'Oh, God. You're just so-o vulgar,' protests Linus, revulsion and hatred advertised all over his face.

'Anyway, I don't know what you're fucking getting all "my body is my temple . . ." about,' continues Jack.

'Tool,' corrects Linus. 'My body is my tool. Honestly,' he huffs. 'Call yourself an actor?'

'Well, you were packing your tool with more coke than a Colombian mule's rectum last night,' laughs Jack. 'It's going to take a bit more than a few happy, carefree carrots to sort that one out.'

Linus looks defeated. 'Oh, piss off, you,' he sighs. 'Just get me some camomile tea, I'm feeling extremely fragile.'

As I start to giggle, I notice James, Wendy and Colin all get up from the far table and make their way towards the door. I frantically beckon for them all to come over. James is the first to make the move. Marching towards the table, his meet and greet hand is outstretched in anticipation.

'James Moore, James Moore, no relation to Roger, unfortunately,' he stammers, his cheeks flushing pink. 'Thought you were great in *French Letters*, really great. I haven't seen it myself I have to say, but my sound-man loves it, loves it, particularly when you get the Patsy Kensit bird at the end. Anyway, great, really great, well done, you. Been acting long? Hard business acting, always lying on your sofa waiting for people to call, terrible, not the most proactive of professions, just a mouthpiece for someone else's script. All you do is read out aloud and get paid loads of money for it. Really, isn't it? Reading . . . Oh, and wearing make-up and wigs, don't forget those. Um, other people's hair . . . terrific.'

Everyone's staring at James. Even the three or four tables in closest environs have been stunned into silence by his bad case of star struck. Jack's eyes are laughing but his mouth is ajar. I can hear Wendy giggling through the sleeve of her cardigan behind me, while Colin's stifled laughter has mutated into a rather painful coughing sound.

'Whaat?' says James at the end of his soliloquy.

'Quite true,' pronounces Linus, with a shiver. 'Nothing worse than other people's hair. Particularly in the bath. So difficult to tell these days if it's pubic or stuff discarded by one's head as part of the miserable ageing process.'

'God, I hate finding pubes on the soap,' announces Wendy, joining in.

'Yeah,' nods Jack. 'Nothing worse than finding pubes on the soap.'

'Oh, God, yeah,' laughs James. 'Or on your toothbrush . . .'

No one says anything.

'Yeah, right,' says Colin finally. 'I think we should be going, actually.' He indicates frantically for Wendy to remove James from his increasingly socially dysfunctional encounter. 'I'm Colin, by the way,' he says, shaking hands with both Linus and Jack.

'Colin's a comedian,' I say, probably a bit too enthusiastically. 'And this is my great friend Wendy, she's a TV presenter.'

Jack gets up out of his seat to shake their hands. 'I thought I recognised you from somewhere. TV presenter, you say.' He grins at Wendy. She smiles right back. Even when most unwell, Jack Morris is very charming.

'Surely you've got more important things to do than worry about organic tomatoes yes or no on morning telly,' laughs Wendy, flicking her hair, a lot.

'Actually between you and me, I haven't at the moment,' confides Jack. 'After the success of *Love Letters* I thought I'd 'ave Hollywood all over me like a cheap suit. But everyone always thinks you're too busy. I've got a shed load of time on me hands at the moment.' He shrugs and takes a slurp of his tea. 'I like your stuff, by the way,' he sniffs. 'You've got a sense of humour, you have. You're wasted on that show.'

'I'll be sure to inform them of that next time "Styling Ascot outfits for the fuller figure" comes up in a meeting.' Wendy smiles, stands and smiles some more. 'Anyway,' she says, 'nice to meet you. Um, we're off.' She points towards the door. 'Urgent engagement with my sofa.'

'Great to meet all of you,' smiles Jack, as I also get up to leave. 'Oh, Abigail?' he asks. 'What are you doing this evening?'

'Me?'

'Yes,' continues Jack. 'It's just that I've been invited to the *What Men Want* Awards. I'm up for best shagging Stud Muffin of the Year, or something dead classy like that, and I wondered if you wanted to come with me?'

'With you?' I repeat moronically, suddenly feeling the whole world slur into a blur.

'Yes,' he says. 'I'll pick you up at around 8 p.m?'

'But you don't know where I live,' I find myself saying really rather practically.

'What are agents for?' He smiles very smoothly indeed. 'See you later.'

All four of us walk out of Coins in a tight little group. Somehow Wendy and I manage to wait until we turn the corner before we start to scream as loud as two queens at a Ricky Martin concert.

'Bet you a tenner you have sex,' says Wendy, jumping up and down in her excitement, holding out her hand to shake.

'D'you really think so?' I reply, a broad grin plastered all over my face. 'D'you really think so?'

★★5★★★★★★★★★★

Eight p.m. and, as good as his word, Jack Morris is on my doorstep. A chauffeur-driven, black stretch Volvo, engine running, is parked in the street outside. Well scrubbed, closely shaven, overly scented, he's sporting a showbiz black tie, black jacket, black shirt. Black tie which, judging by the way he keeps fiddling with it, pinches around the neck. He is still amazingly handsome, if a bit uncomfortable.

I'd spent all afternoon in Wendy's flat. After the screaming incident, we'd gone round to her walk-in wardrobe of an apartment just off the Portobello Road and gone through absolutely everything. It was like a shopping trip to High Street, Kensington. Wendy has so many clothes that she's constantly pleasantly surprised when she opens her cupboards. With me, riffling through my clothes is a barren voyage of perpetual disappointment that ends in the panic purchase of Slim Fast and laxatives. But with Wendy it's a joy. She's got piles of stuff. Not in piles, of course. But in some Technicolored heap in the middle of the floor that could, in less fortunate countries, provide ample shelter for a family of four. But she doesn't really seem to notice the mess. Her car's the same. I've often said to her that she should donate the contents of her passenger footwell to the Museum of Mankind in Moscow. Knee-high, and I'm not joking, with Burger King boxes, M&S prawn sandwich packs, sweet wrappers, cigarette cartons, copies of the *Sun*, *Hello!*, *OK!*, *Heat*, plastic bags, receipts, tissues, and the occasional stray cardigan, scarf or glove, it is a testament to twenty-first-century living.

So we spent the afternoon with me lying on her bed, while Wendy flicked through her pile with navy-blue nail-polished feet. As she flicked, she shared her new aspiration to be Morgan Girl.

'I know it's very sad,' she said, holding up a rather beautiful heavily beaded skirt. 'And I know at twenty-seven I'm way too old to be Morgan Girl and I also know that Morgan Girl takes it vigorously from behind over a Ford Ka, but it's such a cool shop. And so very cheap,' she added.

'I thought you wanted to be Voyage Girl,' I said, throwing a beige thong off the bed which had crept out from underneath the duvet.

'I did,' sighed Wendy. 'It's just so expensive, you need a card to get in and then when you do, you could blow all your rising damp money on a skirt.'

'I thought you did that.'

'Mmm,' she acknowledged, extracting something slinky and black from the pile.

Wendy's always trying to reinvent herself. She's been Joseph Girl for quite a while, having previously gone through a 'Little Miss Sunshine', tight child's tee-shirt phase from Top Shop, a habit that I seem to be finding hard to kick. Before that she'd done Riot Girl, Tank Girl, Joni Mitchell Girl, and even before all that, judging by some of the decidedly dodgy photos that are stuck and curled and covered in Blu-tac grease marks behind the mirror in the bathroom, she was also once Spandau Girl, Brotherhood of Man Girl, Fame Girl and then just plain old Badminton Horse Trials Sloane Girl.

I can't really remember between what stages I actually met Wendy. I think it was probably around the Joni Mitchell stage when she first turned up at Bristol. She was James's best friend from home and seeing as I was James's new best friend, I remember absolutely hating her. She was pretty, thin, funny, incredibly vulgar, sophisticated and studying in London. In short, everything another girl hates. She, irritatingly enough, was generous, annoyingly unthreatened and thrilled that James had found 'such a great' friend. It wasn't until we'd drunk too much retsina on Naxos at the end of the first year and had an hour-long conversation about why breasts float while skinny dipping at midnight that I decided I really liked her. From then on we were inseparable and it was James's turn to feel left out.

This afternoon Wendy had been in her element. Skirt?

Frock? To underwire or not to underwire? Sophisticated? Cultured? Slapper? Glamorous? Trying hard or not trying hard at all? It was a marathon makeover. Thong? No thong? Tits? Tits and legs? Or just plain legs? Eventually, and this was Wendy's decision, we'd gone for a long black evening dress that split up the side and plunged down the front, but subtly. So a sort of low-key 'tits and legs' with a pair of demi-heeled not-trying-too-hard-at-all shoes. Jack is, after all, as Wendy kept on reminding me, quite short and probably weighs the same as me. 'Remember,' she said, as she kissed me goodbye loaded down with her carrier bags, 'don't go on top or you'll suffocate the bastard.' The fact that he had a wife and child was dismissed as an irrelevance by Wendy.

Jack grins as I appear at the door. 'You look great,' he says, ushering me down the steps and along the path. 'It's quite a drive to Ally Pally, so we should really get a shift on.'

I step into the slightly overheated expansive leather back seat and see an orange bottle of Veuve Clicquot on ice. I don't really want to ask him about his wife and baby back in the East End, but a hideous middle class ethical politeness engulfs me.

'How come your wife's not here tonight?' I ask, as casually as I can muster.

'Janine hates these sort of events,' he replies, nonchalantly settling back into his seat. 'She says everyone's rude to her, no one speaks to her, she don't know no one. She went once and said she'd never go again,' he continues. 'You see, you're perfect, you are, 'cos you don't need no looking after. You're a tough journo bird who takes no prisoners,' he laughs.

'Right,' I say, with a long deep sigh, suddenly getting the full picture. 'We'd better open this champagne, then.'

By the time we arrive at Alexandra Palace, Jack and I have finished the bottle between us. Having both been hammered the night before, we've simultaneously developed the toxic pink flushed cheeks of a tramp's tan. As we pull up outside in front of the red carpet and the banks of photographers, we're both feeling a bit over-refreshed.

'Jesus,' says Jack, as he presses his face flat against the smoked glass of the limo. 'I never fucking thought it'd be this fucking big. *What Men Want* has only been around for a few months.' He sighs and turns to me. 'Got a snout?'

'A what?'

'A fag.'

'Oh, right,' I say, slightly embarrassedly handing over half a crushed packet of red Marlboro that is still knocking around in my handbag from the night before.

Jack lights up and inhales deeply. 'Are you ready?' he quizzes. I nod. 'Here goes then,' he says. 'Happy faces.'

Jack gets out of the car first. The flash bulbs are blinding. Everyone's shouting his name. 'Jack, Jack, over 'ere, over 'ere. Oi, Morris, this way, smile, over 'ere . . .' The volume is intense. The atmosphere is confrontational. They're like the baying crowd in the Circus Maximus, gagging to slice and dice a few Christians. Next out it's me. I do it slowly, making sure both my bosoms stay in their sachets and I don't advertise any M&S gusset while I'm about it. A couple of wasted flashes go off. 'Who the hell's that?' I hear someone share somewhat unkindly with the group. 'Abigail Long, what are you doing here?' I hear. I look up along the red shagpile of fame and see a tall dark bloke grinning over his camera lens. It's Andrew Parkes, photographer to the stars and one of my new best friends.

Parksie, as he's known, is one of the chosen paparazzi élite. Neither caged nor penned at parties, he's allowed to roam free, to fraternise and shoot at will. The fount of all gossip and knowledge, he knows all the stars on their way up and on their way down. Although he's never sold a compromising frame, what he has at home in his private collection is anyone's guess.

'No idea what I'm doing here,' I mouth at Andrew, who winks and shoots off a few shots for his own amusement.

Jack puts his arm around my shoulders and smiles.

'What are you doing?' I hiss under my breath.

''Aving a laugh,' he says through his teeth. 'A bit of publicity for the film. Play along. Just smile.'

But in the end his joke falls flat, as one after the other the photographers all start to complain. 'Jack, lose the bird, will you?' 'Can we have a few of you on your own?' Eventually a sequin-clad girl, touting an unfeasibly large pair of breasts and a clipboard, comes to my rescue. Leading me up the carpet to a handy tray of fizzing flutes, we leave Jack behind, putting his best side forward.

Inside, it looks like *What Men Want* have spent a fortune on this, the first ever outing of what they hope will be their annual award ceremony for the country's 'Hottest Talent'. The whole of the dining hall area is draped in gold lamé, giving it a Lebanese hooker's boudoir effect. The rows of fifty or so round numbered tables of ten are all laid with matte gold covers, gilt chairs and huge glass goblets with golden edging. The hovering waiters are decked out like extras from *Spartacus*. Wearing bronze buttock-skimming tunics and slave sandals that criss-cross up their calves, they are huddling in groups for security.

Further inside and the circling cigar girls appear, on first impression, to be totally naked, save for the fine layer of silver car paint. They aren't. For on closer inspection, they're all modestly wearing a pair of paper birthing pants that they've rammed between their buttocks to make them appear more attractive. The luxury of total, full-frontal nudity has been reserved for the boy statues down both sides of the hall. Perched on plinths some way off the ground, like a load of kinky kouroi, they strike different poses. Some with racy devil horns and others with wings dressed as Cupid, they have to be the weirdest addition to the proceedings.

'Fab, isn't it?' gushes the girl in the sequin toothpaste tube.

'Oh, great,' I agree, not really knowing what to say.

'Would you like another glass of champagne?' asks the Tube, handing one over, not listening for my reply. 'So,' she simpers, 'how long have you been going out with the lovely Jack Morris?'

'I'm not,' I reply, taking such a large swig that my eyes start to water as the bubbles shoot up my nose.

'Oh,' says the Tube, sounding put out, bored and disappointed all at the same time.

'He's married,' I add, more to irritate than inform.

She's not listening. Snaking her way through the packed

foyer, she's off to network some other punter. Standing alone, steadily draining my glass, I try to work out who's actually been cajoled or conned into turning up to this bizarre event.

About ten paces away to my left, there are three blokes with long hair, centre partings and flares, all standing together. Judging by the empty semi-circle of celebrity that surrounds them, I presume they are famous. I spy Jackie and Lindy, identical twins, who present something on the Disney Channel. In the far corner by a golden pillar there's some fat comedy bloke who came second in last year's Perrier competition at the Edinburgh Festival. Someone who looks like Sarah Greene is eating a chicken satay stick, I can't be sure. The short girl from *Night Fever* on Channel 5. One of the blokes from *Home and Away* or possibly *Neighbours* who's on the front cover of this month's *Sugar* magazine. H from Steps, Jo Guest, and three Gladiators (devoid of catsuits) are all wandering around in circles waiting to be called to dinner. Never before, I think, as I stub a cigarette out in a useful palm pot, have I seen so many so-called celebrities looking so confused.

'John Humphrys is up for an award. It's either him or Chris Evans for broadcaster of the year,' announces one efficient-looking woman in earphones to another as they stand next to me. 'Oh, and Britain's Hottest Female is either Helena Bonham Carter or Caprice. I've got the press release somewhere. And,' she adds, 'radio station of the year is, now let me get this right, a toss-up between Kiss FM and the BBC World Service.' I empty my glass and start to giggle. This is going to be a surreal evening.

'Finally, there you bloody are,' says Jack, sounding extremely relieved. His eyes are wide, his pupils dilated, he's high on media attention. 'Christ,' he whispers in my ear. 'There's no one here. Not even any of those Brit flick actor tossers who turn up bloody anywhere. I think we should just go on the take and get completely wankered. What d'you think?' I smile. 'Come to the toilets with me now,' he continues, 'and I'll chop out a line of coke. It's the only way you and I are fucking going to get through tonight.'

Every single government health warning comes into my head. They spin around like some pedagogical kaleidoscope.

'Drugs! Just say no! Just say no!' they carp. 'I can handle it.' 'You don't need drugs to have a good time.' 'It was just the once, and then I was hooked.' 'It'll lead to heroin . . . and then you'll be sorry,' my mother's voice suddenly muscles in and joins the internal dialogue. I pause to think for all of three seconds. I sigh out loud with the weight of my decision. There's always a first time for everything, I think. Am I part of this circuit or am I a mere spectator? After six glasses of champagne, cocaine seems such a fine idea. Although I have to admit I am a little scared. Actually, a lot scared. But I'm damned if I'm going to say or show it in any way at all.

I follow Jack to the gents, becoming hotter and sweatier and more silently tense as we approach. 'One minute,' he says as he goes in to check to see if the coast is clear. He comes out beckoning. 'Quick, hurry, in here,' he whispers, pushing me into a cubicle that reeks of warm sweet diarrhoea. 'Jesus Christ,' he says, putting his hands over his nose and mouth. 'That's rank,' he adds, trying not to inhale, his face contorted as he pulls his wallet out of his inside pocket. He stands for a second and looks around for a flat surface. He runs his hands across the top of the cistern. 'Typical,' he shrugs. 'Covered in Vaseline.' Not finding anything else to hand, he pulls down the loo seat and squats down beside it. The floor is covered in wet paper and water, the cistern's still running.

'Fat or thin?' he asks, chopping out the slightly yellow, sticky powder with his new Art House membership card.

'Whatever you're having,' I venture, not really knowing what to say.

'Two big fat ones it is then,' he smiles, lining up two columns the length and width of cigarettes, side by side. He then pulls out a silver straw from his top pocket. 'Cool, don't you think?' he grins. 'Tiffany's. Don't think they do them any more,' he adds. 'Present from the producer of *Love Letters*.'

'What, Vince?' I say.

'Yup,' he says, snorting loudly along the right-hand line. 'Ugh, wow,' he coughs and exhales exuberantly. 'Hair of the dog. That's a shit-load better.' He snorts again, rubs his nose and then throws his head back. 'Can you see any lumps?' he asks, gesturing for me to look up his nose.

'Er, no, not really,' I say. The idea of peering up a celebrity nostril not quite appealing to me, I take one quick glance. 'Um, maybe a bit in the left nostril.'

'Cheers,' he says, picking it with his finger and putting it into his mouth, while handing over the straw.

It's my turn to squat down. My legs are wobbling, either through nerves or alcohol, I can't tell which. I rest my buttocks on the backs of my heels and, putting the cold wet straw up my nose, I snort. Half the coke spills back out again, over the plastic loo seat and onto the floor. I try to finish off the rest of it, snorting away like a truffling pig, but there's still quite a lot left behind. Jack doesn't seem to notice my ineptitude or even care. Instead, he keenly licks his finger and runs it all over the smeared seat, collecting lumps, and puts his finger back into his mouth. I feel sick, imagining how many pairs of buttocks have been there. The coke gags and burns in my throat. My whole body shakes and I retch violently as it trickles down the back of my nose.

'Yuk,' I say involuntarily.

'Strong, isn't it?' pronounces Jack, with a certain amount of pride.

'Mm,' is about as much as I can muster as I fight the desire to puke all over him.

'Lumps, lumps,' he says, taking hold of my chin and pushing my head back. 'You're fine,' he adds, looking intently up my nostrils. 'Let's go.'

Back in the party and everyone's sitting down, tucking into their Parma ham and melon. Jack and I make our way to our seats, a table at the front to the right of the stage. I have Jack to my right and a personal trainer to the Gladiators to my left. Jack's got some sort of showbiz reporter on Sunday morning telly on his left, called Melisse, and a soap star turned pop star, called Benji, next to her. The rest of the table is made up of a *What Men Want* sub-editor called Gary and four of his friends, who are so over-excited about their frisson with celebrity they're sitting in a line unable to speak.

After a Southern Comfort, I begin to find Kelvin, the personal trainer, deeply fascinating. We have an intense conversation about me; where I start to exaggerate animatedly about my previous athletic record and invent BAGA 1 and 2 badges, shot-putting prowess, high jump talent and an illustrious 100-metre career for the county.

'The thing is,' I say, earnestly, 'it could've been me in an England vest had I not popped a handstring in training.'

'Hamstring,' corrects Kelvin.

'Yeah, yeah, one of them,' I nod. 'Terrible,' I inhale loudly. 'A stretcher, stitches and everything. My sponsors were gutted to say the least.'

'You had sponsorship?' says Kelvin, sounding disarmingly surprised.

'Oh, yeah,' I lie, thinking I might have pushed this one a bit too far. 'I was that good. Great shame,' I continue. I don't think he believes me, but quite frankly I don't care.

I suppose that must be the coke. I can feel my heart racing, adrenalin is pumping around my body. I feel the sort of rush that you get when you're on the start line at the beginning of a race. The ends of my teeth have gone numb and my brain seems to have cleared. I'm clever, invincible and very, very funny.

Jack is flirting heavily with Melisse, while at the same time being momentarily distracted by passing topless cigar girls. He's been to the toilet facility twice more since they cleared away the Parma ham and is now playing with his tangerine duck and snow peas with potato rosti.

'So did you enjoy *Love Letters*?' he purrs, leaning forward for more intimate eye contact.

'Oh, ever so much,' she replies, delicately popping a few pods in her mouth with her fingers. 'That Hamish Rowland bloke is ever so sexy.'

'D'you think?' replies Jack, sounding slightly irritated. 'Actually between you and me he's a bit boring,' he confides. 'And a bit up himself. He never mixed with the crew or any of the other lads. Didn't even come to the wrap party.'

'Oh,' shrugs Melisse. 'My mate doing the make-up said he was lovely. A real charmer and ever so sweet.' She takes a sip of her mineral water. 'So what was Gwyneth like?'

'A real trooper,' sniffs Jack. 'We're like that, you know,' he says, crossing the first two fingers of his right hand.

'That's not what you told me,' I interrupt, very amusingly.

'What?' says Jack, looking panicked.

'Joke,' I smile and light up a cigarette. It tastes great. I smoke another immediately afterwards.

Over the other side, Benji, by way of interesting himself, has filleted a few peas from their shells and is flicking them across the table. Benji, known, like Cher and Madonna before him, only by his first name, is the star of a Channel 4 kids' soap. He's recently had two hit records and an album that is rapidly turning platinum. A stage-school kid, he is all-singing, all-dancing with the square pectoral muscles to match. Dressed in a tight white Lycra tee-shirt and combat trousers, with heavily gelled dark hair, he has the sort of face that could launch a thousand teen bras and he knows it. Recently photographed on the front page of the tabloids, stuck to the face of a dancer like a Siamese twin, he's losing his Coco Pops image and developing a bit of a wild child reputation.

'Oi, Morris,' he says, suddenly leaning across Melisse. 'A little birdy tells me they've got lap dancing next door. You know, after-dinner perks. What say you and me go check it out after?' He flashes a straight white smile and then winks. 'Know what I mean?'

'Great,' nods Jack. 'Um . . . ?'

'Benji,' says Benji. 'Pleased to meet you, mate,' he smiles. 'Us celebrities have got to stick together,' he nods, putting his hand in the air for a basketball bonding high five.

'Yeah, course, Benji,' replies Jack, tapping it weakly. 'Hey, mate,' he adds, 'd'you fancy a trip to the toilet?'

'Yeah, right,' says Benji. 'Don't mind if I do.'

The two boys disappear off together, a couple of car show-room models teeter after them in hot pursuit. I'm left with Melisse, who's now smoking her third, Silk Cut Ultra in as many minutes, and the personal trainer, who's busy removing all forms of carbohydrate from his plate, muttering something about mixing protein and starch.

'So what are you doing here?' I smile pleasantly across the empty seat at Melisse.

'Oh.' She exhales. 'I'm presenting an award,' she says, her

head wobbling with pride. 'That's why I'm not drinking or eating and smoking so much.'

'Oh really, which one?'

'Hottest Band of the Millennium,' she announces, flicking her ash. 'Oasis. They're old friends, you see. That's why they chose me to present the award. I've interviewed them three times on my *Rock It* slot on Channel 4.'

'Right,' I say. 'Who were on the panel of judges?'

'I'm not sure. I think it was just the editor of the magazine and, you know, they sort of compiled a list of who he wanted to meet and who they thought might turn up,' she explains. 'I'm dead nervous though,' she cringes.

A brass band suddenly strikes up at the back of the stage. The heady volume drowns out all conversation. A ripple of jaded clapping starts at the back of the hall.

'Ladies, gentlemen and celebrities,' announces a geeky looking bloke in Buddy Holly specs and a Ben Elton spangly jacket from a lectern at the front of the stage. 'Welcome to the *What Men Want* Hottest People of the Millennium Awards,' he continues. 'I'm Adrian Barnes, editor and your host for the evening, and before we go any further I'd like you all to welcome on stage *UK Living*'s Nicky Anthony, my co-host for the evening. Let's have a big round of applause for Nicky!'

As Nicky, clad in a red Lurex mini-sheath, walks slightly unsteadily on to the stage, the *UK Living* table bursts into spontaneous whoops, roars and whistles, while the rest of the hall mumbles loudly. 'Give us a twirl, Nicky,' jokes Adrian, hilariously. Three people laugh. 'Right,' he says, clearing his throat. 'On to our first award of the evening, presented by Nancy Furst of *Smash Hits*. Come on in . . . Nancy!'

On and on it goes. The audience rapidly begins to lose interest. Benji and Jack finally make it back to the table, arm in arm. They practically skip in. They have in the twenty minutes they've been away suddenly become the firmest of friends.

'He's a top bloke,' grins Jack widely as he slips back into his seat and downs a glass of champagne. 'A fucking top bloke.'

Melisse is on the point of spontaneous combustion with nerves. Radio 1 have walked off with an award, as has Helen

Fielding for her Bridget Jones follow-up for Hottest Girls' Book of the Millennium, Irvine Welsh has just said something incomprehensible to rapturous applause, and there are only three awards to go. Melisse has been to the loo twice (under genuine pretences) and is lighting up again, when a clipboard girl taps her on the shoulder.

'Melisse?' she asks. Melisse nods, looking terrified. 'I'm afraid to say that your award's been cancelled,' she explains. 'Oasis haven't showed up and they haven't sent anyone in their place. So we've all had a chat and think that it's better if we just forget it altogether. We hope you're not too disappointed.' She pats Melisse weakly on the shoulder and wanders off to talk to someone else.

'Oh, phew!' says Melisse, raising her eyebrows, looking totally deflated but somehow maintaining a semblance of dignity. 'Saved by the bell,' she laughs rather loudly.

Jack's becoming increasingly bored and belligerent and has started to mix up revolting cocktails with mainly a Southern Comfort core. Lining them up along the table, each in varying degrees of abomination and intoxication, he commences his alternative taste-testers.

'Mmm,' he grimaces, holding a gold-trimmed goblet of Southern Comfort, red wine and Pepsi. 'D'you know, Abigail, da-arling sweetie,' he smiles, coming over all posh, 'that don't taste too bad.'

I take a swig and only just manage to get it down. 'A vintage Benylin,' I surmise. 'A 1956, I would hazard a guess.'

Benji, who has his feet up on the table and is sucking on cigars, pretending to be Al Capone, decides he wants to join in. He asks the dull and increasingly neurotic Melisse (who has told her award story three times in the last five minutes) to swap places. Once sat together, they start mixing drinks with the intensity of deranged scientists hell bent on discovering an alternative to DNA. Jack is halfway through downing a flute of pale lime-green liquid made up of Southern Comfort, orange, white wine and only a dash of Pepsi, when they announce his award.

'And the nominees for the Hottest Man of the Millennium are,' declares *UK Living*'s Nicky Anthony, 'Sean Connery,

Marlon Brando, George Clooney and Jack Morris.' There's a vague round of applause. 'And the winner is Jack Morris, star of the hugely successful Brit film *Love Letters*.'

Benji leaps into the air, screaming and clapping like a lunatic. I, for some reason, get carried away by the occasion and do the same. Kelvin stands and manages to get his palms to meet across his muscle-bound chest, Melisse remains seated but applauds all the same. It takes Jack nearly a whole twenty seconds to realise that he has to go up on stage. Of course, he knew he'd won the award before he even arrived at the ceremony, he said as much in the limo on the way here, but with the amount of cocaine and alcohol he's consumed, he's been somewhat side-tracked and rather forgotten why he and I are here.

'Oh, fuck, right,' mutters Jack as he staggers towards the stage. Climbing the flashing disco steps two at a time he looks a bit unsteady, but recovers his cool as he kisses *UK Living*'s Nicky Anthony on both cheeks. He smiles sarcastically as she hands over the gold plate column. The whole of the hall is on its feet applauding, not out of approval or admiration, but mainly because he's the first familiar face they've seen on stage in the last half-hour.

'Cheers, cheers,' says Jack, shaking his award at the audience. 'I'd like to thank my mother, my father, and my agent,' he smirks, 'my sister, my wife, my son, my mate Skids, my mate Trev, my new mate, Benji over there,' he points towards our table, 'my pal, Abigail, who's also over there, my trainer, my dietitian and of course,' he starts to stage weep, 'my co . . . co . . . co . . . star in the film . . . Gwyn . . . Gwyn . . . Gwynnie Paltrow!' He laughs and leaves the stage to rapturous applause. The whole hall gets to its feet to show its appreciation at the first glimmer of humour or irony the whole evening.

Back at the table and to much more applause, two gladiators deliver a complimentary ice bucket of winner's champagne. Jack runs down the stairs like the conquering hero and immediately sprays the table, Formula One-style, while Benji grabs hold of the award and shoves it between his legs like a golden erection.

'Now that's what I call a head.' He repeats his joke to each member of the table in turn. One by one they shriek with laughter. Benji's such a funny guy.

By this stage I have to admit that I'm in a total daze. I'm high, I'm drunk, I'm disorientated and Jack Morris has just called me a pal to a hall of almost fifteen hundred people. He must be really drunk, I think; either that or incredibly unpopular, I laugh. Or maybe he's just very lonely. How bizarre, a glamorous, handsome young movie star, one of Britain's brightest new talents, and now *What Men Want*'s Hottest Man for the Millennium and he hasn't got any friends. Come to think of it, every time I've met him he's been on his own or with someone who works for him. Occasionally he's arrived with what looks like a friend or a mate, laughing and joking and all over each other and it turns out they only met each other last week. How awful, I muse, reaching for another cigarette, and he's so handsome.

'Oi, Abby,' whispers Jack, squatting down beside my chair as he takes my head in his hands and kisses both my cheeks. 'You're a bit quiet, get a bit more of that inside yer,' he adds, as he pops a neat envelope made from a Lottery slip into my hand. 'Oh, and you'll be needing this,' he winks, taking his silver straw out of his top pocket and handing it over. 'You and I are going fucking mad tonight, baby,' he grins. 'Fucking stir crazy mad.'

By the time I get back to my seat (I took quite a time in the toilet, spilling bits here and there, but I managed it, simply by copying what Jack had done before) our table was two awards up.

'Benji just bloody beat Robbie Williams, Ronan Keating and Jarvis Cocker for Hottest Artist (male) of the Millennium,' giggles Jack, chewing the inside of his cheek, and wiping his nose with the back of his sleeve. He indicates over his shoulder, where, sure enough, Benji's clashing statuettes with Gary, the sub-editor, using them as *Star Wars* light sabres, complete with humming sound effects. 'Finish your drink,' says Jack, holding a flute full of something instantly throwable. 'We're off lap dancing next door.' He raises his eyebrows and grins. 'Oh,' he adds, 'keep the coke. I've just scored a whole load more. Waiters,' he winks. 'Ever so handy.'

I down my drink and instantly regret it as it repeats up my nose. And we're all off. It's a much diminished group – Benji, Jack, me and Gary the sub, who ditches his friends at the first opportunity of a stellar night out. Melisse says she has a rendezvous in town with the All Saints and we all avoid getting eye contact with the personal trainer. As we sneak out the back, a troupe of dancers, and I joke not, are doing some form of topless tribal dancing in faux-plastic grass skirts made from the sort of material normally seen flapping in the breeze on a provincial garage forecourt. Weaving our way through the corridors round the back of the stage, the secret lap-dancing room is tricky to find. Eventually we come across a bloke, the size of a small bungalow, who's guarding a doorway. A nod, a wink, and a £50 note gets us into a darkened room with sophisticated Amsterdam red light effect that's almost entirely empty.

The small stage at the front has two steel poles rooted to floor and ceiling. There are about eight or ten short bar stools covered in red velveteen and half as many tables, plus a mini-bar the length of a radiator in one corner. Apart from us, there are only three other people in there and so far I am, somewhat uncomfortably, the only girl.

Someone, somewhere slips on the Robert Palmer tape and two extremely lithe looking females appear from either side of the stage. Topless, with pert breasts, big blonde hair and silver cheese-wire thongs, they each walk to their respective poles with a sort of hips forward panther-like swagger. They both slowly and provocatively – after a bit of preliminary pole licking with stiff tongues – curl one leg around the steel shaft and pull themselves up off the floor. They spin to face the audience, extending the other leg athletically out at a right angle. Their faces are devoid of any expression.

'Here goes,' salivates Benji, rubbing his hands together, before vigorously scratching his crotch.

They spin, they turn and they arch their backs. They split their legs every which way, always making sure their shiny centimetre-wide gussets are pointing towards the audience. They don't really seem to be dancing to the music, the background beat just appears to be a simple excuse for movement.

It's actually rather hypnotic and strangely unsexual to watch. They writhe like snakes, furling and unfurling themselves, they simulate cinematic sex with their poles like asps on Ecstasy. Benji is really enjoying himself and keeps rearranging his erection in his fortuitously baggy trousers. Jack on the other hand is surprisingly uncomfortable. Embarrassed by his excitement, he minces in his seat and keeps coming up with not very witty asides to compensate for his arousal. Gary is simply gob-smacked. Sitting open-mouthed, with a sweaty sheen on his face, he exudes all the sexual sophistication of a commuter train frotter. He is actually so keen and so revolting, I have to move places.

As I get up to swap seats and move closer to Jack, one of the girls shimmies off the stage to straddle Benji. Her plump pink nipples arrive level with his eyes. All sense of irony or boy-bonding bonhomie immediately drains from his face. Any semblance of cool or post-modern scorn evaporates as she slithers around on his lap, her breasts swinging from side to side, brushing his nose, as they develop a momentum of their own. Just as Benji's penetratively hard, she stands up, turns round, touches her toes and pushes her parted buttocks in his face. It's as much as he can do to stop himself from burying himself between her cheeks. Instead he contents himself with kneading her flesh with an awkward vigour.

Jack leans over. 'Abigail?' he questions. 'Are you OK?' He looks genuinely and gratifyingly concerned. I have to admit I'm touched. Having never been in this sort of tits and arse situation before, I did find the first fifteen minutes or so really rather fascinating. There was a certain amount of communal showers curiosity to it. A sort of mutual muff inspection. But after wondering how I can get buttocks like that, how much saline breasts cost, and what they will look like resting on her skeleton like two defrosted freezer bags when she is dead, I am beginning to develop that rather repulsed feeling like when old people kiss on *Blind Date*.

'I've got the tee-shirt, really,' I reply, trying to look casual. 'Me too, really,' replies Jack and then smiles. 'Anyway,' he says, standing up, 'I don't fancy blondes.' He taps Benji on the back three times to get his attention. 'Mate,' he shouts over the 'eighties disco beat. 'D'you fancy going to the Met. Bar, because I'm out of here?'

Benji looks extremely disappointed and looks round for some sort of group support for a bit more lap. The tragic keenness on Gary's face seems to persuade him otherwise.

'Yeah,' he says, releasing the buttocks and standing stiffly up from his stool. 'I could do with a drink.' Gary springs to his feet, keen as moutarde to keep on the stellar bandwagon, but Benji's too quick for him. 'Gary,' he says, pushing him back down onto his stool, 'stay, mate, enjoy yourself. Look, some of the other guys from our table have just arrived.' He slaps him on the back. 'See you around.' It's true. Gary's friends, who he'd abandoned earlier, have just made it through the door, but Benji's manner of ditching is quite brutal. The sub-editor knows that it is pointless to argue and does exactly as he's told. He sits back in his seat and beckons his friends over. Pursuit is out of the question. Poor bloke. I know exactly how he feels.

Outside and it's the perfect paparazzi moment. It's nearing midnight and the cold damp wait has been worth it. Jack and Benji each know the other's photographic worth and walk out arm in arm towards the cameras, and on to the waiting limousine. I'm left to follow on behind. Head down, I slip in round the other side of the car, while the two boys pose together by the door.

'Jack! Benji!' the photographers shout. 'Where are you off to now? Where are you going to celebrate?'

'Home, of course,' smiles Jack. 'For a good night's sleep.'

'Show us your awards,' yells someone else. 'Put them high in the air.'

'How d'you feel winning the awards?' asks another voice.

'I'm very honoured to have been chosen above Robbie Williams,' says Benji. 'He's a great icon of mine.'

'Jack, how does it feel to be sexier than George Clooney?' asks a hard-faced brunette from behind the ropes.

'I'm amazed,' grins Jack. 'I never thought I was very handsome.'

They slide along the back seat and collapse into giggles after they close the car door.

'Front page?' says Benji, putting his hand in the air for Jack to slap.

'Yeah, front page,' agrees Jack, sitting back in his seat with a long loud satisfied sigh.

The Met. Bar is packed by the time we arrive at around a quarter to one. The music is so loud conversation becomes an irrelevance. As the three of us walk in, there isn't a crimson leather booth in sight and all the smaller tables in the middle of the room are occupied. The boys hang back. They look uncomfortable. The idea of approaching the bar to order their own drinks obviously fazes them.

'Hey, Abigail,' shouts Jack into my left ear, 'will you go and ask the manager to find us a table?' He smiles. 'It's just that we can't really . . .' he says pointing to Benji and himself. Wendy's right, I think, as I weave my way through the tightly packed throng of fluffy, flirting, thin girls and boys in monstrously embroidered jazz shirts, it does look like a school disco. In fact, the place is so small that, in my nervous state, I end up bumping into my own reflection at the far end of the club, as I mistake the mirrored wall for another dance floor. I eventually elbow my way to the bar and try to catch the attention of the Italian stallion who is flexing his biceps in the mirror as he shakes his cocktail mixer.

'Can I speak to the manager?' I yell, cupping my hands around my mouth. He points up the other end of the bar to an attractive short dark man in a black slim-fitting suit.

'Terribly sorry,' I apologise. 'It's just that I'm with Jack Morris, the star of *Love Letters*, and, um, Benji, you know, the pop star, and they've just won these awards and they're out celebrating and there's nowhere for them to sit.'

The manager nods and mouths for me to follow him. Walking up to the first booth with the best view of the door, he pulls a 'reserved' sign out of his pocket and politely clears the table of glasses, ash trays and people. He then stands in the middle of the room and calls the boys over, while ordering a bottle of complimentary champagne from the bar.

Within minutes the girls start to arrive. Nearly always hunting in pairs, they edge along the banquette, stalking with such stealth that it's not until our booth is so full that I'm perched on the end, precariously balancing on half a buttock, that I realise what's really going on.

'Are you Benji?' I hear a girl with a scarlet bob pout.

'That's my name,' he replies, slapping his own thighs before putting his arm round her shoulders and leaning in for full flirting effect.

I start chain-smoking my cigarettes for want of something to do. Lighting one from the other, I wonder if I could fill a whole ashtray without addressing a word to anyone. My legs are bouncing up and down, I do really need to speak to someone. Instead, I look round the bar. I entertain myself trying to see if there's anyone I recognise. Even with my slightly addled *Hello!* head in place, pickings are slim. A Radio 1 group are being loud down the far end of the bar, but are lacking Sara Cox. There are two members of the Chelsea football team, swatting girls, as they have a quiet drink at the bar. But I can't say who they are. Trevor Future's just arrived by the door; a brace of trolley dollies, one on each arm, escort him in. I swear he leaves an oleaginous trail behind. I hide. He makes my skin want to douse itself in Dettox and I'm drunk and I think probably unhinged enough to tell him. So instead, I polish off a glass of champagne and spill the rest of the cocaine that Jack gave me.

By the time I make it back from the loo there's standing room only around the booth. I'm feeling extraordinarily disconnected. I've become irrelevant to the proceedings, I decide, steadying myself on the corner of the banquette, and should really, probably, definitely, while I still can, go home.

I wave to get Jack's attention across the table. He eventually looks up. His smile fades as I make Yellow Pages walking to the door signs with my fingers. Pushing along the row, he manages to extricate himself, brushing himself down, as he stands up.

'Abby, Abby, Abby,' he mutters and mumbles and repeats, snuggling up to my neck, kissing just behind my right ear. 'Don't go,' he pleads, sounding like a small child. 'Stay and play,' he smiles, putting both his hands on my hips, resting his forehead against mine. 'I've just booked a room for the night and we're all going to go upstairs in a minute, what d'you think?'

'Oh, God . . . all right,' I slur, immediately regretting my acquiescence.

'Great, great,' says Jack, running his hands through his hair. His eyes are glazed and drunk, he smells of alcohol and he's sweating drugs. 'Benji,' he shouts across the table. 'Abby's says she's staying. Shall we go upstairs? Room 2010.' He's jigging on the spot, his head's bouncing up and down like a spring-loaded dog on the back shelf of a mini cab. Benji gives a double thumbs and starts flicking off the girls as he barges along the banquette.

'Hey,' he says, as he joins the two of us, his eyes shining, his nose running. 'Shall we leg it?'

By the time we eventually find 2010 and slip the card in the door, we open it to find there's a group of about eight people already in there. The room is full of cigarette smoke, MTV is on the telly, there are four people lying on the bed and they've opened the champagne.

'Jesus Christ, how the fuck did that happen?' says Jack, his eyes wide open. 'I only told a few people downstairs and now we've got a bloody rave.'

Benji sneaks a peek through a crack in the door. 'Well, there are a couple of girls in there worth a squirt,' he surmises. 'And,' he adds, 'there's definitely a drug dealer.'

'How d'you know?' whispers Jack, joining him at the crack.

'He's got a hat on,' he replies. Jack sniggers. 'Whaat?' Benji turns round. 'They always wear hats. It's a fact.'

'Course,' Jack says. 'Like some sort of dealer code.'

The two boys march in ahead. I hold back mainly out of the prospect of no one wanting to talk to me or, if they do, it's only because I arrived with them and I might prove some sort of useful contact. Sure enough, I managed to walk the length of the beige carpeted minimalist suite three times without talking to anyone apart from the prat in the hat – who it turns out isn't a drug dealer but a Christian who works in the record business and he's going home.

Benji's sandwiched between two girls who, by the looks of things, don't mind sharing everything. And without a word really, except an ear-wide smile and three-fingered salute to Jack, he's out and off for the sort of night that would make Larry Flint smile.

From my position on the air-conditioning looking over Park Lane and Hyde Park below, Jack looks like he's had enough. He's got the fixed smile and the middle distant stare of a High Street drunk on the verge of collapse. His brain is working so slowly that you can almost see the thought process travel down his face to his mouth.

'Uerm,' he announces in a loud slurred voice. 'I'm afraid I'm going to bed now, so will you all leave? It is 5 a.m. and I'm calling time, please . . . ladies and gentlemen . . . time, please.' No one moves. The conversation lulls for a second and then strikes up again. A blonde in the corner lights up another cigarette. A bald-headed bloke with a goatee pours himself another glass of champagne. 'Look,' says Jack, raising his voice, as he stands up and lurches from left to right, 'will all you lot just F . . . U . . . CK OFF,' he yells. 'FUCK OFF back to your own FUCKING flats. I've had enough of all you ARSE WIPES.' He then adds quietly, more to himself than anyone else, 'Fuck off, all of you. Fucking fuck off.'

Finally the crowd start begrudgingly filing out of the room. 'What a total shit,' says the goatee as he leaves. 'Who the fuck does he think he is?' No one says thank you or good night as the door closes behind them. The room is empty. We are on our own.

'I should really go home,' I mumble, getting off the window sill.

'Oh, no, stay,' he says. 'Have another drink.'

'I really couldn't,' I reply. 'I think my hangover's kicked in already. I'm feeling really cold.'

'Stay,' he repeats.

'I'll have a cup of tea if you're making one,' I venture, collapsing on to an ash-peppered bed.

'Great idea,' says Jack, stumbling around in the general tea and coffee making facilities area, flicking switches and dropping saucers. 'Milk and sugar?'

'Neither, thanks.'

'That's revolting,' he says, hunched over the tray, spilling sachets as he talks. 'Posh people just don't understand tea. Loads of milk and enough sugar to stand a spoon in. That's tea.'

'Mmm.' I've lost the power of speech.

We both sit in silence as we wait for the kettle to boil. Finally there's a loud whooshing sound and a click.

'I think you're great, by the way,' says Jack suddenly, as he walks towards the bed carrying two mugs.

'So are you,' I say, thinking this is rather late in the day for a chat-up.

'You're the first real mate I made since I became famous,' he says, lying down on the bed. 'You know all that "ears" stuff at the première, I thought you were a real laugh.' He takes a sip, blowing on his tea first. 'And tonight's been a laugh, hasn't it?'

'If a little weird,' I say, warming my hands on the mug. 'All the lap dancing.'

'God, I'd forgotten that,' laughs Jack. He lies there a second. 'Shit, where's my award?' He sits upright, frantically looking around the filthy floor.

'In my bag . . . for some reason you put it there for safe-keeping when we were in the car.' I sniff; the hot tea is making my nose feel freezing cold. I am totally exhausted.

'Oh,' he smiles. 'There you go again, being great.' He flops back onto the bed and sighs.

'I'm going,' I say, determinedly peeling myself off the bed and swinging my feet onto the floor. Even my not-trying-too-hard heels are killing me.

'Look,' says Jack, with the sweetest of smiles and widest and most innocent of blue-grey eyes, 'spend the night with me. I'll put a pillow partition all the way down the middle of the bed. No sex or anything, I promise.'

★★ 6 ★★★★★★★★★★

Persuading Wendy that I hadn't re-enacted the *Kama Sutra* with Jack Morris was going to be a veritable uphill struggle in high heels – exhausting and extremely painful. She'd squealed and slapped her steering wheel a dozen times already in total disbelief at my blank denials. She absentmindedly burnt a hole in her own tights as she begged for details. She even stopped the car at one point opposite the evangelical church on Kensington Park Road, refusing to drive any further until I told the truth.

'Look,' I say, rapidly having a sense of humour by-pass, 'I did not shag him, snog him, or give him a blow job. There was no exchange of fluids, not even a beady string of saliva. We lay side by side and slept. That was it.'

'Did you at least see his willy?' she pleads.

'He's got a wife and child.'

'So?'

'So, no!'

'Bum?'

'No!'

'Chest?'

'Er.' I stop to think. 'Er, yes.'

She yelps with joy. 'Small? Hairy? Pigeon? Or totally revoltingly depilated in a warped André Agassi type of way?'

'Truth?'

'Course.'

'Really rather dull, not dissimilar to my seventeen-year-old cousin.'

'Yuk.'

'Lie?'

'Absolutely.'

'Square and butch and firm with a six-pack gut. A sort

of Peter Andre meets Marky Mark without all the baby oil.'

'God, how sexually threatening.' She shivers with delight as she starts up the car again. 'Are you sure you didn't want to shag him?'

'D'you know . . . no,' I reply seriously. 'They get it all the time, boys like that. Moist gussets hurled at them from every direction . . . must be such a pain.'

'Oh, I don't know,' shrugs Wendy, cutting up a Lexus and giving it a nonchalant finger as the driver stares back in livid disbelief. 'I could think of worse traumas.'

'I think it's good as friends,' I say, breaking into a light smile. 'Um, he gave me his mobile, you know, in case I might need to get in touch,' I add just to wind her up.

'Oh, my God,' she's screaming, 'now that's worth more than chest, bum and full blown sex altogether.'

We're on our way to dinner with Colin and James. It's not long now before James is off to Sri Lanka, and Wendy decided that before all the farewells and family gatherings set in, we should have a quiet evening out together, just the four of us. 'A nice fab four reunion,' she'd insisted on the telephone. 'Where we can all reminisce about old times and tell James how much we love him.' That had been the plan anyway. Arranging it, on the other hand, had been more difficult than organising a Misanthropes' Social Convention. Colin had been evasive about various evenings in such a suspect manner that Wendy was convinced that he was shagging some new nubile, but was too embarrassed about the quality of his pull to share her with the group. James was also being difficult. He complained that he had an acute case of 'financia nervosa' and was only able to show up after we'd all eaten. In fact, or so he bored Wendy, he was in such fiscal dire straits that he even offered to cook at home, just so long as we bought along the wine. In the end, just to shut him up and to avoid what could only be culinary hell, we both promised to pay for him.

Then with everything nearly organised, it was my turn to be the most difficult person to accommodate. I didn't mean to be, but going out three or four nights a week for the column means that I have very little time left for real friends and bona fide social occasions. And even if I do find the time, I'm usually so exhausted all I really want to do is watch *EastEnders* and tuck into a large plate of mashed potato, with my answer machine on screen. The idea of drinking and smoking and talking, trying to be entertaining, is enough to turn anyone on to class A drugs just to keep up appearances, I thought, as I lay on my bed trying to squeeze into my Top Shop trousers that I could have sworn must have shrunk in the wash. Only they haven't been near a dose of Ariel Ultra in three months.

Actually, if it weren't for James, I would probably have come up with some sort of excuse about tonight. Although I haven't seen that much of him recently, the idea of him going away is a lot more upsetting a prospect than I'd previously given it credit for. Now that I really think about it, it's hard to imagine what this Christmas and New Year are going to be like without him. James normally comes down to stay for at least a couple of days on the farm during the festive period. In his own shambolic way, he likes to get out of London. Fill his lead-soaked lungs with grass-infused fresh air, he says. Our modus operandi is always the same. We go on long hearty walks in the afternoons and drink long hefty cocktails in the evening. He does manly chats with my father, warming his backside by the fire, while I slip off and watch an awful lot of telly. My mother loves him and he loves my mother, and her cooking. He constantly refers to her as 'Mrs Long', rather like Dustin Hoffman in *The Graduate*, and she positively pinks up with pleasure at the mere mention of his name. In fact, I've seen her get quite foxy and frou-frou with him after too many Baileys and an extremely competitive game of Trivial Pursuit. 'Such a nice young man, that James,' she says, every time he leaves. 'I really don't understand why you don't go out with him.'

'He doesn't fancy me,' I always have to explain. 'We're just good friends.'

'How very modern,' is her perennial reply.

Anyway, Wendy's parking up outside the compromise dining venue, Pizza Express. She had suggested the Sudanese – Mandola – on Westbourne Grove. Colin had told her where to go, and proposed the more expensive Italian – Zucca – just down the road. But in the end, we all more or less came clean that we were perhaps just marginally more financially flush than James, and we opted for the Pizza Express on Notting Hill Gate – 'for the garlic bread'. Wendy braille parks around the back, clipping both her front and back bumpers just to make sure she's properly in there, and we saunter in, about twenty minutes late.

It is a Monday night and the place is full. Groups of friends are shouting anecdotes at each other across round marble-topped tables. Tight-lipped couples, exuding marital disappointment, sit in muted twosomes, reading everything on the wine list. Gaggles of girlfriends knock back carafes of red, exchanging the weekend's gossip, while a couple of smartly suited City-boy bachelors queue up in the far corner, heads deep in the *Evening Standard*, waiting for their take-aways. Banks of chefs in white aprons frisbee circles of dough, trying to keep up with the orders. The clatter of cutlery is at office canteen level and there's a strong smell of melted cheese.

Winding our way through the maze of white china urine sample bottles and floral tributes, we find Colin and James eating strips of butter-soaked pizza base, halfway through their beers. Colin waves as he sees us approach. His chin is covered in oil. James just smiles.

'Hey, guess who Abigail spent the night with last week?' shouts Wendy from about ten feet away.

'What?' says James, suddenly sitting to attention. Rigid with interest, his eyes flick questioningly from Wendy's face to mine. 'Guess what ... who ... ?'

'Oh, shut up, Wendy, please,' I say, irritated by her total lack of discretion and yet, at the same time, quite keen that she share the news with the group.

Colin could hardly be bothered to look up from his bill poster size menu. 'Oh, God,' he drawls. 'Go on then, bore us if you must.'

'Oh, yes, do tell,' says James, with a weird uncharacteristic curtness, as he takes a swig from his beer.

'Jack Morris,' squeals Wendy, like a jolly assistant hyping Teasmades on *Sale of the Century*.

'Jack Morris,' repeats James.

'Yeees. Can you believe it?' she babbles. 'Only the sexiest film star living on the bloody planet as we speak.'

'What? That short shit we met the other day?' says Colin, taking a swig of his beer. 'The sexiest man on the planet? Are you kidding? He's not a patch on . . . um, not a patch on . . . oh, I don't know, John Travolta.'

'John Travolta?' repeats Wendy, in a manner that suggests Colin should be committed. 'John Travolta? Jesus Christ. You boys have just no bloody idea . . . John Travolta? I'd rather sleep with my own mother than shag that disco dancing Scientologist,' she declares, as she sits down at the table, with a flicking fag ash flourish. 'Now . . . Johnny Depp, that is a totally different story. In fact I'd probably kill my own mother for a night with him.'

'Oh, God,' moans Colin again, lounging back uncomfortably into his red-painted wooden chair. 'It's always sex with you, isn't it, Wendy? It's got nothing to do with talent, or come-backs, or cool, or anything like that. It's pure and simple and really rather basic, isn't it? Oh um,' he imitates in high-pitched girlie tones, 'is he shaggable, or is he . . . not?'

'Are you suggesting that Johnny Depp isn't talented?' quizzes Wendy, taking a long drag on her cigarette. 'Because we all know that's not true.'

'That's not the argument,' continues Colin.

'Um,' interrupts James, suddenly rather quiet. 'So you spent the night with Jack Morris then, did you?'

James seems remarkably persistent in his interest. In fact, his cheeks are slightly pink and I swear the whites of his eyes are slowly filling with blood. He is acting very strangely. You could almost think he cared.

'Are you all right?' I say, sitting down next to him and putting my hand on his knee. 'You look very odd.'

'I'm fine,' he says defensively, shaking his head and flicking my hand away along with a load of imaginary fluff. 'I just didn't know that you knew him that well to, you know, sleep with him.'

'Well, actually,' I sigh loudly, 'what the oracle of all untruths has omitted to add is that I didn't actually sleep with him. Well

I did, but not in the full-blown penetrative sense of the word. We slept together, but didn't, if you see what I mean.'

'Oh?' says James, still looking slightly flushed, confused and even relieved.

'She didn't shag him,' reiterates Wendy, shoving a strip of garlic bread in her mouth and smoking at the same time. 'Which I . . . personally . . .' she continues, through chews, 'find . . . very . . . hard . . . to believe.'

'You see, there you go again,' says Colin, pointing across the table. 'Sex, sex, sex, that's all you think about.'

'Think being the operative word,' mumbles Wendy.

'Rubbish,' says Colin.

'OK, when was the last time I got laid?' announces Wendy, hands in the air, ready for a rough bit of stop and search.

The table falls silent. No one has a clue.

'Um,' says Colin, crafting ash art in the ashtray with his cigarette.

'Ooh,' exhales James, placing a serious thinking finger on his chin.

'Oh, I know,' I announce, with exaggerated delight. Everyone, including Wendy, leans in for the denouement. 'Oh, no,' I say, 'that was just a snog.'

What feels like nearly a whole minute of silence passes.

'Shall I tell you?' says Wendy, actually beginning to sound slightly depressed. We all nod. 'The water skiing instructor, on holiday, with my parents in St Lucia.'

'But that was January,' I say.

'And it's nearly December,' says James.

'Wow,' says Colin.

'Wow,' we all agree.

Fortunately for Wendy, the waitress arrives and cuts short our group contemplation of her arid, barren and practically Maria von Trapp sex life. As she stands with her expectant service industry smile, we all slowly dispense with the menus and order the same pizzas, with the same drinks and the same affected side orders that we do each and every time we come here. That's the strange thing about restaurant chains, they seem to cater for the unadventurous. You only ever seem to go into them with some sort of desperate G spot fix that only a

Big Mac, or Chicken Royale with cheese, will hit. I mean, I've been a Fiorentina girl since I can remember. Wendy always has American Hot, as does James. While Colin is your common or garden Four Cheeses kind of bloke. There is always much humming and haa-ing about deviation and repetition, but we all eventually resort to what we know we like in the end.

'Actually,' says James, after a short pause, as he sits back in his chair, steals one of Wendy's cigarettes and finishes his bottle of beer. 'I can't believe you slept with Jack Morris at all.'

'I know,' I say, leaning in to squeeze both his knees in my excitement. 'Isn't it amazing?'

He shifts uncomfortably. 'No, Abby, it's not amazing, it's very strange indeed,' he replies, beginning to sound slightly like my mother. 'I mean, what were you . . . ?'

'I'm with you there, James,' says Wendy. 'I mean, I could understand you and Abby sleeping together,' she smiles.

'You could?' he says.

'Yeah, well, of course,' she shrugs. 'You know, like brother and sister, in a sort of Babes in the Wood fashion, warm and snug in an us-against-the-rest-of-the-world feeling. Like totally devoid of sex . . .'

'Oh, right, of course,' he says. 'In that way.'

'But you and Jack,' she muses.

'It's only because he's famous, so you took what you could,' surmises Colin, starting to laugh. 'He didn't fancy it, so you went "Oh, OK, Jack, anything you say, Jack, three bags full, Jack, d'you mind if I stay here tonight just so I can tell all my friends." It seems very obvious to me.'

'Oh, my God. Oh, my God, I can't believe you said that,' I say, milking the moment for all its dramatic worth. 'Do you really think I'm that shallow?'

'Yes,' the whole table shrieks in unison.

'Well, that's it,' I say, holding my hands up. 'That's bloody it. I'm chucking the lot of you.' As I stand up at the table, taking rather a lot of time preparing to leave, I wait for them to beg me to stay. No one says anything. 'Well?' I ask eventually.

'Oh God, go on then,' says James. 'Oh, please stay, Abigail . . . we'll really miss you.'

I rejoin the table at the same time as the pizza arrives along with a large carafe of wine and two more beers. We all tuck in, heads down, elbows out, with the ravenous zeal of kill-starved hyenas. The conversation becomes much more fragmented as mozzarella and tomato paste become the priority. Colin fills us in on his quest for a Channel 4 show. Assuring us once again that they are still interested, he says they keep turning up at his gigs, advising him to do the Edinburgh Festival and promising to ask a mate of a mate for a spot at the Jongleurs comedy club. He says he is thinking about doing an open mike slot at the Comedy Club, but someone else on the circuit advised against it, saying that it's about as much fun as throwing yourself to the lions or the sensational equivalent of slowly pouring salt over a slug.

Wendy joins in with a general moan about her televisual career. *Richard and Judy* is not going as swimmingly as it might, and in pursuit of other employ all she ever seems to do is underwire her breasts, wear tight tops and have meetings with biodegrading executives who have eaten too much shepherd's pie at the Ivy and don't sleep with their wives any more. She's even thinking about doing stuff that doesn't air on the telly.

'I mean, can you believe it,' she says, sucking on her cigarette like an extractor fan. 'My agent, the other day, who I am convinced is running a care in the community programme he's so shit, suggested that I go to this audition for what he told me was a British Airways corporate video job. You know, the sort of extremely lucrative money for old rope sort of job that we all have sexual fantasies about early in the morning just before the alarm goes off. Anyway, I arrive in this smelly grey room opposite the London Palladium just by Liberty's, and I walk in and this bloke says to me would I like to put the clothes on? The clothes on! The bloody clothes on! A red and white striped short-sleeved shirt and a doors-to-manual scarf! I couldn't believe it. So there I was, with the words "chicken or beef?" poised to come out of my mouth when they call me in. They don't ask me a single question about who I am. Or what I have done. They ask me to read just a list of credit card names in a pleasant voice. I think I probably stammer over American

Express and then they ask me to go. Outside, all lined up, sitting down in a neat row with crossed legs, and pleasant tights, are a group of Avon ladies all in their doors-to-manual, waiting to go in. D'you know what it was for?' she says, her mouth catching flies in horror. 'Shall I tell you?' We agree we want to know. 'Only the woman who welcomes you on to the Heathrow Express and tells what credit cards you can pay with! Jesus Christ . . . I mean really.'

Colin loses it. The idea of Wendy being in anything that involves the service industry, let alone reading out methods of payment on the Heathrow Express, fills him with such joy that he has to go to the gents to splash water on his face. James also rocks with laughter – yet it sounds slightly hollow in comparison to Wendy and me, who sound like suckling pigs on absinthe. He is obviously a lot more depressed about leaving than any of us first thought.

'You're unusually quiet tonight, James?' I suggest after we've all calmed down post Wendy's story, and dish out the wine which the boys start sampling in lieu of their bottles of beer.

'Oh, I know,' sighs James. 'I'm just thinking really how I'm going to miss you all . . . really,' he says, scratching his chin, his legs bouncing with tension at the same time. 'You know this is the second sort of major time that I've gone away and somehow it doesn't seem so appealing as it did last time.'

'Maybe it's because you know how much work you have to do this time round,' grins Colin, stretching away at his four cheeses.

'Yeah,' giggles James. 'That's certainly true. Last time I couldn't believe I was being paid to hang out in South America. The fact that it was with what remains of the Shining Path did put a bit of a dampener on it, obviously. But two months all-expenses with a bit of beach-bum book-ending was all I could think of at the time.' He laughs, drinking more wine. 'This time it's different,' he adds, looking at me.

'Is it a lot more dangerous?' I ask

'Yeah, probably,' says James. 'Six months with one of the world's best known terrorist groups is not ever going to be incident-free, is it?'

'Sri Lanka's nice,' insists Wendy helpfully. 'Lovely beaches down in the south, perfect for that George Hamilton top-up just before you head home.'

'I know, but I'm away for Christmas and New Year,' he says. 'And I'm going to miss out on all the parties and the fun and going to stay with Abby's parents.'

'Oh, God,' I laugh. 'I'll tell you who is going to be absolutely devastated about that!'

'Who?' he smiles.

'My mum, of course,' I smile back.

'Course,' he says. 'But d'you know that is probably one of my favourite times of year, um, down at your parents.'

'God, is it?' I reply, genuinely surprised. He is a dark horse, James. Sometimes I think I don't know him at all. 'Wow, I never thought you cared,' I laugh. 'Actually, between you and me, I don't think I could get through that period if you didn't come down. My parents would drive me nuts.'

James's face brightens. 'Really?' he says.

'Ah, sweet,' says Wendy, with heavy sarcasm. 'I can't get through Christmas without you. I must ring up my mate at *Tatler* and tell her to put that in next month's "I can't get through . . ." page. Oh, gosh, I feel all fluffed up like a bunny rabbit, I'm so overcome with sentiment.'

'Shut up, Wendy,' interjects Colin. 'Just because we're not talking about you.' She sticks her tongue out.

Wendy famously can't cope when she's being ignored. It used to be probably the only thing that irritated me about her, post our breast-bonding moment. But since both Colin and James pointed it out one evening, it has become a sort of standing joke to be remarked upon at everyone else's comfort and convenience. Since then it's become really rather endearing.

'Oh, I know,' says Colin, mincing about in his chair. 'Let's quiz Abby on her celebrity news and see just how long Wendy can control herself.'

'Oh, actually, please,' says Wendy. 'I'm dying to hear a few bits.'

'Yeah,' says James. 'Just so long as we don't have to hear about Jack Morris.'

'But that's the best bit,' complains Wendy.

'Depends on your point of view,' says James.

'Too right, mate,' agrees Colin. 'Hot-blooded men like us are only interested in the essential questions like – Natalie Appleton, are her tits that great in the flesh?'

'Or,' says Wendy. 'Sean Bean . . . does he have a nice arse?'

'OK, OK,' I say, pretending to referee. 'All questions will be answered . . . one at a time . . . one at a time.'

This is really the first time that any of them has been really interested in what I spend nearly all my week doing. I know it's just the alcohol talking. We're on our second carafe and everyone has gone a bit glassy eyed with flushed faces and loose smiles. James is flopping forward on his elbow as he always does when even the tiniest bit drunk, and Wendy's smoking like it's an Olympic sport. But it's such a relief to be able to talk. In fact, it's a total joy to be able to chat without sounding like I'm some hideous name-dropping Met. Bar tart. And to be honest in the past couple of weeks I have really begun to enjoy myself. The whole thing isn't as terrifying as it was. Like those early days, a couple of months ago, when I used to stand around on the periphery, trying to look busy, holding my pad and pen with occupational purpose. It's all got a little easier. Only the other day I was at some film magazine awards watching Johnny Vaughan and Ewan McGregor fooling around together, pretending to be game show hosts. The conversation quipped backwards and forwards. The jokes flowed as freely as the alcohol. A week later and the photos were everywhere, *Hello!*, *OK!*, *Now*, *Heat*, and in the background of almost all of them you could see my arm.

'OK,' says Wendy, in an extremely businesslike fashion, as if she were ordering a complex takeaway over the phone. 'I want to get a few things straight. Like what was the Elton John AIDS foundation party like? Did you meet Posh? What's Geri like and did they talk? And I want to know all the details . . . frocks . . . food . . . the lot.' Her slim hands are splayed, moving backwards and forwards with each question. Her eye contact is unrelenting. She is deadly serious.

'Um,' I say, slightly flustered to be so put on the spot.

'Actually . . . hang on,' interrupts Colin. 'I want to know, Posh/Geri . . . Posh/Geri, who's the sexiest in the flesh?'

James leans in to the group, keen, if somewhat bewildered. 'Is Geri the one who married the dancer?'

'Ignore him!' declares Wendy, with a sweeping gesture of her fag-loaded hand. 'I asked first.'

'Right,' I say. 'Oh God, um, OK, it was quite a small intimate do, full of Elton's nearest and dearest.' Wendy nods in such a concentrated way that you'd think she was taking an exam in the subject. 'He was there in some Versace number . . .'

'Colour?' she demands.

'Um, pink?' I reply, having no real idea. 'Lilac? It was pale anyway.' She waves her hand to continue, seemingly satisfied. 'Anyway he's there, with his boyfriend David. Um, Posh was with Becks obviously, and Geri was with George . . . and they did seem to have a chat of some sort. But, you know, it wasn't the easiest of parties to do because we weren't given dinner, you know, sat at the tables, because it was a charity do and each ticket was five hundred quid or something. They only had a few for the press . . . like the bloke from *OK!* and Tania Bryer.'

'She gets bloody everywhere,' mutters Colin into his wine.

'She's the one who had a baby relatively recently, isn't she?' smiles James.

The whole table looks at him.

'Whaat?' he shrugs. 'I watch Sky TV,' he explains. 'And I see her sometimes, um, when there's no sport on.'

'Back to the party,' insists Wendy. 'So Posh was in the pink silk dress thing. I saw that in *The Sun*, but . . . and this is really important for detail,' she says, 'was David's tie the same colour as the dress? I mean, did they match?'

'Well, what the hell d'you think?' I exclaim. Singularly unobservant in the wardrobe department, I couldn't recall what Wendy had on under the table right now, let alone what Posh and Becks wore at a party nearly two weeks ago.

'I knew it,' squeals Wendy, lightly punching the air immediately in front of her. 'Like fucking Pinky and bloody Perky, those two. I mean, Christ, the only people who do that are

Beatrice and Eugenie and that's only because they're forced to by Fergie. It's insane. Actually,' she adds after a short pause, 'it's more than that, it's sad.'

'I don't know why you care so much,' says Colin, lighting up a Camel light. 'I find them both rather tiresome.'

'Do you?' I say, intrigued. 'How can you say that? I thought the whole nation was gripped.'

'Well, I'm not,' announces Colin. 'He's all right, I suppose, in a Manchester United sort of a way. He takes a mean corner, and doesn't say very much. But she, on the other hand, looks like a bloody electrocuted scarecrow. That snubby nose, that scrawny neck and pert tits. I mean, I used to quite fancy her at one time. You know, during the finger-pointing stage,' he says, doing the finger-pointing thing, just in case we'd forgotten. 'But she's like that Liz Hurley, you know. As soon as they get all thin like that, they just don't do it for me. They look like lollipops – big heads and no arses. How can they possibly think that's attractive?'

'Yeah, yeah,' says James, nodding along in total agreement like he really cares. 'Dreadful,' he says. 'Dreadful.'

'What would you know?' says Wendy, flicking her ash.

'I don't,' says James. 'But I know I don't like thin girls. Nothing to snuggle up to.'

'Are you suggesting I'm unsnuggleable?' asks Wendy.

'No, not at all,' protests James, his eyes widening as he appeals for clemency. 'No . . . you're gorgeous, as you well know,' he continues. 'It's just that, given the choice between, say, Kate Moss and Abigail, I'd choose Abigail every time.'

'You would?' I say, astounded and rather touched at the same time. 'You'd choose me over a supermodel. I find that very hard to believe.' I start to laugh. I stare down at my old trainers and black Lycra trousers that are springing sprigs of spaghetti, going between the thighs. The comparison is ridiculous.

'No,' he corrects. 'I said over Kate Moss.'

'Ah, over Helena Christensen?' quizzes Wendy.

'Who?'

'It's James, remember,' I say.

'OK,' sighs Wendy. 'Who would you know . . . ?'

'Cindy Crawford?' suggests Colin.

'Ah,' says James, thrilled to have some sort of celebrity recall. 'Now that would be a tough call.'

'Tough?' says Colin incredulously. 'Tough? You are kidding?'

James raises his eyebrows. 'OK, Cindy it is,' he grins. 'Sorry, darling,' he says, leaning over and kissing my cheek. 'She is known as The Body, after all.'

'That's Elle,' corrects Wendy, raising her eyes heavenward.

The waitress comes over again and we all sit back, contemplating coffee and pudding, but eventually opt to just finish off the dregs of red wine. That's the great thing about not really being employable, you can afford to drink too much on a Monday. When the rest of the world is still trying to get to grips with the week, you realise that it's pointless even trying.

'Now where were we?' muses Wendy, rubbing her hands together. 'Ah, yes . . . Elton.'

'Um,' says James. 'Can I ask a question?'

'Go on then,' I smile, waiting for some total non sequitur to pearl from his mouth.

'D'you enjoy it?' he asks, looking at me intently, his eyes slightly shining. He looks concerned and sweet and totally divine. 'I mean, it must be great fun?' he smiles.

'It is amazing,' I agree.

'Who have you met?' he asks. 'Not that I'd know any of them,' he adds, raising his eyebrows. 'But, you know, run a few by me.'

'And when we say met, we mean met rather than seen from some distance. Met means spoken to,' insists Wendy, grinning as she leans in.

I look around the table, ready to start my list. Wendy's pink cheeks almost match the sleeves of her tee-shirt that says 'I like snogging' about twenty-five times across her breasts. She is smiling in expectation.

James is in the same petrol-blue tight-fitting shirt he always wears when he goes out. It's quite endearing really. He has one 'pulling shirt' that I swear I have seen him in at every social occasion, no matter how smart or casual, for the last four months. I even rang the Westbourne pub the other day, trying to track him down. I told them I was looking for a tall slim bloke in a tight-fitting blue shirt. It took them two minutes to find him. James was convinced he must be famous and that they'd seen his documentary. I didn't have the heart to tell him otherwise. Anyway, a lot more relaxed than he appeared earlier, he slouches back in his chair and awaits a list of people who are vaguely familiar.

Only Colin, in huge baggy black polo neck, looks a bit bored. Since his whole Polly Friend incident, and the subsequent trip to celebrity Coventry, he's become a lot less interested in that sort of thing. Partly I think because he must have quite liked her. The idea of Colin taking anyone to hospital is a sign of profound commitment. And also he seems to be getting closer to becoming famous himself. In his words, if you are serious about your career it is not a 'good look' to be seen hanging around stars like some panting dog or a wannabe desperate for the frisson of fame. That privilege is obviously reserved for Wendy and me.

'Oh, I've got a question,' announces Wendy. 'What's Jude Law like?' She looks like she can smell blood. 'Because all those Natural Nylon people get right up my rectum. They swan around, thinking the whole world is applauding.'

'Natural who?' says James.

'Oh, you know, all those sort of Sadie Frost, Jonny Lee Miller, Sean Pertwee and his wife Tadaah people,' she says, scratching her neck with obvious genuine irritation. James looks confused. 'Oh, come on, James,' she says. 'I can't remember her name but I know she's some make-up bird. It's just that in every single photo of her wedding in *Hello!* she looked so pleased to be in there that she looked like she was saying "Tadaah! Look at me!" It made me want to throw.'

'D'you know, much as it pains me to say this, and it really does, Jude Law is delightful.' I smile. 'In fact he's gorgeous . . .'

'Is he?' says Wendy, sitting bolt upright in her chair in glee. 'God, I've always fancied him. How gorgeous?' She inhales and exhales.

'Really gorgeous.'

'Like . . .'

'Like just really lovely lips and eyelashes and skin! He's got lovely skin . . .'

'I think he was really underrated in *Gattaca*,' says Wendy. 'Oh, God, and as for *Talented Mr Thing*, I could hardly control myself in the cinema . . . all that chest hair.'

'Oh, I know.'

'OK, so Jude Law is sexy,' erupts James. 'How about . . . ?'

'No, hang on,' says Wendy, volleying back James's question with the back of her hand.

'What did you say to him then?'

'Oh, God,' I say, flapping both my hands either side of my cheeks trying to cool off. 'Oh, God, right,' I continue. 'First off I said hello.'

'Yeah?'

'Then he said hello right back!'

'Wow.' Wendy's spine spontaneously collapses as she sinks into her chair.

'I don't think I can take much more of this,' sighs Colin. 'James, shall we get the bill?' James looks a little shocked. 'When I mean get the bill, mate, I don't mean pay for it.'

'Thank God for that. You had me going there for a bit.'

'So, after the hello?' says Wendy.

'Oh, I asked him if he was having a nice evening? What he thought of the film? Whether he was having fun? What his next project was?'

'Jesus Christ, Abigail, you should be on fucking *Newsnight*,' says Colin.

'Oh, shut up,' says Wendy. 'Talk among yourselves if you don't like our conversation. So he said?'

'He said he was having a nice evening, how much he liked the film, that he was having fun, and he wasn't sure what he was going to do next, but he had a lot of scripts landing on his doormat every day from Hollywood.'

'God,' sighs Wendy. 'Lucky you, hey.'

'Yeah,' I smile, shrugging my shoulders with delight. I'm so thrilled that Wendy can see the up side of the job and doesn't seem to be at all chippy or jealous.

'Hey,' she says, 'next time you do one of these things, you know, a good one, not some shit book launch, can I come along?'

'Course!' I am so relieved. It would be so brilliant to have an ally to come along with me to share a slice of stellar heaven. 'There is some charity football match next week, you could come too.'

'I don't do football,' she says.

'Not even with Robbie Williams?'

'Deal.' Her hand is across that table swifter than a side-winder snake.

The waitress finally arrives with the bill.

'Now,' says Colin, his hands up like he's directing traffic, 'if anyone says they didn't have a starter and they didn't have any pudding, I will personally garrotte them with my Nike laces, because none of us did. So minus James, who we're all paying for, it's £23.50 each, including tip.'

All paid up, we stand in the wet street outside to say goodbye. It's one of those cold dank miserable nights that the English winter specialises in. Cars splash past and they spray the afternoon's drizzle up against the kerb. Couples walk swiftly along, collars up, faces down, their hands firmly in their pockets. They hardly make a sound except for the tap-tapping of their feet.

Wendy shivers loudly and offers to drive us all home. She is over the limit but it's too inconvenient to leave her car. Colin takes her up on the offer but James refuses, insisting that he wants to walk me home.

'Oh, God,' I yawn. 'Do we have to?'

'Oh, please,' he says, looking through his lashes and doing that special sad dog thing with his eyes. 'I'm leaving in a couple of weeks, and I'm going to miss the rainy streets of London.'

'All right,' I shrug, taking hold of his arm, for warmth and comfort. 'But you really bloody are pushing your luck. But seeing as you're going . . .'

So we walk together along Notting Hill Gate and stand by the cinema waiting to cross the road. The occasional blasts of cold wind slap my face.

'James, it really is bloody cold,' I mutter. 'I can't believe you persuaded me to do this.'

'Sorry,' he says, grabbing hold of my interlinking arm with both his hands and jollying it along, like one might to a tired child. 'I just wanted to talk to you alone.'

'Oh,' I say, slightly taken aback. What is he talking about? 'Um, what have I done now?'

'It's not that,' he says.

'Oh.'

'Um, how long have we been friends?' he says, staring at the road as we cross it.

'God, I don't know,' I shrug, not really understanding what he's going on about. 'Nine or ten years.'

'And we're best friends, aren't we?' he says.

Ever since Wendy announced the Jack Morris thing to the whole of Pizza Express, he's been acting strange.

We walk on some more holding hands. His are warm and slightly damp, mine red raw blocks of ice.

'I'm really going to miss you,' he says suddenly. 'I mean really . . . miss you . . .'

'Me too,' I reply, a bit too automatically for his liking.

'You don't mean it in the same way as I do,' he says.

'How can you say that?' I pronounce with affected offence. 'Trust me, I know.'

We arrive at my front door. I rattle around in my bag for my keys.

'Are you going to invite me in?' he says.

'What . . . in?' I say, looking down at the pavement, the orange streetlight reflected in the puddles, blurring in and out of focus. 'Inside? No,' I exhale loudly. I'm tired. 'To be honest, I'm feeling a bit sick. I think I might have street spin.' The delights of my badly sprung mattress await. 'Can't we do it another time?' I suggest.

'Um, yeah, OK then,' he says.

I leave rather a damp kiss on his cheek. As he walks off down the road, it starts to rain, again.

7

The last week of November and it's blowing an icy gale with the occasional lashing of hail. It's so dark and miserable outside that at 2 p.m. everyone but Wendy is driving with their side lights on. We're on our way to Wembley for a five-a-side celebrity football match for some London children's charity whose name I can't remember. The PR had gushed so heavily on the phone that I'd made sure Wendy didn't renege on her word. 'It'll be so-o-o fascinating for you to see what celebrities do when they're not working or at parties,' she'd said. 'Play Nintendo,' I'd replied. 'Yah,' she'd laughed, breezily trying to move the conversation on. 'But readers of *The News* will be fascinated. Liam and Noel are coming, with Meg, of course, and Robbie, and Max Beesley, and Nick Moran, Damon Albarn, Keith Allen, Jamie Theakston, Ewan McGregor, Hamish Rowland, Vinnie Jones . . . all might turn up. And we've even got some of those Ladettes to put together a team,' she'd trilled triumphantly. 'Zoë Ball, Sara Cox and Denise Van Outen are all playing.'

But as it turned out, Wendy was thrilled to be coming. Ever since some *Blue Peter* presenter shed a stone and came over all trendy, the shopping mall work has been on the wane. And laughing at someone's piles during a Dr Chris Steele phone-in on *Richard and Judy* had also not helped her cause in the studio that much either. 'Fuck it, if they can't take a joke,' she'd shrugged. 'There's always *Taste-Testers* on Granada Breeze. Never too proud to compare sausages with Nina Mishkow, that's my motto.'

So we've been driving around the Twin Towers together for about ten minutes now, trying to work out where we should be. The place is deserted, save for a smattering of cars blown down one end of the car park.

'D'you think it's up there, near that orange car? That looks like something an actor would drive,' suggests Wendy. 'Pop his Jazz supports and codpiece in the back.'

'Hang on,' I shout, face flat against the passenger window, shifting my shoes in Wendy's footwell of filth. 'Was that a sign?'

She slips the car into reverse and without so much as looking behind her accelerates at great speed towards a rather sad and sodden-looking hand-drawn cardboard sign.

'That doesn't bode very well,' sniffs Wendy. 'It doesn't exactly exude glamour.'

Come to that neither do we. Wrapped up in all the scarves and hats and gloves we own, we've both got so many uncoordinating clothes on it's actually relatively hard to move. Prising ourselves stiffly out of the seats, we follow the signs through the tall iron gates and along to the concrete walkway outside. I've only ever been to Wembley for rock concerts in the summer, I think. When the air smells of sweat and fried onions, and the bass takes hold of your kidneys and stir fries them all afternoon. On a winter's afternoon, it's an unsettling feeling being in somewhere designed to cater for hundreds of thousands of people when you are only two. Our wet footsteps echo against the emptiness and there's the stench of urine and the metallic odour of sodden concrete. Wendy and I both quicken our pace. There's an uncomfortable stalker presence around every corner.

'Where the fuck are we supposed to be going?' moans Wendy, waddling along beside me, hardly able to turn her head for the amount of wool and acrylic mix she has wrapped around her neck.

'There,' I say, finding a sign. 'Through there.'

Walking along the darkened tunnel, we finally come out the other side to a glorious view of Wembley Stadium. The emerald-green pitch is divided in half with two mini football matches. Two sets of orange net goals run down the touchlines. This is celebrity-friendly football. The line of play goes widthways, so none of these chain-smoking delinquents exhaust themselves too much in the fund-raising process. Having said that, they do appear to be taking the whole thing surprisingly seriously. There's a large scoreboard down this end of the pitch with a whole list of teams, leagues and what looks like a savage knock-out system in place.

Wendy and I are slightly bemused by the whole thing. Unfamiliar with both football and the etiquette of celebrity football, we don't quite know where to put ourselves.

'Where the hell is hospitality?' says Wendy, throwing a cigarette on the floor. 'I need tea, coffee, chicken soup or a vodka of some description.'

'Oh, hi,' waves a slim brunette, slightly ahead of us on the path. In a pair of tight-fitting black trousers and large black jumper, clutching a brollie, she looks like a spider as she scuttles towards us. 'Abigail?' she asks.

'That's me,' I say, 'and this is my friend Wendy Slater.'

'Great,' she says. 'I'm Antonia, I've been waiting for you to turn up. You've come at just the right time,' she smiles. 'It's been going for a couple of hours now and the Blur, Oasis, Boyzone thing is just about to kick off.'

'What d'you mean?' I say, slightly confused. 'Three teams at once?'

'No, not that,' she says, starting to walk around the pitch. 'Silk Cut?' she asks. Wendy tucks in. 'It's all this fairly pathetic pop star rivalry thing,' she says. 'Someone has said that Blur and Oasis have both got ringers . . .'

'Ringers?' Wendy fortunately interrupts, because I'm busy pretending I know what she's talking about.

'Really rather good semi-professional footballers who are neither members of the band nor roadies or people from the record company. They're friends of a friend who they've brought along simply to help them win the competition.'

'Ri-i-ight,' I say. 'And Oasis and Blur have ringers but Five don't?'

'Yup, so the gossip goes,' says Antonia, flicking her fag ostentatiously into the air as she walks along. 'Don't you just love a bit of chart-topping tension,' she laughs sarcastically. 'But to be honest with you who gives, quite frankly. Just so long as Robbie Williams' team doesn't get knocked out I'll be happy.'

'Oh yeah,' I grin, warming to her more and more.

'He's just so shaggable,' she swoons. 'As is that Jamie Theakston in goal.'

'Mmm, nice legs,' agrees Wendy absentmindedly. 'Will they be in shorts all day?'

'Bloody hope so,' says Antonia. 'It's the only reason I gave Caroline the Gabby Roslin book-signing in Regent Street this morning, so I could come down for a gawp. There have to be a few perks to owning the company, don't you think?' she smiles. 'Cigarette, anyone?' she says, helping herself to another nicotine chaser.

We arrive at one of the many glass-fronted dining rooms with a view of the pitch. Steaming hot in comparison to the chill outside, the place is full of cigarette smoke and celebrities walking around with muddy legs and sweaty socks. Obviously considered one of the more louche, exclusive, corporate entertaining facilities with linen tablecloths and high-back chairs, these pop stars turned footballers for the day are lowering its tone spectacularly. All over the room there are half-drunk pint glasses of lager stuffed with packets of crisps and floating butts. Curling cheese sandwiches with ashtray seasoning are piled up on almost every available table. Styrofoam cups of tepid soup lie abandoned. They've trashed the place, but no one seems to care. Too involved in their ball-breakingly amusing anecdotes, they all flick mud and food onto the moss-carpeted floor. The noise level is amazing. Deep laughter, baritone cheering, whoever thought that boy bonding could be so loud?

'Will you two be OK in here?' asks Antonia with an ironic smile. 'I've just got to go and check on the photographer from *Loaded* magazine who is down on the pitch. Have a few vodkas, tuck in to the crisps.'

The set-up is quite daunting. There's only a smattering of girfriends or wives wafting around. Smooth-haired, lip-lined, they're nearly all sporting funky ski jackets to keep them chicly snug in the inclement weather. Otherwise it is a club house full of men. A whole posturing, bucking herd of them. Although perfectly pleasant at home or in user-friendly groups, en masse they mutate into the sort of fart-lighting blokes for whom women are a bearable irritation, only if they're driving home. Recipie... passing arse pinch or distracted goosing, the w... the whole being ignored, while attention is directed almost entirely on the matches below or the occasional booze cruise to the bar.

For the first ten minutes or so Wendy and I end up standing on our own by the door, on a slow simmer in our layers of clothes.

'D'you know anyone here?' whispers Wendy, as she starts unwinding a rather clammy pink scarf.

'Well, I've seen a lot of them around,' I say, also starting to disrobe. 'I don't normally do music events, I've always found them a bit too frightening. Even something like the Ivor Novello Awards, when it's all the song writers and the singers, is daunting. And the Brits are just terrifying. Pop stars are all too cool. Even the uncool ones are intimidating. They never say anything. They just curl their top lips a lot.'

'So no one in here for us to talk to then?' quizzes Wendy.

'Um?' I look around.

Right at the front by the floor-length window is the Keith Allen and Damien Hirst brigade. All holding pints, all totally involved with the matches outside, they look far too hard and daunting to approach. Next, over the other side of the room, is a bizarre boxing cocktail of Lennox Lewis and Chris Eubank talking to Ant and Dec. The height and size difference is hilarious. Never has such human diversity of form been so obviously on show. Closer to the bar and furthest away from the football is Chris Evans, and the Ginger Productions bunch. Surrounded by his varied side-kick entourage, including his professional friends from his Channel 4 show, Evans is holding forth with Danny Baker. Telling an obviously protracted anecdote, he's commanding the attention of the whole table, a table at which is perched a petite and distinctly less russet Geri Halliwell. Dressed in baby pink football kit, she is playing on the girls' team. The other side of the bar is a gang of professional footballers who are obviously dumbing down for the afternoon. Peter Beardsley, Dennis Wise, Teddy Sheringham and Paul Merson are all dressed in different strips, offering their extremely expensive services to

...owbiz community, bolstering any side in need of extra, rather potent, firepower.

Wendy and I peel off the remainder of our layers of clothes. Walking over to the bar in our matching greying Damart thermal tops, we decide that rather than boy bonding, we'll just sink a few half pints and think about what to do once we have a litre of Dutch courage under our belts. Just as we perch, half-arsed, on two stools in the middle of the bar, taking generous slurps of lager, there's a huge roar from the stadium. The ten thousand or so fans, penned in at one end like battery hens, start chanting and the whole of hospitality legs it to the sliding doors. After about two or three minutes spent viewing the proceedings from above, the whole bar empties at once and stampedes down the stairs.

The two of us are left sitting.

'Where the hell has everyone gone?' asks Wendy, hoovering a packet of Hulahoops with her beer.

'Don't ask me,' I shrug, not overly keen to chase anyone, least of all Ginger Productions, out into the sleet. 'We'll find out eventually.'

'You should go down,' interrupts the barman, surfing the top of the bar with his beer soaked J cloth. 'It's the knocking out stage, loads of stuff goes off.'

We both give each other a reluctant glance and, grabbing a few insulating essentials, we follow the crowd down to the pitch. From the top of the stairs, the stellar players, each in their virulent footballing ensembles, look like boiled sweets rattling around in a bag. Up close while Max Beesley and Ewan McGregor are laughing together, comparing muddy thighs and rips in their shorts, some record company bloke's mouthing off about something.

Out of the twenty teams taking part, only four are allowed into the play-offs. After a whole morning of playing, the atmosphere is roguishly jolly. There's plenty of jocular fighting between the groups but all of it is good-natured in a brash, peppered with swearing sort of way. Eventually, Angus Deayton in an olive suit, with celebrity sheen, plus a navy shirt and telly-friendly scarlet tie, takes the stand next to the scoreboard and starts reading out the results.

The all-girls team is automatically through on a much wolf-whistling, booing and jeering Denise Van Outen, Sara Cox, Geri Halliwell, Zoë Ball and another equally slim blonde friend all run past Angus, a giggling mass of leg kicks, hair flicks and shiny pink ensembles. As they pass the podium, some bloke shouts, 'Get your tits out for the lads!'

'It's intelligent stuff this celebrity football, isn't it?' sighs Wendy.

The girls through, it's down to the serious business of which other three teams are to join them in the final rounds. There's a long wait, with plenty of standing around, stamping with cold and staring at the scoreboard trying to work out who's made it through. Men in blue track suits are efficiently running backwards and forwards with clipboards. Photographers are firing off film of Ewan McGregor smoking, Nick Moran talking and smoking, Robbie Williams talking on a mobile phone and smoking. Eventually, about ten minutes after the All-Girl Stars squeal into hospitality, the other three teams are announced.

'The first team through is Keith Allen's Vindaloo.' The public address system is so loud that it echoes and bounces around the stadium. There's a flurry of applause from the ten-thousand-strong crowd up the other end. The Keith Allen-Damien Hirst gang shout, applaud their own success and mount each other like sexually active dogs. 'The second team through is the Resting Thesps.' There's a stronger wave of applause from up the other end as Hamish Rowland and Max Beesley, Tom Hollander and Rufus Sewell all slap each other manfully on the back. 'And the third and final team are the Williams' Angels.' The scream from the other end of the pitch still has a certain amount of ear-piercing potency by the time it arrives up at our end. I look round for the Williams team made up of Robbie, Jamie Theakston in goal, and two friends, Guy and Charlie, and some bloke from the record company, but all I can see is a group of bouncing heads on the edge of the crowd.

I spot Antonia standing alone, halfway up one of the stands. Her clipboard by her side, she has a broad grin shining across her face. Nothing like a bit of leg to make celebrity football

...ïad more interesting, I think, as I watch her positively skip down the stairs.

Wendy's making very little effort to hide her boredom. Smoking, and sighing long and loud, she starts to bore holes – spinning on her heels – at the edge of the pitch. I take my notebook out, trying to look busy. I jot down Angus Deayton's sartorial style and then make a list of the men with the sexiest legs.

None of it will make it into the column. I don't know really why I'm bothering, I've done my quota this week. A nice theatre opening with Joseph Fiennes. A book launch with Bella Freud. And the European Film Awards where women like inflatable girls walked around with plunging necklines and spoke in Italian – it's a Damon Dupont job and I know which side my bread is larded. But it's all a bit immaterial really. The Abigail's Party column seems to be getting less and less space. Not enough scoops, apparently. Not enough little bitchy, stitch-up stories picked up by the tabloids. Gavin West complains to Marcus every week, so every week they shave off words and every week they make my photograph smaller and the celebrity snaps larger. Eventually it'll be like the coloured section at the back of *OK!* Or a down-market Jennifer's Diary without any words at all. The ersatz scribblings are a way of appearing less bored than Wendy.

'You've got the handwriting of a nutter,' comes a familiar voice over my shoulder. I turn round slightly startled to find Hamish Rowland leaning against the barrier smoking a Marlboro. He looks delicious. His thick dark hair, stiffened by sweat, sticks out in clumps. His long black shorts stop just above his slim grubby knees and his normally wax-white, nightclub skin is flushed through exercise.

'I thought you only spoke to people you trust,' I reply, annoyed to notice he's Cantona'd his maroon shirt and pulled his collar up in an effort to look chic.

'Ouch,' he smiles, his plump lips parting to good close-up effect.

'Um, congratulations on getting through to the last round,' I renege, desperate for something to say.

'I'm more of a cricket man myself,' he laughs. 'It's Beesley who's the football fiend. Ever since he did that film *The Match* he's been a devil with the ball. Runs rings round the rest of us,' he coughs. 'He doesn't smoke, that might be something to do with it,' he grins.

'Oh, good,' I smile.

Hamish Rowland looks almost an entirely different person from the precious thesp I met at the *Love Letters* première, nearly four months ago. Since then, I've read, he's been slaughtered by many an interviewer for disappearing so far up his own rectum you need to be a gerbil to find him. Maybe he's been humbled a bit? I wonder. Either that, or could he have possibly developed, or even purchased, a sense of humour in the interim?

'Um, what are you doing at the moment?' I ask after a couple of seconds.

'I'm doing a small British film in the East End at the moment,' he says.

'A soul-saver for no money?' I ask.

'You could put it that way,' he replies. 'But I'd describe it more as a script-led star vehicle with some good cameos given by a cracking cast. A sort of *Long Good Friday* meets *Lock, Stock and Two Smoking Barrels* meets *Nil by Mouth* meets *Absolute Beginners*.'

'That's a lot of meeting,' I say. 'Don't tell me it's a gangster musical,' I laugh.

'Um, no,' he grins. 'It's just that Patsy Kensit's rumoured to be considering a part.'

'Oh, terrific,' I nod. 'What's it called?'

'*Packing Heat*.'

'I can't believe you said that with a straight face,' I reply.

'I'm an actor,' he grins. 'One of the perks of the job. Ability to lie, feign interest and fake an orgasm at the snap of a clapper board.'

'Men can't fake.'

'Want a bet?' He raises both his eyebrows.

'Are you propositioning me?' I say, attempting to look provocative in my Devonshire home-knit and Angora Dutch cap.

'Now that would be telling,' he smiles and runs his hands

through his hair. 'I'm on in ten minutes,' he says suddenly. 'Meet in the bar for a drink afterwards?'

He walks off and leaves me standing limply holding my notebook and pen, with an extremely puzzled what-the-hell-happened-there? expression on my face.

'That was the most brazen unsubtle pathetic piece of flirting I have ever seen,' announces Wendy, putting her arm around my shoulders. 'It would have been more discreet if you'd just walked up and stuffed your furry little tongues down each other's throats. I haven't seen such pimply adolescent behaviour since some bloke came up to me at Richmond ice rink and said: "My friend fancies you."'

'It wasn't that bad.'

'Abigail, it was crap,' she sighs. '"Are you propositioning me?"' she imitates, in the vacuous high-pitched tones of a contestant on *Blind Date*.

'You're just jealous,' I say huffily.

'Jealous?' She throws her hat back in mock horror. 'Of pencil penis?' She wiggles her little finger. 'No surprise he finds it so easy to fake, it's a wonder anyone knows he's doing it in the first place.'

'How d'you know he is not gifted in the pants department?'

'White wine cork,' she dismisses. 'I checked.'

'You did what?'

'Oh, yeah,' she continues. 'Good things never come in small packages. Or haven't you heard?' She starts walking towards the stairs. 'D'you fancy a short before we go on crotch watch?'

Back in hospitality and it's a whole lot more rowdy. All the teams who failed to make it into the final stages of the competition have more or less given up on the football and have opted for some serious afternoon drinking. The air is choked with smoke and the whole bar is ripe with the smell of feet, jockstraps and sweet sticky booze. The Oasis, Blur and Five contingent, along with the *Lock*, *Stock* crowd of Nick Moran, Dexter Fletcher and Jason Flemyng, have all staked their territory with beer mats around separate tables and seem to be paying little interest in what's going on.

In fact there is very little mingling between the groups. The

Meg and Liza Walker section appear to be smoking a lot and occupying themselves wearing Gucci. Five, changed into long mutually coordinating macs, are on a mixture of soft drinks, halves and a few bottled beers. While the Blur and Oasis crowd are hard at work on pints. Only Sean Pertwee, Jude Law, and Jonny Lee Miller flit between the groups. Sharing a joke here, slapping a back there, they're seemingly the Kofi Annans of the celebrity charity football world.

'Oh, my God, there's Jude Law,' whispers Wendy. 'Let's go and say hello.'

'Actually,' I say, sensing a scene, 'I think we should go back down to the pitch.'

Back down on the pitch and there are enough famous naked legs to maintain Wendy's interest. On the pitch closest to the bar are Robbie Williams' team against the Resting Thesps.

'That Tom Hollander's got a nice arse,' she exhales thoughtfully, like a livestock breeder checking over future purchases.

She smiles as she watches Hollander spring into bouts of intense activity and then give up as soon as he's tackled. Lighting a post-ruck cigarette, he plays the role of spectator to his own team. The larger, more burly Rufus Sewell is all over the pitch like a social disease. Fast and rough, he overcomes almost all the other players, including members of his own team. Thank God that Hamish Rowland says he's happier on the cricket pitch, because playing football he looks as butch as a choreographer. Running as if in an aerobics class, arms outstretched, he chickens out at the mere possibility of a header. In short, he plays like a girl and the rest of the team pass round him. It's Max Beesley who is football-fuelled Robocop, as he ploughs his way up the pitch taking no prisoners. In some deft one-two combinations with Rufus, they regularly cut through the Williams defence but somehow never make it past Jamie Theakston.

For a wine bar boy, Theakston is really rather good in goal. He punches away the strikes with apparent ease, killing the ball dead on numerous occasions and even managing what looks like a rather painful split at one stage to stop the Thesps from going 2–1 up.

But it's Robbie who's man of the match. Every time he so

much as toes the ball a group of young girls, with plump teen breasts, leap into the air and yell, 'Go, Robbie, go!', waving their home-made banners at the same time. Penned in at the far end behind one goal, their attention never strays from the game. So much adoration, encouragement and channelling of pubescent energy into one man has to make a difference when it comes to performance. Robbie's up and down all over the place like a sniffer dog desperate for the ball. He stops only occasionally to take a drag from a cigarette that some rather chilly assistant has permanently lit for him on the sidelines. He scores all the goals, easily slipping them past the goalkeeper, James Purefoy, who I remember as the sexiest stalker I have ever seen on the telly.

The other three members of the Williams team do little. The record business bloke spends most of his time running alongside Williams shouting, 'Rob, Rob, here if you need me, man. Here if you need me,' while the other two chat to the opposition or carve up the pitch with miskicks.

Eventually the final whistle goes and the Williams team celebrate their 3–1 victory with a collection of high fives and cigarettes all round. Over on the other pitch the all-girl team have been beaten 9–1. Apparently the only female goal was scored after someone flashed her breasts at the goalie and Sara Cox slipped one in. But it appears that the Keith Allen team played tough and ran rings round them and, judging by the amount of mud all over their shiny pink strips, the girls spent a lot of their time flat on their backs.

As the girls jog up to the bar, shivering with cold, the Thesps come off the pitch and make their defeated way over to the stand where Wendy and I are sitting.

'There you are,' smiles Hamish, running his hands through his hair as the others stand back and loudly discuss their failure. 'I can't believe you stayed and watched and applauded. Wasn't I just . . . ?' He looks skyward for a muse.

'Crap,' I suggest.

'Um, yes,' he laughs. 'Crap was just the word I was looking for.' He looks up at Wendy and me, who are sitting rigidly still with cold. 'You two look as if you need a blanket,' he says. 'I've got just the thing in my car.'

'You don't feel like getting us a vodka as well, while you're about it?' smiles Wendy, so sweetly that she manages to get away with it. Hamish disappears down one of the tunnels off into the car park. Wendy squeals and kicks her heels with delight. 'You've got him by the proverbials,' she giggles. 'Pucker up and tuck in.'

I don't reply. It's all a bit too exciting to contemplate. I'm sitting with Hamish Rowland, who since the success of *Love Letters* has become the delicious new pin-up, front cover boy on *Arena*, *GQ* and one of those Brit Flick group shots on *Vanity Fair*, and he has just jogged to his car to get me a blanket. A Dempster regular and a man who can command whole page think pieces in the *Daily Mail* is running around worrying about my body temperature. I'm afraid to show any emotion at all, in case the whole world suddenly stops, stares and bursts out laughing at its own fabulous shared joke. So instead I sit rigid like some municipal Telford New Town statue and refuse to join in Wendy's hilarity.

Three minutes later and Hamish is back, clutching a huge ethnic wrap rug thing with an embroidered mirrored border with fuchsia appliqué.

'Year off in Tibet and Kashmir,' he explains, as he tucks Wendy and me in. 'Between Bedales and Cambridge.' He stands in front of us both and inspects his handiwork. 'Better?' he asks.

'Much,' says Wendy.

'Vodkas?' he checks before moving towards the stairs.

'Please,' says Wendy. 'Doubles with tonic.'

And he's off again; taking the stairs two at a time, he catches up with the rest of the Thesp team, who've been ambling up the stairs at the speed of Thora Hird, dissecting their game. He puts his arm around all of them and ushers them in as one large group. Wendy and I, slowly re-chauffing in our ethno-wrap, turn to each other and smile.

'Fag?' says Wendy, a certain amount of triumph creeping into her voice.

'Fag,' I nod and we both light up.

Two cigarettes later Hamish finally returns loaded down with vodka, crisps and a plate of sausage rolls and Scotch eggs. Sidling up next to me, he slips in under the wrap, and dishes out the supplies. Having retrieved a thick jumper from the car and slipped it over his nylon kit, he smells of old sweat and damp wool as he sits next to me machine eating roast-chicken-flavoured crisps. The whole cocktail I have to admit is strangely erotic. I can feel the warmth of his hard thigh as it rubs up next to mine. The right side of my body burns with self-consciousness. I stare determinedly ahead, pretending that such proximity is neither interesting nor disconcerting. The rest of the Thesp team come back down outside to join us all sitting in a row ready to watch the final – The Williams' Angels versus Keith Allen's Vindaloo. The atmosphere begins to build, as team by team, group by group, hospitality empties and the rows in front of us fill up. Hamish starts to shiver. Leaning down the row, he encourages his teammates to place their bets.

'Rufus, man,' he says, turning next to him. 'Angels versus Vindaloo? Fifty quid Allen wins?'

Sewell nods his mop of black curls and slowly Hamish goes down the line extricating money from all his friends, except Tom Hollander and James Purefoy, who both insist that the Angels team will win because of the teen scream factor.

'Right,' continues Rowland. 'So Hollander and Purefoy for Williams and Beesley, Sewell and I for Allen. And the girls? Abigail and um . . . your friend, what d'you think?'

'Wendy,' says Wendy. 'It's got to be Robbie,' she adds. 'This team is so much more attractive.'

'Yup,' I agree. 'So much better to see their winning photo in The Sun tomorrow.'

'Good point,' smiles Hamish, touching the end of his nose like he was playing charades. 'Very good point by the girl in the . . . um, scarves. And the girl . . . in the rather tight-fitting hat.'

I laugh a bit too keenly at his not terribly funny joke, but fortunately my lack of cool goes unnoticed due to the loud scream that emanates from the crowd. The Williams' Angels descend from one side of the ground, dressed in clean Port Vale colours that they've donned for the final. Jogging down the other side of the stadium are Keith Allen's Vindaloo, who have changed into the white Fulham strip.

'Everyone ready?' gushes Hamish in faux-excitement, squeezing my leg. I turn, looking slightly puzzled. 'You've got to get a bit of enthusiasm going,' he shrugs. 'Go, Robbie, go,' he yells, imitating the screaming girls to our left.

'Go, Robbie, go,' joins in Wendy, punching the air, like a member of a chat show audience.

Tom Hollander looks cold. His cigarette hangs limp in his hand; he's forgotten to smoke it and the precariously balanced ash has grown longer than the paper. Rufus is not paying any attention at all and has brought out a copy of some play. His finger running the length of each page, his mouth moving and muttering under his breath, he starts learning his lines, his part apparently underlined in yellow highlighter pen. Max is the only one who's focused. Both legs bouncing up and down together, he is staring at the pitch, alternating scratching his neck or trimming his fingernails with his teeth.

Eventually a professional-looking referee jogs onto the pitch, blows his whistle, tosses a coin, points one way and the play begins. The Angels, it appears, won the toss and kick off. Robbie plays like he did in the match before, steaming down towards the other end, his musicbiz pal at his side. This appears more of a seriously contested match than the one the Thespians lost. For a start the fag-holding assistant waves Lucozade not Marlboro and the Vindaloo boys keep hurling themselves along the ground when they tackle.

To be honest, the match proceedings are wallpaper compared to what's going on under the wrap. I remain rigid as a teenager on her first date. Not quite knowing where to put myself, while Hamish moves his leg up and down against mine. Occasionally using a yell or a shout of encouragement as cover for movement, he puts his hands under the rug and runs his fingers up and down my thighs. I can neither move nor respond. My legs simply don't acknowledge the pulses of electrical sexual excitement that shoot up the inside of my thighs. Only the flushed pink patches burning across my cheekbones display the intense arousal that is building within. My heart is beating so fast and hard that it feels trapped inside my chest, a painful longing grows from the pit of my stomach, my mouth parts as my breath quickens, my lips grow plump.

'Fag?' says Wendy. There's a slightly irritated tone to her voice.

'What?' I reply, somewhat distracted.

'Would you like a cigarette?' she asks tartly.

'Oh, a fag would be lovely,' I mutter, shifting towards her by way of appeasement.

Hamish takes this as a cue to move. 'Any more drinks for anyone?' he says, standing.

'Vodka,' I say, maintaining serious eye contact.

'You'll get what you're given,' he laughs.

'Promises, promises.'

Wendy suddenly gets up. 'I think I might go,' she says. 'I'm a bit tired and I can't really drink any more as I'm driving.'

'Stay,' I say, tugging at her coat.

'Yeah, stay,' says Hamish. 'The football's nearly finished and I've got a gram of coke in my pocket to keep us sharp and witty all night long.'

'You've got a what?' says Wendy, looking more taken aback than I've seen her for some time.

'A gram of coke,' he says, as he walks towards the bar. 'Vodka, was it?' he shouts, as he walks up the stairs.

'Did you hear that?' hisses Wendy, her eyes bulging. 'Did you hear that? The bloke's got coke. Can you believe it? He's got coke.' She shakes her head.

'Yeah? And?' I say, trying to act cool.

'What d'you mean "And?" And? That's sad,' she says. 'Abigail, that's really sad. You can join him if you want to, but I'm definitely going now.' And with that she marches off, leaving a trail of flicking scarves behind her.

I could go after her, I suppose. But I decide not to. There's no point. What could I say? She wouldn't understand. So I sit and stare at the football. The Williams team is winning 2–1. Robbie scored both, naturally, and Jamie Theakston's been sprinting back and forth across his goal, playing the sort of game Peter Schmeichel might have been proud of. Eventually Hamish comes back with a whole tray of drinks.

'Your friend gone?' he asks, in a matter of fact tone.

'Yup,' I say, sounding more hurt than I mean to. 'Yup, actually she had to. She's got to work tomorrow, and can't really afford to get drunk on a Tuesday.'

'Proper jobs,' laughs Hamish, sitting down. 'D'you fancy a line?'

'Sure, that's a great idea.'

We come back to find that the Williams' Angels have won and they're on the podium collecting their cup. Jamie Theakston has been announced goalie of the tournament and receives a rather smart bronze and wooden shield. There's much chanting and applauding by the crowd as Robbie delivers one of his 'too damn right' speeches and everyone's back to the bar.

Hospitality is now so crowded that it's beginning to feel uncomfortable. The music is loud and you have to shout to be heard. The lip-lined ladies have formed a stiff uncomfortable line and are sipping Diet Cokes, waiting for their signal to drive home. In the ensuing alcohol-fuelled chaos, the various teams have split up and are bonding as only famous people can with other famous people. United by paparazzi persecution and public adoration, they don't have to wait for introductions, the fact they are in the public eye means automatic friendship. There's a bizarre bonhomie of mutual appreciation as they each marvel at the other's work. Recounting ever more extravagant stories about where they first saw it or heard it – on an aeroplane in first class, round Sting's house, at the première, chatting to Mick in Malibu. They talk about other famous people they know and then the only other subjects they have in common, fast cars, award ceremonies, parties and the occasional luxury hotel on some far flung tropical island.

It's hard work. Even when on drugs. Not being part of the inner sanctum, there's a lot of hanging around, staring at someone's back, hanging on someone's shoulder, smiling, waiting for the introduction that never comes, laughing slightly too loudly at someone's joke. The thrill is huge. Sit back and enjoy the ride. But never make the mistake of offering up an anecdote, because frankly no one is interested, they don't know who the hell you are.

After an hour of this, following Hamish around the room, as

everyone tells him where and when they saw *Love Letters* – on a yacht, in the back of the bus on a US tour, round Elton's – my legs are beginning to ache from standing and my fixed smile is wearing thin. Hamish, of course, is loving all the stellar chit-chat. Flicking his hair, throwing back his jaw, laughing like a drain, he keeps calling everyone 'ma-a-te' and programs a lot of telephone numbers into his mobile.

I can't really work out if I do genuinely fancy him. Or if I've become a cheer-leading groupie, no worse than any of the other underwired upwardly mobile women, thrusting, pouting and network shagging their evenings away on the leather banquettes at the Met. Bar. Actually, at the moment, I don't really care.

'Hamish,' I whisper into his ear, teasing his lobe to get his attention. 'Can't we go home?' I whine, as schoolgirlishly as I can. 'We could be having so much more fun somewhere else.'

He puts his arm round my shoulders. 'One minute,' he mutters, clipping the edge of my mouth with his lips. 'I just want to get Noel's number. You wait here and I'll be back in a sec.'

As he schmoozes off, I slob down in a chair somewhat defeated and join a group of girls, all busy smoking. I watch as he stands at Noel's shoulder for a good three minutes before he's allowed to join the group. There's some mutual back-slapping and an expansive shaking of hands as he introduces himself to Sean Pertwee, a doe-thin girl and some other bloke in a zip-up utility jacket, who looks like he works in music. Hamish laughs, using the whole of his upper body in the process, and there's a bit of 'hey you' finger-pointing before he pulls out his mobile and punches in the required number.

Five minutes later and we're in his orange Karmann Ghia doing 90 mph on the Westway, on our way to Paddington. Some rave track is on full blast, the heating is on maximum and I'm pretending I know how to chop out lines on a CD. Hamish only slows down a touch as I balance the CD under his nose for him to take a long deep snort.

'Jesus,' he coughs. 'That's better,' he says, wiping his nose. 'Abigail Long,' he says, a curling smile playing across his lips, 'I never knew you were such a naughty girl.'

'I wasn't,' I smile. 'I've just been corrupted by celebrity.' I laugh and, sighing loudly, I lie back in my bucket seat and start running my hand up and down his thigh.

'Mmm,' he moans, squirming in his seat. 'Wait till I get you home.' I let out some girlie squeal, pretending I'm in a fairground. He floors his accelerator and we sweep off the dual carriageway, down into Paddington.

He leaves half his tyres behind as he pulls up outside his flat in a wide white stucco-fronted street. Double-parking his car, we race each other to the door.

'Third floor,' he yells as I push past him, running up the stairs using my hands.

We're both breathing heavily by the time we reach the top. He says nothing as he walks the final two or three steps towards me. His stare fixes on my eyes then slowly moves down to my lips. Pushing me gently up against his front door, he starts to kiss me. His tongue moving slowly across my lips, he descends down my neck, as his hands work their way up under my tee-shirt towards my breasts. I feel hot and rigid; tense through sexual excitement. His cold hands and fingertips burn as they cup my bosom, and my nipples swell and ache as he plays. We both know exactly where this is leading. Resistance is useless. The hall light switches itself off and we're left in darkness. His tongue tastes of tonic and cigarettes, he smells of cocaine.

'Let's get inside,' he exhales down my neck, pushing his hard-on, rigid, up against my thigh.

We fall through his flat door, kissing, and tearing at each other's clothes as we go. We only make it as far as his sitting room, as we tumble onto the hard and unforgiving rug. I lie on my back as he peels off the rest of my clothes. He runs his tongue all over my body. I squirm and moan with desire. Finally he's naked. The light from the street dances along the toned muscles of his back. He leans forward and takes one of my nipples in his teeth, biting it hard. I cry out in pain and thwarted lust. His fingers are inside me. I can't really take much more.

'Go on,' I moan, half-commanding, half-begging. Well, it's been nearly a year. Finally he does. 'Oh, my God,' is all I can manage, as he thrusts. How wrong you were, Wendy Slater. How wrong you were.

Hamish hasn't called for days. Actually to say that he hasn't called for days implies that he's called once. Which he hasn't. Ever. I don't know why I'm surprised. I didn't exactly play hard to get. I wasn't exactly dodging great East End hearses of flowers during a long and protracted wooing process. It's not as if I'd queued up with the dumped fiancées at the Tiffany returns desk, handing back multifaceted solitaires that I thought too rude to accept at this early juncture. He wasn't warming his backside by the fire, discussing EU subsidies with my father, working up to a proposal.

I'd gone to the football, got drunk, taken too many drugs, gone back to his place, fallen on a very uncomfortable Bangalore carpet, spread my legs like I Can't Believe It's Not Butter, and crawled home at 6 a.m., dry retching in the back of a cab. Not the most solicitous of encounters. Not a rendezvous to share with the parents over a Chianti or an amusing anecdote to tell the grandchildren. Just a rather embarrassing slapper moment that no amount of Simple shower gel or Nicky Clarke Lift Thicken and Shine seems to be able to shift.

It's a depressing state of affairs and one that needs sharing with anyone who will answer the phone. James, my first port of call, is completely disorientated when I ring around 12.20. It's the tail end of *Richard and Judy* and there's some rubbish boy band, with a paedophile manager sliming around in the background, playing the credits out. The phone rings about six times; for some reason he picks it up, says nothing and then puts it down again.

'James, what on earth are you doing?' I protest, after I call back a second time.

'Oh, God, sorry. Abigail? Was that you before?' he yawns. 'I thought it was my alarm call. Sorry about that.'

'Alarm call? In the middle of the day? Were you out late last night or something?' I ask, rather confused.

'Er, no, not really.' He stretches in bed. Even on the other end of the phone I can tell his room smells of morning breath and his white body is still steeped in sloth. 'I was on the Net until about three, researching my programme, you know, reading Sri Lankan newspapers. That sort of thing.' He lets out an enormous yawn that sounds like it goes down to his toes and ripples back up his body. 'G-o-d,' he sighs. 'What time did you say it was?'

'Almost 12.30.'

'Christ, is it really? I've got to get to Petty France today to get my passport.'

'But you're going tomorrow,' I say, slightly shocked. 'And it's coming up to Christmas, everyone's going to be on a go slow.'

'D'you think I'm cutting it a bit fine?'

'N-o-o,' I reply sarcastically.

'Good,' says James, totally missing the tone of my voice. 'Because I'd hate to ruin my record of never having missed a plane.'

'What about that trip to Amsterdam?'

'I made it eventually,' he dismisses. 'Even if my girlfriend at the time punched me in the face and we ended up flying Air Kenya. I made it to the wedding.'

'With an enormous black eye.'

'It wasn't that big.'

'James, you couldn't see out of it for three weeks.'

'God, was it that long?' he muses. 'I can't really remember.' He sighs. 'Anyway, hope you are coming to my leaving do tonight.'

'Course,' I say. 'I've got to go to some work thing first but it shouldn't be too long.'

'Make sure it isn't,' says James. 'Because I'm having dinner at 8 p.m. in 192 for ten of my most intimate friends, and I have had to beg for a table.'

'Fine. I'll be there, I promise.'

'Good,' he says. 'Because you haven't been around recently.'

'I know, I know,' I say, sounding tetchy. 'It's this column . . .'

'Yeah, yeah,' he laughs. 'Oh, by the way, how's your drug problem?'

'My what?' I say.

'Oh, yeah, apparently you're a cocaine addict,' he says, obviously climbing out of bed.

'Since when?'

'Since that football match thing. Wendy's very worried about you. She's told everyone.'

'What's she told them?'

'Oh, God, I can't really remember,' mutters James. 'Just something along the lines that you're like some truffling pig, scrimmaging around in gentlemen's toilets, sniffing seats, desperate for a line.'

'Are you winding me up?' I venture, starting to shake with paranoid irritation.

'Might be,' he laughs.

'You bastard,' I laugh. 'What did she say?'

'Oh, only that you seemed a bit too keen for someone who's an occasional user, that's all,' he says, lighting a cigarette down the other end of the line. 'Can't see the appeal of the stuff myself,' he continues. 'It makes people wang for Africa, talk about themselves in repetitive loops, shout, interrupt each other, drink too much and, sadly in my case, stammer and get lockjaw.'

'I never knew you did coke?'

'Once, a long time ago,' he says. 'But I grew out of it.' He exhales. 'Listen, Abby, I've got to go. Petty France is beckoning. See you tonight?'

'Yeah, yeah, see you later,' I say, putting the phone down.

With James unusually nursing a different agenda, and Wendy obviously still angry and spreading rumours, Colin is the only person left to call to discuss the Hamish Rowland incident. As a professional tart himself, I think as I dial, he's certain to understand. And he does, I can tell by the over-excited squeal with which he greets the news on his mobile phone.

'You, you, dirty minx,' he laughs, from the back of his cab on his way to do a voice-over for a breakfast cereal in Soho. 'So are you covered in carpet burns or what?'

'Um, er, a few,' I admit.

'Where?' he probes, not wanting to miss a detail. Colin is worse than a girlfriend when it comes to discussing sexual activity and/or relations.

'Elbows,' I reply, sounding grubbily sheepish.

'Bizarre,' he purrs. 'Do share.'

'Piss off, Colin,' I snap. 'Look, it wasn't that complicated. Did him on the rug, on the edge of the bed and then finally in the bed at about 5 a.m. Slept for about half an hour and felt so revolting and rough that I legged it home.' I lie back on the sofa and light a cigarette. 'But that's not the issue,' I moan, inhaling heavily. 'He hasn't called.' There's a loud cough down the receiver; it sounds as though he dropped his phone. 'Hello? Are you there?'

'I'm here,' he says, and then after a pause, 'Abby, I don't mean to be nasty here but did you seriously expect him to?'

I think about this for a second. 'Honestly?'

'Honestly.'

'Probably not.'

'Well, there you are then.'

'But I quite want to see him again,' I say, beginning to curl my not terribly clean hair around my fingers. 'He's filming in the East End at the moment.'

'Doesn't he go to all those showbiz gatherings that you go to? Can't you just bump into him there?'

'No, not really,' I sigh. 'At least, I've only ever seen him at his own première and then at the football thing.'

'So no chance of a "Whoops I didn't expect you to be here" thing?'

'That's about as likely as a sober dance to "Hi Ho, Silver Lining".'

'Mmm,' he says. I can almost hear the wheels of his wicked brain stirring into motion. 'You could Glenn Close it and pay him a visit on the film set?'

'What? On *Packing Heat*?'

'Whatever the hell it's called,' he replies. 'In a professional capacity, of course.'

'Colin,' I say.

'What?' he says.

'You're a total star.'

'It's been said before,' he smiles. 'Listen, I've arrived,' he adds. 'See you later at 192 for James's thing.'

The sexual stalker visit was amusingly easy to organise. One telephone call to the public relations girl at Phillips and Most, who was so keen on a location report she even offered to send me a car to take me to the old Tate & Lyle factory in the East End. Andrea Adams was slightly more difficult to persuade. I think she's taken my move off her page as some sort of personal insult. After a few minutes on hold at *The News* she finally agreed to take my call.

'Hello, Style,' she yawned.

'Oh, hiya, Andrea, it's me, Abigail,' I said, ever so breezily.

'Abby, baby, long time no speaks,' she said, suddenly slapping her bosom, clearing her cleavage of ash.

'Oh, hi, yes, very well, thanks,' I said, replying to an unasked question.

'How's the wonderful world of celebrity treating you then?' she asked.

'Oh, really well,' I said. 'Very hard work though,' I added, for sympathetic effect.

'So what peachy feature idea have you got for me then?' she coughed.

'Um,' I started to gush. 'Well, it's a fashion location piece, really,' I stammered. 'Along the lines of gone are the days since men in films wore 'seventies floral darts shirts and pink porno shades, now they're in suits. Ozwald Boateng suits to be precise. Smart, simple lines, three buttons . . . collars . . . pockets . . .'

I could hear her heaving and huffing and breathing smoke down the telephone, as she mulled the whole thing over in her embalmed brain.

'Suits, you say,' she said.

'Mmm,' I agreed. 'Sexy attractive men . . . actors, even, in nice smart suits.'

'Ri-ight,' she mumbled. 'Men,' she continued. 'Men in suits . . . Sounds different.'

'Oh, very different,' I encouraged.

'Oh, all right then,' she said. 'You've twisted my briefs. Five hundred words by Monday and no fucking later, OK?'

After quite a lengthy walk from the Docklands Light Railway (I'd decided it was a bit rude to take the car for such a personal mission), I finally arrive at the Tate & Lyle factory in Three Mills Lane. Walking through an arched old-fashioned Victorian gate hewn from what looks like one piece of steel, I walk into an expansive complex of massive cooling towers shaped like oil drums, with corrugated iron out-houses and smaller brick buildings, all interconnected by pipes and flues, on display like intestines and entrails awaiting some Tiresian prediction. Despite the clear blue crisp December afternoon, it is an eerie, frightening place, with dark damp recesses that exude inner city deprivation and sordid violence. It's a perfect backdrop for a slick gangster thriller like *Packing Heat*.

I cross the cracked tarmacked courtyard, almost the size of an airfield. The cooling towers grow larger as I walk towards them. They could easily dwarf a crane. Through the haze of weak sunshine reflecting off the ground, I manage to figure out a small collection of caravans huddled in a circle like the Pilgrim Fathers, protecting them against Indians and the elements. The caravans all have front porches in a sort of mock mahogany wood sticky-backed plastic motif. They vary in size, I presume, according to the glamorousness of the star who inhabits them. In the middle of the caravan circle there's a smaller open-fronted vehicle, with two long trestle tables outside, covered in a lime-green checked tablecloth and dish after dish of food. Lying across the back is a whole poached salmon covered in gelatin and sliced cucumber, next to that is a mound of potato salad decorated with snipped chives. There is a choice of about six different salads, green, rice, apple and sultana, tomato, Greek, or some couscous mix with char-grilled vegetables. There are baked potatoes, French bread sandwiches, plates of cold meats, a bowl of steaming hot rice and a blackboard propped up against the side with the specials of the day listed – beef or vegetable curry, or a chicken and mushroom pie, with a choice of puddings – apple crumble, sticky toffee pudding, or a dainty fruit salad.

'Are you one of the first?' asks a red-faced rotund bloke in a white pinny, leaning through the hatch.

'The first of what?' I ask, overcome with hunger at the sight of so much food.

'You know, the techies, actors, all them lot. Have they broken for lunch yet?' he asks, looking at his watch. 'They said 2 p.m. but it's gone ten past,' he sniffs. 'I'll have to take it all back in if they're not here soon.'

As he spoke, there was a loud cracking and scraping sound as the door from one of the sugar coolers opened behind the caravan circle and a group of about seventy people began to stream out. Inside, the bright studio lights illuminate the tower. The whole of the inside had been lined in a cityscape backdrop. The group all pause outside to change their shoes.

'Some technical thing,' explains the chef, following my gaze. 'Special effects.'

'Ahh,' I nod. 'What are they filming today then?'

'Oh, I don't know really,' he says. 'Some fight sequence when Hamish Rowland kills some other bloke and he falls to his death bouncing off the scaffold,' he coughs. 'They've been at it all morning,' he says, wiping his hands down the front of his apron. 'I did breakfast here at 7 a.m.'

An early group of ten all dressed in jeans and puffa jackets with caterpillar boots, fingerless gloves and the occasional promotional baseball cap crowd round the food, shovelling great portions of pasta and potatoes onto their plate. A couple queue up for the day's specials.

'Not bloody salmon again,' moans some fat ginger bloke with builder's arse and darts players gut, as he helps himself to rice, potatoes and a hunk of bread. 'We had that yesterday.'

While the technical crew tuck in, circling the table like vultures in the bush, a smaller, slower, more strangely dressed group emerges from the cooler. First out is the tiny frame of some seven-stone actress who, smoking a cigarette like her life depended on it, is in deep conversation with a large man with a thicker, more expensive puffa jacket on than the earlier group. With a lens hanging round his neck and his bohemian ponytail swinging down his back and the paternal arm he has around the girl's shoulders, he looks every inch the director.

Next on the tarmac are four young men in sharp suits and highly polished shoes that shine in the sun. Striding towards the caravans, they all stop at one point to share a light as they amble over for lunch. They look remarkably coordinated, like they're in some sort of gang. The two smaller ones are still wearing their costume sunglasses, while the other two have them perched on the top of their heads like girls. They're each wearing a dark coloured shirt, with a bright coordinating suit lining that flashes in the breeze. I recognise two of the shorter actors from a Sunday night BBC 1 costume drama, the other is a well-known stage actor who's been playing at the Royal Court. And at the back, last to lunch, is Hamish Rowland. Black suit, blood red shirt, sunglasses on his head, he is strikingly handsome in the bright afternoon sunshine.

I immediately feel sick. This was a big mistake to think that he might find it amusing or entertaining for me to come and visit him at work. The joke, I have a horrible sinking feeling, is most definitely on me. I decide that avoidance is my only option. A sudden and desperate fascination with the pasta salad is what's required. He walks past me with inches to spare. So much for animal magnetism. I must be as sexually electric as suet. I hunch over, fiddling with the bread basket, looking occupied. Out of the corner of my eye I can see him in the queue for the curry special. He's looking at his reflection in the caravan window, running his hands through his thick dark hair. His suit is beautifully cut around his arse. In his left hand he's holding a script that he lets hang casually by his side. I can hear him laughing with the person next to him.

'Has anyone seen a journalist here from *The News*?' comes a loud plea from a chunky girl with practical hair flicks, jeans, a thigh-length waterproof, sporting a set of headphones and crackling walkie-talkie Velcro-ed to her chest. Standing in the middle of the caravan circle, she scans the crowd for an alien face. Hamish is still talking. Either he hasn't heard or has failed to register her arrival. I look round.

'Um, here,' I smile.

'Abigail?' she booms, worryingly loudly.

'Yup,' I reply.

'Bella,' she announces. 'PR.' She shakes my hand with rough efficiency. 'Everyone! Everyone! Guys! . . . Settle down,' she shouts, clapping her hands together like a nursery school teacher. 'This is Abigail from *The News*.' She points hideously with both hands. 'She's doing a location this afternoon, so let's be very pleasant to her, keep her sweet and . . . give nothing away.' She laughs hilariously at her own joke. A couple of other people laugh out of politeness. The noise level drops.

'Um, hi,' I cringe, giving the most pathetic new-girl wave.

Hamish stops talking and looks straight at me. For a moment his face is shocked and horrified, all at the same time. His jaw hangs slack and his eyes turn spherical with surprise. Two spots, the size of a penny, burn the same colour as his shirt on both of his cheeks. It is a bad idea for me to have come here. He doesn't move. He can't. After a few seconds, his face recovers its cool but the rest of him seems to have caught some vicious post-coital paralysis and he remains rooted to the spot.

'Right,' says Bella, putting a hefty and rather familiar arm around my shoulder. 'I think perhaps you should meet the director first, the producer and then of course the actors. Gemma Knight's gone into make-up so maybe we should do her next and then the boys, Tim, Alex, Miles and Hamish.'

'Um, I'm only interested in the boys,' I say.

'Oh,' she replies, withdrawing her arm. 'What? Just the boys?' she repeats.

'Um, yeah,' I say, somewhat emboldened by her reaction. 'It's been cleared with your head office. It's just a fashion piece really with a few comments from the male actors about their Ozwald Boateng suits. That's right, isn't it?' I check. 'They are all Boateng's, aren't they?'

Bella looks like a deflated party balloon. Devoid of puff, all the energy has gone out of her. 'A fashion piece?' she spits, her face curling like she's just caught her own halitosis.

'Oh, yes,' I continue, rather enjoying her reaction. 'With a few close-ups on the cuffs and buttonholes, maybe. The design essentials. We won't be here for very long. A couple of snaps and a few vox pops with the actors, and we'll be out of your hair . . . Have you seen my snapper?'

Hamish chokes.

'Um, yes,' she says. 'He was wandering around here earlier. I put him in one of the Winnebagos.'

'Which caravan would that be?' I reply.

'The one on the end,' she says. 'I'll go and round up the actors then,' she continues, and then adds hopefully, 'Are you sure you don't want to speak to the director? He's very nice.'

'I wouldn't like to disturb him,' I smile. 'I'm sure he's got lots more important things to do, like, um, look through lenses and stuff.'

As she wanders off to round up the talent, I contemplate making the sharpest of exits. Why on earth did I listen to Colin? Since when has he had a successful relationship to speak of? His life is a series of one-night stands. He's never been any good at the follow-up call, or the cinema date, or anything that constitutes a partnership. Shag and go about sums up his life's philosophy. It would have been so much cooler to have just bumped into Hamish somewhere, wafting through a red-roped area, with a fresh set of highlights and a newly lippo-ed derriere. Neither of which I can afford. Instead I'm in a decidedly too small pair of Hennes trousers looking like a desperate Old Spice who's run out of HRT. So I take three deep breaths, smoke a cigarette right down to the butt, burn my fingers, and frantically try to work out how I might save an iota of face.

Bella returns – special PR smile firmly back in place – with Tim Saint, Alex Hughes, and Miles Grant dawdling along behind her. One of them, sporting a giant nylon bib from wardrobe, has brought his lunch with him.

'Tim, Alex, Miles . . . this is Abigail from *The News*,' she introduces, pointing with her pencil. 'Sorry,' she says, 'I don't know your surname?'

'It's Long,' I say.

'Oh, I know yo-o-o-u,' says Tim Saint, the plumpest actor, with his mouthful. About five feet seven, fifteen stone, and no great beauty, you can understand why he's spent most of his career on the stage. 'I've read your column,' he nods, helping himself to another forkful of heavily mayonnaised pasta. 'Always talking about Jack Morris,' he says, as a rogue shell shape tumbles down his front.

'Oh, yeah,' says Alex Hughes. 'I read it once.' Alex has blond curly hair and Boris Becker eyelashes. He specialises in homosexual artists or nineteenth-century consumptives and distinctly lacks charm.

'Hamish is on his way,' chips in Bella. 'He's popped into his Winnebago for a few minutes,' she smiles.

'Yeah,' agrees Miles. Tall and mousy haired, he used to be the face of Abbey National but has just broken into film. 'He said he had to call his girlfriend. She's filming in the Isle of Man or somewhere like that.'

'Girlfriend?' I find myself saying out loud.

'Oh, yes,' smiles Bella. 'Charlotte Fleet . . . Quite the new golden couple around town, aren't they?'

'Charlotte Fleet,' I repeat, suddenly coming over quite queer.

'You know her,' breezes Bella, starting to fire facts like a machine gun with *Hello!* shells. 'Very tall, pretty, thin, blonde, father's on the Arts Council. Just done that amazing new film with Brad Pitt. Don't think it's out here yet. Won the Palme d'Or at Cannes. What's it called?' she puzzles. 'Oh, I don't know. She's on the front cover of this month's *Vogue*. Gorgeous anyway. And apparently *very* talented.'

'Not thick or bitchy in any way either, I suppose,' I mutter.

'What?' says Bella, just catching what I said. 'No,' she laughs. 'Lovely, actually, and went to Cambridge with Hamish. Law or English. Can't remember which.'

With the glory of his girlfriend's CV still hanging in the air, Hamish saunters over. His jacket flapping in the breeze, his hair neatly gelled, he looks totally unruffled and I hate him for it.

'Hi,' he smiles, his hand out ready for an introductory shake. 'Hamish Rowland,' he says.

'We've met,' I reply.

'So we have,' he nods, wagging his finger, pretending to try to remember where. He's talented at this acting lark. 'Don't tell me, don't tell me,' he says, holding his forehead, shaking it gently for dramatic effect.

'*Love Letters*,' I say, raising my eyebrows in irritation.

'Course.' He holds up both his hands, admitting defeat. 'Right.' He bites his bottom lip. 'Where would you like me?'

'Perhaps you'd all like to stand over there, with those towers in the background. And I'll just go and find the photographer.'

Climbing up the steps of one of the caravans, I walk in to find a small, slim, dark-haired man with an orange tan curled up in a ball of fleeces on the sofa. He's surrounded himself with the moss green cushions, closed the flowered curtains, helped himself to some fizzy water from the tray and is watching the portable telly.

'Abigail?' he mumbles in a thick French accent. I smile. 'I'm Antoine,' he says, offering a pathetic limp and rather unhappy hand to shake. 'I'm very sorry,' he says, shaking his head. 'I went to my first Christmas party last night and I banged so many Es, I feel like a squeezed out lemon.'

'Oh,' I say, feeling strangely wrong-footed, as I sit down next to him on the sofa, staring at the faux-mahogany wall unit. 'Well, if it makes you feel any better, I've slept with one of the actors we're photographing and I've only just found out that he's got a girlfriend.'

'Oh, lo-o-ve that,' says Antoine, with a malicious grin as he props himself up on his elbow. 'Trauma. Recent sex?' I nod. 'Grubby and gratuitous?' I nod. 'You're feeling cheap and just so last week?' I nod again. 'D'you want me to make him look like a shit fuck pig?'

'Can you do that?' I squeal, covering my open mouth in delight.

'Course.' He raises his eyebrows. 'Plenty of the up nose stuff,' he says, tapping the bottom of his chin. 'Three-quarter head, half an eye. Easy. Is he handsome?'

'Very.'

'Take it from me, girl, anyone can be made to look ugly or ordinary. Just as anyone ugly or ordinary can be made to look good. Angles and airbrushing, that's all. I can put kilos on him if you want,' he giggles.

'Oh, the works,' I smile.

'Which one is he?' he says, unfurling off the sofa.

'Hamish Rowland,' I say. 'Tall, dark, in the red shirt.'

Antoine rubs his hands together. 'I'm going to love this. So much more amusing to have an agenda.'

The four boys are pacing around like penned up race-horses by the time we make it back to the group. Bella's huffing on her walkie-talkie about a possible queue in make-up after the shoot's over. And Hamish is still avoiding all eye contact.

'OK, OK, guys, guys,' faffs Antoine. 'We're going to make this a bit of fun, this shoot. Slightly, you know, from below, with the sky in the background. *Charlie's Angels*-style, sil-houette 'seventies retro with Millennium cut suits. Very smooth and cool. So,' he claps his hands, 'complete attention for ten minutes and then it's back to your Winnebagos for Rich Tea and *Supermarket Sweep*, with Dale Winton.'

I laugh. No one else does. They're artistes and they're bored with waiting. Despite the bright sunshine, it's cold and they're irritatedly beginning to hunch their shoulders and put their hands in their pockets, turning their backs to the wind.

'Right, everyone,' announces Antoine, checking his light-meter and adjusting his exposure. 'Special photo faces, boys. Smile, pouty, ever so sexy. Think star, think special, think Hollywood contract, if you can,' he smiles.

'Er, actually,' interrupts Bella, 'Hamish's got one of those . . . A Hollywood contract.'

'Cool, groovy, roger me with a tube of KY,' mutters Antoine, bending down for an up-the-nose special. 'Can the large man in the red shirt put his chin in the air for me a bit,' he shouts. 'I'm getting a bit too much, how you say? Fatty fleshy bit, when I look down the lens.'

'Hamish, chin up,' I add, trying extremely hard not to smile. 'So, Alex,' I say taking out my notebook. 'You're well known for your nineteenth-century drama roles, how does it feel to be sporting such a contemporary ensemble?'

'Oh, right,' he says, not knowing whether to look down the lens, or at me, or both. 'Um, gosh, right,' he flusters some more. 'Um, hang on, um. Obviously,' he says with contentment rapidly growing on his face, as he pouts his moist lips for camera, 'obviously it's great to be in something more "with it". I'm sure a lot of people think that I spend most of my time in breeches.' He rocks with laughter. 'But I'm an ordinary bloke really. I shop in Hackett and spend my afternoons looking for fun furniture for my new maisonette in Fulham.'

'Mmm,' I say, jotting away. 'And Ozwald?'

'Who?'

'Boateng.'

'Oh, terribly fond of his stuff, I think the coloured lining is very racy indeed.' He nods, extremely satisfied with his response.

I ask them all the same questions and receive more or less the same responses. They're all apparently thrilled to look so trendy. To be wearing clothes that they'd all like to wear down Soho House, their partners are all impressed.

'How about your partner, Hamish?' I say. 'Is she impressed by your newfound trendiness?'

'Well,' he says, having the decency to blush. 'I haven't been going out with her very long.'

'Oh, right,' I reply curtly, not looking up. 'How long would you say, exactly?'

'Um, a couple of weeks, maybe a month,' he says quietly.

'Before or after that charity football match you were at the other day?' I quiz. My head's down, but I'm looking him in the eye.

'Um,' he coughs.

'Head up, Hamish,' says Antoine.

'Possibly a bit before.'

'Is this really relevant?' bustles in Bella, putting down her walkie-talkie. 'Only I thought that this was a fashion piece. Not the Spanish Inquisition for *The Sun*.'

'No, no,' I smile ever so sweetly. 'But the readers of *The News* are just a bit fascinated about how long the "golden couple" have been stepping out, that's all.' I push a piece of loose hair behind my ear. 'Anyway – so, Hamish, are you a Boateng boy, or is it just sports casual?'

'Bit of both really,' he says, shuffling his feet. 'It depends on the occasion.'

'Fascinating,' I say. 'That's a marvellous quote. I think we're done here, aren't we, Antoine?'

'Oh, definitely done,' he winks.

'Um, I'm sure I could come up with something a bit more interesting than that,' says Hamish, looking somewhat perturbed.

'No, no,' I say, terribly pleasantly. 'I've got what I came for – well, not exactly what I came for. But a result anyway. So thanks, all of you,' I say. 'Enjoy the rest of the filming. I hope it goes well.'

The group starts to disperse and the actors file back to their caravans, as the technicians start wandering over to the giant coolers for another afternoon's filming. Bella says her goodbyes and rushes over to the Nissen hut next door to the catering bus that doubles as production office. I link arms with Antoine as we decide how we're going to spend the rest of our already highly productive afternoon.

'Just so long as it involves alcohol, I don't care where we go,' he announces, as we make our way towards his car, each with a bag of photographic equipment slung over opposite shoulders.

'Yeah, fuck him,' I say.

'You already have,' screams Antoine, thinking he's just the funniest. 'Tell me,' he whispers, 'was he any good?'

As I stand and contemplate my answer, I feel someone touch my elbow.

'Abigail.' It's Hamish.

'What?' I say, sounding a bit too aggressive, as Antoine makes himself scarce.

'Look, I'm sorry,' he says. 'It's just one of those things,' he shrugs. 'You know, I'm busy filming all the time . . . Up at 7 a.m., back at 8 p.m. I should have called.'

'Called to say what?' I sigh. '"Sorry you're covered in carpet burns I've got a girlfriend."'

'Something a bit nicer than that,' he smiles.

'Well, you didn't,' I say, trying to be brave, digging my nails into the palm of my hand.

'Well, I'm extremely sorry,' he says, looking through his lashes, trying to look cute. 'Friends?' He grins, holding his hand out as a peace offering.

'Oh, BFs,' I smile exuberantly. 'Now if you'd excuse me,' I sigh, not bothering to shake. 'I've got some serious drinking to do.'

Antoine and I decide that we have to go and drown our sorrows. Me, because I've been publicly dumped on a film set in front of a bisexual PR and he, because he's on some post-Ecstasy downer and in need of some upwardly mobile stimulants.

We ended up in a bar with wonderful views, the sort of place where over-made-up women with a public penchant for hair spray sit in silence with short foreign-looking men, drinking champagne. An expensive watering hole with cashew and green olive niblets, there's a late night piano bar where even the most banal of cocktails comes with brollie 'n' cherry accessory. As you tuck into your enforced plate of cheese or meat, there's normally an aged crooner with a steely ponytail, a white tux and a frilly dinner shirt the colour of a prawn vol au vent tinkling the keys. In the past, when monstrously drunk, James, Colin and I have been known to shimmie on our stools, loudly making Lionel Richie 'Say You, Say Me' and Barry Manilow requests.

Tonight at 5.30 p.m. it's almost deserted. Already dark outside, it feels much later than it actually is. In a fecund armchair to our right as we walk in is a Saudi Arabian bloke, in white robes, a red and white headdress, black socks and ginger open-toe sandals. He's drinking what looks like a whisky and Coke, rummaging around in his brown leather suitcase mumbling into a mobile phone. Sat in the middle of the room are two rough looking women in pussy pelmet skirts, each with American tan stockings that have slipped down their thighs. The blonde facing the entrance has bouffed and teased her hair into a candy floss, back combed style rather like a Mr Whippy ice cream. The older, darker one with her back to us has got a short harder biker's helmet of a hairdo with go faster wings. They both obviously talk by the hour.

We walk and choose two low-slung armchairs with a view of the whole lounge.

'Double vodka and tonic,' announces Antoine to the waiter with the maroon bum-freezer jacket, an element of panic in his voice.

'I'll have the same,' I smile. 'And as many crisps, nuts and bits as you can find.' I sigh and lie back into the welcoming armchair. 'Hey, I've got a brilliant idea,' I say, sitting up suddenly. 'Would you mind if I invited a friend of mine, Jack Morris, down here?'

'What, *the* Jack Morris?' lisps Antoine.

'Mm.'

'Fab,' he says, stealing a cigarette. 'Does he like blokes?'

'Not in the way you do, I think,' I say. 'But you never know your luck.'

Jack's mobile rings almost to the point where his answer machine kicks in.

'Hello?' he shouts, over raging background noise.

'Jack, it's Abigail,' I shout back, covering my ear with my spare hand.

'What are you doing?' he yells.

'I'm in a fancy bar,' I tell everyone in the fancy bar, as I fill Jack in on the exact location.

'I'm a bit wankered,' he says. 'I've been drinking and chopping since dinner time today.'

'We'll play catch up then,' I laugh.

'Great,' he says. 'Oh,' he adds, his voice quieter and more conspiratorial. 'I've got your chang.'

'My what?' I shout.

'Chang,' he whispers loudly.

'Oh,' I say, a bit shocked, looking around the room to see if anyone's heard.

'Well, you mentioned you wanted some the other day,' he adds.

'Did I?'

'Yeah.'

'Oh, I don't think we should really be talking about this on the phone,' I say, rather nervous about what I'm doing.

'See you in about fifteen then?' He hangs up.

We've just ordered our second vodka by the time he arrives. He looks a lot more wasted than I was actually expecting. His face is white, yet flushed and covered in a fine layer of sweat. He stinks like a slops tray as he flops down next to me. His black tee-shirt doesn't look fresh and his black leather jacket has food down the front of it, his hair is dirty, and he's got body odour.

'What a day,' he exclaims with a broad grin. 'Lost a part this morning in some Ben Elton project, can you believe it? I've been drinking ever since.'

'Probably not the most constructive of reactions,' I smile. 'D'you want a drink? Or perhaps you want to sharpen yourself up before?'

'Fine plan, Holmes,' he nods, tapping the side of his nose, as he gets up to go to the gents. 'Wossyour name?' he asks Antoine.

'Antoine.'

'Cool,' he replies. 'D'you fancy some powder? Brighten things up a bit.'

As the two of them disappear off to a cubicle together, the lounge bar begins to fill up. A brace of Eastern European-looking businessmen in Prince of Wales check suits drink whisky and water together, obviously sealing an early evening deal. A few more nocturnal-looking ladies come in to take up lucrative-looking positions near the piano. Crossing their legs in their cheap scuffed shoes, one of them has a blue catering plaster hanging off the back of her heel. An ostentatiously thick silver grey wig-wearing pianist starts to play a few bars, eventually working up to 'Lady in Red' by the time Antoine and Jack make it back to the table.

Jack's clicking his fingers as he arrives. More perpendicular than he was before, he's obviously splashed some water on his face and is certainly sharper.

'Lady in Red . . . Get it into your head. . . . I tell you, you look a fright . . .' he sings, shaking his hips from side to side as he takes his seat. 'Antoine's been telling me about you and that Hamish.' He winks. 'Never had you down as the putting out type, Abigail.'

'It was a mistake,' I say, drinking half my vodka and tonic

in one. 'Any of that coke going, by the way? I could do with a lift.'

'Sure, baby, sure,' says Jack, rummaging about in his pockets. 'These are yours, and I've written down Des's number for you and told him to expect your call, so loads more where that came from, if you get my drift.'

He hands over a slip of paper and two small envelopes, folded in the same Lottery ticket paper as always, and I wander over to the apricot marble confines of the ladies. It's difficult to chop out when there's a paper towel attendant manning the make-up counter. But I've learnt that the trick is to make as much extra-curricular coughing and shuffling as I can manage without sounding suspicious or deranged, and then pack away something rather larger than normal so I don't have to come back too speedily.

The table is loaded down with drinks by the time I make it back. The conversation is flowing back and forth. No one has the time to listen to anyone else, their own point of view is too pressing. Jack and Antoine are arguing about how handsome certain actors are and how Bruce Willis has changed how men are allowed to look in the cinema.

'I mean,' says Antoine. 'B.B. – Before Bruce – male actors were having their noses done to make them look refined and cute and facially virginal and untouched. A.B. – After Bruce – you are allowed to look rough like you've been in a fist fight or two.'

'True,' says Jack, holding his hands in the air. 'We all have to take a good fisting to get a part these days. It's the male equivalent of the casting couch,' he shrugs. 'Only last week, I was there on all fours saying, shall we just get it over with because it's always been my dream to work with Sandra Bullock.'

'Shut up,' swats Antoine. 'You know what I mean . . .'

More vodka, more coke, more exchanging of hot air; it's not until 9 p.m. that I realise that I'm late for James's leaving dinner. I fly into a total panic.

'Shit, shit, shit, he'll never forgive me,' I say, sitting bolt upright in my chair. 'I've got to go, I've got to go, James'll never forgive me. It's his leaving party and I'm not bloody there.'

Jack can't see the problem. 'Abby, chill out . . . chill out, he's not fucking going anywhere, is he? His friends are there . . .'

'I'm his friend.'

'Yeah, sure you are,' smiles Jack.

'No, I am, I am,' I insist. 'I'm his best friend.'

'Calm down,' says Jack. 'Take a taxi, they won't have even ordered yet.' He pats the chair. 'Sit down, finish your drink, have a line, calm down, it'll be fine. Chill.'

'Chill? Chill? What are you talking about? My best friend in the world is about to leave for certain death in Sri Lanka and I've forgotten to go to his leaving dinner. Chill? I can't possibly chill.'

'Look,' says Jack. 'Let's order a cab, finish your drink, have a line, you'll be fine. That's my motto.'

So we do. The cab takes half an hour to arrive, I have another drink and one more line before I say goodbye.

'Maybe I'll see you later,' I say to Jack, kissing him goodbye and making that thumb to ear, little finger to mouth phone gesture. 'What are you doing?'

'We're going down the Met.,' says Jack, nodding to Antoine. 'I've got a suite for later.'

'What, again?' I say. 'When was the last time you went back to Mile End?'

'None of your business,' quips Jack, very curtly indeed. 'See you later then.'

It's quarter to ten by the time I arrive at 192. The place is its usual packed and intimidating self. They are three deep at the dark green plastic bar with flashing optic fibre effect, trying to catch the attention of the nubile staff dressed in white aprons like French waiters. Wafer thin girls in expensive shawls drink pink birdbaths of Kir Royale, flicking leaves and swapping sex and scandal stories, using cigarettes for punctuation. Handsome young men in sharp black suits and warm black V-necks pose around the two drinking tables at the front and the booths at the back. Hovering like circling carrions, they pick off the women or try to score vacant tables. The dining room to the left is always full. Tables for six are crammed to capacity with eight. The air is full of talk, smoke and alcohol. Parties of four conspire about the table next door. All movements, all social interaction are monitored by everyone, using the eye-level mirror that runs around the edge of the room for a more discreet form of eyeballing.

Tonight the celebrity count is about average. Minnie Driver is cross-legged in the booth on the right drinking champagne with a girlfriend. Helen Fielding and what looks like her editor are dining on the left at the top of the stairs. The stairs that lead down to sure social Siberia. Like the ladder into Hades, to sup in the basement of 192 is the ultimate of Notting Hill no-nos. Like going to the Carnival and having friends who don't work in the media, it is something to be avoided at all costs.

Needless to say James is downstairs. Actually, to give him his due, parties of over eight are normally filed below stairs and to have managed a table three weeks or so before Christmas means either he booked months ago or still has some sort of cachet with the waitress he took home two months previously. As I walk down the stairs, using the banister for support, the conversation level along the L-shaped table drops.

'Nice of you to show,' shouts James, cupping his hands. He does one of those wide fake smiles. He's obviously upset. Sitting with Wendy on one side, he's kept the place on his left empty.

'Glamorous party?' exhales Wendy, flicking her cigarette.

'Not really,' I reply, frantically looking up and down the table to try and work out what course they might be on.

'Pudding,' says Wendy, spotting what I'm doing. 'Not that you'll probably want any, with your newfound fondness for Colombia's finest export.'

I'm too drunk, wired and tired to react. Instead I smile and crawl underneath the table and squeeze in next to James. Colin's opposite and pours me a glass of wine.

'Good day?' he says with a wink.

'Shit,' I say.

'No-o,' he says, leaning in, intrigued. 'He didn't go for the Glenn Close thing then?'

'Like hell he did,' I sigh, taking a huge swig. 'It went down as well as a cup of cold sick. I felt like Andrew Cunanan.'

'Whoops,' smiles Colin.

'He's got a girlfriend,' I say, drinking again.

'Whoops,' he repeats.

'Who has?' quizzes Wendy.

'Hamish Rowland.'

'Oh, him,' she dismisses. 'Bit of a given, isn't it? Handsome thesp in girlfriend shock.'

'You can always live in hope,' I mutter.

Not listening to our gossip, James suddenly gets to his feet, a large vat of wine in his hand. 'Well, now that Abigail's finally here, I'd like to propose a toast,' he announces, hushing the rest of the table. 'I'd like to start by thanking you all for coming to my going away dinner. I know I keep going away and it's becoming a less glamorous event each time. But I'm thrilled you could make it, celebrity parties notwithstanding,' he adds, glancing down at me. 'I shall be out of contact for the next five or six months, but I will be counting on you not to forget me. And any gossip or letters or bons mots can be sent to the Galle Face Hotel in Colombo, which will be my postal address, and will be gratefully received. Now I know,' he pauses, putting one hand in the air, 'I was nominated for a BAFTA last time around, but this time I intend to win. I promise to come back with a trophy and anecdotes a lot more interesting than the size of Jeremy Paxman's penis. So,' he says, raising his glass, 'to something bigger than Jeremy Paxman's penis.'

Everyone gets to their feet. 'To something bigger than Paxman's penis,' we all enjoy saying rather loudly, except for Colin who toasts his own.

'Don't lie,' I say to Colin as we sit down. 'We all know.' I waggle my little finger.

'I'm not,' he grins.

'He isn't,' smiles Wendy, mincing provocatively in her seat.

'And how do you know?' I quiz.

'Joke,' she says. 'But not that you'd know,' she shrugs. 'I could be marrying him for all you care these days.'

The evening ends amicably enough. Wendy and I don't really speak, but James gets drunk and tells everyone he loves them, especially me. I laugh. He says he's serious. No one believes him. Colin chats up one of James's younger sisters who was sitting on his right, hanging on his every word. And as the boy-girl-boy sandwich of James, Eleanor and Colin weaves its way towards the junction of Elgin Crescent and an elusive cab to the Cobden Club, it looks as though Colin might be in there. Wendy's in another well lubricated group bringing up the rear, as I decide to slip off. I'm not in the mood. Strangely dislocated, depressed and hurt by the day's events, I find myself hollowly laughing at jokes, straining to follow conversations, and drinking too much to take the edge off the coke.

I can't sleep. I move from one uncomfortable position to another. The duvet wraps itself around my legs. My pillows are damp with sweat. It's miserable. I exhale loudly every so often to release the tension. But it doesn't work. The whole evening is replaying in my head. View of the Park. James's face when I arrived late. I'm really going to miss that boy, I think, desperately trying to relax. He's my soul mate. My best friend. He really is. What am I going to do when he's gone? Who will I speak to? Share my secrets with? Oh, God! . . . Wendy's comments . . . I hate myself, and all I've said and done, and everything . . . I'm useless and a bad friend . . . Selfish . . . unreliable. Self-loathing engulfs me like a damp towel. It's 5 a.m. and I'm still staring at the ceiling. The room is spinning like a Whirlitza when my mobile rings. The name 'Jack M.' flashes neon in the dark.

'What?' I say, finally deciding to answer.

'Abby, I feel terrible,' he mumbles. I can hear giggling in the background.

'Jack?'

'Mmm? I feel really . . . really . . . terrible.'

'Who are you with?'

'I dunno. Girls,' he says. 'Girls . . . Girls . . . I picked up from somewhere.'

'Well, can't they look after you?' I sigh.

'Abby, they don't seem to be taking me seriously.'

'What's the matter?'

'I'm not joking, man. It's fucking hard to breathe. My heart really fucking hurts. It's beating in my ears. I'm fucking racing, man . . . It's horrible.'

There's a high-pitched squeal and the sound of someone falling off the bed. Jack laughs.

'Morris, stop winding me up,' I say, really quite annoyed. 'Go to sleep. I'll see you in the morning.'

'When?'

'Oh, I dunno . . . breakfast?' I yawn.

'Done,' he says. 'Here? When you wake up?'

'Night,' I snap, switching off the phone. Tosser, I sigh to myself, as I lie back, alone, and carry on staring at the ceiling, hating myself some more, thinking of James.

9

It was the smell that hit me first, I later tell the police. Have you ever smelt death? At close quarters? It's a weird, heavy, hot, airless smell. Death. Sweet, warm, high. Horrible. As soon as I opened the door to the de luxe room, I could smell it. Like the windows had been closed for decades, sealed for an eternity and all the oxygen used up. I knew something was wrong as soon as I walked in. The hairs on the back of my neck told me that. My shoulders hunched by way of self-protection. Strange. For some reason, I knew not to touch anything. My toes curled as I walked in. Moving on the balls of my feet, I picked my way across the carpet. The weak winter sunshine was coming through a crack in the curtains. It shone across the lower half of his sparsely haired legs. I made my way towards the window. Curiosity drove me on. I ripped back the curtains, to let the day in.

He was lying flat on his back. Naked. Arms outstretched, legs apart. His dark curls on the pillow, his face contorted in pain. His lips were pale powder blue, his cheeks shiny. I could still see lumps of cocaine up his nose. He'd obviously been having sex. There were condoms and split turquoise wrappers all over the bed. The room was a mess of broken glass, filthy smeared mirrors pulled off the wall, razor blades, towels and clothes everywhere. A half-empty bottle of champagne. A collection of flutes. I called hotel security from the phone by the bed. Told them something was wrong. I sat down in the armchair next to the chest of drawers. I stared at him. Poor Jack. Beautiful, talented Jack. Jack with a wife and baby Ray in Mile End. I promptly threw up into my hands.

Within minutes the room was full of people. Police uniforms, hotel staff, running around like rats, rattling in and out of the room, sharing what they'd seen. Someone had the decency to put a sheet over the body. I couldn't. I couldn't move. I sat in my chair, the acrid yellow vomit growing cold in my hands, unable to feel any part of my body, or hear anything that anyone was saying. I was like a passenger on a macabre merry-go-round, the stream of faces, the caught voice or phrase, the brusque efficiency of all concerned and always that terrible, haunting, putrefying smell of a departed soul. Eventually – it seemed like hours – a policewoman with a round hat, huge brown eyes, blackheads and soft voice manoeuvred me out of the chair and into another outside in the hall. She gave me a towel for my hands and a warm cup of highly sugared tea. I remember holding the mug in both hands and thinking how much I hated the maroon tracksuit bottoms I was wearing.

'Are you all right, love?' said the WPC, putting her hand on my shoulder.

I couldn't reply.

'Someone's going to drive you home to get a few things together and then I'm afraid you're going to have to come down the station to answer a few questions.'

'I didn't kill him,' I said, looking her in the eye, suddenly terrified. 'I found him. I only found him.' I was beginning to burble uncontrollably. 'I didn't kill him.' I rocked back and forth in the chair. 'I'd never do that. He was my friend, my mate. I didn't kill him. I promise. I swear. I couldn't.'

'We know you didn't kill him,' said the WPC, her nylon tights swishing against her skirt as she sat down next to me. 'It's just that you found the body, so we have to fill in a report. When forensics get back and we have a word with the pathologist, then we'll know what went on a bit more, but so far you are all we have to go on.'

As she spoke, a team of some five or so men dressed like an 'eighties dance troupe, in crisp white jumpsuits, filed into the room in front of me. Within minutes the room emptied of hotel staff and uniformed police and they sealed it behind them. Another ten minutes later a four-man stretcher team came down the corridor, dressed in pistachio surgical suits and rubberised shoes. They negotiated through the door, before entering the suite. After a few minutes inside the room they left with the partially rigor-mortised body of Jack Morris zipped up in a black rubberised body-bag. I let out a rather pathetic squeal as they paraded past.

'Ready to go now?' asked the WPC, leaning over with a smile. I remember standing up and willing myself to stagger to the lift. The lift I'd taken less than an hour previously. I'd been quite irritable and aggravated at the front desk. Jack wasn't answering my calls to his mobile and they wouldn't tell me which room he was in. So annoying of them, I'd thought, like I was some star-struck groupie.

'He's my friend,' I'd insisted. 'We had a loose arrangement that I'd come for breakfast. He might even have left a key card. He's done it before. He can't be bothered to get out of bed to answer the door. He's lazy like that.'

Sure enough he had. In an envelope under the front desk. It even had my name on it. 'Abby.'

Even on the way up in the lift I think I knew something was wrong. I remember not being excited about seeing him. I remember a feeling of dread. I don't quite know why. Maybe because last night I hadn't been that kind. Perhaps I expected him to be angry. I wasn't looking forward to it, that's all I know. It was going to be a negative experience. And on opening that bedroom door I now know why.

'Um, Abigail,' said the WPC as the lift doors closed behind us. 'There will be some press photographers outside the hotel and there are also a few, so the unit says, reported to be around and outside your house. So might I suggest that you keep your head down and say nothing at the moment and me and a couple of my colleagues downstairs in the foyer will escort you to the van. We will be moving quite fast,' she smiled. 'But you can trust us to get you there.'

Nothing I have ever seen in my life could have prepared me for what happened next. Not even that jolly encounter with Jack and Benji and the limo at the *What Men Want* Awards. There were banks and banks of them, on ladders, up trees, suspended off lamp posts, shouting my name, yelling at me, pushing and shoving and fighting and screaming. Flash bulbs popping everywhere. They were blinding. The orange after-glare repeated each time I blinked. You can understand why in some countries they believe that the camera snaps your soul. Here, they were tearing away at it, mauling it, ripping off great chunks, fighting over the entrails, pecking at my heart. Up until this point I hadn't cried. It hadn't really been appropriate. I wasn't his wife, or his son or his lover. We were friends, pure and simple. Recent friends at that. But suddenly tepid salt tears ran down my cheeks.

The police were very nice. They buried me, like a sex offender, in the back under a rough grey blanket that smelt of dust and disinfectant. But still paps came after us, banging on the windows with their fists, running down the street, sticking their long fat lenses up against the car. It was only when we reached the Bayswater Road that they took the blanket off. Driving at speed with blue light flashing but no sound, we flew along past Hyde Park. The pubs and restaurants along the way were all lit up with fairy lights, their windows edged in swathes of cotton wool, but Christmas could not have felt further away.

Pulling up outside the flat, I was offered the opportunity to stay in the car. It was the WPC who went inside the flat to collect some warmer clothes, trousers and a thicker coat than the one I was wearing while the Panda car toured the area.

'I'll keep you moving round,' said the copper at the wheel. 'That way they won't be able to get a good shot of you.'

It seemed an age before we arrived at the station.

So here I am at Paddington Green. The fortified station where they used to detain IRA suspects under the PTA. Modern, high walls, small windows, it's designed for security not comfort. I'm on my third cup of PG before they decide they're ready to take my witness statement. They've been keeping me waiting for over two hours in a pale blue-painted room with black Formica-topped desk, four plastic padded chairs and one of those double-spooled tape recorders I've seen on *The Bill*.

'Sorry to have kept you waiting, Miss Long,' says a rather good-looking policeman with mousey hair short as suede. 'It's just that we're rather busy and we had to inform his wife, and with the run-up to Christmas, we tend to be a bit short staffed.' He smiles. 'Anyway we're here now and

I wonder if you can tell me in your own words exactly what happened.'

'Aren't you going to switch the tape on?' I mumble. 'And shouldn't I have a brief or something?'

'Um, hasn't it been explained to you that you're not under arrest or anything? I'm just after a witness statement.' He shows me his pen and paper to prove the point.

'Oh.' I slump back into the chair.

My gaze fixed on a broken plastic floor tile in the far corner of the room, I tell him the story. From the phone call at 5 a.m., with the giggling girls, to me arriving at the hotel and actually discovering the body.

'But what was he doing there?'

'I don't know,' I say. 'He stayed at the Met., the Metropolitan Hotel, quite a lot. I suspect that his marriage was not going very well. He used to go out drinking late sometimes and he stayed there instead of going all the way home. They loved him there. He got on with all the staff. You see, the bar next door closes at three and Jack would like to carry on drinking.'

'Who were the girls?'

'I've no idea,' I sigh. 'All he said to me was that he picked them up. I don't know where he met them. Either at the fancy bar where we were together earlier or the Met. Bar. Actually,' I pause, 'who knows where he went after that? I left him and a *News* photographer, Antoine, in the bar at about nine to nine-thirty.'

'D'you know where he got the cocaine?'

Jesus, shit, my heart starts pounding in my chest. They know about the drugs. 'I couldn't tell you,' I say, feeling a muscle can-canning in my left cheek.

'Are you sure, Miss Long, because until we have it analysed we'd like to keep if off the streets. It could be a bad batch, you know, cut with something toxic. But we won't be able to tell that for a couple of days. In the meantime we don't want it knocking around,' he smiles, 'killing other people.'

I took a load last night and I'm fine, I think. 'Jack always arrived with drugs on him,' I say. 'I've never seen him buy them from anyone before.'

'Right you are then,' he says, jotting away. A silence hangs in the room. Des the dealer's phone number burns a hole in my bag. I have no idea if he believes me. Maybe he even thinks I supplied him. I panic, my hands start to sweat, I can feel beading on my top lip. I wipe my mouth with the back of my hand.

'W-w-what d'you think happened?' I stammer, eventually trying to break the accusatory quiet.

'To be honest, I'd rather not say,' he says, stacking up my statement on the desk. 'But between you and me it looks like a classic case of death by misadventure,' he says. 'But we'll have to wait on the autopsy and then, of course, what the coroner says. But we get quite a few of these a year,' he continues. 'Cocaine-induced heart attacks, it's a lot more common than you think, particularly in that young party set.' He hands over the statement. 'Now if you could, Miss Long, I'd like you to read through your statement, just to check on the details. Fill in the top here,' he points, 'and sign here, here and here.' He indicates at various dotted lines on the form. I lean forward to read his round, fat, surprisingly feminine writing. He's circled the dots on 'i's. 'Um,' he adds as he walks towards the door, 'because of all the press, we will be escorting you home. Is there someone who could come and stay? It's probably not a very good idea being on your own at a time like this.' He coughs, somewhat embarrassed. 'Depressing thing . . . finding a body.'

I ring Wendy. Despite her recent sharpness, she's the only person I know who would actually enjoy dropping everything to come to my aid. Wendy loves a good crisis, illness or just general poorly sick malaise. Any excuse for back-to-back videos, sausage-rolled under a thick duvet on the sofa with bowls of chicken soup, and she's in a cab and at the intercom before you've made the choice between *Nightmare on Elm Street IV* or *Ghost*.

She's predictably delightful when I call.

'I suspected half as much,' she says, sounding soft and sympathetic. 'Chris Tarrant's been banging on about it all morning. It's the lead on the news that film star Jack Morris was found dead by his journalist girlfriend.'

'Girlfriend?'

'Oh, yes.'

'But I never . . .'

'That's what they're saying.'

'Oh, God.'

'I know.'

Thirty minutes later she's on my doorstep dressed in dark glasses and a black pashmina wrapped tight around her head. It's not, I have to admit, a very good look.

'Quick, quick, quick,' she stage-whispers frantically as I open the door. 'Paps everywhere. Don't show your face.' She slips through the crack in the door and, breathing heavily, pins herself flat against it, like she's just dodged snipers and a hail of bullets. She thrusts forward an old orange and white Sainsbury's bag containing a frozen Tupperware container. 'Chicken soup,' she says. 'Went via my mother's on the way here and stole it from her freezer.'

'Thanks.' I take the bag and walk slowly up the stairs.

Normally I'd laugh at Wendy's over-dramatic reaction to my state of photographic siege. But it's actually not that funny. They've been shouting through my letter box ever since the police dropped me off about an hour ago, using the paedophile blanket again for protection. It's a strangely isolating feeling being locked away in my own house for my own protection. A prisoner in one's own home: you hear the expression but you never really understand what it means. I don't really feel like I live here any more. What were once attractive idiosyncrasies, like a cracked hand basin, are now just plain ugly. It's like being burgled. My small flat has been defiled and I feel dirty just sitting in it.

'Oi, Abigail,' shouts another voice through the letter box. 'Were you having sex with him when he died?' The accusations drift up the stairs, through my own front door and into my sitting room.

'God,' says Wendy, finally taking her scarf off and releasing her cheeks. 'How long's that been going on?'

'Ever since I got back from the police station.'

'Poor you,' she smiles, putting her arms around me. 'Are you OK?'

It's amazing how just one drop of kindness can release a tidal wave of self-pity. I bawl like an unselfconscious toddler on her shoulder. I don't really know why I'm crying. Whether it's for me, or for him, or for the wife and the child he's left behind. All I know is that it makes me feel better. After about three minutes of mulling and snotting all over Wendy's lemon yellow cashmere jumper, I move into the bathroom to splash water on my face. Staring at the mirror, I hardly recognise myself. Skin the colour of glazier's putty, eyes puffy and narrow like silverfish, mouth bloated like Marlon Brando, I'm a piteous sight. But there's something else. I get eye contact with myself and I'm afraid. The blackness of my own pupils is disconcerting. I inch in, resting my chin on the shelf. I stare at me staring at myself. There's no light shining back, just an infinite darkness. It shocks me, and sends a jolt down my spine. I decide not to look that closely again.

Coming back out of the bathroom, I can still hear the banging downstairs. Wendy's turned the lunchtime news on and is heating up her mother's soup in an enormous pan that she must have found at the back of the cupboard somewhere.

'It hasn't come on yet,' she says, hacking away at the hissing frozen chunks with a wooden spoon. 'You don't mind, do you?' she adds, pointing to the pan. 'It's just that it's the only one that's clean.'

'Course not,' I say, pouring myself into the sofa. 'That smells delicious.' I collapse exhausted, realising that the last thing I'd eaten was a mouthful of mayonnaise-coated pasta at the *Packing Heat* photo shoot the lunchtime before. How unimportant the whole Hamish Rowland thing appears now, I sigh.

'Actor Jack Morris was found dead this morning . . .' announces Kirsty Young in a special sincere death voice on the ITV lunchtime news. 'Star of the romantic hit film *Love Letters* with Gwyneth Paltrow, he is believed to have died of a drugs overdose in a top London hotel . . .' They're showing footage of the film and of Jack smiling and laughing in his romantic lead shirt and breeches. He looks devastatingly handsome. He smiles. He laughs. He is in a clinch with Gwyneth. 'A spokesman for Miss Paltrow says that the actress is shocked and devastated at the loss of someone so talented, so young.' They cut to footage of him arriving at the première in his black tie, linking arms with Hamish Rowland and Vince Graham. 'His body is believed to have been discovered by his close personal friend, society journalist Abigail Long, seen here leaving the hotel earlier this morning ...' And there I am, looking white and terrified, surrounded by screaming, shouting people, a grey blanket over my shoulder, flanked by police with their arms out, pushing a route through the crowd. '... He leaves a wife and two-year-old son.'

'Wow,' says Wendy, chicken soup dripping from her wooden spoon. 'I had no idea it was that fucking heavy.'

'Neither did I,' I reply, equally shocked. 'Somehow on the television it looks so much more real. I had no idea that's what it was like. It all happened a bit too quickly really for me to take any of it in.'

The hammering on the front door continues unabated. If anything it's getting louder and more persistent. The phone rings.

'Shall I answer that?' suggests Wendy. I nod. 'Abigail Long's phone? ... Mmm? ... Oh? ... Right ...' She puts her hand over the receiver. 'It's your mum,' she mouths.

Oh, my God, my mother. I hadn't even thought about my mother, my father, my elder sister Joanna, or how the hell any of this is going to affect the rest of the family.

'Abigail?' The tone is familiar Home Counties clipped. 'It's your mother.'

'Hi.'

'Don't you "hi" me, young lady. What the hell is going on? I've got reporters at the end of the drive. Taking photographs of the house. Your father's pissed off to do the cattle, leaving me to deal with the whole thing. I can't cope. It's a nightmare mess. What's happened? Are you hurt? Are you a drug addict? Because if you are, Mrs Morton-Prescot has just rung and her son, you remember him? Rory. Good looking? Went to Eton? Anyway he's a heroin addict, or is it smack? I can't remember ... But she says she knows this place in Cornwall where you can dry out and ... go cold thingy. D'you want me to book you in? Or d'you want to come down here? Or shall I come up there and look after you? What's going on?'

The tirade is nonstop. She barely pauses to draw breath. The only reason she eventually stops is because I haven't been able to get a word in and she has nothing to argue against.

'No, no, don't worry. I'm fine,' I say, trying to sound calm, rational and not like a drug addict.

'Fine!' she screeches. 'Fine! You don't sound fine to me. I love your definition of fine. Having an affair with a married man who happens to be a drug addict. Drugs!' she sighs. 'It's just so embarrassing.'

'I wasn't having an affair with him,' I say very slowly and quietly down the telephone. I'm actually too exhausted to deal with her hysterical tweedy outpourings of frilly-collared angst about what they're going to be saying in the local butcher's in Taunton.

'Oh,' she replies, somewhat deflated. I can hear her Vaselined lips glueing together in shock. 'So you weren't his lover?' She sounds disappointed. I suppose I must have reached the age when she's stopped hoping I was a virgin.

'No, we were friends,' I explain. 'Good friends, but new friends. I'd only known him for three months. I was supposed to be meeting him for breakfast.'

'Breakfast?' she says. 'At ten-thirty? On a Thursday? Don't you have any work to do?'

'No, I'm too busy injecting crack cocaine up my rectum to do any work,' I reply, extremely sarcastically. Wendy sniggers into her chicken soup.

'There's no need to be rude,' she continues, quietly. 'I'm just worried about you. It's all very upsetting.'

'I know.'

'Listen, your father wants to know if you're coming home for Christmas? It's just that there's a choice of bird he's rearing.'

'Tell him yes.'

'Oh, good,' she sighs. 'He will be pleased. Shall we discuss all of this then?'

'Yeah, yeah,' I reply. 'I'm fine, honestly. Listen, I must go, my phone's bleeping.'

'If you're sure you're OK . . . ?'

'Fine, 'bye.' I hang up. 'Hello?'

'Abigail?' comes another less clipped female voice.

'Mmm.'

'Brenda here, on the *Mail*.' She's got a voice like Jack Daniels and Embassy. 'Now I know you've been through a terrible, terrible shock,' she starts, her voice cracking with pseudo emotion. 'Finding the late Jack Morris's body and all that awfulness, and I wondered if you'd like to share your traumatic experiences with the readers of the *Mail*? You know, like in a problem shared problem halved sort of a way.'

'Um, no, not really, thank you,' I say very politely.

'Not even if we compensated you for your trouble?'

'Um, not really.'

'A grand?'

'Um, no.'

'Five then.'

'You want me to sell my story for five thousand pounds?' Wendy's eyes have left her head and are doing a tour of the room, she's so excited.

'Oh, all right, ten then,' sighs Brenda down the telephone. I can hear her sipping her regulation Femail black coffee in irritation. 'But that's my final offer.'

'I'm not selling my story to anyone,' I say. 'I think it's an ugly and revolting thing,' I add pompously. 'And it's immoral.'

'You'll change your fucking tune,' she barks, 'when no one wants to fucking employ you.'

No sooner has she slammed the telephone down than there's another newspaper on the line, wanting me to sell the great romantic story of a love affair that never happened.

'I understand you're not ready to sell the story,' sympathises some sharp geezer from *The Sun*. 'But d'you have any of his "Love Letters" that we could print; you know, last words for his fans to read? You know the sort of stuff. Packed full of emotion, a real tear-jerker. All very tasteful, obviously. It's all in the public interest, of course.'

It goes on and on. Even some bloke calls from the News

Desk on *The News* and starts talking about newspaper loyalty and how I owe it to them to tell them first, if I value my job in any way at all. Refusal to share a story, no matter how personal, was a sackable offence. Or was I not aware of that when I signed my contract?

'I don't have a contract,' I shout before slamming the phone down again.

Wendy switches off halfway through all the telephonic comings and goings. She even turns up *Ironside* so she doesn't have to hear my ever more offensive replies to the ever more offensive offers. By the fifth or sixth call I'm simply yelling 'Fuck off!' down the telephone and then hanging it up. Then suddenly I hear a voice that I recognise.

'Don't hang up! Don't hang up!' I hear it cry in the distance like a small child as I'm about to put the receiver down.

'Hello?' I say tentatively.

'Abby?' smooths the voice.

'Yes?' My brain is frantically fumbling through its atrophied filing system trying to work out who it is.

'Hello, darlin',' it says. 'Remember me?'

'Course,' I lie, just in case.

'It's Trev . . . Trevor Future.'

'Oh,' I cough, revolted that he should have got hold of my number.

'You sound like you need my help,' he breezes, oblivious to my unenthusiastic response.

'Oh, yeah?' I say, immediately defensive.

'Well, it's only a suggestion,' he says. 'I just suspect that you might have your hands full . . .'

'Well, um . . .'

He can smell me weakening and is in there, like a ferret down Richard Whiteley's trousers.

'Lots of telephone calls from newspapers?' he starts.

'Yes.'

'Wanting your story?'

'Yes.'

'Offering money?'

'Yes.'

'And you have no idea what to do? Who to speak to? What to say? Or whether you should say anything at all?'

'Yes, yes, yes, yes.' I feel myself succumbing to his beguiling empathy.

Wendy looks over from the sofa. 'Who is it?' she mouths, with a gob full of obviously hot soup. I don't answer. I'm too appalled and too interested in what's being said down the other end of the telephone.

'Have you got people banging on the door?'

'Yes, those too,' I mutter, the feeling of responsibility for all that is happening ebbing away.

'Right,' he says authoritatively, 'you sound as if you really need my help. You never know, these things can really run away from you and, before you know it, they're writing all sorts of stuff that bears no relation to anything that happened. What you really need, my darlin', is to be in control from the off. Control the media, don't let it control you.'

'D'you really think so?' I say, confused. The banging on the door downstairs is getting louder. I'm beginning to feel actually quite frightened.

'Think so?' His laugh is so fat, it sounds calorific. 'I fucking know so, mate.'

'Right, so what do you want me to do?' I catch myself saying.

'Nothing, fuck, nothing.' He is suddenly sounding extremely efficient. 'I'll release a statement to the media, and then either me or one of me assistants will be round at about five this afternoon to discuss matters further. In the meantime, you don't speak to no one, you tell no one nothing and you don't get snapped down the pub having a drink. You don't want any image of you in the next twenty-four hours that isn't grief-stricken. Stay at home, watch the telly and don't answer the door. We'll be around in a couple of hours to sort the lot, OK? Oh, and I'll be wanting twenty per cent of everything for my trouble.'

'OK,' I repeat, pathetically. He hangs up.

Wendy looks at me quizzically. Like what did I just agree to? I flop down into the sofa next to her, completely drained. Suddenly with Trevor in charge, the whole thing seems so much less threatening. I feel I can cope and I suddenly start to relax for the first time since I found Jack.

'Who was that?' says Wendy, getting up to serve herself another bowl. Paper clip thin, the one thing that tempts her off her steamed rice, vodka and boiled vegetable lifestyle choice is her own mother's soup. Consequently she goes home as little as possible.

'Trevor Future,' I try to say as nonchalantly as possible, but his name, after months of sublime hatred, still gags in my throat.

'Not the biggest media sleaze in Christendom?' She's standing there with both shock and revulsion writ large all over her face.

'Mmm,' I say, not having the energy to argue. I lean forward and take the remote control off the old trunk covered in a sarong that constitutes my sitting-room table and turn the volume up, even louder, on the telly.

'Did I hear you right that you agreed to meet him?' quizzes Wendy from over my shoulder in the kitchenette.

'Mmm,' I say again.

'Why?'

'He says he can help.'

'Help? In what way can he help? He's the most revolting piece of lowlife. I mean, look what he did for Polly Friend. She became a laughing stock. Her bits on show like that all the time. That man is trouble and you should have nothing to do with him.' She sits back down next to me.

'I'm not taking my clothes off.' I sigh loudly at her brazen stupidity. 'He's just going to help me deal with the press.'

'But you are the press,' retorts Wendy. 'Is he going to save you from yourself?'

'What do I know?' I snap, my voice beginning to falter. 'I've never found a dead body before,' I mumble, 'let alone a famous dead body. I'm not really sure how to proceed from here. It's not really one of those handy little life skills that you pick up on the way, is it?'

'I suppose not,' says Wendy.

'Actually, can we not talk about this any more?' I venture.

'OK,' she agrees. 'Soup?' she asks.

I nod, she serves and we end up sitting side by side, slurping, in silence, channel hopping through *Blue Healers*, the end of *Ironside*, the beginning of *Supermarket Sweep*, waiting for *Fifteen To One* and *Countdown*.

'I've never been able to do a Conundrum, have you?' says Wendy, adding to the pile of butts she's collecting in her ashtray, balanced on the right arm of the sofa.

'Not often,' I reply, adding to the collection of ash in my saucer, balanced on the left arm of the sofa.

'When you say not often,' she says, her eyes not moving from the screen, 'how often does that mean?'

'Well,' I say, also staring straight ahead, 'never . . . actually . . . if I'm being honest.'

Suddenly the downstairs banging gives way to a brusque ringing of the front door bell. The sound resonates throughout the flat as Wendy and I sit rigid on the sofa, in the hope that, by not moving, whoever it is in the street will move away. It rings again. A series of six or so short sharp angry bursts. They really mean business.

'D'you think you should answer that?' whispers Wendy, glancing furtively at the grey plastic intercom.

I shrug and stare. It goes again. Louder and longer this time, its urgency ever more apparent.

'Right,' I say with uncharacteristic decisiveness. 'Whoever it is, is going to get the shock of his life.' I walk to the hall mirror and, riffling through the stack of swinging *objets* that have been filed over one corner, I find my carnival whistle hanging on the end of its red, green and gold shoelace. Picking up the receiver, I wait for a voice down the other end to announce itself before blowing viciously. I hear the stalker scream as I relieve him of one of his eardrums. Putting back the phone, I positively skip to the sofa before flopping over the back to rejoin Wendy who, I have to say, has gone slightly hysterical. As we both sit back faintly pleased with ourselves, thrilled by our glamorous pro-activeness, the telephone rings. I decide to leave it for the answer machine to pick up.

'Hi, this is Abby,' my plummy voice kicks in. 'I'm sorry I can't take your call at the moment . . .'

'Abigail,' starts the familiar voice, 'it's Trev here and I'm downstairs on the mobile, recovering from the pleasant little trick you just played on me through the intercom . . .'

'Shit,' I say, picking up the call, through a whistle of feedback. 'Trev, I'm sorry, d'you want to come up?'

Three minutes later and after a few scuffles outside the front of the flat with whole reels of film being fired off at the back of my hand, Trevor Future is finally sitting on my sofa. Pink, sweaty, short of breath, with puffy bitten fingers, he's still got the same plump moist carp lips that I remember from Art House. However, on closer, sober, daylight inspection they reveal not only a downward curl to the mouth but also an uneven shape. Like badly puffed sofa cushions, they give him the tendency to snarl even when he's trying to be perfectly pleasant. Which he is when he first arrives, desperately pleasant. He compliments me on my nice flat, commiserates with my terrible loss, he tells Wendy she's wonderful on the telly, her pride shows all over her cheeks. He tells me again how much he hates to be here in such inauspicious circumstances.

'It's a tragedy, it really is a tragedy. Such a nice bloke, I met him a few times. With a wife and a kiddie and everything. Just terrible. Poor you, Abigail.' He carries on to such an extent that I really begin to believe he cares. Eventually Trevor sits back, orders some coffee from Wendy, lights a short Cerrute cigar and, crossing his legs to reveal white hairless calves in short pale blue towelling ankle socks, he suggests getting down to business.

'Right,' he says, coughing as he exhales. 'What you want is not only a bit of damage limitation, but also the correct advice to manage this to a career advantage.'

'Sorry?' I say, the wind rapidly leaving my sails. 'What? Work it to my advantage?' I am surprisingly shocked by his lack of scruples.

'Oh, yes,' he replies, blowing on his coffee and slurping it loudly. 'Have you put sugar in this?' he says to Wendy. She nods. 'Well, not enough,' he announces, handing it back.

'Are you seriously suggesting that I make capital over someone else's death?' I say, horrified, leaning forward on the brown corduroy pouffe I'm perched on.

'Well, someone's going to, and it may as well be you,' he sniffs, taking another sip of his coffee. 'That's better, thanks, darlin'.' He winks at Wendy. 'White and sweet like myself.'

'I think that's morally bankrupt behaviour myself,' I announce, extremely hurt, uncontrollable emotion bubbling to the surface like a pan of boiling milk. 'Jack was a dear sweet friend, whom I loved very much, even though we hadn't known each other very long. He was mad, and vulnerable, and kind, and very talented, and I'm going to miss him very, very much. I can't possibly even contemplate anything else at the moment other than the terrible waste and tragedy of the situation.' I'm pacing the room, shaking my head from side to side, hugging myself, getting hotter and hotter with rage and sorrow and my intense hatred for this man. What was I thinking ever answering his call? Letting him into my house? I'm such a fool. My eyes sting with tiredness, there's an acrid metallic feeling at the back of my throat through lack of sleep.

'Hang on, hang on,' says Trevor, scribbling away on his notepad. 'I've only got as far as "who I loved very much". What did you say after that?'

'You're not quoting me?' I say, suddenly coming to a standstill.

'Well,' he says, struggling to sit up as he flicks his stinking cigar into the saucer in front of him. 'I have already promised the showbiz editor of *The Sun* some sort of exclusive statement from you and a photo. And you know how I hate to break my word.'

'I wasn't aware you were the sort of bloke who had a word to keep,' I mutter.

'Now, Abigail, you offend me,' he replies, holding up his palms in mock shock.

'I think I might leave you two to it,' says Wendy, looking around for her coat and black cheek-clincher of a scarf.

I am totally horrified that she can even contemplate leaving me alone with this social pariah, this leech on the face of human decency, whom I have somehow half-wittedly invited into my flat. I stare and silently will her to stay, my eyes bulge from their sockets, my arms stiffen by my side. But she seems oblivious to my pleading, either that or she chooses not to notice.

'You don't need me here any more,' she announces breezily, wrapping her scarf tightly around her face. 'Abby,' she says, hugging me, 'I'm so sorry about what's happened today. He looked like a sweet person.' She kisses my left cheek. 'Be careful,' she whispers. She turns to kiss the other. 'Don't let him talk you into anything.' She stands in front of me and smiles. 'James got off OK,' she adds.

I inhale dramatically.

'Oh, James,' I say, feeling very unsteady.

'Ssh,' she hushes. 'He'll understand. James always understands. Anyway, he sends you, in particular, lots of love.'

And with that she's gone, leaving a trail of Jo Malone Grapefruit behind her as she goes down the stairs and braves the paps on the doorstep, who shout first, 'Abigail!' and then, 'Oi' after her as she walks on towards the Portobello Road. So in the end it's just me, Trevor Future and the cabal of snappers in the street who, encouraged by the sortie of fresh meat, start to really sense their prey and hammer harder and louder on the door, with more brazen ringing on the buzzer. The noise is intense. Each knock or call begins to reverberate through my brain, already addled through grief. Patches of sweat circle under my armpits, seeping through my jumper; my hands are so lubricated that they slip off each other. My whole body, right down to my intestines, is shaking.

'Abigail, Abigail, Abigail, what are we going to do with you?' Trevor Future shakes his head. A fine dandruff frosting peppers his jacket. Cigar in one, he rests his other dimpled hand on his expense account paunch. 'I'm only trying to help, you know,' he says, sounding like a gynaecologist warming up something hard and silver in his hands.

'I don't know what to do,' I say weakly, feeling whatever iota of fighting spirit I have left deserting me. 'Just make all these people go away,' I sigh, as the banging continues

'Fine . . . we can do that very easily,' smiles Trevor. Much like a python goes in for the kill, his beguiling hypnotic smoothness belies his vampiric intentions.

'What do I need to do?' I'm exhausted. The whole momentousness of the day has finally taken its toll. I feel like a rag doll pancaked by a passing family saloon.

'Leave it all to me,' says Trevor, extricating himself from the sofa. 'Can I borrow your phone?'

I nod slowly and pathetically as I watch Trevor move around the house with efficient purpose. Soon he's on to his office and my aged fax machine is grinding into operation. Future PR are on my case. A statement is already pouring through the fax. Judging by the speed of its arrival, Trevor had penned it before his departure from the office. The man has confidence, if nothing else. He's talking to me about exclusivity contracts, with whom I can talk, what I can say, etc., etc. I can't hear or understand what he's saying. He's become an irritating 'wa . . . wa . . . wa' sort of sound in my ear. To be honest, all I'm looking forward to is *Home and Away*.

'Right,' he says again. 'Abigail, what I'd like you to do is dress in something extremely sombre. Sexy and sombre, you know, tight black cover-all jumper thing and a pair of dark glasses,' he says, standing in front of me, flicking my fringe. 'Fix your hair a bit, nice and smooth, neat, and put, you know, a nice shade of lipstick on.' He nods. 'And then I want you to follow me outside, we're going to face them.' He grins, the anticipated thrill of confrontation making his nostrils flare.

'What d'you mean face them?' I say, fear making my legs shake again.

'When I say "face them", well, you don't say anything, not a word. I'll stand, you know, read a statement, then, of course, they'll take a few snaps and then they'll leave you alone. You're in the public domain, the story's out, simple.'

'But I thought you'd make them go away.'

'I'll make them go away, baby,' he says. 'It's either this way, or you stay in here for the rest of your life, forever paranoid that someone will leap out at you from the bushes, put ladders up to your toilet window, pay your friends for topless shots of you when pissed.' He takes my shoulders and shakes them, trying to make his point sink in. 'You're the girl who found Jack Morris dead, from a drugs overdose, naked in his hotel room. People wanna know what you look like, darlin'. They wanna share your grief, they wanna see your pain, d'you understand?' I nod, change into the gear he suggested and join him at the front door. 'So are you ready to go out there then?' I nod again. 'You don't say a word, remember?' I manage a half-smile. 'Ready?' he says.

'Yes,' I whisper.

Trevor checks himself in the hall mirror, smooths down his hair, and straightens his tie, shifting about a bit in his beige trench coat. He opens the door to go down the stairs.

'Oh,' he says. ''Ave you got a handkerchief?'

'A what?' I say, bewildered.

'You know, a hankie. Just hold it next to your cheek for the photos. Run along and get one, there's a good girl.'

We open the front door and a bomb goes off. The shouting is loud and aggressive and continuous. The noise is terrifying. The flashing, even through my sunglasses, repeats with each blink at the back of my eyes. My name is called from the lips of some two hundred strangers. I hide behind my glasses and hang on to Trevor's arm for support. 'Were you lovers?' 'How long had you known each other?' 'Is it true that he was naked?' 'Are you carrying his love-child?' The questions come thick and fast and from every angle of the semi-circle that has naturally formed around my front door.

'Gentlemen, gentlemen,' says Trevor, holding out his hand for silence. 'I have 'ere a statement from Abigail Long that she wishes me to read out on her behalf. So I'd like a bit of hush while I read it and then you will be allowed one minute to take photos of Miss Long before she goes back inside and that, I'm afraid, gentlemen, will be that. She has signed up with me and any deals or requests will be handled by Future PR, all right?' he sniffs.

No one says a word; the reporters are leafing through their pads ready to write down the statement and a couple of photographers have already peeled away from the pack to talk to their news desks on their mobile phones.

'Ready?' says Trevor. 'Are you rolling with those cameras?' He nods towards various cable networks, plus the BBC, ITN and Sky crews. 'Right,' he says again, clearing his throat. 'Abigail Long expresses her deepest regret at the sudden death of her close and,' he pauses for dramatic effect, 'very special friend Jack Morris. He was a great film talent and even better confidant. The world of cinema will miss him very much as, of course . . .' another pause, 'so will she. Her heart goes out to his wife and his young son. She will most definitely be attending the funeral, as well as helping the police with their inquiries. Thank you very much, gentlemen, that is all.'

Shouts go up for more. Trevor raises his hands.

'That's it, guys, that really is it,' he announces.

I'm horrified. Three or four minutes of non-stop photography later and we're both inside the front door, Trevor punching the air at his success. 'Yes, yes, yes,' he says, turning on the spot in joy.

'What the hell did you do that for?' I shout, tearing off my glasses and throwing my hankie down in disgust.

'Do what?' he says.

'Make out that I had a relationship with the bloke, what with his wife and everything?'

'I know,' he grins. 'What a master stroke that was, don't you think?'

'But I didn't have sex with him.'

'No one else knows that,' chirps Trevor. 'Anyway, you knew each other, that's good enough for me. And there are photos of you together. I checked before I came here. The *What Men Want* Awards. Black dress,' he says, making an hour-glass shape with his hands. 'Very sexy, on their way to *The Sun* as we speak.' He winks. 'Abigail Long . . . the New Girl Next Door,' he laughs. 'Enjoy it, sweetheart, because it won't last long.' Whistling through his teeth, he picks up his ginger leather briefcase. 'Now any calls, problems, etc., give me a call,' he continues, without missing a beat. 'Card,' he adds, handing one over. 'Meeting tomorrow, eleven-thirty. I'll send a car. See ya.' And with that he's gone.

Crawling back upstairs to the sitting room, I lie back on the sofa feeling very alone and wretched. How did I end up here? What am I supposed to do? Jack . . . I'm so sorry to have used you and let you down. I go to the fridge and find a half bottle of vodka. I fill a white wine glass with the stuff and knock half of it back in one. I then remember the gram of coke still in my coat pocket from the night before.

'Fuck it,' I say out loud to myself. 'Oblivion, that's the answer.'

I chop out six. Each the length of a CD. I resolve to watch television and toast Jack every hour on the hour with a line. He'd find that funny. I smile. That much I do know.

It's amazingly quiet. The banging has stopped. The telephone is silent. They're running repeats of *Birds of a Feather* on the telly. Maybe the whole thing was a dream, I think, seeing if I can pour vodka down my throat without having to sit up. It stings as it dribbles down my cheeks. Only one line left. My empty alcohol-packed stomach is swirling and rumbling like an old tumble dryer. I'm smoking old butts when *Newsnight* comes on.

'Paxo, it's you!' I laugh, lying back, thinking of James. Dear James, sweet James, uncomplicated James. It would be so nice to have him here. He'd understand. Isn't it amazing that you only realise how much you miss someone after they have gone?

'And now a look at tomorrow's papers,' sneers Paxo with his collection of front pages and photocopies off the fax. 'The *Telegraph*, *The Times*, *The News*, and the *Mail* all lead with the Europe story,' he says. 'The *Mirror*'s got "Cabinet Minister in Suspenders Shock", that political hot potato, and *The Sun* leads on "Coke Death Actor's Mistress Will Go to Funeral", the story of the controversial death of young British actor, Jack Morris, found by his alleged mistress, Abigail Long, in a hotel room earlier on today. Anyway, that's the news . . . this evening . . . Good evening.'

I sit and stare at the television, my heart pounding, my pulse racing. It's real. The whole fucking thing was real. There I am. On the front of *The Sun*. The sunglasses and the white handkerchief. Paxman read it out on the news. It definitely happened. The phone starts to ring again. I hold my head in my hands. Oh, my God, I think, what the hell have I started?

★ ★ 10 ★ ★ ★ ★ ★ ★ ★ ★ ★

It's been ten days since the funeral at St Paul's in Covent Garden. It's Christmas Eve and I'm on the Taunton train on my way to spend the festive season with my parents. I'm in first class for the first time. Bigger seats, less garish upholstery, but I still can't see through the smudged windows. It's raining hard outside. The water is running diagonally down the window like the furrows of a ploughed field. Jack's angelic face – extensively airbrushed to look younger and more female – is on the front cover of all the magazines I have piled up in front of me. 'The Death of an Icon', says one. 'Exclusive Photos of the Funeral', says another. 'The Nation Mourns as a Bright Light Goes Out', announces a third. I'm not sure if I can look.

The whole funeral thing was such a surreal and insane affair, it's difficult to think about it even now. The cobbled streets outside the church were packed with screaming, weeping teenagers all waving special *Hello!* or *OK!* black-framed photos, pulled from the stapled centre pages of speedily published souvenir issues. Whipped up into a tabloid frenzy of grief, as newspaper upon newspaper, magazine upon magazine, called 'tragic' Jack Morris the new Leonardo DiCaprio – with the fate of James Dean – the hormone fuelled hysteria was enough to make the hairs on the back of your neck stand rigidly to attention in a state of emotionally heightened protest.

Not since Princess Diana – said *Hello!* and *OK!* afterwards – have Britain's youth been so united in their despair. Not since Princess Diana have the nation's teenagers so openly and publicly wept as they did for the People's Actor – Jack Morris. Much was made of his East End roots, his chance discovery on Oxford Street. His was a truly modern day tale of rags to riches. He was the beautiful talented youth who lived fast and died young. The nature of his passing was not something that many people cared to dwell on. But *Love Letters* reopened in some selected cinemas, so people could remember Jack, and his one film, and sign a book of condolence afterwards.

Over time, Jack Morris began to epitomise the modern day truth that everyone has the potential to be a star. All you need is someone to recognise your talent and soon you too are welcoming TV cameras into your lovely home. He was the shining example of how, in the land of docu-soap celebrity, hard work, dedication, sacrifice and single-mindedness are tantamount to nothing in a culture where everyone can be famous and everyone is special. You can do anything you want, just so long as you shout loud enough, take your clothes off quickly enough and have been to stage school. Only boring people do boring jobs. We all have a talent. It's just a question of someone else telling you what it might be. It doesn't matter what you look like, it's the person inside who counts, or at least that's what they were saying on Trisha! Or was it Esther! Oprah! Or Kilroy! I can't quite remember.

I met Jack's wife, Janine, at the funeral. She turned up with Ray, dressed in a black child's suit and black tie. She cried as we all watched him put the white 'Daddy'-shaped carnation bouquet on the coffin. But she remained dignified throughout, even while they played 'Stairway to Heaven', which was when most mourners sobbed hysterically. Jack's mother, in a black pillbox hat with feathers like three flaccid arrows, had a bit of a turn and had to be escorted out of the church. Even at the wake in the upstairs dining room in Soho House, while they played the *Love Letters* promo in a loop in the private cinema next door, and the Back Street Boys sound track behind the bar, Janine had been surprisingly stoical. Pretty, with dark curly hair to just below her shoulders, a plunging black jersey dress and unfeasibly high heels, she was petite, big-breasted, with eyes the colour of lavender. Instead of an aggressive slap, a public snubbing, or bereaved wailing of Middle Eastern magnitude, she calmly muttered something along the lines that she didn't blame me for his death and that, despite all what the papers were saying, she knew I wasn't having an affair with Jack. 'He wasn't really capable,' she'd muttered. 'What with all the drink and the drugs and that . . .' And that was it. No recriminations, no snide remarks, no nothing. It was like the life had been drained from her and she didn't really have the energy to fight. I liked her. She said Jack had talked about me. 'Made some joke about "ears" or something,' she'd smiled. But it was obvious we would never be friends.

Despite all the public mourning, it's amazing what a grubby untimely death does to a funeral turnout. Fantastically popular on the canapé circuit while alive – turning up at the opening of a door, a regular at Art House, Teatro, Groucho's and Soho House – his funeral was, I suppose, predictably devoid of those familiar party faces that turn up when the going is good. Beyond the teen scream, anyone with a career worth speaking of avoided it like herpes. Hamish Rowland was nowhere to be seen. Publicly dumped by Chariotte Fleet after he'd unwisely shared with the *Express Magazine* that his ideal woman was Winona Ryder, he'd sent his condolences along with a tasteful bunch of lilies and had taken the opportunity to announce that he was filming with Sandra Bullock in Canada and therefore unable to attend. Gwyneth was also surprisingly absent. She'd shed a tear on *Letterman* in his honour and then cited Jack as a reason for kids to say no in 'the war against drugs'.

Tom Blend and Miles Renton, the co-stars who had been both filming Stateside with Tim Roth and Pacino when *Love Letters* first opened, did, surprisingly, turn up. Wearing uniform wraparound Oliver People celebrity shades, they'd waved to the young crowd outside the church. Shaking hands and signing autographs, they'd seemed more like they were attending a film première than a funeral. In coordinated thin-collared, black Prada suits, with white shirts and black ties, they looked like two Reservoir Dogs, as they worked the crowd, again, on the way out. Someone cynically suggested that they'd been forced to attend because *Love Letters* was out on DVD and needed a final push in the last run-up to Christmas. Whatever the reason for their being there, they didn't manage to make it to the wake afterwards.

Vince did. Less of a porky truffling pig than he was when I last saw him dancing under the lamp post in Trafalgar Square, he looked positively haunted. His face was chalk white and he had two huge fleshy purple boxing gloves under each eye. Actually, he looked like a junkie. Lack of sleep had affected him so much that on closer inspection his eyeballs looked dry and his lower lids shone scarlet and raw in the early afternoon light. Rumours that he'd checked into the Meadows in Arazina, where they dish out large bronze coins to remind you how special you are, were obviously unfounded. Upstairs in Soho House he launched himself on the vodka and tonic, holding his glass with both hands, either out of fear that someone might relieve him of it, or because his hands shook so badly he needed a double hand grip for stability. Anyway, he looked positively relieved when I walked into the room.

'My God, it's you,' he said, placing a moist kiss on both my cheeks, with the inside of his lips. 'Fuck me, I'm pleased to see you. One of the few friendly faces around,' he sighed. His breath smelt acridly of old alcohol. 'Half the people here didn't even know him. I knew him though,' his voice quivered. 'He was my mate.' He punched the air weakly with semi-clenched fist. 'We were such mates on *Love Letters* . . . the times we had.' He sighed again. I moved a step back.

'I understand it was you who gave him that silver Tiffany straw,' I said, slightly sharper than I intended.

'Yeah,' nodded Vince, staring at a patch of wooden floor that seemed to contain some romantic memory for him. 'Certainly did,' he added proudly.

'Very classy,' I smiled.

'Well, I thought so,' he grinned. 'So, um, Abigail,' he sniffed, 'how are you then? Saw you in the papers.' He nodded, tucking into his drink.

'Yeah,' I said. 'It was all a bit terrifying, to be honest, and a bit of shock,' I found myself sharing amazingly candidly. I suppose despite all that had gone on I was a bit pleased to see Vince, as he was one of the few people whom I knew who knew Jack. 'Didn't quite know what to do actually,' I said. 'What would you have done? D'you think it was a bad move?' I smiled. 'You know, all the press interviews and stuff.'

'No-o-o,' said Vince, opening his throat to drain his glass in one. 'You go for it, girl,' he grinned. 'So,' he coughed, 'did you, um, well, you know, did you, um, have a bit of how's yer father going on with old Jackie boy then?' he said. 'Eh? Eh? Eh?' He jokily jabbed my elbow with his. 'Go on, Abby, a tenner says you did 'im. Shared fluids,' he sniggered. 'If you know what I mean?'

I was stunned. Vince of all people. 'Why don't you just piss off,' I whispered under my breath. I said it so quietly that I don't think Vince heard it. But the expression in my eyes said it all.

'This man upsetting you?' said Trevor, immediately coming to my rescue.

God, Trevor's been such a support. The day after finding the body I was on the front page of *The Sun*, page four of the *Mail*, three of *The News* and the *Mirror* and *The Times*, page seven of the *Telegraph* . . . In fact every newspaper in the country wrote the story in some way. Total coverage, according to Trevor. He's got a whole load of cuttings, kept in a file for me.

I went to the meeting the day after. I had a terrible hangover, I remember. But Trevor was just so great. Buns, coffee, Resolve, it was all there waiting for me, in this big black leather and chrome office on Conduit Street – framed magazine and newspaper front pages all over the walls, the lot. Trevor's PA, Lorraine, had come to collect me in a white Mercedes with the blacked out windows in the morning. There were still a few photographers hanging around in the street outside, but nothing Lorraine couldn't handle. Apparently, Trevor had been delighted with the initial media coverage. Much better than the start he'd made with Polly Friend. But, as he'd explained to me in this long complicated meeting that went on for hours, where I signed papers and things, we needed to keep the momentum going. It's a snowball effect, he revealed, and we were just beginning.

So a few days after Jack's death, I did a Close Up and Personal in the *Mail*. Heart-to-heart stuff all about my deep friendship with Jack. I then did a similar sort of piece in *The Star*. *The Sun* had refused, I remember, because we'd given it to the *Mail* first. But Trevor had explained that we should go for the *Mail* first because it's got a mainly female readership and they'd be sympathetic to what I was feeling. And he was right. I received so many letters of condolence. Trevor put them all into a book for me, after he'd showed them to *The Sun*, of course. Apparently he's got some magazine shoots lined up for me when I come back after Christmas. At Home sort of things, with photos of Jack, all very tasteful, apparently. He's got a whole plan worked out on my return.

'Telly,' he keeps saying to me. 'We've got to get you on the telly and then you'll be sorted.'

Trevor's persuaded me that I should go home for Christmas. After my conversation with Mum, it was not really my first choice, but he says that it will look good. Going back to the bosom of one's family after a crisis. Makes me look like a home-loving girl. So he bought me a first-class ticket. Amazingly the vodka's free all the way to Taunton Station. So I've hoovered more than my share of mini bottles on the way down, and we're almost there.

Pulling up on the platform I can see my mum and my sister staring into each of the windows, trying to find me. They look mildly shocked when they see me step out of the first-class carriage at the front. The first to move is my elder sister. A couple of shades darker than I, with a rounder, softer, altogether prettier face, she has pale eyes, the colour of wet stone, with a large 'W' of freckles across her nose. She is five months pregnant and just beginning to really show. Normally a good stone and a half lighter than me, she has elegant wrists and long fingers that used to play the piano but have since been blunted through working on her husband's farm.

'Wow, Abby, very snazzy, arriving first class,' she laughs, galloping gauchely towards me, her arms outstretched, her glossy, healthy aura shining in the neon strip lights of the station. As she comes closer she slows and her expression changes. 'Jesus,' she pronounces. 'Abby, darling, you don't look at all well, are you all right?'

Her sudden concern is disconcerting, and I can't work out how to react. Half of me feels like collapsing into a heap on my heavy suitcase of dirty washing and wait to be gathered by Joanna and Mum. The other half is brave, defiant and coping.

'I'm fine,' I say, sucking in my cheeks. 'It's just that I haven't been able to smoke all the way down here and I'm gasping.'

'Awful,' says Joanna, pretending to understand. Her two-armed stance reduces itself to one and she puts an arm around my shoulders as she kisses me on both cheeks. Her unborn child gets in the way.

My mother's expression is altogether more tight-lipped. In a smart pair of navy trousers with black patent loafers and a navy round-necked jumper with a scarlet silk scarf, she has just blow dried her silver blonde hair and is looking very Christmas Eve. She takes a couple of steps towards me, but waits for me to approach.

'How could you afford to travel first?' she asks, with a hint of sarcasm.

'My agent paid,' I smile, knowing it would piss her off.

'I didn't know you needed one of those,' she says, bending down to pick up my suitcase as she kisses one of my cheeks. 'Euch.' She flares her nostrils with disdain. 'Joanna's right, you don't look very well,' she says, raising an eyebrow. 'Or is it heroin chic?'

'Mum,' laughs Jo, coming to my rescue as always, 'you know perfectly well Abby's been through quite a lot recently and what she needs is some early nights, proper food and a few walks and she'll be right as rain.' She puts her arm around my shoulders again. 'Isn't that right, Abs?' she jollies.

'Probably,' I sigh.

I don't know what it is about coming home, but no matter how glamorous or interesting anything I've done in the past has seemed, as soon as the car tyres crunch on the gravel drive into Hope Farm, I regress to the surliest of teenagers – monosyllabic answers, sloping shoulders; I lose the use of my forearms and let them flail around in front of me, taking the place of conversation.

Jo somehow manages never to come across as childishly petulant as I. Perhaps because during her youth she was far too busy over-compensating for the fact that my father desperately wanted a son. Either that or she was a natural insomniac with an affection for straw and cow shit. Whatever the exact reason, she was always well behaved and displayed a keen interest in the farm. She'd be out in the sheds in the middle of the night with Dad, helping him with the calves, while I'd be upstairs dancing in the mirror with my hairbrush, fantasising about having sex with Rob Lowe.

Jo married Adrian, one of the driving forces behind the Young Farmers' Association, when she was twenty-three. The youngest of three sons, he had stupidly – according to my dad, who knew about these things – gone to Cirencester Agricultural College. It wasn't Cirencester that was the problem but his choice of career. As the youngest of three, he didn't have a hope in hell of inheriting his father's farm. So he and Jo had started from scratch. Built up their small place fifteen miles away from almost nothing. Renting milk quotas off the surrounding farms, they'd done fifteen-hour days for almost seven years. Just as they began to go into profit, Jo decided she could allow herself to have a baby. And everyone was thrilled.

On the way back in the car we talk about anything other than Jack Morris.

'Oh,' says my mother in a strained jovial voice, as we pause at some traffic lights, 'James has sent you a postcard and called a couple of times from Sri Lanka.'

'He has?' I say, leaning forward in the car with over-excitement. It is the best news I have had in weeks. I thought he might have forgotten about me, all those miles away, holed up with the Tamil Tigers. But he hasn't. It is such a relief to know that someone, somewhere, is on my side. Someone is thinking about me. Unsullied by all the whole fame game thing, James is that shining light at the end of my long dark tunnel.

'He says he will try and call at Christmas,' she continues.

'That would be great.' I smile.

'It's a shame he hasn't come down with you this time,' she says. 'You are always so pleasant to be around when he is here.' She sighs. 'Such a lovely young man.'

'What?' I say. 'I'm more pleasant when James is around?'

'Oh gosh yes,' says Joanna. 'It's famous. Everyone thinks

so. Why do you think we all like having him around so much?'

'Because he's so nice, such a laugh and rather handsome?' I suggest.

'That too,' says my mother. Our mutual appreciation of James is one of the few things that we agree on.

The car falls silent. The conversation drifts back to the perennial Hope Farm topics. Apparently beef sales are picking up, pork is down a bit and Jo and Adrian's choice to go totally organic is supposedly an extremely smart and lucrative idea. Can you believe that the people down the road might have to plough their new potatoes back into the ground because the winter's been so mild the market might well be flooded later in the year?

'It hasn't felt mild,' I say, leaning over the two seats from in the back. 'It's been fucking freezing in London.'

'Darling,' sighs my mother from the driving seat, 'stop swearing.' She exhales loudly. 'Have you been drinking?' she adds.

'Might have been,' I say, flopping into the back seat.

'I think we need to have one of our talks,' she says, efficiently snapping the indicator to turn right.

Back at the house and the atmosphere doesn't change. It's only when I throw myself on my large white fluffy bed that anything feels better. It's that clean sheets smell of my mother's detergent that swings it. That and the collection of fluorescent stars that are still on my ceiling, despite my mother's effort to de-twee the room after I left home. Stripping off the apple and white flowered wallpaper, she's tried to make it more spare room than bedroom, and opted for that safe Thatcher yellow that every estate agent painted their flat in the mid-eighties when they wanted to sell at a profit. She's even added some tasteful border effect she'd read about in *Women's Journal*. She's re-covered my dressing table that my godmother gave to me on my thirteenth birthday. But the smell hasn't changed, and the way I'm feeling at the moment that's some sort of consolation.

Being away from it all doesn't really help. I feel even more disassociated down here than I do in London and I've stupidly brought only one gram with me to last all of Christmas. Why haven't I thought ahead? I've been doing quite a lot of coke recently. Calling Des up. He comes round to my house and we talk about Jack and get high together. For some reason I find it helps. I lie on my bed and scratch with worry. I'll be fine, I think, getting up and walking over to my dressing table. Rationing is the key. I chop myself out a small sharpener on a patch of the glass top next to the silver hair brushes that were a christening present from my grandmother. Something to keep me going through early evening drinks and the inevitable tree decorating before dinner.

'Hiya,' I say, as breezily as I can, entering the snug, scruffy sitting room. Jo's already there, warming herself against the log fire, struggling with the tinsel.

'There you are,' she smiles. 'I was just about to come and get you. I'm not doing all of this on my own,' she laughs. 'You look as though you've cheered up a bit,' she adds, fluffing out an angel's skirt.

'Definitely a bit perkier,' I say, sitting down next to her on the carpet, clearing a patch in the baubles with my feet.

'We've all been terribly worried,' she says, her head moving to one side with concern. 'Mum's been on the phone every day,' she continues, 'reading out all the stuff in the press. She's beside herself.'

'Really?' I say, shredding silver plastic icicles.

'I know she pretends,' says Jo. 'But take it from me, she's very upset.'

'Upset?' I repeat. 'How d'you think I feel. My mate dies and suddenly the whole world's in my face, asking me ridiculous questions.'

'I know, I know,' she says, not really knowing. 'Mum had two reporters here as well, you know,' she says rather curtly, and then pulls herself up. 'But you realise I'm always here if you need me,' she says, softly. 'You know that, don't you?'

'Yeah, yeah.' I nod. 'Anyway,' I change the subject, 'how are you?'

'You know, fine, feeling fat . . . Not as sick as I was. Adrian's thrilled, obviously, and he's being ever so sweet, and kind and lovely. Keeps fussing all the time. Giving me breakfast in bed ... little presents, that sort of thing. He can't keep his hands off my bump ... He wants a boy,' she says dreamily. 'I don't really mind ... Just so long as it's healthy. We aren't going to find out. We both want to keep it a surprise ...' She stops suddenly, thinking she's being tactless.

'No, I'm really happy for you,' I say, leaning over to kiss her on the cheek. 'Really I am. You've worked really hard for what you've got.' I sigh, unwinding some more tinsel, staring at the floor. 'It's all real and honest and everything. I think I might be a bit jealous.'

'Jealous?' she laughs. 'But your life is so glamorous, film stars, parties packed with celebrities. It must be such fun.' She sighs wistfully.

'Not really,' I say. 'It's actually quite boring and, um, very lonely.'

'Don't be silly,' she tuts dismissively, sounding exactly like Mum. 'Everyone down here thinks you're so-o-o famous. They're always asking about you.'

'Are they really?'

'All the time,' she says. 'You're quite the local celebrity. I'm always being introduced as your sister. Now,' she asks, holding up two baubles, 'd'you want to do red and gold this year or blue and silver?'

'What?'

'Colour-scheme-wise.'

'Oh,' I say, 'whatever you want.'

'Red and gold it is then,' she says, getting up slowly and making her way over to the tree. 'We had blue and silver last year.'

I have had two vodka and tonics, plus another quick one, by the time Dad and Adrian turn up for supper. Huge, red-faced, with fat hands like rump steaks, Dad seems to have aged since I last came down at Easter. He's lost more of his once thick dark hair and gained more weight. The red broken veins on his nose stand out like scarlet twigs growing across his face. He's not wearing well.

'Too famous to kiss me now,' he says, as he walks in and takes his boots off, hanging up his cap.

'Course not,' I say, kissing him on both cheeks. He smells of cows.

'Hello, trouble,' says Adrian, placing his coat on the next door peg to Dad's. He's always treated me like I was six.

'Hello,' I say sarcastically, 'busy day on the farm?'

'It took me ages to get here, Sue,' he says to my mother. 'There's a lot of traffic coming through Taunton. I tried to finish early so I could, you know, be of assistance, but it's that new roundabout intersection – can you believe they're doing roadworks at this time of year?'

'Mmm, no, terrible,' says Mum, stirring a bread sauce on the stove.

'Who's for a drink then?' says Dad, rubbing his hands.

'Abigail's had enough already,' says Mum, not taking her eye off the pan.

'No I haven't.'

'Yes you have, young lady, I've been watching.'

'You've been what?'

'Watching,' she says, turning round with the wooden spoon still in her hand. 'And actually I'd like to point out that since you were last here, you've become a rather embarrassing lush.'

'A lush?' I'm beginning to shake now.

'A lush,' she repeats.

'A lush?' I repeat back.

'Yes, darling, a bit of a drunk' – her voice softens slightly – 'and I think perhaps you should call it a night and move on to something soft.'

'I'm twenty-eight years old,' I snap. My body is now shivering uncontrollably. 'And I think I know when I've fucking had enough to drink, all right?' I'm shouting now and I can't really see any more; an over-emotional miasma has descended and I have no idea what I'm doing.

'Don't you swear at your mother,' says my father, his hands on his hips, the temperature rising on his cheeks, the branches on his nose filling with anger.

'I'll fucking well swear at who I fucking well want,' I shout, the rush of adrenalin sending me slightly out of control.

'No you fucking well won't,' my father shouts back.

'Will,' I whisper loudly, flashing the whites of my eyes, hunching my shoulders, behaving like some cornered rabid dog.

'That's it,' announces my father, standing with his arm outstretched pointing towards the stairs. 'You can go to your room.'

'Go to my what?' I say, mouth open, horrified at the belittling nature of his punishment.

'Your room,' he says quite calmly. 'If you're going to behave like a child we will treat you like one.'

So off I huff. Arms flailing by my side, exhaling loudly as I reach the bottom of the stairs. Taking one at a time, I hammer my feet on each of them in turn, making as dramatic an exit as possible. When I finally reach my room, I slam the bedroom door behind me with such force that the frame shakes, and a fine stream of dust pours onto the carpet like a serving of icing sugar. I stand leaning on the door for a while, not entirely certain what to do next. My heart races at the rush of uncharacteristic confrontation. Tears of anger trickle down my cheeks. There's no great urgency or reason for them, but they drip off the end of my nose all the same. I'm breathing heavily, my hands are clammy. Wiping my palms down the legs of my trousers, I wander over to the edge of my bed and flop back onto the mattress. Staring back are my pubescent fluoro stars. The ghost of arguments past stirs under the bed.

Fuck them, I think. Fuck them all, they've never understood me. They've never liked me. I've always been the odd one out. The youngest. The mistake. They were always more interested in Joanna. She was always the one, they liked her best. She was always better at school. More responsible, perfect, with better reports. She was made deputy head girl. How pleased they were. There she was up there on stage, while I still spent assembly sat on the floor with all the other unranked, unrecognised members of my year. It was always the same. Why can't you be more like Joanna? Why can't you work hard like Joanna? Why d'you need to go to university? Joanna didn't. Why can't you be married like Joanna? Why can't you have a baby like Joanna? Bloody Joanna.

I'm now totally enveloped in self-pity. The thick duvet marshmallows with empathy. I lean over to find a postcard sitting on my bedside table. My mother must have put it there, I think, as I pick it up and turn it over. 'The Temple of Tooth at Kandy' it says on the back. It's the one from James. 'Love u, miss u, think of me alone this Xmas – James,' it says. For a man who makes a living in communications, James isn't half brief. I smile. Oh, God, where is he when I need him?

There's a gentle knock on the door.

'What?'

'It's me,' says Jo.

'What d'you want?'

'Oh, I don't know,' she says. 'A chat probably, just to check to see if you're OK. We're all very worried about you.'

'Good,' I manage defiantly, as more tears flow sideways down my cheeks.

'Can I come in?'

I think about her request. 'Um,' I sniff, 'OK then.'

She needs no prompting, and within five seconds the weight of her fecund behind is lowering one corner of the bed. She tucks the loose curls of her unsmoothed hair behind her ears and smiles. It's a benevolent smile with a certain hint of patronising big sister blended in for good measure.

'Now,' she says, 'have you come to your senses a bit?'

'What d'you mean?' I reply, sitting up in the bed. I catch a glimpse of myself in the mirror. It is not the most beguiling of sights.

'Well, we've been talking downstairs and we've come to the conclusion that you might need some help or something.' She nods, keenly trying to get eye contact. 'You know, counselling, rehabilitation or something like that. Mummy says you've become a bit of a handful.'

I deliberately stare down at the duvet and, after bending the postcard, resort to pulling off clumps of imaginary fluff. 'Help?' I scoff. 'Counselling? Rehabilitation? I'm a handful? You lot have no idea what you are talking about. I'm by far and away the most sane person I know. In fact I'll go so far as to say that you have no fucking idea what you are talking about. It's not tricky,' I say. 'I'm tired, my friend died and I've come home to chill out, kick back, have a few drinks and hang out with my family. You hardly need to be Dr Raj Persaud to understand that.'

'If I knew who Dr Raj Persaud was I could disagree with you,' says Jo, getting up off my bed. She looks tired. 'Do what you want,' she mutters. 'But I just want you to know that I'm there for you,' she smiles.

'That's about the fifth bloody time you've said that to me this evening,' I bark, getting off the bed and flouncing around the room.

'Well, what the fuck else am I supposed to say?' shouts back Joanna. 'You're an impossible bitch and I wish you'd leave before you spoil Christmas for the rest of us.' Her aggression shocks even herself as she stands, rooted to the spot, both her hands over her mouth, trying to catch the words she's just said. 'I didn't mean that,' she whispers quietly.

'Too . . . bloody . . . late,' I whisper back. Licking my top lip, I raise an eyebrow with malicious intent. 'Why don't you just leave . . . and inform our mother that I shall be doing the same.'

She closes the door quietly behind herself as she leaves. I hear her sob all the way down the stairs and shut the kitchen door. The house falls silent. The vulgar clatter of canned laughter on the telly occasionally makes its way up the stairs, but apart from that I remain utterly undisturbed.

It takes Trevor a full three goes on his mobile before he eventually picks it up. It's a bad line, but I can tell he's pissed already. He slurs his words and calls me 'baby' a couple of times as I recount the appalling nature of my homecoming. He offers to send a car to pick me up and promises that no one's eating before midnight, so there'll be plenty of food left.

'Not that you'll be eating much,' he sniggers. 'Cos have I got a packet for you?' He coughs, choking on the hilarity of his own joke. 'See you in a few hours, baby,' he adds before putting the phone down.

Actually, it's more like four and half by the time the blacked out Mercedes collects me from Hope Farm and speeds me up the M4 back up to Little Venice in North-west London. The driver and I exchange a few words just as we hit the motorway and then I crash out in the back, the heavy stitching on the leather-backed seat almost indelibly imprinting itself on my right cheek as I sleep as far as the Talgarth roundabout. Stirring myself through Chiswick, I only just manage to resist chopping out on the mahogany arm rest as we come off the flyover again and on to Blomfield Road.

As we pull up outside the huge white stucco house which Trevor appears to own in its entirety, a few second thoughts about what the hell I am doing here windsurf through my head. But they are soon dispatched by another wave of anger towards the ineptitude of my family and disappear off into the horizon. Steeling myself, I walk up his palm-fringed path and ring the shiny brass door bell.

It only takes two blasts of *William Tell* before Trevor opens the door with drunken exuberance. 'Abby, babe,' he smiles, fat cigar in fat hand, as he leans on the door handle for support. 'Welcome to the home of the Future.' He laughs at his own well-worn joke and, running his hands through his oil-smoothed hair, he slowly looks me up and down. 'You look like you've had a few,' he opines, 'and could use a few more,' he snorts. 'Come in and say hi to the rest of the gang,' he says with a flourish, bowing slightly as I cross the threshold. 'I'm afraid you missed the main meal but we're on the disco dandruff, if you know what I mean.' He chuckles to himself again as he weaves his way along his gold-disc-lined hall.

As I follow him I realise that it's the first time, I think, I have ever seen Trevor really drunk. And judging by the high colour of his face and the bitter sweet smell of the beads of sweat smeared all over his forehead and upper lip, he's a whisky man, and he's not stinting on it tonight. For Trevor's in almost as festive a mood as his Christmas outfit. Sporting a maroon velvet jacket, with black silk lapels and large yellow Chinese dragon heavily embroidered on the back, he resembles a Triad-backed boxing promoter on his way to an award ceremony. In black patent pumps, with an overly tight white shirt, he's kicked back enough to have undone his bootlace tie with silver rodeo tips. In fact, he looks almost as charming as his house.

Walking past the bank of gold discs dating back from Sam Fox to Sabrina, Kim Wilde, Anita Dobson, Stefan Dennis, right up to 'Oh yeah' by Caprice, the full horror of Future's home unfurls. The whole place has obviously been interior designed by someone with a hefty cheque book and limited taste. With acres of gold leaf and rolls of flocked wallpaper, it looks more like the Presidential Suite in the Dubai Hilton than a place someone would actually choose to call home. The discs give way to Bond movie posters, and framed celebrity snapshots that are blown up and mounted all over the walls like wondrous star-studded achievements. The clotted cream carpet is so thick that Trevor and I leave Ranulph Fiennes-like footprints as we walk into the dining room.

I'm a yard or so behind Trevor, tucked in behind the six-foot plastic Darth Vader statue that guards the entrance to the dining room, when he demands his guests' attention, with a long, loud, drunken 'ssh'.

'Ri-i-ight, everyone, a bit of hush please for our new arrival,' he says, waving his pink plump hands in front of him. His sovereign ring catches the candlelight. 'This is the girl I was telling you about,' he grins. 'My new Girl Next Door . . . after you, of course, Polly,' he adds swiftly. 'But this girl has a huge future ahead of her, and I'm the bloke who's going to make it happen, aren't I, darlin'?' he says, cuffing my arse and kneading it slightly, as he pushes me forward. I smile stiffly as he clears his throat, with faux-showbiz aplomb. 'Ladies and gents, I give you . . . Abigail Long,' he smiles, arms out like a showman, '. . . the girl who found Jack Morris!'

The sea of faces burst into spontaneous whoops and wows, followed by a lengthy handclap worthy of any daytime TV show. 'In yer come, in yer come,' says Trevor, patting my behind again, as his pushes me further into the darkened room. 'Don't be shy,' he mocks. 'We're not going to bite,' he says. 'Or not very hard, anyway.' Everyone rocks with laughter. It's clear that Trevor is very much in control of the evening and everything he says or does is marvellous.

It takes a while for my eyes to get used to such darkness. The room is painted black and lit only by two outrageously opulent silver candelabra in the middle of the table that are dripping with scarlet wax. The tablecloth is a dark blood red and covered in bowls of sugar-glazed fruit, none of which has been touched. The guests' side plates are piled with various discarded leaves and their main courses of plump breasted quails have been picked at. Each has a large goblet of Burgundy, except for Trevor, who has his own half-empty bottle of malt.

'Right, right, meet 'n' greet, meet 'n' greet,' says Trevor, patting a high-backed zebra-skinned chair with chrome lion's feet for me to sit on. 'Sit yer arse down there,' he adds.

I fall down into the chair, desperate for some alcohol. The long car journey, the catnap on the back seat, coupled with the parching combination of heating and air conditioning, make me feel like I have a tongue made of crispbread. I rapidly scan the table for a spare glass. In the low candle-light it's difficult to work out who is who and what is what.

'Let me help you,' snuffles a squat man to my right with curly dark hair and black-rimmed glasses. As he leans across the table to retrieve me a glass, I notice his shoulders are so bizarrely hunched that he actually looks deformed. He is also short on sartorial style; his shirt gapes around the neck and his black bow tie's a clip-on.

'Red?' he says, handing over something the size of a small paddling pool.

'Please,' I smile, as he pours away.

'Fucking 'ell. Jesus, Keith, you're quick off the mark, aren't yer?' shouts Trevor as he leans back in his chair to release his gut and puff away on his cigar. 'One glimpse at a pair of tits and you're in there, mate, like a fucking rat up a fucking drainpipe,' he screams with porcine laughter. 'You want to watch this one, Abigail,' he says, his short legs swinging free of the floor as he leans back and runs his hand the length of his tight waistband. 'Keith used to work on *OK!*, but since he got fired, he's now number two at *Wow*,' continues Trevor, raising his eyebrows in admiration. 'So he's Mr Showbiz interview, if you see what I mean,' he adds, knowledgeably tapping the side of his nose.

'Oh, right . . . good,' I say, nodding away.

'And before you ask,' chips in Keith. 'I was fired for fiddling my expenses.'

'Oh,' I say, not desperately interested.

'Bollocks,' snorts Trevor. 'It's because you bit some girl's arse at the Christmas party, and you fucking well know it.'

'Look, shut it, Future,' says Keith, with surprising aggression. 'Or not one of your piss-poor clients will get a *Wow* front cover.'

'Wooo ... ooo,' says Trevor. 'Not even the lovely Polly Friend?' He points opposite to a rather fine underwired pair of scarlet sequin breasts I had failed to notice earlier.

'Oh, go on, Keith,' she says, plumping her assets on the table. 'Not even for little old me?' she smiles, her heavily glossed mouth shining.

'Well, maybe just you,' he says, his hand crawling across the table to stroke hers.

'Coke?' quizzes the brunette the other side of Keith, as she passes on a large square mirror covered in lines, a credit card, some curled notes, with a large white mountain in one corner.

'Cheers,' replies Keith, his attention immediately diverted as he places it all on his mat.

'Have you two not met?' he says, using the credit card as an introductory baton.

'Um, no,' I venture, really beginning to think that I might have made a mistake coming here.

'Hi, I'm Claudia,' purrs the brunette, with a slight American twang in her voice.

'Claudia,' I say, shaking her hand across the drugs.

'Claudia's just come back from the States,' says Keith, as he sneaks an extra rock off the mountain.

'Oh, really?' I say, suddenly coming over all Home Counties polite. 'What have you been doing out there?'

'I'm a fluffer,' she replies, matter of factly taking a swig of wine.

Keith snorts as he snorts and comes up for air with a large smile on his thick-skinned face. The whole table, including Polly Friend, Keith, Trevor, Claudia and the two silhouettes at the other end, all stare at me for a reaction. A quiet 'Oh' is about all I can manage.

'Claudia firms cocks for a living,' explains Trevor, as he flicks his cigar ash onto his plate. Everyone laughs, including Claudia.

'It's more complicated than that,' she whines, mincing in her seat. 'It's a very qualified job, don't you know.'

'Yeah, yeah,' dismisses Trevor. 'Give this cigar a quick Lewinsky and we'll see just how talented you really are.'

'No,' she flirts, flicking her hair off each shoulder in turn.

'Go on,' he dares, leaning in across me. I get a waft of his hot cinnamon aftershave.

Claudia doesn't quite know whether to rise to the challenge or not. The more she procrastinates in her chair, the more Trevor dangles his wet, half-chewed, half-smoked cigar in her face.

'One little suck,' he whispers, his drunken eyes shining lasciviously. Claudia smiles slowly, licks her lips and makes as if to take it in her mouth. Trevor breathes more deeply the closer she moves her lips towards his cigar.

'Actually,' she says, suddenly leaning back in her chair, 'we all use our hands these days. It's very old-fashioned to use the mouth.' She purses her lips and looks heavenward. 'You know, post-AIDS and everything. So much has changed in the porn industry, you know, Trev, since you knew it,' she continues. 'Most fluffers have graduated from hairdressing or beauty school, at least. It's none of your old porn stars still hanging around on set any more, trying to get a job doing anything. It's all very professional.'

'Oh, very professional,' laughs Trevor, as he flops back down in his seat somewhat deflated. 'Look,' he says brusquely, turning to me, 'me and my manners, me and my manners. Abigail, let me introduce you to these two at the end of the table. That's Alan.' He points with his cigar. Alan leans into the candlelight, smiles and gives a little wave. His thin hair is dyed mahogany black and fuzzes up like a merkin. All his teeth are capped. 'And next to him is his lovely wife, Sandy.' She strains her face into a Debenham's make-up counter smile. Even from the other end of the table you can tell she's had a cheap lift, so even in repose she appears to be sitting on a pencil.

'Alan's in the music biz,' informs Trevor, bowing his head at the splendidness of his friend's credentials. 'He's a hit-maker, you know.' He sits back in his chair and belches through his back teeth. 'Choosing and mixing covers for soap stars and the like.'

'He's doing me,' announces Polly, with a kittenish giggle.

'He is indeed, love, he is indeed,' confirms Trevor, rubbing his hands together, sniffing metaphorical tenners.

'That's right,' says Alan in flat northern tones. 'I've been in show business for a very long time, me. Cut my teeth in Butlin's in the late 'sixties, I did, and if I can't sniff an 'it at an 'undred paces no one can.'

'Oh,' I say, smiling at Polly, 'what are you going to sing?'

'Um,' she giggles. 'What is it, Trev?' She looks terribly puzzled.

'Oh, um, Alan and I don't rightly know yet, do we, mate?' he says.

'Well,' says Alan, 'it depends on the rights really. I've always thought that "Hey, Jude" is ready for a remix meself. But that's very dear, ever since Wacko Jacko bought the rights. Very dear indeed. But I've got a few on me list,' he says. 'A few on me list. Like "Ra-Ra-Rasputin", that's ever such a good song, or "The Reflex" by Duran Duran, or maybe even F.R. David's "Words", you know, "Don't Come Easy to Me". All you need really is a drum machine for a bit of a modern beat, and a few backing girls in shorts with pom-poms, and you're Top Ten.'

'Sandy was one of his 'eighties creations, weren't you, Sand?' smiles Trevor. Sand looks constipated. 'But now she does catalogue lines.'

'Great,' I say, finishing my wine and shoving the glass in front of Keith to pour me some more. 'Catalogue lines?'

'Yeah,' replies Sandy, inspecting her square-tipped French polish, totally uninterested in talking to someone of the same sex.

'What are they exactly?' I'm not giving up that easily.

'Oh, you know,' she sighs.

'No?'

'Tell her, love,' says Alan, digging his wife in the ribs.

'Oh,' she says, 'it's like when you take a celebrity, like Polly . . . or yourself, for example.' Sandy speaks very slowly, slurring, as she searches for words. 'Well, anyway, you get the celebs and you photograph them in various outfits, suits and tops, etc., then you put their name on the clothes like, for example, the Anthea Turner Collection, or the Denise Van Outen Collection, or the Carol Smillie Collection or the Jenny Powell Collection, or the Ulrika Thingy Collection . . . and then you sell them in the catalogues, and then you make money, and so do I. You know, we all take cuts of the profits and stuff. I don't do them a lot but you get the idea. Sort of. Kind of. You know.'

'Great,' I say, downing another full glass of red. 'It sounds really interesting.'

'Chop, chop, Abigail, with all that coke,' says Trevor. 'The other side of the table's waiting.'

I hack away at the mountain and help myself to a huge rock. Squashing it with Trevor's gold card, I chop out a fat line. I role up a £20 note and put it right up my left nostril. It's damp with either Keith or Claudia's snot. I can't tell which, but by this stage in the evening, I don't really care. I'm sitting at a table loaded with alcohol and drugs. I can't feel very much any more. The conversation is not exactly tricky, so I'll just sit quietly and consume.

'Cheers,' I say to Trevor, as I cough and let the acrid cocaine trickle down the back of my throat.

'So what d'you think of my team?' he says, taking hold of the mirror.

'Your team?' I say.

'Yeah,' he grins. 'With this lot you've got almost every avenue covered.' He raises his eyebrows and gives another conspiratorial smile.

'Oh, I see,' I say.

'There's nothing I can't do,' he announces. 'Welcome to the gang, Abigail. Welcome to the gang. I'd like to propose a toast,' says Trevor, getting the attention of the table. 'To Abigail.' He raises his glass. 'No need to get up, anyone,' he laughs, 'because I certainly can't.'

'To Abigail,' they all say.

'To my new mate,' says Polly, offering up her glass. We chink.

'Oh, hang on there a sec,' says Trevor suddenly, 'I've got a present for you.' He smiles as he leans down and pulls out a small turquoise Tiffany bag with white cord handles from underneath the table. 'Tadaaah,' he says as he hands it over and places it on the table in front of me. Inside the bag is a long thin box, tied up with white satin ribbon. I put the box on my empty plate and pull on the ribbon. 'A silver straw,' announces Trevor proudly, before I've opened it. 'They're very hard to get hold of these days.' The table applauds. I smile weakly but feel overcome with nausea. 'Every star should have one. Happy Christmas, babe,' he says, leaning over and planting a wet kiss on each cheek. 'You're going to do great with the Future.'

I spent the whole of Christmas and almost up to New Year with Trevor. We took so much coke that Trevor woke up twice with a nosebleed and came down to breakfast with cotton wool plugs up his nostrils. The house partied every night, but I didn't really get involved. I sat on the sidelines, locked my door at night and smiled most of the time, taking more than the occasional great slug of sense-dulling wine. Anyway, the whole thing was mad. Crazy. But Trevor was so nice to me. More like a father really than anything else. He let me moan on for hours about my family and about how they don't care. He kept me in cigarettes and drugs. Whenever we ran out he just went to get more. He's a very generous man.

But I'm back at my own flat now and I'm feeling really rather terrible. I've got full body shakes and I'm definitely sweating alcohol. After our three- or four-day binge my New Year's resolution is to seriously cut down on everything because it's all getting a bit out of control. I've got to get back to work. I haven't written anything in ages. *The News* gave me a couple of weeks' compassionate leave after Jack's death but they've since left three messages on my answer machine asking for my column. Thankfully Trevor managed to help me knock something together this morning, plugging a few new bars he's got shares in. So it's just this week that I have to worry about.

My flat's freezing cold. I haven't been here in so long, the kitchen sink's full of old washing up and cold water from the permanently dripping tap. Even the air is damp and unwelcoming and, apart from the messages from Marcus at *The News*, no one else has called. Not even Wendy. I suspect she's still with her family doing Christmas stuff. She's big on that. But Colin hasn't called either, which is strange for him, because he's always around in that barren period between Christmas and New Year. While the rest of the city is slothing on its sofa digesting, he's normally desperately looking for someone to watch videos with and share a family packet of Kettle Chips.

I'm lying on the sofa smoking butts because I can't be bothered to go to the shop. I start to replay the last couple of weeks over like some bargain bin, straight to video movie in my mind. Jack's death, the row with my parents, the long weekend with Trevor. It's all so strange and depressing. I'm suddenly overcome by an appalling wave of filthy, grubby revulsion, closely followed by a deep self-loathing. I feel totally wretched. I sit bolt upright on the thin cushions. My legs start to shake. 'What the hell have I been doing?' I say out loud. 'I must have gone insane.' I have. I've gone mad. I spent Christmas with Trevor Future. I must need my head examining. I haven't seen my real friends in weeks. Instead, I've been hanging out with the most extraordinary collection of lowlife ever to inhabit the under-belly of society. Horrible. They're worse than horrible. Fleas on rats. Herpes on fleas on rats. I need a bath. I'm really shaking now. I desperately miss James. I miss Colin and his jokes, and Wendy. I really miss Wendy. I know I'm in the throes of some virulent cocaine downer but there is nothing I can do about it. I crawl over the cushions and reach for the phone. I dial Wendy's mobile. It rings.

'Hi,' says the familiar voice.

'Hi,' I say right back, grinning with excitement, my heart racing.

'Fooled you,' it says. 'It's only an answer machine but please leave a message and I'll call you back.'

'Hi, this is Abigail,' I mumble. 'Desperately seeking Wendy. Please call, I miss you ... 'bye ... um, Happy Christmas, er, etc.'

It sounds pathetic but that's how I'm feeling. The world as I know it has done some extremely athletic Olga Korbut flick-flack with Torvill and Dean flourishes and I have no idea what the hell I'm supposed to be doing. Or indeed where I am. Or who I am any more. The phone goes and I'm on it, keen as a Customs and Excise spaniel after smack.

'Hello.' I sound breathless.

'Abigail Long?' goes a laconic, handsome male voice.

'Yes?'

'Damon Dupont here, from Descartes.'

'Oh, hello. Long time no hear,' I say half-wittedly, for lack of anything else to say.

'Um, yes,' he says, sounding confused. 'Now, I don't know what your plans are tonight,' he continues, sounding uncannily like a PR, 'but we've got a small party on, you know, very exclusive, VIPs only. Bruce Willis is in town for his new film . . .' I can hear he's frantically shuffling paper, 'um, called . . . called . . . well, anyway. Bruce is in town for his new film, and I know this is short notice but we've only just been asked to do it ourselves, last minute, as a favour, and I wondered if you'd like to come, to the film, of course, and then to the aftershow at Planet Hollywood? He'll be playing the mouth organ with his band. It should be great . . . loads of people are coming down.'

'Um,' I say, not sounding too enthusiastic.

'It'll be very good for the column,' he insists. 'I'll send you a car and you can have a plus one.'

He's beginning to sound a bit desperate. It's obvious that he's been more than metaphorically grabbed by the balls; his voice has gone up a couple of octaves and he's even dropped a call on his mobile while he's waiting for my answer.

'When you say everyone . . .?' I query, enjoying my momentary whiff of power.

'Well, Barbara Windsor, Dale Winton, Chris Eubank, Boy George . . . you know, um, everyone,' he says.

'All right then.' I sigh dramatically, like it's some dreadful chore.

'Great, great,' he says. 'We'll send a car at six-thirty, and Abigail . . .?'

'Yep?'

'I owe you,' he adds, shockingly.

'Don't be silly,' I blurt with an irritating yet predictable lack of cool. 'I've got nothing else to do.'

'See you later,' he smooths and puts the phone down.

*   *   *

I haven't mixed in a large group of people since Jack died and I'm suddenly really rather nervous. Apart from the funeral, that is. But that doesn't really count as Trevor organised it all for me. The transport to and from the church. He even escorted me in and out of the church and he only really ever left me alone at the wake and that was it. It wasn't exactly an ordeal. Trevor Future. His name is enough to make my bone marrow shiver. Peeling myself off the sofa, I wander into my bedroom and flop back down onto my bed which sags like a fat bloke's gut as I lie there. But then again, I smile, Mr Future is extremely useful. It's just a question of not getting too involved. Boxing clever, as Colin would say, boxing clever.

But still, it is weird the idea of going out alone. I should be used to it by now. Slipping in unnoticed, weaving through the crowds, looking very busy indeed, like I'm on my way somewhere, rather than doing yet another lonely tour of the room. Landing myself on people with clipboards who have a contractual obligation to talk to you. Leaving without really talking to anyone, after waiting in a queue for half an hour to get some fascinating quote from Antonio Banderas about his sword fighting capabilities while standing there, grinning, like someone's lodged a cattle prod in your rectum. But I haven't done it in weeks and I'm suddenly amazed at quite how out of practice and vulnerable I feel. In fact, if I hadn't had Marcus barking in my ear this morning about deadlines and money and future employment prospects, I really wouldn't be going at all. The idea of a quiet night in fluffy pyjamas with a big pizza is suddenly incredibly beguiling. The phone goes.

'Wendy?' I wish.

'Er, no, actually it's Polly.'

'Polly?'

'Yes, you know, Friend, we spent Christmas together?'

'Oh, yes, of course,' I say, thinking how did she get my number?

'Anyway, Trevor suggested I call you, about *The Feds* party tonight,' she says.

'*The Feds* party?'

'Yeah, you know, Bruce Willis's film and the party afterwards?'

'Oh, right,' I say.

'Anyway, Trevor says they're sending a car for you and he suggested we should go together.'

'Did he?' I mutter.

'So I thought if I came round to yours, we could have a couple of drinks before we go out? What d'you think? Trev's given me the address so I could be with you in a while.'

True to her word, Polly Friend turns up on my doorstep, in considerably less than a while.

'Hiya, you,' she says, kissing me on both cheeks like we're old mates. She's doused herself in Christian Dior's Poison and obviously spent the whole afternoon being got ready. Her elbow-length blonde hair has been ironed straight, her lips have been lined and she's got white tips to her nails. She's wearing a black sequin cropped top and calf-length skirt. She's showing her navel, complete with golden belly ring.

'I didn't know you had your stomach pierced,' I lie, as she stands on the threshold, her sculpted four-pack all toned before me.

'I tried to do it myself once,' she shares, flicking her hair. 'But this is a professional job.' She shoves it forward. 'Sexy, dontcha think?'

'Very.' I nod.

'Anyway, can I come in?' she says. 'I'm freezing my tits off out here.'

'That would be expensive,' I mutter.

'What?' she says, leaving her mouth hanging open.

'Course,' I say, ushering her in. 'Come in, come in.'

Polly marches confidently up the stairs, in a pair of stratospherically high diamanté mules. She perches half an arse on my suddenly very scruffy looking sofa and starts to rummage around in her clutch bag.

'Um, Abigail,' she starts, 'I need a mirror, cards and a note, and . . .' she turns around, 'you don't have any vodka, do you? I find I always need a drink if I've got to sit through a film.'

'D'you think coke's a good idea if we're watching a film first?' I say. 'You know, jigging legs, gagging to chat, that sort of thing, when we're supposed to be lying back and thinking of Bruce.'

'Nah,' she dismisses. 'It'll keep us awake.'

'Fair enough,' I say, opening the fridge in the hope of finding some vodka.

The stench of the indeterminate rotting greets me as I squat down to take a closer look at the cartons of cottage cheese in various stages of putrification. I somehow always end up buying cottage cheese. Wendy's the same with Greek yoghurt. In the door is a sealed carton of orange juice on the verge of exploding. I'm about to give up on the vodka front when I hear the tell-tale rattle of miniatures in the egg compartment. As I retrieve all three of them from underneath the plastic cover, I realise I must have stolen them from a mini-bar or something, because I certainly don't ever remember buying them.

'I can only offer you neat vodka,' I say, clutching my hoard. 'I think the orange might be off.'

'Fine,' says Polly, sniffing a line off Zoë Ball's face on the cover of *Elle* magazine. 'Couldn't find a mirror,' she says, wiping the end of her nostrils. She coughs. 'Christ,' she says, 'that's just what the doctor ordered.' Her eyes are watering as she hands over the magazine. 'Be a love and hand us over one of those vodkas,' she says.

'It's one and a half each,' I say territorially.

'Cool,' she says, draining the small bottle in one.

We've managed to fit in another couple of lines each before the car to take us to *The Feds* finally turns up. So by the time Polly and I are sitting together on the back seat of the black Mercedes on the way to Leicester Square, neither of us is making that much sense.

'God, I like your dress,' she gushes, pawing Wendy's tight black frock which I'd failed to return after the *What Men Want* Awards with Jack. 'It really suits you.'

'Thanks,' I say, leaning over to touch her arm. 'I like yours a lot too.' She recoils, but not before I notice a multitude of razor thin lines peeking through from underneath all the foundation.

'I'm so glad Trevor suggested I call you tonight,' she chats, changing the subject. 'He's such a great guy, Trevor, you know,' she babbles. 'I mean, when he found me I was doing nothing really, just presenting the football results on my local cable channel. We met at Stringfellow's.' She continues her confessional without pausing for breath. 'When I was out with a group of girls from Theydon Bois. My folks are from Nottingham but I've been there a while, you see. Anyway, he picks me up, buys me some Bacardi and Cokes, and the rest, as they say, is history.'

'How long has he managed you then?'

'Oh, about ten months, or is it a year?' She wipes her nose. 'I can't really remember. It was his idea to do the full bush shots. Well, everyone else, you know, like Caprice, Gail Porter and what's her name? Big tits, the one who did the *Big Breakfast*?'

'Kelly Brook?'

'Yeah, that's the one, well, none of them have done the full bush. So I thought, just so long as it's tasteful.'

'Oh, and it was,' I say, lying reassuringly.

'Well, anyway, it worked, I've got calendars, I do PAs, and soon I'll have a hit record and it's all down to Trevor, really.'

'So, d'you sleep with him?' I suddenly heard myself not so much asking as checking.

'Co-o-urse,' she squeals, her feet coming off the floor as she throws herself back in the seat, like I was the stupidest fool in the world. 'You've got to, haven't you?'

'But those horrible bitten fingernails and his fat hands.' I'm rambling.

'Put it this way,' she confides, 'he's not that demanding.'

As we approach Leicester Square, the traffic starts slowly to grind to a halt. It's backed up as far as Eros, but in the distance I can see three giant searchlights combing the night sky. There's an airship floating above the Square with '*The Feds*' emblazoned across it and a huge close-up of Bruce Willis's grittily determined face.

'This looks like a big do,' I say to Polly, inhaling deeply, as we crawl towards the edge of Leicester Square.

'Certainly does,' she smiles. 'Look, stick with me,' she adds. 'At least until we get inside.'

We pull up at the edge of Leicester Square and a policeman opens the car door.

'Evening, ladies,' he says. 'Going to *The Feds*?'

'We sure are, officer,' purrs Polly, letting her coat hang open to reveal her stomach.

'Evening, Miss Friend,' replies the policeman. 'No need to check your ticket.'

Polly and I walk arm in arm through the extraordinary mêlée of people who hang around Leicester Square on a cold winter evening. Past the Army of Jesus squaddies standing on their soap boxes, sporting their red scarf bandanas, recruiting drunks and the homeless. Past the illegal Eastern European immigrant cartoonists sketching tourists who are uncomfortably digesting a sickly cheese fondue from the Swiss Centre. Past the Peruvian pan-pipe bands in their multi-coloured ponchos. Past the man selling roast chestnuts and the bands of drunk girls with mini skirts and bare blue legs on their way to a 'top night out' in Equinox. And eventually we find the red carpet.

'Thank God for that,' mutters Polly, as she smiles at Security. 'Bloody hate Leicester Square. Right,' she says, turning to me at the end of the carpet, 'are you ready? Head up, shoulders down and back, walk slowly and smile.'

I nod. I've got no idea what she's talking about. I'm here to work. She's a relatively famous person, but who really cares? Anyway, she grabs hold of my arm and we're off down the red carpet. It's actually quite a walk, and, all along, the barriers are heaving with people. Even right at the beginning they are as thick as six or seven deep, doubling and then tripling in number as we approach. It's not until about two-thirds of the way along that they start shouting Polly's name. It starts off with a few random yells from the crowd and the occasional flash from a disposable snappy snap. But by the time we turn the corner towards the banks and banks of professional photographers, standing on their ladders, arranged in groups of ever-increasing importance the closer you get to the door, the noise is frightening.

'Polly! Polly! Over 'ere, over 'ere, Polly, over 'ere. Show us what you're wearing, Polly. Give us a twirl, Polly! Get your kit off, Polly!' Polly laughs off the last comment but does as she is told. She takes her coat off and slowly twirls for the cameras, smiling into each and every lens.

'Who's the bird with you?' shouts someone from the far side. Polly rushes up to my side and, pointing at me with an exaggerated finger movement, yells, 'This is my best mate, Abigail Long.' She smiles. You can almost hear their brains slowly cranking into gear, flicking through their Rolodex of faces. Then suddenly there is a flash of group recognition which translates into my name being shouted from every which way and an explosion of bulbs. 'Abigail, this way! Oi, Abigail, over 'ere. Polly, Abigail, stand together, get closer, over here, the two of you. Oi, Abigail. Polly, put your arms round each other, kiss, go on, kiss.' Polly bends down off her heels and plants her lips on my cheek. The photographers go mad and let off a leery cheer.

'Right, shall we go in now?' smiles Polly, taking hold of my hand. All I can really do is follow. By the time we're inside I'm seriously disorientated.

'Jesus Christ,' I say. 'I wasn't expecting that. What were they thinking? I can't believe it.' I'm now shaking, looking in my coat pocket for a cigarette. 'That's almost as bad as when Jack actually died, but they were shouting the most revolting stuff.'

Polly's not really listening. Her eyes are shining and she is bouncing around from heel to heel, looking over my shoulder.

'Wasn't that great?' she gushes, taking hold of both my shoulders and shaking them with excitement. 'Trevor was right,' she grins. 'They always go for the two girls together photo op. It's irresistible. Bet we're in all the tabs tomorrow. Look, there's Ant and Dec!' She gallops over to the two diminutive Geordies whom she's just spotted talking to a honey blonde publicist dressed in Betsy Johnson and a push-up bra.

I'm in total shock at the manipulative turn of events. I lean against the velveteen wallpaper opposite the popcorn stand and take deep drags on lots of cigarettes. Outside the Metropolitan Hotel I could understand, I think, inhaling and exhaling. The funeral was fair game. It's not as if I did that much publicity after Jack's death . . . a few things here and there. But that was incredible. The real thing. It takes me a good five minutes to calm down and realise that I'm supposed to be working. The amount of alcohol and drugs in my system isn't really helping matters but eventually I place myself in a good spot to see the arrivals. Not that I have to be that attentive because anyone who can so much as command one of those hilarious caught unaware shots in the Sunday tabloid magazines, as I just demonstrated, is being flash-bulbed tonight. So all I have to do is wait for some lights and a bit of a kerfuffle before getting out my notebook.

I lean and smoke and smoke and lean and watch Polly and the push-up publicist giggle and flick their hair at Ant and Dec. Patsy Palmer and Sid Owen walk past, doing their old celebrity televisual couple bit. Then through the crowd I spy the familiar navy cashmere coat and Madonna mike ensemble of Damon Dupont walking towards me.

'Hey, Damon,' I say, throwing my cigarette to the floor.

'Oh, hello,' he replies, visibly ransacking his brain for my name.

'Abigail Long,' I smile. 'I spoke to you on the phone today. I met you a long time ago, doing *Love Letters*,' I add helpfully.

His reaction to my name is extraordinary. 'Oh, my God, Abi–ga-a-ail L-o-o-ong,' he smiles, his oleiferous glands shifting into lardy overdrive. 'Abigail,' he publicly relates again, just to make sure he remembers my name. 'Wow, what a lot has happened to you since we met.' He nods earnestly. 'Well, we must have lunch. I'll get my secretary to ring and sort something out. We could be very useful to each other.' He shoots me with his right index finger.

'Um . . .' I say.

He holds up his right hand, making a stop sign. His left index finger is now stuck in his ear as he strains to hear what's being relayed in his headset. 'Sorry, what?' he says. He mouths another sorry in my general direction as he listens. 'Sorry, who was that again?' he shouts, unable to hear. 'Oh . . . right.' He nods efficiently. 'Right, of course, on way . . . Roger, roger. I repeat, on way. Over. Do you copy?' He smiles. Apparently they copy. 'Very sorry, gotta go.' He sucks in his cheeks with self-inflated importance. 'Problems with Dale Winton's plus one. See you at the party, OK?'

As Damon walks off officiously in one direction, there's a

tornado of excitement outside as Bruce Willis arrives. Dressed in his usual tee-shirt, jeans and promotional leather jacket and baseball cap combination, he walks into the cinema with more heavyweight security than a prize fighter about to enter the ring. He is much smaller and actually, if I'm being honest, weedier than I ever expected. But then again, I surmise, I've only ever seen him sixteen feet across – in a vest – as he single-handedly destroys a whole terrorist organisation with nothing but his New York cop badge and no shoes. Anyone with that sort of advance publicity is going to be a disappointment. Anyway, he stands around with his beefcake entourage, not really knowing where to go, or what to do. Fortunately he's wearing shades, because it must be hard to maintain star quality while hanging around in front of a popcorn stand. The stellar loitering only lasts about three minutes, because sprinting and elbowing his way back through the crowd is a very flustered Damon Dupont, who'd obviously PR-ed himself in the wrong direction at the wrong time and is falling over himself with contrition by the time he reaches the Willis posse.

With Bruce and his entourage settled we are all ordered to take our seats. The multi-coloured light show stops in the auditorium and the film begins. Polly Friend rattles her legs throughout the performance. She giggles and whispers and comes out with bland asides and irritating comments. In fact she spends most of the film twisting and turning in her seat, trying to catch the eye of any famous person in the vast room. A wave to Peter Stringfellow. A nod to Dale Winton. A kiss blown in the direction of Sophie Anderton and Caprice. Fortunately for all concerned she is far enough away from Willis and his gang that no amount of thrusting her bags of saline solution is going to get her noticed.

'D'you think he's back with his wife?' she whispers loudly in my ear, just as screen Bruce is about to blow up a whole building.

'I've no idea,' I mutter back, trying to concentrate on the complex plot of crossing and double-crossing with Chicago mobster overtones.

'Who d'you think I could get to introduce us?' she continues unabashed.

'No idea,' I hiss.

'I know,' she says, with such a thrill you could almost see the light bulb igniting above her head, 'he's playing later, I'll just stand below him and swing my hips and get to meet him that way.'

'That'll take him by surprise,' I say.

But Polly is as good as her word. As soon as we'd run the gauntlet of the wannabe paparazzi who hang around outside premières and chase people through Leicester Square, she was up the stairs in Planet Hollywood and, after a quick coke sharpener in the ladies and a few slurps of a Long Island iced tea for Dutch courage, she's out at the front working that belly ring for all its classy charm. Bruce, I have to say, at the moment doesn't look particularly interested. With his beatnik trilby perched on the back of his follically challenged head he's high-fiving the band a lot, smiling sweatily above the audience, and giving us blasts on his mouth organ to the delight and delectation of the eclectic crowd.

Meanwhile I'm relaxing in the corner. Once inside the synthetic confines of Planet Hollywood, beside Monroe's dress and Madonna's conical breasts, my colleagues seem to leave me alone. Only Parksie and Ben Old and their mate from the *Evening Standard* magazine are allowed into the inner sanctum of celebrity anyway and they are not interested in nobody material like me. Parksie meanders past with his smokeless plastic fag and wide smile and shoots off a few frames just for a laugh. 'You never know.' He winks. '*Wow* magazine might be really desperate.' I flick him a V and he fires off a few more.

'Go and do Bruce Willis,' I say, ushering him along. 'You won't get 25p for me.'

Watching him go off, I decide to get my celeb interviews out of the way so that I can do some serious drinking. Walking past Henry Dent Brocklehurst and his lovely wife Lili Maltese, I find Damon.

'Hey,' I say. He turns round and shoots me. I shoot him right back. 'You're just the person I was after,' I smile. 'I need to get into the VIP area to do some celeb stuff.'

'You're wearing a pass,' he says, pointing to the stiff piece of laminated card swinging between my breasts.

'I am?' I say.

'Course,' he says. 'Everyone knows who you are.' He shrugs. 'It's over there to the right of the band.'

'Um,' I smile pathetically. 'Will you come with me?'

'Why?' He looks at me strangely.

'To do introductions and things.'

'All right,' he says, looking down at his clipboard to see if he has enough time in his schedule. 'Bruce isn't off stage till midnight.'

We weave our way through a crowd of possessed looking people who are all standing rooted to the ground like foie gras geese, their mouths open, staring at Bruce on the stage. Walking up two steps we reach the red-roped-off area that's guarded more keenly than the Styx. We both flash our passes and are given the appropriate Masonic nods in. One side of the red rope bears a striking resemblance to the other. The same bitza bitza pizza are doing the rounds served on the same tin trays, accompanied by the same fast food smiles. In fact the only thing that is strikingly different from the proletarian party space is that it is a hell of a lot more crowded in VIP. It's packed. I spend the first five minutes in Lennox Lewis's armpit before being rescued by Damon, who's found a space next to Pasty Palmer on the banquette. Damon does his introduction thing.

'Patsy, this is Abigail Long,' he nods, eyeballing the significance of my name to her. She's not really concentrating.

'*All right*, hiya,' she says, flicking her long red hair and sticking her hand out.

'No, no,' he adds. 'The Abigail Long, you know, the one who . . .' He raises his eyebrows.

'Oh, r-i-i-i-i-ght,' she says. 'Gawd, poor you,' she adds. 'Sid,' she says, leaning over. 'You'll never guess who this is,' she says, pointing. 'Abigail Long, you know, the one who . . .'

'All right,' says Sid. 'Poor you, are you all right? It must have been terrible.'

From then on in I'm passed down the table to Barbara Windsor, Dale Winton, Martine, from there off to two of the All Saints, to a couple of actors, to the guy who used to dance for Frankie Goes to Hollywood and then along to the blonde girl from Steps, and back to Damon. Each of them in turn said how sorry they were about Jack, how awful it must be for me, how terrible the press were, how dreadful those paparazzi boys were and that they were all only too happy to give me a comment on the film. 'Seeing as it's you and that . . .'

I smile in a slightly bemused fashion at Damon.

'Are you OK?' he says.

'D'you know,' I reply, 'I think I'm going to go back through the other side and have a few drinks.'

One Long Island iced tea later and I'm shovelling in mini veggie burgers and the occasional passing chicken satay plus the odd bag of mini chips in an attempt to soak up some of the alcohol. But it's not going down particularly well. There is something fairly rank about pared down fast food – not only is it simply not satisfying but it doesn't tap dance on your taste buds like a tizzed-up canapé. It is, in short, the worst of both worlds, bland and without bulk.

'Um, excuse me,' says a languid voice next to me, 'are those tomatoes genetically modified, because I simply can't eat them if they are. I've potentially got a possible ulcer and they'll play havoc with my immune system. I can only do organic.'

'Linus?' I say, turning round to see a vaguely familiar face dressed in the same open-necked chest-displayer of a shirt that he was wearing all those months ago. 'I'm Abigail,' I smile. 'I met you with Jack? Jack Morris? Over egg and chips? You were in the same . . .'

'Outfit?' He nods. 'Always am, always am,' he repeats. 'Find something that suits you and stick with it, that's what they say.'

'I'm sure they don't mean it literally,' I laugh.

'Well, you know.' He shrugs. 'Abigail, ah, yes,' he continues. 'I remember you. Where are all your nice friends?' he says, looking around me.

'Um,' I say, 'I'm on my own tonight.'

'Oh, well,' he smiles, 'that makes two of us. D'you fancy a drink? So much better for you than GM foodstuffs,' he laughs.

I follow Linus to the bar, where he orders two of the strongest cocktails they have and we walk over to the special seated area, away from the party.

'God,' he sighs, taking a huge sip of his dark green drink. 'Aren't parties a bore?' I nod sympathetically. 'Here we all are again, out, pretending we like each other, smiling, having our photos taken. It's such a chore. I don't know why any of us bother, d'you?'

'No,' I say.

'I mean, the only reason I'm here is I've got some shit show in the West End and I've been told by the publicity department that I've got to get my face around a bit, up my profile, get some bums on seats. It's all so ghastly.' He lights up a cigarette and exhales with one long dramatic stream of smoke. 'I mean, they ship us in here like veal calves, blind us with flashlights, feed us fajitas and then send us on our way again. Like one big celebrity sausage factory. And for what? Something that's going to be covered in puppy shit in two days' time. Honestly.' He rolls his eyes. 'What is it you do again, Abigail?'

'I write stuff for puppies to shit on,' I smile.

'Do you?' he grins. 'That's fantastic.' He hunches his shoulders and rubs his hands together. 'God, what fun to meet a social pariah. Does everyone hate you or is it just actors?' he laughs.

'Pretty much everyone,' I reply.

'Great,' he smiles. 'It must be really interesting to be hated. You see,' his head cocks to one side, 'everyone lo-o-o-ves actors. You think I'm joking,' he says, 'but I'm not. They think we're marvellous. They ask our opinion on everything.' He paints a huge circle with his arms. '"Oh, Linus,"' he imitates, '"now that you're in *Lolita*, what d'you think about paedophiles? Oh, Linus, I note that you kill someone in your next project, should the American gun laws be repealed? Oh, Linus, what's your recipe for apple pie? Oh, Linus, do you think Tony Blair's doing a good job? What's your favourite colour? I note you don't have a girlfriend at the moment, are you gay? I mean, I don't f-u-u-u-cking know!"' He is standing up at the table, his voice loud and raised.

'Sit down,' I hiss. 'Everyone's looking.'

'Let them,' he says with a flourish, before sitting down.

We sit in silence and both drink more of our Green Duchesses, or whatever they're called.

'So,' I say, 'I didn't see you at Jack's funeral?'

'Yup,' says Linus, holding his head in his hands. 'I wasn't around.'

'Oh?'

'I was filming some art house piece of rubbish that will never see the light of day in Romania,' he huffs, sounding like a surly child. 'But it was a terrible, terrible business. He was such a sweet bloke. Not a brilliantly talented actor,' he mumbles, 'but a lovely bloke all the same.'

'I was the person who found him dead.'

As I say it, I don't quite know why I do. Am I showing off? Am I just trying to make conversation? Or just proving that I know more about the story than anyone else?

'Really?' says Linus, not as enthusiastically as I'd hoped. 'That must have been very upsetting.' He finishes his drink. 'Awful, in fact.' He doesn't ask for details. He's not keen or impressed; in fact, he leans away from me. 'Death,' he mutters. 'How dreadful.'

'Um, Linus,' I say, desperate to change the subject, 'd'you want another drink?'

'Oh, yes, indeed I do,' he smiles, clapping his hands. 'Call me Line, everyone else does. Oh, talking of which, you haven't got any, have you?'

'Sure do,' I smile, feeling for Polly's wrap in my pocket. 'And I've got a special silver straw.'

Linus and I go on to disappear into a Bermuda Triangle of debauchery, with trips to the lavatory combined with pit stops at the bar and then back to the table. Bruce is blowing his organ with increasing dexterity and the crowd around his stage is thickening and swaying with augmenting agitation. Out of the corner of my eye I occasionally spot Polly Friend's black sequined cropped top, shimmying and corkscrewing away at the front of the crowd. Every so often she seems to pogo stick above the rest of them, in a terrifying 'look at me' sort of way. She is nothing if not persistent. Even when Bruce leaves the stage at midnight she doesn't come and join us. She gives us a wave as she walks past on her way to the ladies. I offer her back her wrap which she refuses with an Asda pat on her arse. 'Loads more,' she mouths. Five minutes later she is teetering back up the stairs on her way into VIP. 'See ya,' she smiles, with a double hair flick combination. 'I'm on a mission.'

'Christ,' says Linus, leaning forward, clasping both his hands as he slips his feet up under his behind. 'She's fucking terrifying. Like an automated Barbie from hell who's programming is stuck on "shag". Who is she?'

'Polly Friend,' I explain.

'Who?' he says, looking puzzled.

'You kno-o-w,' I smile. 'Takes her clothes off in men's magazines.'

'Oh,' says Linus, looking very confused now. 'But what does she do?'

'That's it really,' I continue. 'Oh, and she guest presents on a few things, opens supermarkets, has calendars made, that sort of thing.'

'And you can make a living like that?' says Linus, his jaw almost dragging along the table with surprise.

'Oh, yeah,' I say, flicking my ash.

'Interesting,' he says, raising an eyebrow. 'I never knew that.'

The drunker Linus and I become, the more strange I realise he is. He doesn't seem to know very much, yet knows an awful lot and is very entertaining. He tells wonderful self-deprecating stories and name-drops celebrities like he's playing some sort of personal hot air balloon game, soaring higher and higher into the stellar atmosphere. The only problem is that he calls everyone by their first name, so by the time I'm impressed, he's moved on to someone else. It's Hugh (Grant) this, Vanessa (Redgrave) that, Tony (Hopkins) the other. And then there's some bloke called Jonathan (Kent) who is apparently frightfully amusing. And he's BFs with Cate (Blanchett) and Kevin (Spacey). At the end of it all I feel like I've been force-fed a *Vanity Fair* and *Variety* baguette and I want to throw. Or it could be the third Green Goddess, I'm not sure.

I'm on my way to the ladies, and not by the most direct of routes, when a brunette with a sensible bob walks up towards me, wagging her finger.

'I know who you are,' she says, with a wide lip-lined smile. 'You're . . . don't tell me . . . don't tell me.' She's grinning and approaching and still shaking her finger. 'Derek!' she yells. 'Over 'ere.' Suddenly some five burger a day bloke, with a builder's crack and a heavy camera with a bright light, swings round. 'Claire Newcastle, GMTV,' she says, sticking out a small, short-fingered manicured hand. 'So here I am at *The Feds* première party, and I'm joined by Abigail Long who, as many of you viewers know, is the unfortunate lady who found Jack Morris dead. So Abigail . . .?' she breezes. 'Are you having a nice time?'

'Um?' I know I sound and look confused, but there's very little I can do about it. 'No, it's smashing,' I smile.

'Great,' says Claire. 'Have you seen Bruce Willis play before?'

'Um, no, not really,' I say.

'Great,' says Claire. 'Did you enjoy the film?'

'Um, yes, lots,' I say.

'Great,' says Claire. 'Tell me, are you a bit of a Bruce Willis fan?'

'Um, no,' I say. 'Oh no, actually yes . . . big fan . . . I'm a very big fan. He's very . . . good.'

'Great,' says Claire. 'Thank you, Abigail Long.' She turns to face the camera. 'Coming up after the break an interview with the man himself, Bruce Willis! So don't go away now.' The camera sweeps past us both and Claire turns to me and throws her head back, doing an enormous, hilarious, silent laugh. 'Got that, Derek?' she says with her hand on my shoulder. Derek nods. 'Thanks ever so much,' she says to me. 'You look after yourself.' And with that she's gone.

Feeling dazed and distinctly untogether, I finally make it into the ladies and deposit the contents of my stomach as quietly as possible in the toilet. In fact I fill the bowl with the sort of electric green-coloured vomit last seen when I overindulged at a children's party, and I feel a whole lot better. While on my hands and knees I take the opportunity to finish off Polly's coke. God, I laugh, I've got so much more efficient at this since the *What Men Want* Awards. Out with the wrap, chop out the line, lick the edge of the credit card, wipe the rest of it on my gums, pull out Trevor's straw and up it goes. Gag slightly. Always gag slightly. Flush, push the seat back up and leave the toilet to check in the mirror for lumps. Wendy. Oh, my God, it's Wendy.

'Aaaaaaaah,' I'm screaming, quite forgetting where I am or what I'm doing. I grab her by the waist, lift her off the ground and swing her round. 'I can't believe it, I can't believe it, I can't believe it.'

I know I'm gibbering but the excitement is too much. Wendy looks positively shocked by the time I put her back down.

'Hi,' she says stiffly, smoothing down her hair. She looks very different. She's cut her hair much shorter and put red and white Marti Caine stripes at the front. She's also lost a lot of weight and is wearing some skin-tight ankle-length transparent silver dress. You can see her knickers, and her nipples are sticking out like raisins on top of two fairy cakes. I'm obviously staring.

'What d'you think?' she says, striking a show girl pose and running her hands up and down her sides. 'Pure slapper, or what?'

'Um, foxy as hell,' I lie. 'Wow, you look, um, great, amazing, great. Where have you been? What have you been doing? I rang you today and left a message on your mobile.'

'That doesn't work any more,' she says quickly.

'Oh?'

'Cut off!' she laughs. 'Well, it was either that or this dress. Good choice, don't you think?'

'Yeah, wow,' I say. There's a long pause. 'Wow,' I say again.

'Have you been taking drugs?' she asks.

'No,' I say defensively.

'Don't lie,' she says. 'I can see a bloody great lump of the stuff hanging out of your nose.'

'Oh,' I say, immediately wiping the end of my nose. 'Um, so what have you been doing?' I quickly try to change the subject.

'Nothing much,' she replies. 'In fact, if I'm being honest, it's all going a bit pear-shaped. *This Morning* aren't using me any more, they prefer their younger, firmer model. But you know, fingers crossed, I've got a few auditions. That sort of thing.'

Wendy's arms are crossed as she stands in front of me. She's leaning on one hip and her jaw's thrust forward. To all the other women queuing up, we must look like we've just met.

'Great,' I say. 'That's good.'

'I've got a new agent,' she boasts.

'Really,' I smile. I take a step forward, she takes one back.

'Yeah,' she says. 'You know, he does loads of good people.'

'Oh, good,' I say. 'That should help.'

'I'm doing the cover of *What Men Want* next week,' she says, looking at the floor.

'What?' I say, staggering back two paces at once. 'Bra and pants?'

'Course,' she snorts. 'A girl's gotta do . . . Listen, I'll see you. I've got to go,' she says with a stiff smile. And she leaves.

I follow her out but she doesn't look back. She is greeted by another girl who I don't recognise and they leave together. I wander back to the table to find Linus fiddling with a mountain of cigarette butts.

'God,' he moans. 'You were ages.'

'Yeah, listen, I'm sorry,' I say. 'I've got to go home.'

'Great,' says Linus. 'All back to yours.'

'Um, no,' I say. 'I think I want to be on my own for a bit.'

'On your own?' Linus looks horrified. 'Well,' he says, 'I suppose I've got another party to go to anyway.'

12

Trevor's been looking after me for three months now and to say that it's going well is a bit of an understatement. I mean, he's totally revolutionised my life. First off, when I was fired from *The News*, he immediately sorted me an advice column on one of the Sunday tabloid supplements. For more money and a whole lot less work. Actually, the whole thing was extraordinary. I remember walking into the offices of *The News*, the same grey carpet tiles, the same bio-degrading spider plants doubling as ashtrays. I hadn't been there in such a long while it was a very bizarre experience. I didn't take my sunglasses off the whole time I was there. Well, I didn't really want to catch anyone's eye and all they did was stare.

Andrea had been all of a fluster. The nice bloke, Marcus, who'd been looking after me, was fired weeks ago and was now apparently working on the *Pink Paper*. So it was Andrea who welcomed me with an almost open shirt. She had cigarette ash almost three inches long on her B&H, which I think she must have deposited down the back of my new Joseph jumper, because after she'd hugged me hello it had gone. Maya, the swizzle stick work experience with boardroom connections, appeared to have put on weight, either that or my weekly vitamin injections from my special doctor in Harley Street really were working. But I swear she looked fat.

Andrea had invited me in on the pretext of a girl's lunch to talk about the future of the column, but I'd arrived forty-five minutes late, so we had to skip the pleasantries and get straight to the sacking. She ushered me upstairs to the fourth floor and to Gavin West's eunuch of an office. The red tiles and the stiff little secretary with elasticated shoes. I couldn't believe I'd been frightened of all of this seven or eight months ago. He ushered me over to his sofa with a wave of his hand, Alison smiled, delivered her sacrificial lamb and, I promise, she walked out backwards. I sat down and crossed my legs with a loud squeak of my leather trousers. I coughed, sighed loudly and he carried on typing. I recrossed my legs. And then did it again. To be honest I was rather enjoying the noise my trousers were making. Eventually he pressed the 'send' key on his computer with a dramatic flourish and got up out of his seat, manicuring his revolting thin little brown moustache as he went.

'Oh, dear, oh, dear, oh, dear,' he said, walking towards me, shaking his head and smoothing his facial hair with his thumb and forefinger. 'Abigail Long, what are we going to do with you?' he said.

I couldn't be arsed to reply. All I could think was that I was about to be fired by a man who got a pair of hovercrafts strapped to his feet. 'What are we going to do with you?' he continued. 'What are . . . we going to do with you?' Surely he was even boring himself. 'You started out with such promise,' he said. 'I mean, you weren't the most talented writer we've had through our doors by any stretch but, you know, you weren't bad. No obvious style but, you know, perfectly adequate. We looked after you, nurtured your perfectly mediocre talent and how do you repay us?'

He stopped mid-pace. I checked his crotch for signs of life. He must be enjoying all this by now, I thought. He's almost got to the 'letting you go' stage. But there was nothing. Not a stir. Maybe he couldn't any more. Maybe he's reached that stage in a man's life where that sort of action only comes at birthdays and Christmas. Or maybe I just wasn't being afraid, or contrite, or humble enough for him. Either way he was officially devoid of any form of Egyptian monolith in his pants that afternoon.

'And how do you repay us?' he repeated.

'I don't know, surprise me,' I said.

'What?' he said, releasing his 'tache in shock.

'Surprise me,' I repeated, maintaining eye contact through my Guccis.

'Um,' he said, suddenly wrong-footed. 'You . . . you . . .

never got us any stories that were followed up by tabloid newspapers.'

'Whoops.'

'Never.' He was beginning to raise his voice.

'Except the Jack Morris story. I got you that one,' I smiled.

'Well, except for that one,' he acknowledged. 'But' – he stood, his finger raised in the air – 'But, none of my friends, or my wife, or daughter ever said your column was any good, or commented on it, or ever mentioned it to me . . . ever.' He sounded triumphant. I didn't reply. 'So . . . so,' he said. 'Also your copy is sometimes late and often it's simply not funny. And I am very humorous.' He was pacing again. 'So when I say something isn't funny, it isn't . . . funny.'

'Ri-i-i-ght,' I said.

'So, so . . .' He spun on his aerated pumps. 'I'm going to have to let you go.'

'OK,' I said.

'You're fired!' He was on the verge of shouting, his hand thrust in the direction of the door.

'Fine,' I said and got up to go to the door.

'Sacked!' His face was scarlet. But still nothing stirred.

'Picture me giving a shit,' I smiled and walked out.

Striding back up the road, I rang Polly.

'Hey, Pol,' I said. 'Guess what?'

'What?'

'I've just been fired.' I laughed.

'No, really?' she said.

'Yeah. On coke, brilliant, you must do it some time.'

Interestingly, after I was fired the invitations didn't dry up. Trevor and his assistant, Lorraine, organised all of that, making sure that I was put on the mailing list of all the PR companies like Descartes, Avalon, Cake, Pink Fish, MacDonald & Rutter, all those sorts of things. Obviously the events I go to now have changed. Book launches are a pointless exercise. Who wants to meet an author, as Trevor says, who's been in their garden shed for months, their arse expanding into a pair of track suit bottoms, and who falls on a glass of box wine and a packet of cheese and onion crisps like a grateful prisoner recently released from the gulags? Unless, of course, it's Martin Amis, Will Self, Jay McInerney, Brett Easton Ellis, Helen Fielding and, um, Poor Salman, in a venue like the Pharmacy. Then I turn up, on my way somewhere else, just to remind people that I had a university education.

Theatre is also out these days for similar sorts of reasons. According to Trevor, no one really goes to the theatre. We all say we do but most of the time we're parroting reviews we've read somewhere else. It also takes too long. In an evening when I have three or four launches, shop openings and award ceremonies to go to, I can't fit it in. I've slipped into an aftershow party before. But Trevor does keep having to remind himself that sometimes big Hollywood names come to London and tread the boards, so occasionally he puts Lorraine on the case, trying to get first-night tickets, but Future PR's connections don't really stretch to the Almeida and the Donmar Warehouse. He's always kicking himself for not having predicted the fashionable rise of the Fringe. Any Andrew Lloyd Webber, on the other hand, or 'seventies disco revival event, or big musical opening in the West End, Polly and I are dispatched together, to ensure something in the *Mirror* or *Bizarre* the next day.

Otherwise, I go to the things I used to go to, but I don't have to write about them any more. My new column is all about other people's problems, so these evenings out are now pure pleasure. Parksie and the rest of the paparazzi gang are beginning to snap me more and more. To start with I used to get a few rude remarks along the lines of 'Oi, Abigail, found any more corpses recently?' But they've begun to get used to my new role. A couple of the new cable TV shows have begun using me as an agony aunt. Trevor pulled a few strings to start off with, but it's now more of a self-perpetuating thing. Normally what happens is some showbiz story breaks about Calista Flockhart being too thin or Posh Spice losing weight, or some other star being caught with drugs, checking into rehab or their nose collapsing and I'm asked to come on to talk about the 'agony of celebrity'.

Trevor now insists that it's written into my contract that Jack Morris isn't mentioned. Before, they used to introduce me as 'Abigail Long, who found Jack Morris dead' but since

I'm well known in my own right now, I'm simply known as 'Abigail Long, Celebrity Commentator'. I've done the *Lorraine Show* twice and there's even talk of me doing *Richard and Judy*. Since Wendy no longer works there, I keep saying to Trevor that there must be an opening. There is some other girl who's taken over her roving reporter slot but she really isn't very good. But Trevor says we've got to up my personal appearances before we can think of approaching 'Dick and the Dog'. He's currently in talks with the producers of *Wheel of Fortune* to see if I can step into Jenny Powell's shoes when she's on holiday. And the same goes for a slot on *The Big Breakfast*. Although I'm not holding my breath, because the competition is tough out there. As Wendy found out to her detriment.

Trevor's of the new opinion that you've got to be very careful who you put forward to do a bra and pants shoot. Any girl can apparently take her clothes off but it doesn't always work. As well as all that girl-next-door appeal, you have to have the figure for it which, he says, I don't. And secondly you have to look like you're enjoying it, which plainly Wendy did not. It was the worst selling front cover in the history of *What Men Want*. Everyone predicted the end of men's magazines and said that laddism was dead. Until the next month's issue with Polly Friend on the cover outsold Wendy's twofold. Then, of course, there was a spate of 'what's wrong with this girl?' articles and a few compare-and-contrast competitions in the tabloids, eventually resulting in a blonde versus brunette debate. All that happened in the end was that Wendy lost her job on *Here and Now*, the current affairs programme that she was about to start, and I hear she's doing some dating show on cable.

But the whole thing is exhausting. It's not so much the partying that's difficult, because I worked out long ago how to get through that. Des still turns up but now he delivers four grams to my door every Tuesday and that just about does the week. Unless I go out for fun on Friday and Saturday, then he's only too happy to make another trip round. It's not the socialising that kills me, it's the preparations beforehand.

I have my highlights done once a week – regrowth really

shows in photos. And I have a brushing every time I go out – ironing tongs, the works. Antonio (real name Mark) at the end of my road does it, 'the full Aniston' for £25 a pop.

But apart from that I have my teeth bleached once every two months, CACI electronic face lifts once a week, regular waxes, pedicures, manicures, body brushings, eyebrow pluckings, massages, seaweed wraps, de-toxes, Cellophane wraps. I've had a full acid facial peel to make me look younger, collagened my lips and my laughter lines, frozen my forehead with some deadly chemical, and I still insist, when I do 'Me and My Health' in the *Daily Mail*, I just do yoga and drink plenty of water.

Naturally, I borrow most of my clothes. Although there are quite a few designers who won't lend clothes to any of Trevor's girls, for some unknown reason, he always manages to get some outfit biked round to me before I go out. They're a lot more revealing than I would have worn in the past, but since I've lost some weight, I don't see any reason for not flaunting it.

Tonight is an interesting evening, because I'm going to the launch of Colin's new TV show – *Chapman Discovered*. Not exactly the sexiest of titles, but I suppose it just about sums up what the show's about. Colin's been incognito for months. In fact the more I think about it, the more I realise I haven't seen him since before the Jack Morris incident. Every time I've rung him and asked him if he wants to come to a Pepsi Chart Party or the Cable TV Awards do, he's made some lame excuse like he's been working. I heard that he'd stopped going out altogether because finally he's been given a break by some Channel 4 producer who'd managed to extricate his tongue from his secretary's throat long enough to realise that Colin was, in fact, quite amusing and worth investing some money in. So after years of the rest of us joking that 'Channel 4 say they're interested', they are, and he has a six-part series on Tuesdays just before midnight to prove it.

I'm really quite excited. Despite fighting the hangover from hell after a long session in Art House with some indie band after the Kerrang! Heavy Metal Awards, I'm looking forward to seeing Colin. Wendy might even be there. I've had a couple of vodkas to settle my stomach, a coke sharpener, and I'm in the same red sequin dress and red strappy heels I wore the night before. Well, it's not going to be that glamorous an occasion, I think, as I pace around my flat, lighting one cigarette from the next. I'm only really going out of friendship.

My cab is ten minutes late, so I give the driver the silent treatment all the way to Old Compton Street and the corner with Soho House. Arriving at the club, there's no one outside to take my photograph, so I hand in my invitation and make my way upstairs to the private room where they held Jack's wake.

The lounge and bar area is more packed and choked with cigarette smoke than a first-year student party. As I barge my way towards a waiter standing with a heavy tray loaded down with glasses of white wine, red wine and orange juice, I look around for Colin or anyone else I might know. It all seems very Channel 4 comedy to me. And, seeing as I spend most of my nights out these days, no one is instantly recognisable.

I drain a glass of white wine and stand by the entrance, smoking cigarettes, searching through the crowd for Colin. Everyone seems very animated and friendly towards each other. Nearly everyone is dressed in black. Black polo necks, black shirts with black jeans or black combat trousers. There are a few executive-looking types in black round neck tee-shirts and Conran jackets. I'm beginning to feel distinctly over-dressed and extremely disassociated. I contemplate leaving but plump for another large glass of white wine instead. As I lean against the door frame and try to look as inconspicuous as a red sequin full-length dress will allow, a short dark woman with a PR clipboard enters the room.

'Hi,' I say with my special happy engaging smile, 'I wonder if you can help me?'

'Yes,' she says, suspiciously eyeing me up and down.

'I'm Abigail Long,' I announce.

'Yes?' she says.

'Abigail Long,' I repeat more slowly this time so that she understands. She evidently does not and shrugs her shoulders slightly. 'Um, I used to write for *The News*,' I say.

'Oh, yes?' Her eyes show some sign of recognition.

'I used to be best friends with Colin,' I add.

'Oh, he's lovely,' she smiles. 'And so-o-o good looking.'

He's obviously had her, I think. 'I wonder,' I continue, 'is he here?'

'Not yet,' she says. 'He's just finishing off an interview on Capital, but he'll be here in a minute. Can I get you a drink?' she offers.

'Um, thanks,' I say, finishing off the last one. I follow her to the bar. 'Great party,' I say for lack of any other opener. 'Who are all these people?' I laugh.

'Who are they?' She looks extremely confused.

'No idea.' I put on what I think is a crazy comedy face. She takes a step back. 'Like that bloke there with the bleached blond hair?' I laugh.

'That's Ben Miller from the comedy duo Armstrong and Miller,' she says in a deadpan voice.

'Oh,' I shrug. 'And that dark bloke?'

'Steve Coogan,' she says.

'Course,' I laugh. She is not finding my company amusing. 'And that dark bloke?' I point across the room.

'Neil Morrissey,' she sighs.

'Go-o-d,' I smile. 'I'm not really with it today.'

I'm halfway through another glass of wine and another cigarette by the time Colin walks through the door. He looks wonderful. His thick dark hair is longer than I've ever seen it before. Wild and unkempt, it curls as it hits his shoulders. He's wearing a black suede jacket and a pale blue shirt that matches his eyes. Standing by the door, he looks slightly bowled over at the number of people who have turned out in his honour. He appears surprisingly nervous as he surveys the scene. A muscle is twitching in his top lip. PR bird is the first to spot him and calls everyone to a loud efficient hush. The beery crowd at the back of the room ignore her pleas and carry on joking with each other.

'Hey, everyone,' she says. 'Colin Chapman is in the building.'

There's a load of whooping and applause. Colin remains in the doorway, executing a series of little stage bows to each corner of the room, his arms folded across his stomach like a waiter.

'In you come, in you come,' says PR bird. 'Vodka and tonic?'

'Please,' says Colin, with a wide smile.

One by one the crowd around him gets more and more dense. Everyone wants to shake his hand, rogue arms are launching themselves over other people's heads in an effort to press his flesh, or just to pat him on the back.

'Great show, man, great show,' everyone keeps saying. 'Fucking funny, man. I mean, full of just really great jokes. You're a genius.'

Armstrong and Miller both go up and each shakes an arm simultaneously. Colin blushes with the intimacy of his celebrity encounter, and grins like a cool cat with a pint of cream. His vodka and tonic appears over the crowd. I find that I've moved so far away from what's going on that I'm almost under a lamp in the corner. This is ridiculous, I think. He's one of my oldest and best friends and I'm suddenly nervous of approaching him. I finish my drink, take a deep breath and make my way through the crowd.

'Colin!' I exclaim loudly, standing in front of him, with my arms outstretched, a smile on my face. His face is a total blank, for all of three seconds until he recovers.

'Abigail,' he says in the same enthusiastic tone that I had used. But somehow it sounds flat. 'God,' he says. 'God,' he repeats, running his hands through his hair, 'what are you doing here?' He grabs hold of both of my shoulders and kisses me on my cheeks.

But the whole thing is awful. The three-second delay, the running of his hands through his hair, it's all gone terribly wrong. I don't know what I was expecting, really. We've grown apart but I would have thought he would recognise me.

'I can't believe I didn't recognise you.' He smiles, more warmly this time. 'It's just that it's been so long and you look so different. To be honest I wasn't expecting you here. I didn't know you were invited.'

'Well,' I sigh. 'Here I am!'

'Here you are indeed.' He whistles through his teeth.

'Yup,' I say. 'Oh, well done with the show, by the way,' I say. 'I hear it's very good.'

'Oh, thanks,' he says. He's looking over my shoulder. 'Hey,' he says to some dark bloke who runs over and gives him one of those all encompassing male bonding bear hug things that culminates in the two of them jumping up and down and turning around in a circle while still intertwined.

'He-e-e-ey,' says the bloke, shaking both index fingers at Colin.

'He-ee-ey,' replies Colin, shaking both index fingers at the bloke.

I smile and drink some more wine.

'Oh, sorry,' says Colin eventually, as I haven't moved. 'This is, um, my friend, Abigail . . . Abigail, this is my producer . . . Andy.'

'Hi,' says Andy, looking me up and down. 'Um, great frock.'

'Er, yeah,' says Colin. 'You look like Jessica Rabbit on drugs.'

They both crease up with laughter. I just stand there.

'I'm sorry, I'm sorry, Abby,' says Colin, wiping away a tear. 'But you do have to admit it is a bit much . . .' I don't say anything. 'Well, it is, Abby, isn't it, come on? I've never seen you in anything like that before. I mean really . . .'

'Probably,' I say more curtly than I intended. 'But I've got a première to go to,' I lie. 'I've just popped in really to say good luck and actually, in fact, I should go now really.' I'm mumbling and lying and going red and trying not to cry all at the same time.

'Stay,' says Colin, realising the magnitude of the situation. 'Really, stay, I'd love you to stay. Wendy's coming down later and I know she'd love to see you.'

'No, no, really,' I say. 'I'm late already.'

It's all I can do to stop myself from running out of the door. He doesn't come after me.

I wait until I'm in the street before I burst into tears. I don't really know why I'm crying. I'm over-tired, slightly drunk and I suppose I'm furious and humiliated. Bloody Colin Chapman, I think. I've never been made to feel so small and insignificant and such a total fool in my entire life. Doesn't he know who I am? I'm beginning to feel more indignant than anything else. Fuck him and his shit show, I think. I'm going to call Trevor and have some fun.

When I finally track Trevor down he is on his way from the aftershow party of one of the spring's hottest new films, *Hard Crime*, an espionage thriller about the Russian Mafia and a Colombian drugs cartel, starring Hamish Rowland and a new half-Puerto Rican model turned actress, Carmen Weltz. The DPM (deaths per minute) were among the highest so far this year.

'Carmen's not here,' he whispers on his mobile. 'But Hamish is and a whole load of Brit Pack actors and the like. It's kicking,' he says. 'Get your little sequin-clad arse down to the K Bar. I'll leave your name on the door.'

I'm suddenly feeling a whole lot better as I walk down Old Compton Street and take a right up to the K Bar. Trevor sounds on form and it's exactly what I need to make up for the unpleasantness of earlier. Turning the corner into Wardour Street, I can see there's a very over-excited crowd already gathered outside. Climbing all over each other, they jostle and elbow for a better vantage point on the red rope that cordons off the length of red carpet from the club to the street.

Walking up the road I can see that familiar frame of Parksie in his black waterproof puffa jacket, a selection of cameras thrown over his shoulder, as he fires off a few frames at Tamara Beckwith's arrival. This is obviously quite a glamorous event for Parksie to be outside. Either the film's promoters have a blanket ban on photographers inside the party, or he's banging off the arrivals for the first edition. As I get closer there is an almighty scream, as the crowd surges forwards, and the line of bouncers all link arms in the hope of some sort of containment. The photographers are all over each other snapping away. I never knew Ronan Keating had such a following outside aurally challenged prepubscent females. I let him go inside before making my entrance.

Despite the drizzle, I take my coat off to reveal the red

sequin sheath. Polly taught me how to work the carpet. She gave me a lesson once in the sitting room at home, one afternoon when we were quite drunk. But she was really serious about it. You walk slowly, she said, moving your head in a series of semi-circles, smiling to each and every camera lens on your way to the front door. Swing your hips as much as possible, your feet crossing in front of you as you walk. Even large girls can look attractive with a good use of angles. Put one arm on your hip and push your shoulder forwards, it makes both you and the arm look thinner. And don't forget to put highlighter across the top of your collarbones, it reflects the flash and takes pounds off you.

So I Friend it up the crimson carpet of fame. The reaction is not as frenzied as with Ronan's arrival, but it's a perfectly satisfactory number of flashes, coupled with some 'Over 'ere, Abigails' and I sign a few autographs on the way in. I'm not sure the second person's pad I write in knows exactly who I am, but she's just keeping up with the anorak next to her.

Inside, and it's difficult to work out where to go. The upstairs bar is relatively empty and lit rather brightly in comparison to the rest of the club. The pale wood floor and banquettes give the place a feeling of an 'eighties wine bar in the City, rather than somewhere cutting and kicking. Downstairs and the noise levels increase to the point that conversation is as stimulating as chatting up a former Miss World – an awful lot of repetition, followed by a series of non sequiturs. The temperature also soars to the sort of heights only reached by a nuclear reactor in total meltdown. The lighting is low and red. It takes me a whole twenty minutes of weaving around downstairs and approaching people to the point of almost touching noses to find Trevor. Eventually I see him, sitting at a table in the corner next to the VIP enclosure, with a girl on each seat either side of him, nursing a bucket of champagne.

'Trevor.' I wave from three yards away. He doesn't see me until one of his dates points me out. Shielding his eyes from what looks like emergency lighting in a submarine, he ripples his fingers in my general direction.

'Baby, baby,' he smiles. 'Sit down and have a glass of

shampoo, on me. Well, when I say on me I mean Warner's, naturally. Free bottles of champagne, can you believe it? They must be radio rental.' He bores into his temple with his right index finger just to reiterate his point. I'm still standing, as I smile and look around for a chair. 'Oi, Becky,' says Trevor, leaning over to flick the long demi-waved curls of the girl on his left, 'be a love and go and get our Abigail a chair, will you? She's been busy working that derrière of hers all day and she needs to rest it. Am I right, Abigail? Or am I right?'

'You're right,' I smile. 'And it's been a terrible day, Trevor, it really has.'

'You put your cheeks here' – he pats the warm seat next to him – 'and tell me all about it.'

He fills me a flute and lights me a fag and I have a good old moan about Colin and everything.

'Well, you're all right now,' he says, running his hand up and down my leg. 'You're with the Future, and it's looking rosy, if I don't say so myself . . .' He laughs. 'Now are you all right for star dust tonight?' he asks, his face so close to mine I can feel his breath on my cheek. ''Cos I've got this tasty packet in my pocket if you need any.' He runs his short finger along my lips.

'I'm fine, actually,' I smile, shifting away a bit. He's never normally this tactile. 'More alcohol is what we need.'

'Then more alcohol is what you shall have,' says Trevor, with exaggerated ebullience.

Becky comes back with a chair and eases herself in between Trevor and me. I'm actually quite relieved. I haven't seen her before so I presume she's a new addition to Future PR. Either that, or Trevor just fancies her and has promised her a career in showbiz and he's just bringing her along for a ride, later tonight. She seems keen on a taste of the Future, because she hasn't addressed a word to her friend since I sat down. Poor girl. She is so obviously the friend, you can't help but feel sorry for her. She looks miserable. While her mate is all over Trevor like an octopus on E, she's stirring her rum and Coke as if her life depended on it. In a tight black top with an extra pair of breasts pouring over the top of the ones she's encased in an overly small bra, she's got a bad double side flick haircut and cottage cheese forming on her upper arms.

'D'you want a cigarette?' I shout across the table. She smiles.

'Don't mind if I do,' she replies.

'I'm Abigail,' I shout again.

'I know,' she shouts back.

'Oh!'

'Chantel,' she shouts.

'Right,' I nod.

I pour myself another drink and decide that since Trevor is obviously rather involved I should do a round of the party. I wander back upstairs into the quieter wine bar room. Standing by the bar, there is some large American in a loud check suit and pale yellow open-necked shirt, nursing the sort of stomach that makes you think male pregnancy is a distinct possibility. I could have sworn I'd met him before. He's telling a long anecdote to three other men.

'Hi, I'm Abigail,' I say, interrupting slightly as I lean up against the bar and blindly crunch on a crudité that unfortunately turns out to be a spring onion. 'I'm sure we've met before?'

'Really?' he twangs. He looks apologetically at the rest of the group. 'I'm sure I'd remember. William Wellstein,' he smiles. 'I'm Carmen Weltz's agent.'

'O-o-oh,' I smile. 'We've definitely met then,' I laugh. 'At the première of Coloured Sun and we had a good old bitch about how Miles Renton was gay and kept some go-go-dancing boyfriend from the IT Club in Amsterdam in a flat in Bruges.'

'I don't think so,' says William.

'I know it was you,' I smile. 'Because we laughed about how the rest of the world could possibly think that he was straight.'

'I'm Miles Renton's agent and I can assure you that he is not homosexual,' says William, extremely slowly and with a certain amount of irritation.

'Right,' I say. 'We haven't met before then.'

I walk further up the bar and order myself a large vodka. Over in the corner Noel and Meg are sitting with Eddie Izzard and Anna Friel. They seem to be having a very animated conversation about the film. Two of the All Saints come towards the bar.

'God, it's so much better up here than down there,' says one of the girls in mid-Atlantic tones.

A bit of inter-celebrity waving follows as the table acknowledges the bar. I take a sip of my drink just as Stephen Fry walks in with two other blokes and heads straight for the bar. *Hard Crime* has received some rather spectacularly good reviews, so I suppose a good star turnout is inevitable. It's almost as if they gain some sort of by proxy credibility by turning up to the event. There's talk of Hamish being nominated for an Oscar, along with Carmen Weltz, who's now so hot she doesn't even turn up to her own launch party.

The wine bar area is soon so crammed it's almost impossible to move for stellar talent. Judging by the amount of celebrity jostling for bar space upstairs, I decide this might be a good opportunity to chance making it into VIP. Getting up from my stool, I'm surprisingly unsteady as I walk towards the door. I wave at various groups of people on my way – the All Saints, the *Lock, Stock* . . . boys, Ewan McGregor and the gang. I see them all around at openings and award ceremonies, so we're all old showbiz friends. The corridor that leads to the stairs is draped in silver net, lit with fairy lights and packed with fat-necked bouncers in black tie. Ben Affleck, who's currently filming on the south coast, has just been whisked by and straight down the stairs into VIP.

I follow. Clasping onto the handrail for support, the noise and red darkness are extremely disorientating – it's like re-birthing, but the wrong way round. The crowd seems to have slimmed down. Trevor's still in the corner wrapped around Becky, I can see her silver handkerchief top from here. Her girlfriend doesn't appear to be at the table; either she's in the loo or gone home. Before making an assault on VIP, I decide to have a quick sharpener to take the edge off all the alcohol I've consumed. As I walk into the ladies and look at my reflection in the mirror, I realise quite how drunk I am. My face has fallen off its bones. My eyes are glazed and dull. Normally almond-ish, they've mutated into these great round spheres staring back at me. The backs of my hands are fat. My rings are too tight on my fingers. I've got to have a line.

I sit on the floor of the cubicle chopping one out. I'm too drunk to squat; every time I do I fall backwards against the door. As I squash the rock on the seat, Tamara Beckwith and Tara Palmer-Tompkinson come in to repair their make-up and have a long conversation about suede skirts. I flush the loo as I snort my line so no one can hear what I'm doing. As I come out of the cubicle Anna Friel walks in. There's some sort of girl group hug in the corner as they all meet and greet. They give me a wide birth as I tweak my face in the mirror.

The VIP area is guarded by two large blokes with walkie-talkies, clipboards and bow ties. Beyond the red rope, the place seems almost deserted. Then at the back of VIP I notice an inner inner sanctum. Screened off from the rest of the VIP section by diaphanous curtains full of Middle Eastern promise is another section. A low-lit cave, full of silk cushions and, from the occasional glimpse you get, with at least three ice buckets of champagne.

Even for someone as seasoned as I, entry to the inner inner sanctum looks a fairly daunting prospect. Anyway, when you're in there who are you going to talk to? I think I see Kate Moss, but as to who else is lounging around on the silk cushions, it is anyone's guess. Certainly not Ben Affleck, because he's arrived at the party and has since disappeared. Such anti-social behaviour, really. It's a wonder any of these people bother to come out. If they don't want to talk to other people, why don't they just invite their friends over for a pizza and a video at home?

I'm standing near the red ropes when Anna Friel breezes past straight through the cordon into the inner inner sanctum area. I follow on her Voyage tails. A bow tie stops me.

'Um, I'm with her,' I mutter.

'Oh no you don't,' says the tie, blocking my way with his not insignificant forearm. 'What's yer name?' He starts running his finger down the list on his clipboard.

'Um, Abigail Long,' I say, rapidly realising the pointlessness of the exercise.

'What did you say?' asks the tie, going down his list again.

'Long . . . Abigail,' I sigh, holding on to the rope.

'Um.' He's reading each name in turn, his lips moving at the same time. 'Er, no,' he says finally. 'You're name's not down, you're not coming in.'

I roll my eyes. 'But I'm with her,' I say.

'Look,' he says, getting more aggressive, 'I've been doing this job for two years now and nothing you can say will change the fact that if you're not on the list you're not getting past me. So why don't you do yerself a favour and move away from here. Go and enjoy yourself somewhere else, all right?'

'But . . .?'

''Op it,' he says.

As I start to walk away, there's a commotion on the stairs and the crowd of people on their way down are parted by two burly-looking blokes. Through the half-light I realise it's Hamish Rowland. My stomach tightens. In a black suit with petrol blue shirt and matching shiny tie, he looks fabulous. He's got an expensive-looking haircut that's been styled and tweaked at the front. His eyes are fixed on the floor as he walks through the crowd. He exudes both confidence and embarrassment. As he approaches the VIP, I suddenly find myself stepping forward to block his path.

'Hi, I don't know if you remember me?' I'm swinging like a pendulum, my arms are hanging slack by my sides. 'Abigail . . .' I'm slurring my words. His head divides into two and then rejoins itself. His face breaks into a half-smile, a vague recognition of intimacy past.

'Um?' He raises a finger.

Just then his blonde publicist in a slim fitted skirt, with breasts like firmly clenched fists of blancmange, catches up with him and ushers him through.

'Um, hang on a sec, Ciara,' he smiles, putting his hands up in the air, trying to slow her down.

'For chrissake, Hamish, you don't talk to her,' she sniffs. 'She's a frightful little tart with a coke problem.'

I walk slowly back to Trevor's table, people bumping into me as I go. I pour myself a large glass of champagne and let the tears of anger and humiliation slowly run like drops of acid down my cheeks. Trevor's not paying me anywhere near enough attention. Becky is now sitting on his knee, her arm round his neck, her bosom like some underwired bouncy castle, offered up like a handy chin rest device. I could have been shot through the head by a herd of passing ninjas for all he's noticed. I really start to cry. My shoulders are heaving, my mouth is making strange wailing noises. It's Becky who notices first.

'Are you all right there?' she enquires, like she's offering a free spritz of Chloe in Terminal 4 Duty Free.

'Don't be nice to me . . .' my voice is warbling.

Trevor somehow manages to get Becky off his knee. He pulls his chair along the floor towards mine. He puts his arm round me. He smells heavily of alcohol, and the acrid mix of whisky and champagne. Added to that his jacket is impregnated with old sweat and cigars. He's really quite drunk and having had Becky on his knee for the past half-hour, there's an aura of sexual excitement about him.

'There, there,' he says. 'It can't be that bad.'

'It is . . . it is . . .' I say. 'She called me a tart.'

'There, there,' he says. 'It's all right now.'

Any attention is better than no attention at all and I really let go. Tears are pouring uncontrollably down my face, my nose is running, my make-up is running. It can't be a very attractive sight. Becky is hovering at the table; she doesn't quite know what to do, or where to put herself. Neither does Trevor, for that matter. He keeps squeezing my shoulder, massaging it, kneading it in a rather irritating manner. I'm causing quite a scene and Trevor hates scenes.

'Look, Becky, babe,' he says finally, reaching in his check jacket for his wallet. 'Here's twenty quid, love.' He nods, leafing through a great wad of notes. 'Take a cab home and I'll call you later.' She looks annoyed but takes the cash anyway. She opens her mouth to protest, but before she can say anything Trevor adds, 'Look, babe, I'm sorry, but you know, business is business. Run along now, there's a good girl,' he says. 'I'll call you . . . I promise . . . when I've taken care of this.'

She flounces out of the club, a mass of big brunette hair and silver, closely followed by Trevor and me. He has his arm around my shoulders and covers my face with his jacket. He shields me along the red carpet from any photographers, who immediately start to snap away as we weave our way to the kerb.

'Look, guys, guys, leave it out, will you? Leave it out,' he orders, as we stand on the pavement waiting for a cab.

Finally Trevor hails one down and we fall onto the back seat together. I'm so drunk and disorientated I think I'm going to be sick, but instead I nuzzle into his chest and close my eyes.

'Trev,' I mumble into his black shirt, 'are you taking me home?'

'Course I will, princess,' he says. 'Course I will,' he says. 'You just sit there and relax and let the Future sort everything out.'

He's running his hands through my hair. I am lying across the back seat like a bag of old clothes, incapable of moving. He keeps running his hands through my hair. I don't really understand what he's doing. I don't really understand why he's doing it. What is he doing? I try to move. It's impossible. My limbs have turned to lead. I feel impotent. Then I feel his tongue in my ear. It's hard and dry like sandpaper. If I ignore it, it'll go away, I think. If I ignore it, he'll stop. I pretend I'm asleep. It's just the ear at first but then he starts making big circular motions, dragging it down my neck and across my face. All over my face. He's forcing my lips apart, sticking it in my mouth, like some foul probe. I can taste the whisky and champagne on his breath.

'Trevor? . . . What are you doing?' I can't really speak, the taxi is spinning, the streetlights are flying past, my body won't respond to anything I want it to do.

'Abby, baby,' he mutters, his left hand going up my dress. 'You know you want it . . . you know you do . . . you've always wanted it . . . ever since I met you . . .'

His heavy weight is on top of me now. His erection is jabbing away at my thigh. His rough chin is grazing my face. His right hand's unzipped my dress and he's grabbing at my bosom. It's all horrible and painful but I can't make any noise.

'All right in the back there?' yells the cabbie.

'Yeah, mate, yeah,' says Trevor. 'Blomfield Road, right?'

13

It was my mother who admitted me to Pastures. Apparently I'd swallowed enough vodka and Temazepam almost to kill a small pony. But being about the size of a small pony, I'd survived. It was Jo who'd found me. Lying on the sitting-room floor in a Snoopy tee-shirt and Donald Duck pants surrounded by pills and bottles and a very full ashtray. We were supposed to have been meeting for lunch, she was going to show off her new baby, Max. But when I'd failed to answer the door she'd let herself in with a spare set of keys to try to find any clues as to where I might be.

The sight, she says, was terrifying. Sprawled across the floor like a victim in *Columbo*, hair all over the place, arms above my head, legs akimbo, she originally thought I was dead. But predictably enough I hadn't even managed to pull that one off. She rang an ambulance, and then our mother, and while they were both on their way, so she says, I came round. I muttered some sort of rubbish about 'tarts and drugs' and 'Hamish' and 'Trevor'. She couldn't really understand what I was going on about. I was taken to St Charles's Hospital just down the road for observation, but seeing as I'd come round of my own accord, pumping my stomach wasn't necessary. Then two days later I was admitted to Pastures.

An old manor house in Hampshire, set in about four acres of formal gardens, Pastures could easily be mistaken for a rather nice country house hotel, were it not for the bars on the windows. Not that we're locked in, explains Karen, when I'm admitted. We're free to leave any time we want, apparently, but just don't expect to be allowed back a second time. So it's the fear of their disappointment that keeps us all here and, of course, our deep-rooted desire to get better. Although I have to say that some of us are keener to step down that road to recovery than others. Patients – because that's what we are, rather than inmates – patients who admit themselves are more leniently dealt with than those who are forced through the door by concerned relatives or parents.

Although taken there by my mother, following a hideously silent car journey serenaded by Radio 2, I admitted myself under my own steam and was therefore spared the ignominy of a full body and luggage search. No drugs of any sort are allowed on to the premises. Not even aspirin. Although quite how Alexa (the lead singer of an indie band) managed to get enough heroin and cocaine for her speedball is anyone's guess. I've never seen anyone keel over so dramatically in early morning Group before. She made quite a statement before she was asked to leave. But she was not the only person to try to break the rules. Margot, a very plummy woman from Sussex who was admitted by her husband after he found her taking an axe to the wine cellar door, had a vanity case full of booze. Each and every one of her toner, cleanser, and pore refiner bottles was full of gin. How she thought no one would smell it on her breath at the Ten o'Clock Club, when we all have to sit around and chat over tea and biscuits, I don't know.

But then again, you can hardly blame her, for at Pastures there seemed to be two distinct groups of patient. The ones who think they shouldn't be there, and the ones for whom this is their last and only chance. They have no other option, nowhere lower for them to go, except perhaps internment.

When I first arrived I fitted into the first category, obviously. I had a bit of a coke problem but nothing that a holiday in the South of France or a few nights in wouldn't cure. I remember sitting there on my institutional candlewick bed cover, feeling as low and miserable as I had ever felt in my life. But I was also furious that I was being forced to stay here. The smell of dust, old clothes and the faint waft of boiled cabbage in the air conjured up images of incontinence pants and an old people's home. I simply didn't need to be here. My room was small and characterless, like a youth hostel dormitory. Three single beds in a row, each with the same chair and a slightly differing chest of drawers, undoubtedly picked up from some cruddy car boot sale somewhere along the line. In fact that's what the rest of the place looked like. It exuded car boot sale chic and had all the allure of an institution for the insane. Fire doors full of security glass divided what I presume must have been perfectly good corridors and rooms in half. While the upstairs sported an extremely short pile biscuit carpet, the whole of the ground floor was fitted out with a faded and cracked red lino floor that was mopped down with a weak chlorine solution every morning. Such a distinction was not shown in the paintwork; the whole place was painted in a faux-sunny yellow that most normal people would mistake for bile.

I could have coped with the ugliness of the interior, the shabby furniture, the smell of cremated greens, the one biscuit tin a week that somehow always seemed to arrive devoid of bourbons, had it not been for the group element to rehabilitation. I can't stand anything to do with groups. In fact, I find anything 'group' offensive and irritating. I didn't even have a gang at school, so the idea of having to become part of a group and share my innermost secrets with a bunch of strangers filled me with pure horror. Especially when I saw them.

As my mother and I sat in stiff silence on the bed, they came and introduced themselves. They each wore the generous smile of the insane, which of course they were, and they circled the bed like lobotomised vultures, which they could have been, luring me off the counterpane, desperate for new flesh to join their world.

'Hi, my name's Vanessa,' said the first girl. 'I'm an obsessive compulsive and your group leader for this week. Welcome to Pastures,' she smiled. 'I like your hair.'

'Hi, I'm Patrick,' said a bloke in a Noel Edmonds jumper (an executive at Channel 4). 'I'm addicted to power. Welcome to Pastures. It's really nice to meet you.'

'Hi, I'm Debbie,' said another woman. 'I'm a food obsessive, and a depressive. Welcome to Pastures. I hope you'll be happy here. I am.'

'Hi, I'm Freddie,' said another man with a red spotted kerchief wrapped around his neck like an air hostess. 'I'm a crack addict. Welcome to Pastures. It's great to have you here. Really, really great.'

They all did that. Came up, said who they were and what their 'problem' was and then said something 'nice'. Half the group were desperate to be friends with the new girl. In need of love and affection, they were hoping that I'd fill some sort of void. They all hung around like over-enthusiastic spaniels, willing to please. And the other half were just plain terrified. Jacqueline was the worst. An unemployed actress in her sixties from Hampstead, she was incapable of any form of eye contact, let alone conversation, and would spontaneously take exception to the furniture in her room. Each day a different item would 'upset' her. It was a long and protracted process that involved stomping, screaming and then the sudden and dramatic removal of a whole range of objects – her chair, bedside table and then eventually on one very bad day her whole wardrobe and bed were moved out onto the terrace.

With so much dysfunctional behaviour going on around me, it would take a complete fool not to realise that I didn't deserve to be here. Especially when I worked out who I was sharing with. There were two other women in my room. The first was a heroin addict called Melissa whose parents lived in Brighton. She worked in the music business and was in rehab for the third time. The other was a woman called Dred, a meths drinker with a 'wet brain'. At the age of forty-five she'd managed permanently to drink away whole tracts of her brain so, even when sober, she appeared totally pissed. She'd spent some time on the streets and would wake up in the middle of the night slapping her own face, yelling, 'The spiders, the spiders.' I gave her a bit of a wide berth. Especially where my property was concerned. She had this commune idea, born from her days sleeping rough, that anything that strayed into her environs automatically became her property, and no matter the weather, she'd put it on. I remember coming back to the room after one-on-one therapy to find her wearing my Nicole Farhi fringed waistcoat over three tee-shirts, a jumper, cardigan and coat.

Melissa, on the other hand, became my mate. Well, inasmuch as you can have real mates in rehab. Initially quite a disturbing personality, she spent my first three nights keeping me awake, throwing up as she went cold turkey. I found it hard to look her in the eye for a while. I hadn't seen so much puke since my dad made a mistake with the fruit punch measurements on New Year's Eve in 1987. But we'd caught each other's eye over the communal toaster and sniggered slightly together at Debbie, the food obsessive, as she guarded her loaf of toast like a lion with its kill. Melissa and I had decided to take the piss. We'd edged along the bench together, a buttock at a time; the closer we got to Debbie, the more she hunched over her food. I swear she growled.

But we bonded more in Group, when we were forced to paint together in Art Therapy. Our counsellor, Angela, said that the meeting of her orange cloud with my turquoise one was symbolic of the meeting of our minds and inner anger. Which was obviously bollocks. It was just that Melissa and I had been painting 'anger' and 'loneliness' all week and thought that we'd have a bit of abstract fun when it came to 'dreams' and 'bonding'. Well, there's nothing else to do for entertainment. Three hundred quid a night and they've got a worse video collection than the local village shop near Taunton.

Not that there is much time for anything else other than discussing one's problems all day. We're up at 8 a.m. and into breakfast by 8.45 a.m. There's a rota system as to who cooks the eggs, makes the tea, lays out and washes up breakfast. It's all done under the guise of Occupational Therapy but everyone knows that it's a way of cost-cutting. It's the same with mopping the floors and cleaning the loos. The philosophy is that if you can humble yourself, if you've reached the all-time low of cleaning the toilets, but cleaning them for the good of the community, then the only way is up. But I'm sure it's just because it saves them a couple of grand a week.

Anyway, after breakfast it's Group, where we all sit around in hard high-backed chairs, say who we are, and what we are, and how we feel. I have to admit I'm not the most communicative of people in this situation, so for the past six weeks I've said something along the lines of, 'Hi, my name's Abigail, I'm a cocaine addict and today . . . I feel fine.'

Angela, herself an ex-cocaine 'user', would always find this mildly irritating and tell me that I wasn't trying hard enough. So I'd usually invent some sort of problem that I'd managed to sort out in between listening to the loud wailings and shoutings that go on throughout the night.

'Hi, my name's Abigail, I'm a cocaine addict and today I feel better than I did yesterday because I don't miss book launches as much as I used to.'

That used to get her off my back until the next session. But others like Patrick took to it like an attention-seeker getting attention. He was always itching to step in. Literally. He'd scratch the back of his hand, swing his leg, and bounce his foot maniacally until it was his turn.

'Hi, my name's Patrick, I'm a power addict and today I feel good about myself because I let Debbie use the toaster before me.'

'Good,' Angela would reply.

But then Patrick would always have to interrupt again. 'Um, no!' he'd say. 'I've got something to add. However, I did have to suppress my anger at not being asked to speak first again in Group. So I suppose I don't feel so good about myself now.'

Freddie's morning Group chats were normally the most frank. They were swift and to the point.

'Hi, my name's Freddie,' he'd say, tugging on his red kerchief. 'I'm a crack addict and I feel shit because I want some now . . . Right now.'

Shit, strangely enough, was Vanessa's obsession. She was into washing because she believed that everything contained shit. And she meant everything.

'Hi, my name's Vanessa,' she'd say. 'I'm an obsessive compulsive and today I feel better because I've only washed my hair twice so far this morning.'

But Debbie's were the most bizarre. Quite how someone was supposed to feel that much emotion all at the same time, without having a multiple personality, I shall never understand.

'Hi, my name's Debbie, and I'm a food obsessive with depression,' she'd start. 'And today I feel happy . . . and a little sad, um, angry . . . and calm . . . euphoric . . . quite depressed . . . and um, nervous.'

Nervous I could understand. I think we were all nervous. Nervous about being in here in the first place. Nervous about never getting out. Nervous about what our friends would say when, and if, we did get out. Nervous about falling off the wagon and getting into the state that originally brought us all here in the first place. Nervous of the future and not being able to cope. Nervous of such a radical change of lifestyle that we'd never be the same again. But most of all nervous of becoming one of those desperate therapy bores who wang on for hours at a party, on the corner of some slowly emptying sofa, about how they found themselves, and embraced their inner child, and realised they were really special after all. Now that was a truly terrifying prospect.

And judging by the texts that we were subjected to at the Daily Reading after Group, I realised quite how stultifying those voided sofa conversations could be. First off there was *Promise of A New Day*, which took the whole of the first week to read. That was swiftly followed by *How To Be Your Own Best Friend* and my own personal favourite, *Getting the Love You Need*. For someone who can't be bothered to flick through *Men Are From Mars, Women Are From Venus*, even as a joke, I spent most of these sessions biting my cheeks.

My sister came to visit me in my third week of being here and brought me a couple of novels and a giant teddy bear for company. I never really had any time to read the books and the bear was pummelled for twenty minutes by three nurses convinced it was a ploy for smuggling in vodka.

But I got used to it in the end. The regimented atmosphere and the lack of privacy and spare time were a small inconvenience compared to the whole-hearted embarrassment of the swimming excursions. Obviously no one is allowed to leave the premises during their first ten days of near total detox. Just in case you run into some handy smack salesman on your way to the village shop. Then, by the end of the second week, we were allowed to go to the local shop. The first few times you make the fifteen-minute walk you are accompanied. And to be honest, the first time you leave Pastures you are quite glad that someone else is there. The outside world seems a strange and disorientating place. It's amazing how heavy shoes become after you have been in slippers for nearly two weeks. Your sense of perspective also disappears: your head aches and you really don't want to look anyone in the eye. The world seems to have speeded up since you were away and Karen or Angela are the only people who understand. Despite the proximity of the shop, it's easy to comprehend why most of the patients, even when they earn the right to go out on their own after three weeks, still prefer to buy their cigarettes at the tuck stall in the main hall.

But swimming was the worst outing of all. Once a week, on Thursday afternoons, the whole centre, of some thirty to forty patients, was bused to the local swimming baths about twenty-five minutes away. And they really were the local swimming baths. For someone like Margot, who had her own indoor and outdoor at home, the whole experience was enough to send her back to her vanity case. They were revolting. The sort of baths where lumps of phlegm and plasters regularly keep pace with your lengths, matching you stroke for stroke as you work your way up the pool. The changing rooms boasted thirty-five different types of verruca, the air smelt of out-of-date chlorine and the water was full of pre-teen urine and pubescent sex after they'd all heavy petted round the side of the pool.

Add to all of this our arrival and you can imagine why it wasn't a very popular place for the middle-class residents of the area. We must have looked terrifying. Actually, I know we looked terrifying because most women called their children out of the pool upon our arrival. A veritable hotch-potch of body shapes and ages and sizes. Old flesh, loose flesh, fat flesh and track-marked flesh – all of nature's amusing little foibles were on display. As were the creative efforts of the bathing suit industry. Monstrous flowered costumes, skinny Speedo briefs, parachutes of rotting elastic, plus the occasional black Calvin Klein number. The middle-aged alcoholics wore rubber floral caps that lapped the pool like expensive wedding bouquets. The anorexics always chose to swim in tee-shirts, the bulimics had to be prised from the changing rooms and the heroin addicts always shivered down the shallow end, finding the water too cold. But everyone was forced to swim, at least one length, no matter how unbuoyant they were. Patrick usually completed a competitive forty and told everyone all about it on the coach on the way home. I usually managed to rattle off a good fifteen, with my neck stretched to capacity, trying to keep the blood warm water as far away from my mouth as possible. Not since sub-zero hockey on the games pitches at school has exercise been so unappealing.

But I've now done six of my Twelve Steps. I've cried and dug deep and examined my childhood, my present, my past, my current and old relationships with the best of them. I've performed ball-throwing exercises in Drama Therapy, proving I can trust someone to lob me the correct colour ball, if only Melissa would stop fooling around. I've examined my self-destructive tendencies, my lust for fame and recognition and my obsession with celebrity and the desire to feel special and different and I've come out the other side. I've finally admitted that I have an alcohol problem as well as a drug fixation and I no longer want to be famous or frot the famous, or talk to them, or sleep with them or anything else so loaded with low self-esteem. Alcohol is insidious and canapés revolting. I'm marvellous and special and ready to go home.

So here I am, sitting on my bed, picking at the fluff on the yellow candlewick counterpane, staring out of the window all packed and ready to leave. My mother has promised to come and collect me around midday. She'd said she'd take me back to the farm and we'd have a quiet week together and we'd more or less take it from there. I've still got my flat but I haven't got a job of any description to go back to. To be honest, having been so desperate to leave this place, I have no idea what I'm leaving to do. I don't really have any friends to speak of any more. My real mates went long ago and who can possibly talk to the likes of Polly Friend unless they are pissed or wired to the tits on cocaine? London doesn't really hold much allure at the moment. A few quiet nights with my parents and the television for company are about all I can probably manage.

Mum actually came into her own during the last six weeks. Apart from Jo and her giant teddy, she and Dad have been my only visitors. Every Sunday on the dot of midday they came for their allotted hour. They suffered the embarrassment of having their bags searched for drugs with total calm and dignity. After I handed in some rogue gram I found in a trouser pocket halfway through the programme, the staff were a bit more lenient on them. I don't think either of them have ever seen the stuff, let alone know where to buy it. But therein lies an irony. They were sweet when they were here, they never asked why or how, and they never looked sad or disappointed. I was never put in the position where I might feel that I had let them down. Instead, they joked and talked of insignificant things that were happening at home, about Jo and Max. They're very proud to be grandparents. It shines through every pore.

But now she's late. Nearly half an hour late, and I'm beginning to get worried. It's most unlike Mum. She must know the journey like the back of her hand by now. The number of times she's been here. It's a beautiful June day so it can't be the weather. The scent from the climbing rose underneath my window fills the room. Everyone else is in Individual Group, so it's totally quiet as I sit and wait, staring down the long gravel drive, longing to leave.

Far in the distance, I spot a car. Without even checking if it's the right one, I gather together all my stuff and almost run down the stairs. I've already said all my goodbyes and promised to find a sponsor and enrol in AA, or NA, or both, to finish off the Steps as soon as I know where I'm based. So I'm straight out of the door, leaving the jaded red lino behind me. But as I stand on the steps, my bags at my feet, I realise it is the wrong car. It's a rubbish Fiat Panda coming up the drive, the exhaust tearing holes in the ozone layer as it comes towards the house. I sit on the steps and watch it approach. I've got nothing better to do. As it pulls up outside the door, something inside me leaps. The long legs, the Caramac coloured tan, the long messy streaked hair, the beaming smile, the arms outstretched wide as can be. It's James. It's bloody James. Trust him to be late.

'Darling,' he shouts, breaking into a run. 'I'm so-o-o sorry I'm late. I got lost on the way. I never could read your mum's handwriting,' he smiles.

I can't really say anything. Tears are running down my

cheeks. What's he doing here? I'm so pleased to see him, so overjoyed he came to collect me, I can't believe it. I run towards him and within seconds I'm being given the tightest, warmest, most delicious hug I have ever had in my entire life. It's so wonderful, I genuinely sigh with happiness.

'I've been planning this for weeks with your mother,' he laughs, as he hugs me even tighter.

'God, I've missed you,' I say from somewhere in his armpit.

'You have?' he says, sounding delighted and surprised. 'I've missed you too,' he smiles. Taking hold of my shoulders, he pulls me away from himself for closer inspection. He kisses me hard on both cheeks and squeezes me again. 'D'you know,' he says, taking my suitcase in one arm and putting the other over my shoulder, 'you look really rather beautiful?'

'Do I?' I smile.

'Gorgeous,' he winks. 'Hop in.'

'Where are we going?'

'We've got a few people to see,' he smiles.

'Like who?'

He taps the side of his nose. 'Never you mind,' he smiles. 'Oh, careful,' he adds, as I sit down in the passenger seat. 'There's a little something I picked up for you in Sri Lanka.'

'Oh, wow, thanks,' I say, unwrapping the heavy unwieldy present. 'It's . . . it's a very strange wooden carved statue.'

'Isn't it wonderful?' he beams over the steering wheel.

'Um . . .' I pause. It's in fact the most monstrous piece of carving I've ever seen. A heavily ornate peasant or shepherd of some sort with flowers, ivy and fawning beasts curling around his robes. The detail is too regular to be pleasant, even the wood itself is like some heavily stained Victorian church pew. 'It's, um . . .'

'You hate it, don't you?' He's still grinning. 'I can tell.'

'Um.'

'Abby, how could you?' He rolls his head. 'Look at the work on that . . . look at the quality of the carving on that . . . look at the craftsmanship on it . . . go on, look, look.'

'James?'

'What?'

'Is that how they sold it to you in the market?'

He doesn't even reply. He just starts to laugh. It's one of those huge knowing laughs accompanied by a shaking of the head that usually follows the realisation that you've been had. He turns to me smiling.

'It's shit, isn't it?'

'Yup.'

'The carving's rubbish, isn't it?'

'Yup, all done by machine.'

'The wood's horrible, isn't it?'

'Really horrible.'

'Shall we get rid of it?'

'Where?'

'Out of the window?'

'Can I?'

'Darling, you can do anything you want.' He's winding his window down with his right hand at great speed. 'Hey, give it here,' he says, a wonderful schoolboyish smirk curling his lips. I hand it over. 'Ready?' he smiles. The wind is in his hair. It's snaking around his head like a bleached blond halo, his eyes are shining in the midday sun. James doesn't just look handsome, he looks like a Greek god hurling statues from his extremely environmentally unfriendly Fiat Panda. 'OK? Are you sure?' I nod keenly. 'One . . . two . . . THREE!' As he throws it out of the window, we both scream, close our eyes and then immediately turn round to inspect the damage.

'It didn't even break,' says James in shock and total puerile disappointment.

'That figures,' I smile. James looks confused. 'It takes quite a lot to break plastic. Particularly a bloody great lump of it like that.'

'No-o-o,' says James, his shoulders collapsing as he drives, his head hanging. 'God, I'm a mug.'

'Quite a handsome, amusing, clever mug,' I smile.

'God, I've missed you,' he says again, leaning over to kiss my cheek and squeeze my knee. The feeling's mutual.

I find myself being driven back to London. The week in the country is obviously another yarn spun by James and my mother together. I don't mind, I spend the journey singing along loudly and badly to James's homemade tape that he has somewhat enigmatically entitled 'Positive Chunes'. We have both the windows open full and the volume on high as we shout along to 'On Top of the World', by the Carpenters. In fact, the only problem is that James keeps doing crap dancing in the driving seat and every time we go over a bump the cheap tape-deck cuts out. But apart from that it's blissful. Actually, then again, perhaps, because of that, it's really blissful. I rest my chin on the window. I can feel the smell of disinfectant being blown out of my hair as we drive along. I feel really happy. The English countryside for once is living up to its reputation. We drive past yellow fields of flowers spread across the hillside like great servings of lemon curd. There are banks of poppies and cornflowers along the roadside and chocolate-box cottages groaning with roses. Every so often, as we wind our way along the narrow village roads, the smell of freshly cut grass fills the car. I flop back into my seat.

'Happy?' says James.

'Oh, yes,' I smile. He looks pleased.

About half an hour into the journey, James pulls into a petrol station. It's an old village station with a swinging metal sign, two round yellow pumps with no distinguishable company logo and an old bloke with a limp who insists on serving. As he ambles back and forth, slowly, very slowly, going about his business, there's total silence in the car. James turns to look at me.

'Abigail,' he says. He sounds very formal.

'What?' I say, turning to look at him.

'What was it like?' he asks.

'What?' I'm slightly taken aback. I wasn't really expecting that as a question.

'Being in there?' He nods towards the back seat.

'Oh, that? Um,' I say, feeling a horrible wave of great sadness engulf me.

'Honestly,' he says.

'Honestly,' I reply. 'Honestly it was probably one of the worst experiences of my life. I've never felt more miserable and alone as when I was in there. It was pure hell.'

We both sit in silence. I must be crying because James is

wiping tears off my cheeks, he wipes the hair off my face, he's moving closer and closer and suddenly I realise he's about to kiss me. He does. His lips are soft and gentle and really warm. His arms are around me. This is heaven. Like drinking honey. I'm amazed at my reaction. I melt. There's no other way to describe it. Never has a kiss felt more wonderful and perfect. Never has such an amazing happiness grabbed the pit of my stomach and run around with it. Never has such an erotic charge shot through every nerve of my body. Why didn't I realise all this a long time ago? Why didn't we do this a long time ago?

'I've been wanting to do that all morning,' says James as he rests his forehead against mine and stares into my eyes.

'You have?'

'Actually I've been wanting to do that for about five years,' he says. 'But as you know, Abigail Long, I'm rubbish, truly . . . truly . . . rubbish.' He takes my face in his hands and kisses me again.

There's a polite cough behind him.

'Excuse me, sir,' says the old boy with the limp. 'Do you want your change?'

James laughs. 'I would say keep it,' he says. 'But I'm totally broke.'

I smile. He starts the engine and we head off back up to London. The rest of the journey is quieter. A sort of serene joy has settled on the car. James holds my hand all the way home. He alternates between kissing it and squeezing it as he drives along.

It's about 2 p.m. by the time we drive along Ledbury Road, W11. James drives past the turning to my house.

'Where are we going?' I ask.

'I thought you might like a coffee in Coins before we go home,' he says, including himself in the returning to the flat process.

'Um, not really,' I say. 'To be honest I'm a bit nervous about noisy places and crowds of people. It's a long time since I've done that sober.'

'Don't worry,' he says. 'You've got me now. I'll look after you.'

'Only if you promise,' I say.

'Cross my heart and hope to die,' he says, turning right down a side street and parking the car. 'Come on, out you get,' he hurries. 'Things to do, deals to make, orgasms to fake.'

'All right, all right,' I say.

As we walk to the end of the road, he stops and takes my head in his hands and kisses me hard on the mouth. He stares into my eyes.

'Right, Miss Long,' he says, his nose touching mine, 'I love you. You're wonderful. We're going to walk into this place together and if at any time you feel you can't handle it, I promise I'll take you home. I've been gagging to do *that* for five years as well.'

It's a warm lazy Saturday afternoon in June and the terrace at Coins is packed. The green metal tables are overflowing with thin brown girls in cropped tops and shorts, lounging around drinking frothy coffee, smoking cigarettes and talking on mobile phones. A multi-coloured hippie spins past on a silver scooter. A couple of handsome young men in tight white tee-shirts and cargo pants tuck into huge club sandwiches, while one of them keeps an eye on a pushchair. It's a scene I know so well. Yet I'm strangely apprehensive. I squeeze James's hand some more. Walking along the pavement I hear my name being shouted from the far table in the sun.

'Abigail, over here, over here,' shouts a pencil-thin girl jumping up and down waving, in a pink dress with the largest pair of sunglasses I've ever seen. She looks like the Fly; either that, or Jackie O's optically challenged sister. It can only be Wendy.

'Me first . . . me first.' She hops from one leg to another, as she pushes Colin back down in his seat. 'Oh, oh, oh, oh,' she says, giving me the largest and tightest of hugs. 'It's wonderful to see you, it really is, and you look great. Really, really great.'

'My go,' says Colin. 'Look at you . . . you foxy thing.' He grins, putting his arms round me. 'We've really missed you, you know, we really have. I'm so glad you're back.'

'I'm really glad to be back,' I smile, taking hold of James's hand.

Wendy's sharp as a cut-throat. 'No-o-o?' she says, taking a long drag on her Marlboro. 'He hasn't finally told you, has he?'

'Told me what?'

'That you're all he ever thought about on those long hot steamy nights all alone with a gang of sweaty, naked-to-the-waist men in the jungle?' She raises her eyebrows. I look at James.

'Well,' he shrugs, 'I had to share it with someone and Wendy's always been so discreet.'

'Truth be known,' announces Colin, lounging back in his chair, 'he beat me to it.'

'Liar,' I say. 'You drew straws and James's was the shortest.'

We all start to laugh. It's just like old times. We order big glasses of iced coffee and smoke each other's cigarettes and talk about the first thing that comes into our heads. Actually, it's more like the second or third thing that comes into our heads, because the first couple are a bit too tricky at the moment. It's about an hour before anyone brings up the rehab question and, of course, it's Wendy.

'So anyone sexy in there?' she asks, exhaling. Everyone stops laughing. 'Wha-at?' she says. 'I only asked.'

'No, actually,' I say, 'I'd prefer it if you did ask.' I smile. 'And d'you know? There wasn't. Locked up night and day with twenty men and not one of them was handsome. In fact I'd go so far as to say they were all hideous.'

'What, all of them?' says Wendy. She looks very disappointed. 'But you always hear about people, well, celebrities meeting each other in rehab and getting married. Or at least having sex. Surely there must have been someone worth snogging.'

'Nope.' I smile at James.

'Just as well he collected you,' says Wendy. 'You must have been desperate.'

'She'd have to be pretty desperate anyway,' laughs Colin.

James slaps him on the back of the head. 'You can talk. When was the last time you even got to first base?' he smiles.

'I've been wo-o-rking,' says Colin, stealing one of Wendy's cigarettes.

'Boy, has he been doing that,' sighs Wendy, tapping the back of his hand. 'Talk of boring bastard. Yawn, bloody yawn.'

'No one's seen you for dust,' says James.

'And how would you know?' asks Colin.

'I've got my sources,' smiles James.

'I'm sorry I've been so out of touch. What happened after you ignored me in my red sequin sheath frock thing?' I ask.

Colin sniggers. 'It was awful,' he says. I hold my hands up in total agreement. 'I got great reviews and I'm doing another series.'

'No-o?' I say.

'Oh, yeah,' says Wendy, flicking her ash in her saucer. 'And d'you know? I don't begrudge him a bit,' she smiles. 'Well, maybe just a bit. But you worked really hard, so you deserve it.'

'You sound like my mother.' He raises his eyebrows in mock boredom.

'And you, Wendy, what's happened to you?' I ask.

'How long have you bloody got?' She sighs, leaning back in her chair.

'Two minutes,' says James.

'OK,' she says, sitting up straight. 'Career's down the toilet. Took my kit off, big mistake . . .' I open my mouth to say something. 'No,' she says, making a stop sign with her hand. 'Don't even try . . .' I close my mouth. 'Worst fashion error I've ever made,' she laughs. 'No one would touch me with a bloody great seven-hundred-foot barge pole, even with a six-inch-thick prophylactic stretched over the end. Anyway, nightmare, rotted on cable for a while, doing some shit show about trying to get fat pond life off with spotty pond life. It was called *Desperately Seeking*, or *The Sad Twat Show* as I called it . . .'

'Wittily,' says Colin.

'It's bloody hard to be witty when you're surrounded by people with as much intellectual spark as an ironing board,' she sighs. 'Anyway, fuck it.' She holds her hands up in mock surrender. 'I'm retraining.'

'Retraining?'

'Oh, yes,' she says. 'I'm done with fame and fortune and interviewing tossers in shopping malls. I've got a place at the Courtauld and I'm going to do a post-grad in History of Art. Where will it lead to? Who gives a shit? But all I know is I can't be a wannabe all my life. I mean . . .'

'Two minutes,' says James.

'So that's the deal. I plan to get a great tan all summer and then, come September, it's new pencil cases all round. Meanwhile I'll content myself star-fucking Colin, and James after you've finished with him.'

'I'm not really interested in fame,' muses James. 'From what I can see it doesn't look like a whole load of fun to me.'

'What would you know?' says Wendy.

'Well, I don't think Abby had that much of a good time,' he says.

'Yeah, well,' I say. 'Does anyone want any more coffee?'

We all sit back and lounge in the sun waiting for our round to arrive. I close my eyes and sigh. It's just wonderful to be back with them all again. I smile. None of us has changed that much, I muse, stealing one of Wendy's cigarettes. Still rude and rubbish with each other. Perhaps a bit wiser and less naive.

'Hey, Abigail,' says a familiar voice behind me. I turn round to find Linus, cigarette hanging from his lips, posing in the sunshine, his fecund chest hair poking out of his trusty old cream bouffant shirt. 'Long time no see,' he smiles.

'Yeah,' I smile. 'I've been out of it for a while.'

'Right,' he laughs. 'So have I . . . Been to any good parties recently?'

'Not really,' I say. 'I've been in the country.'

'Oh.' He shrugs. 'Great idea the country . . . There's a big bash on tonight if you fancy coming?'

'Um?' I hesitate. The whole table sits to attention.

'I hear Johnny Depp's supposed to be there.'

'No, really,' I say. 'I really couldn't. I think I've had enough vol au vents to last me a lifetime.'

Some time later . . .

Abigail Long still doesn't take drugs. She drinks wine, but since she moved in with James Moore, eighteen months ago, she doesn't feel the need to get out of it any more. James still makes documentaries and he keeps hoping that one day his gong will come. Wendy Slater is still glamorous and amusing and badly behaved. Having just started at Sotheby's, she already has half the contemporary art department wrapped around her little finger. And Colin? Well, you've probably seen him on the telly. He's won awards and the respect of his peers, but he still faffs around, talks rubbish, tries to bed girls, and drinks lots of frothy coffee on Saturdays with a group of very loud friends just around the corner from where he lives. Future PR is still very much in business. But Abigail cut all ties with the company, immediately after Trevor sold her 'My Drugs Hell' rehab story to the *News of the World*. And Polly Friend? Who the hell is Polly Friend?

1

It is the beginning of the long hot summer of 1976 that sweats in the memory, and Madeleine has been in the kitchen nearly all day. Radio 4 is on full volume and various pots and pans are steaming away. The atmosphere hums with hysterical creativity. It's her thirty-second birthday and she has been doing battle with an avocado ring all afternoon. She is overtired and emotional by the time her husband, Larry, comes home from work. Up to her elbows in grated avocado, gelatine, Hellmann's and prawns, she looks more like a vet wallowing with the contents of a cow's stomach than someone following a cordon bleu recipe with naïve, yet Masonic zeal.

In Solihull society Madeleine is not known for her culinary expertise. With little interest in food, thanks to the amount of amphetamine-based slimming pills she takes, she tends to exude enthusiasm in the first furlong, only to lose interest and eventually burn things. So much so that Larry has recently sent her on a cookery course in the hope that some improvement in the home entertainment department might help him further up the corporate ladder.

As he comes in through the front door Larry – unlike his other half – is rather pleased with himself. Hurling his summer checked driving jacket in the vague direction of the hatstand, he almost trips with delight up the hallway towards the kitchen.

Larry is not the most attractive of men. In fact, truth be known, in his expansive middle age, he is possibly the most unattractive of men. Wide girth, wide arse, wide thighs, mean mouth, he has the sort of fat-boy forearms more genetically suited to pulling pints. He is pure Birmingham. Well, more of a heady cocktail of Black Country and Redditch, or just plain Solihull, depending on whom he is talking to. Solihull to Madeleine's parents and Norfolk friends, not that they can distinguish the subtle nuance of this white lie. But Larry persists anyway. Birmingham to the other swingers in tyre trading circles, and Black Country/Redditch down the pub. Where he is, often. As Larry has a backside bar stools are made for. His well-padded buttocks make it possible for him to spend whole evenings knocking back pints of unreal ale with gin-tonic chasers, without much need for movement, save for a return trip to the fag machine and/or an infrequent toilet facility break.

And he is ginger. Not the sort of sandy ginger that generous people would call strawberry blond, but the sort of fluoro ginger that requires heavily smoked sunglasses on a summer's day. Fortunately, or unfortunately depending on your gingerist point of view, Larry also has lots of hair. On his head, legs and chest. The fact that his collars and cuffs match is one of his favourite cocktail boasts. He has thick, heavy sideburns that reach towards his layered chin like splayed fists, and a leftward-leaning fringe that covers his forehead in a soft feathered line to just above his eyebrows. He also sports a bushy, almost fecund, David Wilkie moustache that squats like some flavour-saving device on his top lip, dipping and dunking itself into soups, sauces and alcoholic beverages with such frequency that it is nearly always moist. His daughters hate it, and refuse to kiss him unless he dries his mouth first.

'Hey,' he says. 'Guess what?'

Madeleine looks up with a faint smile, a sweaty blonde curl in the middle of her forehead.

Larry grins a wide smile and chucks a fistful of one pound notes up in the air, letting them fall around him like confetti. 'Can you believe it!' He laughs. 'Bloody love ... bloody British ... bloody Leyland.' He leans against the door frame, slightly exhausted. 'Can you believe it,' he repeats, inhaling and exhaling over-exaggeratedly. 'Got the order of a lifetime this morning; well, this afternoon, over lunch in fact. Want more tyres down Leyland's,' he gasps. 'The Rotarians are splashing out. Shifting more Princesses a year than they thought. So we, my dear, are rich,' he pronounces.

Larry raises an imaginary glass in the air and then hugs his wife. He squeezes Madeleine so tightly that she feels much like the piping bag of whipped cream she is now holding. With her nose and cheek in Larry's armpit, she inhales the suburban cocktail of body odour, stale cigarettes and slops. It makes her feel quite queasy.

But she is actually, genuinely pleased for Larry. He's been working at J&C Rubber Company ever since he moved south to Solihull from the Black Country almost twenty years ago. Starting out on the shop floor, he is now deputy managing director and doing rather well for himself. No, she is pleased. Really pleased. But there is still a rather stiff plastic Charlie's Angels element to her smile. Since Larry has managed to get himself rather over-lubricated at lunch, the new tyre deal will obviously be the only topic of conversation at dinner. Her birthday dinner. The dinner she has spent all afternoon cooking for.

And she is worried. For Madeleine knows just how much the subject of heavy industry makes Angela's skin crawl. Angela is the Johnsons' neighbour, in so far as one actually has neighbours when you are rich and live in seventies Solihull. She and her husband live just up the road in Lapworth, in a heavily interior-designed, mock-Elizabethan manor. Angela talks about money constantly, but finds it vulgar to discuss where it comes from. Her neck stiffens and those endearing little acronyms just come careering out at a ROK – rate of knots. Truth be known, Angela only gets on with Larry when she is tight. But since Larry always fills her full of drink every time they meet, it is normally only a matter of cocktails before they finally bond.

'You know, Larry,' she usually insists, holding on to her plaited hairpiece as she leans forward to light a cigarette from the long, thin, orange, tapered candle ensemble, organised into a crown motif, that *everyone* is decorating their tables with in 1976. 'You're QSAA – quite a scream after all,' she pronounces, taking a drag from her fag through her lip-lined pan-sticked circle of a mouth, and exhaling like a pair of industrial bellows. 'But no . . . but no . . . really,' she repeats. 'QSAA.'

The main problem, however, is Angela's husband James. Quite like Larry, in a sort of new-money, rabid Tory type of way, he has the affected chinlessness of someone who has been to a minor public school in Oxfordshire. An insurance broker, he finds the subject of money more distasteful than his wife, yet at the same time seems irrevocably drawn to it. So instead of letting the subject drop like most polite people do in polite company, he becomes fiscally competitive. He will boast about the size of his garage, the amount of glass in his greenhouse – which mutates into a conservatory depending on whom he is talking to. His latest was the expense of his wife's pedigree toy poodle. It was almost worth buying stock in, the amount the price went up in one evening.

Madeleine is therefore determined to calm Larry down a bit before the guests arrive. 'Why don't you go and have a Badedas bath?' she suggests, leaning over the sink to pick up her spare cigarettes and green plastic daisy lighter from the windowsill. 'The girls are in their nighties. You could go and tell them the good news, read them a story or something, and get ready before everyone arrives.'

Larry looks strangely stunned. He even wobbles slightly in his slip-on pumps. He never reads his daughters stories. Why on earth should he start now?

'What?' he asks, recoiling slightly with the energy of his protest.

'Oh, I don't know,' mutters Madeleine, lighting her cigarette. 'They're coming in an hour. Just go and get ready. Or organise the drinks tray. Make yourself useful. I've got the rice to do yet and the table to lay.'

'Ah,' says Larry, sticking his finger in the air. 'Drinks tray. Good idea.' And he is off with the enthusiasm of a lab technician assigned some very interesting mixing to do.

Madeleine heaves a sigh of relief and leans back against the kitchen unit. She smokes her cigarette and looks down to check out the sharpness of her hipbones. How did she end up here? she wonders, inhaling deeply.

A shy, skinny, middle-class girl from Norfolk, under-educated, under-optioned, never employed, she married flash Larry because he asked her, and she thought she had no other means of escape. He was the most glamorous man she had met in her short and sheltered life. He earned his own money and drove a soft-topped car. He smoked small short cigars, wore sharp suits and smoothed his side-parted hair with some sort of pomade. And her father really disapproved of him, which, of course, more or less doubled his charm. A product of fifties parenting, where girls were taught nothing and told to dream small, the idea of anything other than motherhood terrified her. Hitched at nineteen, pregnant in the sixties, Madeleine has never really been young. Like thousands of other women before her, she married for necessity yet dreams of love. She understands mother love. Mother love tears at her very soul when either of her two daughters is ill or unhappy, but romantic love has well and truly passed her by. She sees young couples in the street, giggling, holding each other's hand, and stealing kisses as they walk along. Her eyes follow them with a wistful longing and suffocating tightness in the pit of her stomach. Hedonistic love doesn't happen to people like her. Mad passionate love doesn't happen to suburban housewives in Solihull. So Madeleine watches films, reads books, pops her slimming pills and loves her children more than ever.

Breathing in, she lifts up her maroon T-shirt and verifies the gap between her stomach and her hipster jeans with flared ankle insert. Two babies and still thin, she thinks, smiling to herself. 'Not bad, not bad at all,' she reassures herself, stubbing her quarter-smoked cigarette out with a sizzle in the kitchen sink. She fills her ring mould with avocado mousse, puts it in the fridge, then goes upstairs to change.

Larry is predictably at the drinks tray when Madeleine reappears. She has bouffed up all her hair on top of her head, using a whole packet of Kirby grips and one faux doughnut ring hairpiece. She has also tonged three fair strands of hair into curls on either side of her head. She is wearing a lethal pair of silver sandals that make her slip slightly as she teeters rather tentatively into the sitting room. She looks amazing.

'Mummy, you look lovely,' says Lara, as she helps herself

to a handful of the salted cashews Madeleine has put out for the guests.

'You look like a real princess,' adds Sophie, so over-excited at the prospect of a party that she has both fists full of cocktail eats, and can't decide which to shove into her mouth first. 'Daddy?' she says, covering her father's navy light cotton slacks in a fine mist of moist cashew bits as she bounces up and down near him for attention. 'Doesn't Mummy look just s-o-o-o pretty?'

Larry looks up from the gin martini he is concocting and checks out his wife as one might do a new motor: up, down and round the back. 'Not bad,' he says, tweaking his moustache and handing over what is effectively half a pint of gin with silver cocktail onion garnish. 'Who's coming then?'

'I told you this morning,' says Madeleine, taking a slurp and whistling a gentle 'wow' through her teeth as she swallows.

'I know, I know,' admits Larry, bent over the silver-plate drinks tray again, trying to get the correct amount of vermouth in the glass. 'But I can't remember. You organised the whole thing. It is your birthday supper after all. Angela and James?'

'Angela and James always come,' replies Madeleine, looking round for her cigarettes. 'Liz and Geoff . . . and Valerie,' she continues distractedly out of the corner of her mouth.

'Valerie?' Larry snorts his cocktail. 'You could've told me she was coming.' He frantically brushes his slacks. 'I'll have to go and change now.'

'Whatever for?' says Madeleine with an innocent smile. 'You're not rich enough for Valerie. New deal or no new deal, you simply don't have enough flexible friends to keep Val happy.'

Larry, of course, knows this to be true. He doesn't have a slush puppy's chance in hell of getting anywhere near relieving Valerie Roberts of her underwear. And although he is most certainly joking, a bloke could dream, couldn't he?

'C-o-o-ey?' comes a familiar shout from the kitchen. 'Anyone home?'

Angela and James have arrived.

Madeleine knows it is them. Angela and James are always first and they are always early. They march straight into the living room and after some cursory kissing take up their usual positions: James next to Larry at the drinks tray, and Angela in some tantrically skilled cross-legged position on the leather pouffe beside the glass-topped table, where she can stash her cigarettes and alcohol without moving. Wearing an extraordinary scarlet, feather-fringed jerkin with matching feather-trimmed bell-bottoms and a silk shirt whose collar reaches to her nipples, Angela is so thin and so overdressed that she looks like a highly decorated gift shop pencil.

'Oh, gosh, nearly forgot,' Angela exclaims, flicking her smooth blonde bob and leaping up from the pouffe. 'Here you are, Maddy, happy birthday, darling. Happy birthday,' she says, proudly holding aloft the sort of itsy bag that is normally reserved for diamond rings, or a box of four truffle chocolates.

'Oh, thanks, you shouldn't have,' replies Madeleine, brushing cheeks and squeezing shoulders. Putting her drink down on the table, she opens the packet with theatrical trepidation. 'Oh . . . wow,' she says enthusiastically.

'Let's see, let's see,' chime in Lara and Sophie at the same time, tugging at their mother's cheesecloth ensemble.

'It's a . . .'

'Sellotape-end finder,' pronounces Angela, flicking her ash purposefully, obviously thrilled by her own generosity.

'Is it?' says Madeleine. 'Oh. Of course it is. How silly of me. Look, girls,' she continues valiantly. 'A Sellotape-end finder, isn't that great?'

Lara and Sophie are unimpressed. Aged eight and six they have yet to acquire that social veneer that allows people to mask their true feelings. They lost interest almost as soon as they saw it tumble out of the bag and embarrassingly are already back at the sideboard digging into the nuts and crudités.

'Larry?' says Madeleine, using an especially high-pitched, jovial voice. 'Look what Angela bought . . .'

Larry has been showing off about his new tyre deal to James. James has been monosyllabic in his responses, running his hands through his blond flyaway hair, staring at the drinks tray, secretly willing Larry to shut up and make the gin martinis more quickly.

'What?' says Larry, looking up and over his shoulder.

'A Sellotape-end finder.'

'Where on earth did you get that?' says Larry, laughing. 'It's—'

'Lovely . . . very, very kind and very, very lovely,' interrupts Madeleine. 'Angela bought it.'

'Oh, so it is,' says Larry quickly. 'Um, lovely . . . Drink, anyone?'

'Oh, JWTDO,' says Angela, settling herself back down on the pouffe, arranging the feather fringe on her bell-bottoms attractively.

Larry looks confused.

'Just what the doctor ordered,' says Angela, pronouncing each word as if Larry were some aurally challenged relative.

'R-i-i-i-ght,' he says. 'Onion?'

'What?'

'Oh, silver cocktail onion garnish?' he embellishes.

'Please,' replies Angela.

'Nuts?' offers Madeleine.

'Oh, Lord! No,' says Angela, patting her Twiggy-slim stomach and reaching for her packet of JPS. 'A moment on the lips, a lifetime on the hips.' She laughs heartily at her own well-worn joke, disturbing her blow-dry in her enthusiasm. She lights a cigarette. 'So,' she says to Larry. 'Business good?' She takes a slurp of her gin and whistles through her teeth as Madeleine has done before her. Larry's cocktails are always too strong.

'Funny you should ask,' says Larry, puffing up his paunch with pride. 'Today the most amazing thing happened—'

'Was that the front door?' chimes in Madeleine breezily. 'Larry? Off you go, don't want to keep our guests waiting.'

'Tell you in a second,' says Larry, pointing his finger in the air on his way out of the room. 'And I promise it really is worth waiting for.'

'Ooh, how exciting,' replies Angela, mincing in her seat with anticipation. 'I do so enjoy a good story. Don't I, James?'

James doesn't reply.

'James? Don't I enjoy a good story?' she repeats at greater volume.

James pretends he can't hear and wanders over to the

eight-track cassette player, where he flicks through the Neil Diamond and Demis Roussos collection. 'These are all terrible,' he complains. 'Whose are they?'

'Mine,' replies Madeleine. 'You say that every time you come, James,' she says, looking at her collection protectively. 'Why don't you just put *Ipi Tombi* on and be done with it?'

'Oh, I love *Ipi Tombi*,' pronounces Angela from the pouffe. 'Went to see it in London. Such a hoot.'

James fumbles through the stack of tapes for a minute and finds a dark green cassette with a pair of naked breasts on the front. He momentarily peruses the cover with the clammy frustration of a pubescent. His flyaway hair flops forwards as he slips the tape on.

'Hey, look who I found outside,' announces Larry, coming back into the room holding an empty glass. 'Liz . . . and her lovely husband, Geoff.'

Madeleine smiles. She is trying hard to enjoy herself.

'Oooh, new necklace?' says Angela, tugging at her jerkin as she stands up.

'What d'you think?' replies Liz, offering up her gorge for group appraisal.

'Looks terribly expensive,' says Angela, getting indecently close.

'From that new shop in Stratford,' announces Liz.

'Jewellery quarter in Birmingham,' whispers Geoff to Larry as he smooths down the sleeves of his lemon-yellow sports jacket and pulls the sweaty waistband of his trousers up around his girth. He turns and pops a carrot and cream cheese combination in his mouth, ruffling Lara's hair as he does so.

'Secret's safe with me, mate,' says Larry, winking to Geoff. 'Gin martini?' he adds in an extra loud voice.

'Don't mind if I do,' replies Geoff, as if he's some extra in the village panto.

'Gin martini?' Larry asks Liz.

'Just tonic for me,' she replies, making a steering-wheel motion with her burgundy-tipped hands.

They all stand, hold their drinks and smile pleasantly at one another.

SHAGPILE
Imogen Edwards-Jones

If you enjoyed reading this extract from Imogen Edwards-Jones's new book, SHAGPILE, you can take advantage of SHE Magazine's exclusive offer and order your copy of the trade paperback edition of SHAGPILE at a special price of £7.99 (£3 off rrp £10.99).

Don't miss out on this fantastic offer, order your copy now.

Please send a cheque/postal order payable to Linton Healy Ltd (CO208), to SHAGPILE Promotion (CO208), PO Box 69, Leighton Buzzard, Beds, LU95 1ZD, along with your full name and address, including your postcode and daytime telephone number and details of how many copies of SHAGPILE you require at £7.99. Alternatively, if you are paying by credit card you can call our 24-hour order line, (01525) 851945, or you can fax your order through to (01525) 372774.

Terms and Conditions
Readers in ROI or Europe wishing to order, please pay using Sterling, and add £0.50p per book to cover additional Post and Packing.
Offer closes 31st December 2002
Please allow 28 days for delivery. Proof of posting is not proof of receipt.
Offer subject to availability. If you have any queries about your order after you have applied, please contact ou Enquiries Department on (01525) 853399.